STAR-SPANNING,
SWASHBUCKLING ADVENTURE

"Best known for his libertarian science fiction (*The Probability Broach*), Smith offers a change of pace with this swashbuckling space adventure loosely patterned in the spirit of Rafael Sabatini and C. S. Forester. The powerful imperial conglomerate of the 31st century spans the star systems, extorting from those under its rule. When young Arran Islay decides to live as a brigand, he declares war on "Those who live by stealing property—life and liberty—from its rightful owners." Adopting the name of his murdered friend, Henry Martyn, he sets sail in search of fortune and revenge. Other Islay family members are fully delineated and play important roles in this story, written in an evocatively archaic style reminiscent of both the classic adventure tales familiar from childhood and the space operas of 1930s pulp fiction. The author has a flair for inventive future terminology and imaginative concepts. Smith blends intergalactic action, heroics and derring-do into a futuristic political thriller, and the result is a delight."

— *Publishers Weekly*

Tor books by L. Neil Smith

The Crystal Empire
Henry Martyn

L. NEIL SMITH
HENRY MARTYN

A TOM DOHERTY ASSOCIATES BOOK
NEW YORK

HENRY MARTYN

Copyright © 1989 by L. Neil Smith

All rights reserved, including the right to reproduce this book, or portions thereof, in any form.

A Tor Book
Published by Tom Doherty Associates, Inc.
49 West 24th Street
New York, N.Y. 10010

ISBN: 0-812-50550-6

First edition: August 1989
First mass market printing: August 1991

Printed in the United States of America

0 9 8 7 6 5 4 3 2 1

Acknowledgments

IT WOULD BE CHURLISH (to say the least) not to acknowledge the works of Rafael Sabatini, Michael Curtiz, Errol Flynn, and C. S. Forester. Bedad, you can do it *again,* but you can't do it *better.*

TABLE OF CONTENTS

PROLOGUE: HANOVER
YEARDAY 278, 3008 A.D.
DESSE 36, 509 HANOVERIAN
SECUNDUS 12, 1566 OLDSKYAN

BAD NEWS, BAD NEWS TO THE WOODSRUNNERS BOLD,
BAD NEWS FROM BLACK HANOVER CAME.
THAT THEIR DEAREST SON HAD BEEN MURDERED MOST FOUL,
  MOST FOUL,
  MOST FOUL,
AND DARK DISHONOR BROUGHT TO A GOOD NAME.

Wheels of spreighformed pneumoplastic rolled along the carpeted corridor beneath a pale blue perforate ceiling of acoustic insulation. Nor did the technicians, laboring by twos and threes in dozens of small bays upon either side of the corridor, look up as the wheels passed. They represented an accustomed presence in this place.

The figure folded into the wheeled chair gave a nod in signal to the hulking servant-creature pushing it, almost the sole physical gesture of which his wasted body was capable. Suspended upon a silken ribbon about his graying thatch, he wore a masque—an unprepossessing flesh-toned schweitzer —which, by contemporary convention, ought to have been held upon a wand that it might be whisked away in moments of disarming truthfulness. Yet he was incapable of the gesture, even had he been capable of the candor. The servant-creature, unmasqued save by a countenance frozen into perpetual neutrality, man-shaped, man-colored, yet well in excess of the height and bulk an ordinary man might have attained, paused—the sole response of which it was capable being obedience—and brought the wheels to a halt.

"This has a familiar look, what have we here?" The crippled figure spoke to blue-smocked workers in a bay to his right, regarding the naked body of a young human male, by look a commoner, stapled through the bones of his arms and thighs to the nichromium surface of an examination table. With precise care—the man in the chair tolerated no inelegant butchery here—the youth's fingernails had been removed, the outer layer of skin at the fingers, hands, and wrists slit and flayed back, the better to expose more sensitive tissues beneath. Upon a freestanding tray beside the table, an array of probes and palps of various sizes, shapes, and substances lay ready to explore this sensitivity. Yet the chairbound figure's eyes gazed upon a scene beyond this, visible through a broad transparency behind the technicians.

No dank basement, this, the man in the chair thought with proprietary satisfaction. Others of the Drector class might choose to skulk about in cellar and attic as if there were something about their amateurish pursuits to feel guilty of. His facility was the finest in private use upon the planet, the equal of anything available to official intelligence, and lay upon ground level, where the sun of a rare beautiful Hanoverian afternoon shone in through great windows reaching floor to ceiling. Outside, his artfully landscaped personal gardens were to be seen, with their exotic trees and flowering bushes collected from a hundred thousand worlds, kept in balance by skillful and expensive labor. Birds and colored insects whirred and fluttered among them, although nothing of their activities could be heard. This wing was soundproofed to three hundred decibels. It was often necessary that it be so.

Upon a tiled wall, as in each of the other bays, was displayed a fanciful poster representing a man, its head gigantic, fingers, toes, nose, and lips swollen in grotesque proportion to arms and legs which, in comic atrophy, illustrated the relative occurrence of nerve endings throughout the body. The poster was for the edification of visitors—ladies tittering and titillated behind fashionable masques and strutting popinjays sick but afraid to manifest it before one of his position—always surprised at the insignificance afforded the genitalia, as well as by the absence of sensation in the brain. The technicians required no such reminder, knowing their art as they did and having benefitted from much opportunity to practice it.

Movement caught the cripple's eye as the aesthetist left her valves and tanks of pain-enhancing gases to peer over her own masque—no mere social convention this, even had her station in life permitted it—at floating lines of barquode from a datathille inserted in a reader at the table's foot. Muttering inquiry to a smock-garbed assistant bent over a cautery intended to stanch unplanned bleeding, she received a single word in answer and gave the data brief attention again before looking up.

"A Skyan peasant, Drector, discovered traveling without sponsorship and diverted here as you ordered all such should be. You put the question to him yourself, sir, yesterday a week."

A nod, "So I did." He was a busy man with many duties here upon the capital of the grandest civilization in recorded history. He could not expect to remember everything, even regarding personal schemes as long in preparation as these. "I had purposed rescinding the order, as, thanks to this youngster, among others, there is no further need. It slipped my mind." The boy's brown eyes were desperate above the temporary gag forced into his mouth upon the chairbound man's arrival. He had long since betrayed such data as the names and duties of key servants, geography and plans of strategic sites, movements of products and supplies, transportation and communication, and, most vital, descriptions and characterizations of principal members of the family in question. The man shook his head as if in dismissal of an errant thought. "Ah well, what glimmerings have we torn from him today, then?"

"More personal information, sir," replied the aesthetist. "You may recall he names himself Henry Martyn, seventeen Monopolitan years of age, colonial bondsman and stowaway, bored with home and harvest, looking for adventure." The aesthetist shook her head, brown curls bobbed beneath her surgical cap. "That last, sir, corroborated by the captain of the *Plover,* a lugger of eleven projectiles out of the Autonomous Drectorate of Prudentalis. What our poor Henry got, in place of adventure, was a pressganger's needle in the back of his skull and a free voyage to Hanover. A runaway, under death sentence by rights, though it says here suchlike aren't prosecuted upon Skye." A pause. "What sort of barbaric back-eddy will not punish runaways, sir?"

Behind the chair, the servant-creature gasped, startled from its torpor by the directness of the question. Indeed, thought the crippled man, it bordered upon insubordination, coming from one of the aesthetist's class. Yet she, like each of the others garbed in his surgical livery, were superlative technicians. And the patron to whom they gave much gratification pampered them, making allowance for artistic temperament.

"That," he answered, "is but one of several quarrels with Skye's Drector-Hereditary which we shall settle before the year is out." He gave a different nod this time, one sensible to mechanisms within the chair itself, the being which had pushed it here mostly serving purposes of ostentation appropriate to its master's class and, in rare need, acting as bodyguard. The chair's servodevices emitted a thin whine and trundled closer to the table, so that, through the wise and benevolent eyeholes of the masque he wore, its owner might witness proceedings the better. "Prod him somewhat," he ordered, "I wish to hear the villain speak for himself."

"Sir." In dutiful—and compensatory—acknowledgement, the aesthetist resumed her position at the subject's head and replaced the gag with one of her transparent algesic masques. She signaled her assistant. Gases began flowing, amplifying sensations, as the exacting treatment afforded the subject's upper extremities was repeated upon his toes and feet.

"Kill me and have done!" The boy's scream tore through the masque, which had been designed not to muffle words. His breathing would have been ragged but for the flow of oxygen. *"I'll tell whatever you want to know!"*

Another nod, and the chair's owner leaned closer to the boy's face, masque, as it were, to masque. "Dear boy, you mistake me. If I wished to know anything more from you, I would simply have you kept awake three days and nights as I did before. As you know, you would tell me anything, anything at all, in gratitudinous exchange for a single hour's sleep." Servos whined and the crippled figure backed up. "It is the very fact that this procedure is unnecessary which transforms it into art. I am having this done to you for nothing more than the pleasure it gives me." He looked across the table, past the helpless form which lay upon it, at the aesthetist. "I have an appointment within the hour and cannot wait for things done in proper order."

"Sir?" Failing to take his meaning, she looked a question at her master over her pale blue masque. In answer, she received an impatient scowl.

"Do the eyes *now,* while I can watch."

PART ONE: TWO WEDDINGS
YEARDAY 113, 3009 A.D.
PRIMUS 6, 1567 OLDSKYAN
IRSSE 1, 509 HANOVERIAN

THERE WERE THREE BROTHERS WHO DWELT UPON SKYE.
'ON SKYE DID THEIR HOLDINGS THEY KEEP.
AND THEY DID CAST LOTS AS TO WHICH ONE SHOULD GO,
  SHOULD GO,
  SHOULD GO,
ROVING AND STAR-ROBBING OUT IN THE DEEP.

CHAPTER I:
ARRAN ISLAY

"Pray tell, my dear Forbeth-Wethinghouth, which ith it to be with the gell, gavage or gavelleth?"

An appreciative titter arose from an unseen audience. Lightyears—and another way of life—further away, twelve-year-old Arran Islay shook his head. "Gell" was the snotty way denizens of the capital world pronounced "girl," but what was this about "gavage or gavelles"? Gavelles were units of Monopolitan currency, of course, but if he were to look up "gavage" in the dicthille lying among his school references upon a shelf across the bedroom and Mistress Lia or Old Henry were to catch him out of bed . . .

Arran shook his head again. With his father gone pleasure voyaging (against better judgment, he had complained until the moment of departure), that conscientious pair were all the more serious in the execution of their duties. This meant, from a point of view unique to the object of those duties, considerable annoyance.

In Old Henry's case, Arran's annoyance was doubled. Since his namesake and only grandson had run away offplanet last year—the youth had been in Old Henry's charge since his parents had been killed alogging—the old man had "adopted" Arran with the family Islay's approval, cared for him through this sickness, and begun teaching him many of the ancient Skyan ways passed down, father to son, mother to daughter, over the century which had seen this planet redis-covered by the Monopolity of Hanover, one of a handful of great imperia-conglomerate which dominated the known reaches of—

The viewer caught Arran's eye again. Across a too-color-ful, make-believe drawing chamber, past overembellished furnishings and garish fixtures, a second actor, the juve-

nile lead, having waited through the audience reaction, ran a
slender hand through his elaborate hairstyle. He grimaced at
the question Arran had found incomprehensible, an embarrassed blush revealed behind the masque—a conservative
(some might have maintained, unimaginative) silver kennedy
—he had let drop in momentary display of vulnerability.
He offered nothing more in answer, but raised the masque
again upon its stick, the more decently to conceal his emotions.

The speaker, a blond, aristocratic figure in chartreuse
culottes and lavender doublet, half lifted an arm, his pale
wrist bent at the lacy cuff. His masque, a classic bronze
machiavelli, lay upon the parqueted surface of the secretary
before him, demonstrating what a forthright, modern fellow
he must be. In the background a synthechord was playing.
Notes fell like metallic raindrops as if timed to the glitter of
the lumitory sconces upon the walls, or the chandelabra
making their own tinkling music overhead. Standing at his
secretary, the fictional and famous Piotr Megrim-Boutade
produced an expensive hand-wrought inhaling tube, gave its
knurled ferrule a delicate twist of adjustment, and thrust it up
each elegant, flared nostril in turn.

Megrim-Boutade, Mistress Lia had explained when she
lent him this thille, was second son to an imaginary Drector-
Hereditary of Capriccio and a celebrated character in parlor-
pieces such as this. He was the soul of wit (in theory, Arran
added for himself), the spirit of his times (whatever that was
worth), and, she had claimed, the unanswerable social arbiter to far-flung Hanoverian civilization and all who admired
and wished to emulate it. He would not have lasted a single
hour, Arran thought with scorn, in the everblue forests
or the mist-shrouded shroom bogs of his own birth planet,
Skye.

Not realizing what harsh and final judgment had been
passed upon him, the elegant Megrim-Boutade slipped the
inhaling tube into his ruffled sleeve, exposing the polished
collimator of a gold-chased kinergic thrustible strapped to
his forearm. "'Pon my thoul," he observed with a delicate
sniff, "there can be no middle courth with her ilk, nay, nor
even clavitheth, for I have it upon good authority your

enamorata ploth her own courth, toward thome Jendyne gentle of a germane gender." The audience erupted with laughter.

Clavises! With a snarl, he jerked the dramathille, criminally misnamed, the thought flashed through his mind, from the viewer upon his blanket-covered lap. The images before his eyes dissolved in a shower of incoherent sparks. He hurled the cylinder across the bedroom. It struck the spotless wall beside rough-cast door timbers—a flower garland, beginning to brown and dry, hung from a peg there, souvenir of a festivity which, in his illness, he had been unable to attend—and fell to the polywood floor, frightening the boy's pet triskel which had been lying upon a hand-hooked oval rug. With a squeak, the triskel leapt to all three feet and burrowed under the rug.

Arran's room was at the apex of a tower, built of graniplastic blocks by the Islays' predecessors and long disused, at one corner of his father's Holdings. Arran had claimed it for himself as soon as he was old enough to state his preference in this or any matter. With help from Old Henry and Mistress Lia, he had pried the door from the frame to which it had long been nailed, driven out the night-fliers, cleaned the place up, and seen the walls beadblasted until they shone translucent white.

That had been before he had fallen ill.

He glanced up at the long, slender precolonial weapon they had found while renovating the place. Its metal parts were rough and pitted, stained with oxides. No maker's mark remained, if ever there had been one. Here and there a patch showed of the original dull-gleaming blue-black tint. The thing was much too heavy for strapping to the user's forearm, as was the custom with thrustibles. It had been mounted in a length of grainy, unplasticized wood, carven, where broadest, with the figure of an alien animal, long extinct, which Old Henry said had once been brought to Skye by hundreds for riding, but which had not prospered upon the forage found here.

In the old man's opinion this symbol had been personal to the owner and indicated that he or she had been among the planet's first human inhabitants, long and long, as Henry put it, before the Monopolity had come. They had found other things in the tower room, a toothless comb, a bristleless brush, the top of a small plastic chest which had been in similar manner carven.

Cleaned and oiled, though still unworkable, the weapon, topped with a dented sighting tube which placed its time before that of laser designators, hung from its sling, with a dozen of the tarnished chemenergic cylinders it had used, upon the wall between the broad sails of a pair of modern full-rigged model starships, products of Arran's mentor-guided hands. The boy was filled, as he had often been before, with a feeling of curiosity about the first Skyans, wondering what it must have been like here before the thrustibles of Hanoverian Oplytes had overridden ancient arms like this.

Outside the arch-topped tower windows, thick polymer with calmed and beveled borders, the morning sun shone in a sky of faultless azure. A ghostly thumbnail sliver of the Broken Moon was visible, horizon to horizon, above the close-spaced tops of trees which marked the near edge of the forest. Between the everblues and the Holdings, Islay retainers would be harvesting groundberries in a meadow where they grew year round. Birds would be singing. It was, upon those accounts and others, he thought, a terrible day, the worst kind of day for a boy to be bedridden, sentenced to remain indoors.

"Waenzi—Waenzi, it is all right, come here." Arran whistled to the little triskel. Thus encouraged, the three-legged creature emerged from its hiding place and hopped onto the bed beside him, where the boy stroked its short, coarse fur in an attempt to soothe it, sneering down, as he did so, at the dramathille where it lay at the edge of the rug.

Weighing less than a gramme (it was but seven siemmes in length, less than a tenth that in diameter, barquoded to—misindicate—its contents), its arrival at the wall had produced no racket to satisfy his frustration. It was, in essence, indestructible, promising him no emotional compensation had he been the sort to delight in its destruction, which he was not.

They were all like this, each thille his tutor, Mistress Lia Woodgate, received from the capital, a tendentious hodge-podge of effete mannerism and incomprehensible fuss.

Clavises? What did the currency of the Jendyne Empery-Cirot have to do with anything? What did any of it mean? Half the time Arran could not understand what that bugger Megrim-Boutade was saying through his cultured lisp and egg-shaped tones; the other half, his features were concealed, like those of the other actors—indeed, if Mistress Lia were believed, like those of every fashionable gentle-being upon Hanover—behind masques created in the likeness of obscure historical figures whose proverbial qualities were supposed to reveal something of the mood or intentions of the characters. Mistress Lia, also instructor to Arran's brothers, Robret *fils* and Donol (and something more than this to the eldest), had shown him one of her own masques, avowing she favored a pale lavender portia, which, for some reason he had never understood, was supposed to be clever.

"Wanque!" Arran pronounced the word aloud, startling Waenzi again and dismissing the Megrim-Boutade once and for all. He glanced round with a guilty expression to see if anyone had heard him utter the boyish obscenity.

As it happened, someone had. A perfunctory pair of raps sounded in the small room. Startled again, the much-abused triskel hopped from the bed and vanished beneath it. Arran hoped he had not wet the floor. The door opened, spreading dessicated flower petals as it swung into the room. Old Henry Martyn followed, bearing a handworked tray the mere sight of which—rather of the tankard upon it, an original from this room and in likewise carven with an animal's form—made Arran shudder with recent but deep-grained reflex. Upon the tray, beside the hated flagon, lay another object which the boy thought he recognized, although the reason for its presence was a mystery.

Noticing Arran's expression, the old man stepped over the throw-rug, set tray, tankard, and mysterious object upon a table, bent and picked up the dramathille. He gave a conspicuous nod toward the waste-chute in the wall across the room from the bookcases. "Methought I'd taught ye throwin' straighter'n that, young master." He gave the boy a broad grin and a blue-eyed wink. "Then, ye'd been touch sickly, ha'n't ye?"

Waenzi reappeared to bump his torso, which served as the

only head he owned, against the old man's ankles in greeting and hopped upon the bed again. Despite himself, Arran answered with a laugh. Old Henry had that effect upon him. Stooped and withered until he was scarce taller than the boy himself, the old man was the most ancient being Arran had ever known. Old Henry's sky-colored eyes twinkled among the furrows of a face like a dried apple, and a thick shock of pure white hair stood upon end like his brother Robret's thissbristle shaving brush. For all his venerability and apparent decrepitude, he moved with smooth alacrity and energetic purpose, without a hint of the tremble Arran had seen afflict many a younger man than Old Henry Martyn.

"Yes, Henry," he answered, giving the timid animal an absent stroke, "I have been." He looked down at what he was doing. " 'Sick as a triskel'—though in truth I have never seen Waenzi sick a day. And I have been missing all the fun." He nodded toward the garland upon the door, although he might have meant the dramathille by his complaint. "A poor plain substitute such a thing as that, for games, and food, and music—"

"Aye, an' noise an' excitement—"

"The visiting nobility . . ."

"An' common folka Skye, come t'pay respects, more welcome at it in whole wide imperium-conglomerate'n they might'd been 'neath any other Drector's roof." The old man shook his head. "Aye, an' alla that. But even childhood cancer virus be serious matter, lad—had it m'self at yer age—an' serious matters must be seriously treated, ha'n't they?" Old Henry raised his thick and snowy eyebrows, nodding toward the dreaded flagon upon the table.

Arran made a grudging face. With Old Henry's help, he lifted the heavy container, gulped down quick as he could the vile mixture it contained, and which was, he admitted, step by gradual step, making him well once more—though with less rapidity than he hoped it would.

Scarcely remembering his own mother, dead these eight years, he thought it a good thing, his father's taking wife again, as had occurred the previous week while he lay wracked with drug-induced delirium. He was uncertain how he felt about his father's bride, the Lady Alysabeth Morven, but he had hated missing his father's wedding. Time enough to decide about his new stepmother once she and Father were back from honeymoon travels. Likewise, he would hate missing his eldest brother's wedding, due to take place upon the senior couple's return in another month and a half. He was as fond of this particular bride-to-be as if she were already the sister she was about to become. Or the mother he had never known. Now that he felt better—which in contrast to the time of his father's wedding meant only that he was conscious—he would begin worrying about a gift. It must be appropriate both to the occasion and his feelings about those celebrating it.

Old Henry took the flagon from him, inspected it to make sure it was empty, and set it back upon the tray. Curious, Waenzi leaned over to sniff at the container, gave out a strangled, mewling noise, and vanished beneath the bed again. Old Henry and Arran laughed.

"Valorously done, lad," the old man commended the boy. "Valorously done. An' there be rewards for heroes." He made no move toward the other object lying upon the tray, as Arran might have expected, but, grinning his wrinkled grin again, took a step back. "Ye're t'get yerself outa bed now, an' take such exercise as ye feel capable of."

A thrill went through the boy. "Henry! You are not having fun with me?" Not waiting for the old man to reveal that his words had been a joke, he sat up straight in bed. "I may, really?"

"That ye may." The old man offered Arran a hand as the boy threw off the blanket and swung his legs past the edge of the bed for the first time in nine long, nightmarish weeks. What dizziness or infirmity he felt was more from prolonged involuntary rest than any disease afflicting him. When at last Arran stood upon the floor, both shoeless feet cool from the contact, Old Henry tapped an age-polished finger upon the object he had brought with him. "This, young master, be but firsta many surprises this day an' those t'come'll bring ye." He straightened, of a sudden formal, and cleared his throat. "Beginnin', as y'might someday swear, best an' busiest time ayer young life."

Standing, his knees still weak, Arran looked down at the object with its ancient, unintelligible embossery of flaked gold metal. Not certain how it was done, although he had seen these things referred to in dramathilles about the ancient and romantic past, he picked it up, spread it open in his left palm, and let a gentle right thumb riffle through the brittle, symbol-covered sheets of which it consisted.

His guess had been correct, although he had not known such objects to exist within his father's Holdings or even upon the planet Skye. He realized they were unique in one respect: they had been invented long before *ulsic,* an inbuilt property of artifacts which allowed them to perform complex functions without human attention. As many words and ideas as this thing might contain, it was nowhere near as "smart," say, as the most idiotic thille, or even the flagon keeping his medicine well mixed and at proper temperature.

Still, he had been right: it was a book.

CHAPTER II:
THE ISLAYS OF SKYE

"Let it rain," Robret Islay declared to no one in particular, "I am none the less content."

It was a remarkable confession from one unused to speaking his feelings. Tall, broad of shoulder, he claimed that mixture of brown skin, fair hair, and dark eyes under coal-black brows which marked him son (firstborn and principal heir) to the famous warrior-nobleman, Drector-Hereditary of Skye. He gazed out the many-paned windows of what an earlier age had called a library into the meadow surrounding the Holdings.

The day, having dawned unnaturally brilliant, had deteriorated into light drizzle drifting from a gray overcast more typical of the planet. Oblivious to the weather, half a hundred of the Holdings' croppers stooped in the meadow, gathering groundberries and lawn-herbs which, later in the season, would sustain them during the arduous shroom-harvest. Excepting the quaint hats they wore, streaming with moisture, their clothing was the same as the younger Robret's. Had Robret Senior been here, he and his family might have joined them in their labors.

"For I ask both of you," Robret turned and faced into the room, "how could family affairs be more gratifyingly concluded? Our father, eight years the widower, remarried this week amidst all the splendor and ceremony which our age, and his station in the order of things, afford . . ."

"And into a rich connection," intruded a male voice from across the room, "offering untold political advantage."

Robret concealed the sour expression this cynical utterance might otherwise have cast upon his face. What had been asserted was true enough: Tarbert Morven, second son of the Drector-Hereditary of Shandish, Drector-Appointee in his own right, father of the bride, was an old acquaintance of the family Islay. In past decades, he had become a powerful figure in the Monopolitan 'Droom. Less lucky than Robret "the" Islay, he had been crippled in the conflict which had made Islay a hero and given him a Drectorate of his own, establishing the current dynasty upon Skye. That Morven lived at all was to the senior Robret's solitary credit. Nevertheless, that did not constitute a reason—he broke off the diatribe he had been about to deliver, smiling instead at a female figure seated nearer by.

"And, heaping fortune upon fortune, leaving me at liberty to seek my own happiness." He lifted a hand toward the voice which spoke of connections. "My younger brother is awarded new responsibility, in which, perverse though it be, he finds as much satisfaction as I in the prospect of marriage." He glanced up, through the ceiling as it were, toward the old tower. "My baby brother, at death's door not long ago, is now upon the mend. Old Henry Redshirt had him up and about this morning, were you two aware?"

Upon a low stool beside the room's modest firegrate (another the size of Arran's bedchamber dominated the great dining hall) Mistress Lia Woodgate glanced up from the cleverwork held in the lap of her voluminous skirts and smiled back at her fiancé. Her hair, unbound and soft upon her shoulders, was a glossy brown. Her skin, over a frame of delicate bone, was fair where it was not heavily, and not unbecomingly, freckled. Her eyes, blue as Robret *fils'* were brown, upon this account were close to black. A hardpine log within the grate cracked with a startling noise and split from end to end, releasing a thousand short-lived fireflies to dance up the ancient chimney.

Above the fireplace hung the cadet Arms of Islay. Upon the shield, against a field of native everblues, the tusk-jowled Skyan *thiss* crouched in wrinkle-snout defiance within a frame of *steyraugs* (thrustibles being considered modern by the heraldrists, and gauche). Cadet as might be, the Arms of Islay had just been redesigned to incorporate a silver pick-axe at each corner, juxtaposed with an ebony-and-golden miner's lamp. This device was symbolic of the Morven family, therefore also of the senior Robret's bride, Alysabeth. Decades younger than the Islay—and, some avowed, inhumanly beautiful—she was the golden-tressed daughter of Tarbert who had been a fighting comrade to the senior Robret.

Above the shield, upon hooks cast from ancient cartridge brass, hung the original from which the pictured *steyraugs* were conceived. An awkward mass of metal and green polymer, it represented precolonial arms which, a century ago, had been overcome by the thrustibles of invading Hanoverians. Both sides had collapsed from mutual exhaustion, the invaders' maladaptation to the planet, and the vicissitudes of a larger war which had so far lasted a thousand years. The Holdings were hung about with many such outdated artifacts.

The burning log settled in its irons, scattering sparks. Lia pulled her skirts from the foot of the firescreen and inspected them for scorch holes and embers before speaking. "Pray do not permit Old Henry to hear you call him thus. It would distress him. He repents of youthful days misspent amongst rebellious woodsrunners."

Robret shook his head. His hair was straight, and, being somewhat longer than was the vogue, brushed the collar of his well-worn brownish-green outdoorsman's jacket. "Ought I call him by the name the Unsurrendered among his kinsmen give him, 'Henry the Uncled'? It is an ungainly calling, though I have heard it claimed it was a custom in those ancient times, which saw this world first settled by our Predecessors, that a weaker foe must cry 'uncle'—why, I do not know—for mercy from stronger."

Lia made a gentle noise denoting scorn in one of her gender and breeding. "'Unsurrendered' do they call themselves, while making mock of one such as Old Henry? Your father, I think with too much kindness, names them 'Holdouts.' Are they not those who have retreated, unmolested, to the deepest forest and the mountain fastness, partaking in full of the great unwritten Bargain he first put to them—thereby bringing unprecedented peace and happiness to Skye—one of tolerance and, at an arm's length, coexistence?"

"And therefore," Donol gave his tutor's logic a cynical twist, "who is uncle-ing whom?"

"Uncled." Robret repeated the awkward word as if he had heard neither his brother nor fiancé. "You know, that might be a corruption. 'Cravens who have purchased their survival through submission.' The *unculled*. Ugly thought! You are quite right, my dear, I shall never call Old Henry by such a name again, he who was first henchman to Ianmichael Briartonson," Robret had pronounced the name *Bronson,* "leader of the genuine rebels upon Skye!"

"And," added Donol, "our mother's father."

This time Lia expressed involuntary and uncharacteristic surprise.

"Knew you not," Robret explained before his brother could lecture, "that my mother, Glynnaughfern née Briartonson, came to the Holdings not only out of love, but as a highborn hostage? She, the only offspring of the rebel leader, dwelling in the heart of Hanover-Upon-Skye, as it was then known?"

"It was your vehemence which moved me, darling," answered Lia. "I thought this to have been part of the Bargain. She must have been a great—"

"A great *something,*" he interrupted, "so the Holdouts called her. It hurt her all her life. Sometimes I think that this—not the genetic drift the boffins speak of with such eloquence, which made her birthings of us and our unborn siblings difficult—was what killed her at the last."

Silence followed for a time. Never upon previous occasion

had such delicate and sanguine matters been discussed between the brothers, let alone with someone else who was, however temporarily, not yet of the family.

"However . . ." Robret continued as if there had been no intervening period of silence, as if the thoughts of all three had not wandered elsewhere, but still lingered upon the same subject, which indeed they did. "I brought it up to tell you something else you may not know, nor Arran, either." He glanced toward his middle brother. "Nor even you, Donol, at a guess."

"What could it be, elder brother, that you have learned that I have not?"

Robret smiled. Even his love Lia could not guess what feelings the expression intended to convey. "When Ianmichael Briartonson had died—to his surprise of old age and of natural causes—and likewise our mother before her time, peace was still fragile and in need of husbandment. Old Henry Red—Old Henry Martyn, not so old in those days, who had been Briartonson's chiefmost lieutenant—came here afoot, of his own accord, willing to become a humble servant in order to take, in some small way, our mother's place as hostage."

Donol's expression was a puzzled one. "Robret, you were quite correct. I had not known. Why would anybody do such a thing?"

"Have I not just explained?" He turned to Lia. "Perhaps you will see that when I called him 'Redshirt' it was in token of respect. Perhaps we all—myself included, who has not thought upon these things in years—will henceforward respect Old Henry the more for it."

Lia nodded and began to speak, but was by Donol interrupted. "Upon the contrary, brother, I disrespect him more who steps from leadership to servitude preserving a bargain made by others, decades old, which perhaps did not require it. To 'Redshirt' and 'Uncled,' let us add 'Wastrel'!"

"Only," Robret suggested, "if we grant you the honorifics 'Cynical' and 'Blackhooded.'" He observed his beloved suppress a grin.

Donol frowned. "Unlike you, my sage and elder brother, I speak of none of these affairs with any authority. They all transpired before my time, not to mention yours. I do

wonder why savages everywhere resist those pragmatic phi-
lanthropists intent upon bringing them the benefits of superi-
or culture."

"Perhaps they believe," Lia offered as if Donol's voice had
not been laden again with sarcasm, "the asking price of those
so-called benefits too dear, even were they given opportunity
to bargain or demur." Before Robret could add whatever it
was he planned, she turned to him. "Nor have I ever heard
you speak with very high regard for the benefits of culture,
your ordinary term of preference being, as I recall, 'effete
thiss excrement.'"

Robret's reply was half chuckle, half snort. "Much exists,
my darling, of which Old Henry might repent himself and
does not." He attempted imitation of the ancient servant's
voice. "*'Mon didna always sail 'tween stars in mighty
shipses . . .'* Thus he fills young Arran's head with romantic
tales of sailing the galactic Deep, enveloped in colorful and
subtle auras, propelled by insubstantial sails bellying in the
tachyon wind, sometimes being dashed to pieces in neutrino
storms." This time the snort was unmixed with humor. "He
pursued the selfsame folly with his grandson and namesake
and has none but himself to blame for whatever befell the boy
in the end."

Lia sighed. She knotted off a stitch, wielded the fiberaser
without which no human fingers could have severed the
tenacious thread, pocketed the implement, and folded her
work round its hoop. "You are the best of men, my darling. I
cannot help myself but to love you most immoderately—"

A faint, ironic cough interrupted her. Robret's brother,
seated across the room at the secretary which had become his
sovereign domain, was of lesser stature and lighter build than
Robret. His hair was thin, sandy-colored, his eyes a paler
shade than normal to the family Islay. In his bridegroom-
father's absence—as, in truth, was more and more the case
even in the elder warrior's presence—he was attending the
estate's complex accounts. Running the index finger of
his free hand along the bands of barquode in the ledger,
he paused, adding this brisk notation, correcting that careless computation, turning his flat-tipped *ulsic* smartbrush
one way and then the other, making each precise, vertical
stroke the proper width to be read by man or machine. Hav-

ing heard Lia, he looked up, favoring Robret with a wry glance.

In Robret's expression were mixed embarrassment and pride at Lia's confession before a witness. He grinned back, foolish, at his brother, addressing his reply to her. "Pray, Mistress Woodgate, how could you resist?"

The scowl upon her face was only mockery in part. "If you please, sir, forbear to interrupt. I love you well. Else, after three dreary years in which to sample it, I would never have contemplated dwelling the rest of my life upon this damp and gloomy world you Islays all adore so."

She set her cleverwork aside upon the woven lid of a native basket, rose, and, brushing at imagined wrinkles in her skirt, joined Robret at the window. Donol kept his head bent over the ledgers spread before him, but was, without insincere pretense to the contrary, giving them an attentive ear.

"'We Islays,' perhaps I ought to begin saying," she continued, taking Robret's hand. "Yet, for all of that, and more besides, you are most charming in your naiveté—"

"Wait now, my girl!" The warrior's son brought himself to full height and shook her hand off.

"Sir," she insisted, catching his hand again, "if you will not take offense at your tutor saying so out of a humble sense of her bounden duty."

"Well, it is true enough and true again," he shrugged. He laughed, seizing her small, soft hand in both his larger, rougher ones. "Although I might with justification claim my naive appearance to be sophisticated dissimulation. Old Henry says they have no masques upon Skye, and must fashion their disguises out of words. The truth is, I had never a head for history, for politics, for economies of any kind. Like my father, I am—"

"A warrior?"

"Not I. A farmer when you boil the froth down, albeit with a fancy title. Would you undertake, despite the obvious difficulty of the task, the unsuitability of the material at hand, as it were, to educate me?"

She laughed. "Is this not the thing which I was brought here to accomplish in the first place?"

He nodded, smiling as sweet memories welled up in his

mind of having fallen in love, unexpected by none but himself, with the "old maid" hired from the capital to be teacher to his brothers and himself. "Aye, and I confess that you have educated me in ways I had never before anticipated."

"Robret!" Lia blushed a darker color than her freckles and was compelled to turn aside for a grace-saving moment, although a pleased smile touched the corners of her lips. Donol conspicuously ignored the pair, finding deeper interest in his accounts than had been the case the previous moment. After a time Lia cleared her throat and assumed a tutorial tone. "For that, darling farmer-when-you-boil-it-down, you shall pay forfeit, and, naiveté being a curable condition, permit me to earn my keep as teacher a final time . . ."

Robret, knowing her well, shrugged in resignation to the inevitable.

"In the matter," she began, "of cultural benefit and precolonial resistance, few individuals at present appreciate the extent to which ours is an unprecedented period of historic contrasts, of wide-ranging exploration, remarkable invention, intellectual innovation—"

"Amounting," Robret interrupted, disdain sincere and heavy in his voice, "to no more than the filching and in-smuggling of 'foreign' ideas."

Lia shook her head. "You are the country squire, are you not? Have it your way, for the nonce we shall reverse the polarity of evaluation. Set against all I have described, a dreadful philosophical stagnation threatens our vaunted civilization, political corruption too base to speak of in decency, a general moral decay which besets long-established institutions—"

"Take care, lass," Robret aped a sternness of address learned from his father which, in that individual, was no more genuine, "lest you speak treason toward the interstellar Monopolity to which the family Islay pledges fealty, and whence derive our power, prestige, and privileges."

She ignored him. "—and the territories, spatial, geographical, and otherwise, they have controlled for centuries." Of a sudden, Lia brought herself closer to Robret, as if beseeching warmth against the weather outside, which could not touch them in this cosy room, or perhaps from weather of a different kind, further away and colder. "It is a time, my love, of reason and brutality, of heroism and villainy, of virtue and depravity."

"In this," he asked, "does it differ from any other time?"

"Agreed," she answered with a sigh, "it is not unique in that regard. What sets it apart, I think, is the degree to which conflicting qualities are found among us, perhaps in the fact that they are less to be discovered in conflict with one another than in combination within the same individual."

"Sentimental moralistic nonsense!" Donol sealed his smartbrush with a fastidious flourish, closed his ledger, and turned in his seat to face them. His expression was one of disgust. "Personalities have nothing at all to do with history. Nor, I warrant, do they—"

He was interrupted by a gentle knock at the room's double doors. Without awaiting an answer, a girl entered with a tray, set it upon a table intended for the purpose, and departed, closing the doors behind her. Lia poured three cups of the steaming drink, known hereabouts as "lawn tea," brewed from the same stimulant herbs which the croppers gathered in the meadow outside the window. She offered one to Robret who took it in both hands, another to Donol who accepted it without rising, and took one for herself.

"Donol," Robret asked after he had emptied half his cup, "you were warranting something?"

Donol's momentary blank look vanished as memory overcame the effect of interruption. "That I was: the human personality is constant. It never changes over the eons, and cannot, upon that account, represent a significant factor in the path history takes. The human personality understands only wallowing self-gratification and the brute force of authority necessary to temper it—to print a phrase—into constructive mettle. Thus your savages have no right to resist that which is its own justification."

Warming to a subject they had previously disputed, he cleared his throat. "Let us eschew sentimentality and be analytical. As is well understood, civilization is characterized by the source whence it derives its energy. In previous ages, animals and slaves, steam and the combustion engine, fission and fusion, powered the fundamental machinery, and thus determined all else of politics and economics, even of personality. So, in our twenty-seventh-century civilization is everything desirable accomplished by means of '§-physics'—"

"'A technique,'" Robret jumped into the recitation, "'of discriminating between fundamental properties of matter—mass, weight, inertia, potential and kinetic energy—and exploiting their separate characters.' Broward and Kearney's *Matrices of the Civilities,* Chapter Three, if memory serves. I know the catechism as well as you, younger brother, Lia taught it to us. And your logic leaves somewhat to be desired, as well. Do not lecture."

Wise in the ways of brotherly disputation, Lia uttered not a word.

"Save your advice," retorted Donol, "for those who have need of it. If Lia taught us, by the Ceo, she should know the lesson better herself."

Robret opened his mouth to respond, but never got a word out. The doors flew wide. In the hallway entrance stood, beside the girl who had admitted him, a cropper, wet from rain and dripping upon the carpet.

"Beggin' pardon, yoong mahster," the cropper touched his forelock, self-conscious of his clothes and accent, "Toddy McCabe's poot tail af glass-lizard through foot. We've needa Old Henry 'fore poison's after spreadin'."

"By all means." Robret's answer was brisk. In truth, he was relieved to be given an excuse to leave this pointless argument. He did not appreciate Donol's not-so-subtle chaperonage. The Hanoverian custom—that what he and Lia had pursued with the greatest joy and vigor earlier was now, with the announcement of their engagement, denied them until their wedding night—was an increasing burden and annoyance to him.

He nodded at the servant girl. "Find Old Henry Martyn and send him straightaway." To his brother and fiancée, he added, "I am going myself, to see if I can be of assistance."

CHAPTER III:
THE HOLDINGS OF ISLAY

Boxes, bales, bundles, and bushels.

Dust, decay, dehydration, and death.

All round Arran, the block-constructed walls, draped in clinging webs and the cloying miasma of abandonment, shone in his lampwand—which gave no visible light of its own, nor cast a shadow, but made the plastic about him glow from within—exuding moisture of disquieting color and viscosity.

Arran's pet triskel, Waenzi, bumbled underfoot, following in front of him, weaving between Arran's ankles, collecting cobwebs and dust bindles in his short, stiff fur, never venturing outside the safe locus of the soft light excited by the lampwand. Almost, the boy regretted bringing him. Never before this had he been able to persuade the triskel to accompany him upon such an exploratory foray. Perhaps his recent illness had made a difference in the animal's attachment to him.

Legos: the architectural style was still referred to by its legendary name. Much the commonest method it had been, of building in precolonial times, with their primitive machines and less-sophisticated spreighformers. In hindsight it made perfect sense, yet what a surprise it had been to early explorers, who should have known better, that petroleum was everywhere abundant, even upon those planets which had never known life, formed, as it was, in the process of each world's condensation from a disk of primordial gas rich in carbon molecules. It was a method of construction still in universal employ because it was so cheap and simple, and because it worked.

The great translucent blocks had been extruded, fresh and new, from spreighformers the estate still used, where they had been assembled *in vacuo* a molecule at a time. Each block, a measure upon a side, had been moulded with deep locking grooves and matching ridges. Each had been slid into place and welded, using ultrasound, to its neighbors, forming a solid mass, indestructible by time or the elements. Never had Arran been able to scratch or mar one such, nor separate it from adjoining blocks. But here, deep within the Holdings' foundations, their once-polished surfaces were dulled, their once-sharp edges softened—"rounded" would have exaggerated it—by the weight of centuries and the punishing load they bore. Arran noticed that the faces of the blocks bulged outward. Those which made up the walls of his tower bedroom, many stories above, otherwise identical in every respect, were concave, carrying, as they did, a lighter burden.

He had wandered these passageways before, where dust and mildew alternated, chamber to chamber; where small, multilegged things—some not so small, from the sound—scurried at his approach. All three of Waenzi's eyes bulged with comic tension, trying to look everywhere at once as unsavory creatures of an even more unsavory darkness fled the alien influence of his master's lampwand. Some were native to Skye, others man-brought by inadvertence or intention, altered in subtle detail by the stressful voyage or by subsequent exigencies, and which nature—or his imagination—now endowed with poison fangs or tail-barbs, glowing eyes of variable size, number, and arrangement, slime-tracks smeared behind them upon the floor, or other attributes and habits even more despicable.

Each time he passed beneath a low-curved dripping arch, brushing legger-weavings from his face, he dreaded that something finger-sized and brittle-bodied, with countless needle-pointed appendages, would drop down his unprotected collar. Yet Arran was drawn, despite vague terrors of the place, by a comforting certainty that no adult he knew of had come here since he had been born. Therefore, he would not be bothered, nagged, or interrupted in his explorations. He felt a certain gratitude toward Toddy McCabe, whose recent injury made him the estate's new "sick-boy" to be fussed over and watched, leaving Arran free to pursue important boyish business.

Today it seemed he had never before seen what these ill-lit tunnels stored. He had taken, he thought, the dust-covered crates and barrels which surrounded him, in many chambers piled to the low-groined ceilings, to be one with the walls and beams of what he enjoyed believing was a dungeon.

Twice each day the past week, upon walks Old Henry had intended to help the recovering boy get exercise—walks which at first, had Arran been willing to admit it to the elderly Skyan or himself, had been exhausting—his self-chosen mentor had pointed with mixed pride and sorrow to coats-of-arms which decorated the Islay family Holdings. Over fireplaces, propped in niches, strewn about the great hall where Arran's father had been wed, ancient—now useless—weapons, once the property of defeated enemies, could be seen upon the walls: *steyraugs, remwins, arpeegies, smithwessons.*

Dauntless pioneers those first men upon Skye must have been, the old man had often whispered to the boy, boiling up, as they had, off a used-up mother planet, the now half-mythical "Earth," seeking fresh opportunity and new adventure. Nor—Old Henry always peered about them to see he was not overheard—when men began to ply the star-lanes, were their liberties at first circumscribed by the whims and vagaries of the imperia-conglomerate.

Many a great war had it taken to achieve that in a time of legend long before Arran's father had been rewarded for his prowess upon behalf of Hanover with elevation to the Drectorate. Long before a previous Drector-Hereditary, bitterly stalemated with Skyan rebels, had died without distinction or heirs. Long before these ancient Holdings had lain vacant for a century of neglect by the faraway and, at the time, preoccupied Monopolity. Long before, despite the stalemate they had won (or as its price), Skyans had been reduced to a state of ignorant and fearful serfdom or the brutish existence of Holdouts running wild through woods and mountains, robbing travelers and raiding villages during the harsh Skyan winters. Even long before the sons and daughters of those dauntless pioneers Old Henry spoke of had been surprised and nearly overwhelmed by those they considered looting second-comers.

And, to appearances, it had taken something more than war. The trappings of the torture chamber were all about him. Chains rusted in reptilian coils upon the gritty flags.

More hung stapled to thick plastic walls, bleeding red-orange oxide into the interstices. Or pigments, perhaps, more sinister. Iron-plaited archways leered as he passed, age-tarnished interwoven bars whispering of lifetime after hopeless lifetime of imprisonment and obscene abuse. Welded square-stock gratings swung to his reluctant touch upon shrill hinges, everywhere partitioning room from room and hall from hall.

Or perhaps this was nothing more than his imagination, fired by Old Henry's stories and by dramathilles. So unfamiliar was young Arran with the clumsy, complicated precolonial machinery about him that what he took in pleasant, grisly fancy for a bone-breaker or stretching-rack could, he admitted to himself, have been a lady's hobby-loom, a printing-press, some arcane contrivance for producing wine. Metal baskets hung with the remains, corroded to near-anonymity, of what might once have been tongs and irons designed for the wringing-out of confessions. Yet they may with equal ease have been implements of (to Arran) far humbler and far less romantic utility. Even at his age, he was sophisticated and introspective enough to detect within himself a tendency to see what his imagination would have him see. This facility within him thirsted for adventure, for escape from what seemed—as home does to every boy—a drab, mundane existence. In a manner which would have surprised most of the adults who thought they knew him, he made appropriate allowances without abandoning his fancies. Nor was he entirely conscious of the complex process by which he kept his impressions balanced.

Now, however, Arran ignored the rooms themselves, along with their dubious furnishings. He had a purpose. His mind fastened upon their contents, the discarded bag and baggage of an earlier era, stored in these dim hallways, for the first time separating it from the walls which supported it in towering piles, sorting it into various categories of possibility.

Anything might be found here. All this mouldy rejecta, tonnes of it, was already here when his father had taken formal possession of the Holdings or had afterward been hauled down, Arran appreciated with wry humor, against some hypothetical day when some hypothetical someone should discover time and inclination to dirty his hands, get rid of the unquestionable trash, and restore what might be useful—or simply interesting—to the upper floors, daylight, and fresh air. Like all such resolutions concerning cluttered basements, memento-choked attics, bulging storerooms, and crowded outbuildings, the day of redemption was never likely to arrive.

Nonetheless, these mountains of offcast trivia, the impedimenta of another century (to Arran their mystique would have been quite as strong had they been but the leavings of another decade), presented to the bright and curious boy a vast and promising frontier. He might never fathom its fullness. Its inexhaustibility being an attraction in itself, it might never cease providing him with something interesting to see and do.

The useless weapons hanging everywhere above had come from here. Rather, they were among the few articles not relegated to subterranean darkness. Yet Arran, today, was intent upon another quarry. The book with which Old Henry had gifted him—in which he was beginning to make gradual progress, sounding out each painful syllable with frequent reference to the phonetic key the old man had barquoded for him upon a flyleaf—was of the same vintage as most of this refuse. Perhaps he could ferret out another of its kind which had survived the vicissitudes of abandonment. Would not Old Henry be surprised?

Thus this was no occasion for mere idle poking about, Arran reminded himself. He was here to a purpose. Robret was to be married in a few more days, and to Mistress Lia, whom the boy loved full as well as his brother. In his illness, he had missed his father's wedding, missed gifting that union with something from his own heart, his own mind, perhaps even his own hands. He would not be cheated of the honor and the pleasure now. His energies, those of a recovering boy, and thus his time, were limited. To say nothing, he thought, of the capacities of his sun-charged lampwand. He shuddered with imaginary chills at the idea of being stranded down here in the darkness.

To business. But where to start? Everywhere he looked, everything he saw was covered with dust, draped in cobwebbery, coated with mildew. Some of the things down here, he knew, had been mouldering away for centuries. Attempting to be of assistance, Waenzi gave each item they encountered a cautious sniff, making curious noises, often backing up in sudden, disgusted retreat, straightaway into Arran's legs.

The odd pair's random footsteps carried them at last into a low-arched vault not larger than Arran's bedroom. Here a few things had been stacked against a wall and covered with a sheet of plastic, now dark and brittle with age. Watchful for he knew not what slithery horror to jump out at him, he pulled the disintegrating plastic away. Dust and musty odors welled up in his face as he spied a dozen large plastic boxes in a somewhat better state of preservation than most of what he had seen thus far. One of these, a solid-looking chest, mottled green and brown, was perhaps half an arm's length upon a side. Rounded corners it had, and was guarded against intrusion by a pair of heavy black clasps, also of plastic. An efficient sealing ridge thick as Arran's index finger wrapped about its circumference.

At sight of such a chest, many another child of Arran's time would have seized upon thoughts of brigands of the Deep. Of treasure. What caught the boy's eye was a detail of the lid. At no small effort it had been incised in careful, artful strokes, with the selfsame riding-animal design he knew from those several objects in his bedroom which also bore it. Countless years had filled the deep-scribed lines with grime, enhancing, with a certain irony, the contrast of the well-executed carving. This chest, if Old Henry's surmise was correct, had belonged to the same unknown individual who had once occupied, and perhaps loved, the tower room centuries before Arran had made it his own.

Hesitating, wondering whether he ought to open the chest here or upon an upper floor where cleaner air and better light were to be had, Arran lifted an edge of the thing where it rested upon the half-collapsed crate which brought it to the level of his waist and let it down again, not wishing to crush the supporting container further. It was too heavy for a small, recuperating boy to carry up hundreds of steps into the inhabited area of the Holdings. Nor did he relish asking for adult help and getting a lecture about being down here in the unhealthy dust and dampness.

Arriving at a decision, he turned a knurled ferrule in the middle of his lampwand, doubling the amount of warm yellow light it caused to be spilled into the small room. This made him feel a deal more comfortable. Waenzi, too, made noises of appreciation. However, at this level of output, the light would not last many more minutes. The wand would have to rest a good long while, soaking up sunlight upon his windowsill.

As curious as the boy, the triskel tensed its short trio of legs and hopped up onto the crate, threatening to topple everything. Absorbed with his find, Arran gave it scant notice. He nestled the wand in a fold of crumpled plastic sheet and pried up the first of the clasps upon the carven chest. It gritted with the sound of dust, made a loud clacking noise, and snapped open. The second clasp yielded, and with this the chest gave a sigh, releasing or taking up air—Arran was uncertain which —to equalize pressure between its interior and the exterior world.

The lid, deep as the bottom, hinged back. Arran was disappointed. Inside lay a litter of mouldering scraps. Something which had once been a book was now a foul-smelling stack of flaking debris. Most of the contents were beyond identification. He thought some of this mess might be the remains of various articles of clothing and was about to give up when he remembered the weight. Its sides and top were thick, but something in the chest besides the ashes of slow-motion oxidation must account for its mass.

Sifting with careful fingers, he discovered something soft and yielding at the bottom, withdrew his startled hand—it had felt much like a lump of flesh—then realized it had been a cushion of plastic he had touched. He placed his lampwand in the chest-lid, which began to shed a better light than the walls, gulped, and searched again until he retrieved a rectangular pouch no larger than both his flattened hands. Along one side it had an odd kind of sealing edge and was heavy for its size.

The seal parted. Contrived, it had been, with cleverness. A ridge in one sheet comprising the pouch fit into a matching groove moulded into the other. From its appearance, the pouch might once have been transparent, the dark strip along the sealing edge a brilliant blue. Now the plastic was cloudy, yellowed to near opacity. The invisible influence of his lampwand brought no glow from it, as if whatever it had to give in the way of light had long ago been used up. The strip had faded to a nondescript blue-gray.

Inside, to his surprise, Arran encountered yet another pouch, thick and yielding black plastic this time, almost triangular, with yet another sort of sealing edge, one fashioned from alternating teeth set along most of the circumference. This was *old*. Recognizing the fastener from history texts and period dramas, he pulled its tab with elaborate care past metal tooth after interlocking metal tooth until the pouch split apart.

What he found within, coated with dusty traces of what was once a colorful plush liner, was older still. It was, he knew, a weapon, much smaller, and in far better condition, than the trophies upstairs. Fine markings, visible through a reddish-brown patina thinnest along the wear-polished grip surfaces and sharper edges, were not altogether incomprehensible thanks to those others within the pages of the book Old Henry had given him:

—WALTHER—
Carl Walther Waffenfabrik Ulm/Do.
Modell PP Cal. 22 l.r.

He sounded out the first word, startling Waenzi. The creature flailed about, almost falling off its precarious crate perch. It was the first the boy had spoken for a while. The word had been engraved within the stylized outline of a sort of banner. Beyond being easy to pronounce, it was quite without meaning. The remainder of the ancient writing lay nearby in two neat lines upon the metallic upper portion of the weapon. The banner word was repeated upon each of the black plastic handle surfaces, with their subtle curves, which were otherwise filled with decorative knurling. Upon the frame, just ahead of one of these plastic panels, were stamped the additional words: "Made in West-Germany". This was a great deal more satisfactory to the boy. Arran wondered where the planet Germany might be. He had never heard of it. In the corresponding location upon the other side of the weapon was a five-digit number, followed by the marking "LR".

Pleased with himself that he could read this much, he noticed several minute markings which appeared to be birds or bats, spreading their wings over the letter "N". In another place, upon what would be called the "axis" of a kinergic thrustible, beside another miniature bird, something like the leaf of a lawn-shrub appeared, along with the number "67".

Having exhausted the newfound object's literary merits, Arran turned to its mechanics. Upon one side was a round, check-patterned button and a small striated lever. Who knew for what? In the midline were two more levery things. One, forward of the handle, was a simple curve within a large, protective ring, an obvious fit for the index finger. The other, a small ring in itself, serrate about most of its circumference, sat high at the back.

Additional irregularities and projections which he could not begin to fathom interrupted the artifact's eye-pleasing contours. Moreover, several smaller objects, arcane supplies and accessories, odd-shaped and mysterious in themselves, occupied space within the cushioned pouch. He would have liked to examine the weapon further, but realized it must wait. These things could be dangerous, he understood, obsolete as they might be. They were rumored to be capable of retaining their power charge for a long time.

He would wait until Old Henry could help. But perhaps, after all, he had found a fitting wedding gift for—the light excited by his lampwand flickered in warning. Waenzi emitted a low, miserable moan.

And by these presents, did Arran know it was time to climb back up into the weary, unfree world of the grownups.

CHAPTER IV:
THE SPREIGHFORMERY

"Waffenfabrik, be it?" Squint-eyed and straining every muscle in his wrinkled forehead to achieve focus, Old Henry Martyn peered at the shallow-graven lettering on the weapon Arran had discovered. "Now there be word I've no knowin' of. Historical ancient lingo. We'll just find ourselves dicthille, after we finish here, an' look it up."

Outside, summer lightning flared, blue-white and blinding, followed by a grumble of thunder from the nearby forested hills. The air was perfumed with ozone, thick with anticipation of the rain to come. Inside—the two were in the spreighformery, a low, modern outbuilding not far from the Holdings proper—light emanated warm and steady from the walls. This illumination required no lampwand to excite it, although one such could have been used, had power failed, which, in Arran's memory, had never happened.

The obscuring film of orange rust which had covered the object of their present attention had yielded to a cursory swipe with an offcast rag saturated in aromatic spirits. (Otherwise Arran's constant companion, Waenzi had departed in olfactory disgust, preferring to brave the fury of the natural elements.) Old Henry had observed, for Arran's benefit, that half a dozen ventilated capsules, filled with moisture-absorbing crystals and placed in the pouch with the weapon, had done their work well, even over what must have been a period of seven hundred years.

In the end, merely wiping down the weapon had not satisfied the meticulous old man. He had taken it apart, piece by minute piece, guided by Arran knew not what arcane knowledge, examining the condition of each component, cleaning it with a small brush, reassembling everything as if he had always known how it should be done. The number and variety of pins and springs and levers had been bewildering. The process had consumed an hour, impressing Arran once again with how *complicated* the ancient people's artifacts had been, and how clever Old Henry was to fit dozens of odd-shaped puzzle pieces back together in anything resembling the original arrangement.

For his own part, although he did not say so (opinions might have varied as to the wisdom of this course), Old Henry was impressed with Arran's display, during the prolonged process, of an observant patience many an adult he knew, Skyan or Hanoverian, could never have demonstrated. He had been more impressed that the otherwise independent-minded boy had waited for his help instead of initiating any dangerous experiments himself.

"That'd be m'guess, anyways. I take this '67' t'be date, likeliest in nineteenth, twentieth, or twenty-first century. Canna guess closer."

"But I thought—"

The ceiling was low overhead. Along two outer, intersecting walls, the windows were grime-filmed, dusty-silled, always the case in a utility building not occupied for continuous periods, where the infrequent occupant's attention is upon tasks other than housecleaning. Workbenches lined the windowed walls.

Arran's face contorted as if in agony. Old Henry could see he was in the throes of a painful struggle against preconceived notions. It was clear he did not enjoy the sensation, although the old man entertained hopes the boy would someday come to relish this most bitter of conflicts.

"Another language?" Arran demanded at last. "What else could there be but *the* language?"

Old Henry suppressed a chuckle. "Tell Old Henry now, were ye p'raps born aspeakin' *the* language, young master?"

Arran was uncertain that this constituted a logical answer, although proving it was, for the present, somewhat beyond his abilities. Staring sightless across the room, he strained his faculties to recall what seemed to him the remotest past, a time even he realized must feel like no more than yesterday to his elderly companion. What he was looking at, without seeing, was an inner wall, holding bins of raw materials: soil, wastage from septic tanks and a dozen of the Holdings' crops, ores from various locations upon Skye, valves for an underground reservoir of petroleum. Spreighformers could be made to fabricate any object their memories held plans for, but cost and complications varied. Nor could they fabricate from nothing. In practice it was easier to begin with complex compounds, readily available, than to build these one tedious transmuted atom at a time.

"Indeed, I do not think so, Henry," he answered after a time, "I seem to remember having to learn, to ask the words for things. I recall once asking someone . . . perhaps my mother . . . about the decorative scroll-work carven upon the edges of a secretary. She—whoever it was—mistaking my meaning, told me 'desk.' I remember the frustration of not being able to ask properly. The answer caused me much confusion for a time."

"Aye," Old Henry was pleased by Arran's reasoning and his open, healthy memory. "An' suppose, lad, if y'can, some other place, some other time, other people usin' different words for things like 'secretary' or even 'mother'?"

"But why," Arran protested, "would they bother, when perfectly good words already exist for . . . oh. I believe I see what you are getting at. They would feel the same about our choice of words, would they not?"

Old Henry laughed, knowing it was time to express pleasure with the boy's achievement. "Amounta life-blood's been emptied over such trifles'd fill every loch an' spillet 'pon Skye, boy. Pity most folks be not as quick as ye."

The final wall consisted of the spreighformers themselves, a pair, each the size of the fireplace in the great hall, indeed somewhat resembling giant ovens. The ultimate accomplishment of the ancient *ulsic* craft, everything young Arran had ever possessed, every item save perhaps the book Old Henry had given him and some of the precolonial artifacts he had salvaged—including, it was to be presumed, this walther-weapon they were examining—had come from these or other spreighformers. Between them lay the §-field annihilator in whose unreal heart naked atoms danced to different laws, reversing their identities to immolate themselves in the presence of normal matter. This process generated light and heat for the Holdings proper, for dwellings in the countryside roundabout, as well as providing occasional rare but necessary elements the spreighformers required.

For the most part, the annihilator was a simple machine, as were the spreighformers. Unattended, it performed its several tasks without the dubious benefit of moving parts. As with all products of the *ulsic,* any sophistication in the machinery's character no longer lay in mechanical complication, but in a thousand years of careful thought directed toward its gradual simplification. To Arran's knowledge, indeed to Old Henry's as well, none knew how to build such devices any longer. They had themselves been created in even larger spreighformers which in turn had come from spreighformers even larger. The regression must have had an ending somewhere, but neither of them had ever thought about it.

The two were quiet for a time. Despite Old Henry's commendation, Arran had missed the happy pride in the old man's voice. But no matter. The ancient Skyan knew the boy would give him reason again to praise him soon enough. Another flash was even more dazzling than the one which had come before. Another muffled roar, and rain began to fall in fat drops upon the courtyard flagging outside.

"So this . . ." Arran stumbled over the unfamiliar word. ". . . this *'vahf-fen-fahh-reek'* means something sensible in the—*our* language?"

"Aye," Old Henry nodded, "likeliest 'pistol-makin' place,' I be thinkin'. 'Carl Walther' might be famous maker. We'll find out. Meantimes, I'll teach ye t'make sure this toy be safe afore ye begin t'playin' with it."

His gnarled thumb pressed the checkered button upon the left side, behind what he had told Arran was the trigger-lever. A black plastic projection at the bottom of the handle, constituting the end of a section within the grip itself, slid out, falling into Old Henry's ready palm.

"Charge cassette," Old Henry offered, "what they usta be calling 'magazine.' Holds makin's for more thrusts after first be gone. This one be empty though, it seems." He winked at the boy, who realized full well this had already been established, indeed had been the first priority, when Old Henry had cleaned the weapon.

"And the first thrust?" Arran's eyes were bright with piqued curiosity. Never had it occurred to him that the ancient weapon might be made to function, that, unlike all other precolonial artifacts he was familiar with, this might serve a purpose other than to hang upon a wall and be wondered about.

Old Henry tapped the section of the axis—"barrel" he insisted—showing through a sort of window in the upper portion of the weapon. "Never take for granted nothin' about weaponry. We han't looked for a while now. Charge could still be here an' dangerous. Shall we be after takin' a look?"

With these words he replaced the empty magazine, held the grip in one hand—keeping his finger off the trigger—with the front of the weapon pointed away from both of them. He placed his other forefinger and a thumb upon the shallow serrations at the rear of the upper portion and drew it toward him. The upper half slid backward until it locked in this position, all the beauty and symmetry of its flowing lines lost.

"Is it broken?" Arran asked, unable to suppress a disappointed quaver.

"No, young master. Stone-cold empty it be, an' atellin' us so. It'd be fair important if your life depended upon this toy. Ye'd know it be past time t'slap in another cassette an' be ready t'thrust again or be thrust." Indeed, a second "magazine" object lay within the pouch, along with the crystal-containers and a few other, less recognizable, objects. "Now this here," Old Henry poked a flat, colorless finger at one of the unidentified objects still in the black pouch which lay upon its once-transparent wrapper upon the oil-stained bench before them, "will be testin' of our luck."

"What be—is it?" Without waiting for the old man's answer, Arran reached an eager hand toward a small rectangular solid of a crumbling material he had never seen before and yet which looked familiar. It was covered, every siemme squared, with lettering, once bright-colored, now dirty and faded.

Old Henry brushed his hand away. "Have care, young master. It be pasteboard, as they usta be callin' it, same as books be fashioned from, an' never intended t'last single century, lettin' alone any six or seven."

Indeed, the box had begun to crumble at the boy's touch. Neither had its condition much improved by his handling of the pouch in the cellar. Where it had been tucked into the box, Old Henry prised a fragile end-flap away. Inside, within an unprinted, lidless half box, was visible a row of five green-brown metallic cylinders, each at least two siemmes long and half again the diameter of a thille. Arran realized they were analogous to the larger cylinders which hung upon his bedroom wall with the *steyraug*, yet half of the objects visible in the box were topped with elongated domes of an unfamiliar, frosty, almost mildewed-looking substance.

"Our luck be aholdin', young master m'lad. These be power charges for yon antique weapon. Hmm—aged, I think me, beyond usin'." He gave the boy a broad wink and laid a finger beside his nose. "Still, with bitta fiddlin', we may be after obtainin' some good athem."

With elaborate care the old man took a pair of forceps from the bench and lifted one cylinder out. Arran could see that all five in the end row, perhaps all fifty or so in the box, were identical, being stacked top-to-bottom alternating with bottom-to-top. The end opposite the mildewed-looking tip had been flattened in some fashion, like the head of a nail.

Old Henry took the object across the room, opened a metal-framed window in the face of the right-hand spreighformer, and placed it inside, careful afterward to seal the window. He placed a palm over a light-sensitive area, touched a colored grid with his forefinger, and waited as the colors changed. Then he nodded, whether to himself or to the machine Arran could only guess.

Crossing to the row of ore-storage bins, Old Henry pushed a small hand-scoop into one of them, retraced his steps and emptied it into a hopper low in the spreighformer face. He checked the readings again and added a cup of petroleum and a scoopful of odd-colored dirt from a different bin. The spreighformer hummed a while, afterward falling silent.

What Old Henry afterward removed from the manifesting chamber bore only the most superficial of resemblances to what he had first placed in its analyzing window. In place of the dull-surfaced and corroded brown-green cylinder from the faded pasteboard box, an object of metallic gold appearance now glittered in the proffered hollow of his wrinkled palm.

"Brass it be," Old Henry explained as they examined the object. Arran observed how, like almost every artifact he had seen from this period of antiquity, the thing bore lettering. How the ancients loved to write and read! This time it was fine, eye-straining scratches upon the flattened head. "Alloyed copper an' zinc. Aluminum-titanium likely'd done quite as well, or many another mix Old Henry can think of, but perhaps they didna have knowin' athat in ancient times, else 'twas after provin' too expensive for them."

The great wonder to Arran was that the floury tip of the walther-charge—"Cartridges they were after callin' 'em . . ." —was also golden, dull of luster, and waxen to the touch. "Aye, but it be thinnest platin', wot they usta be callin' 'wash', though I canna say why. Underneath be nothin' but purest dross. Lead, buttery-soft t'take t'riflin'—I'll be explainin' that anon—an' expand upon contact with target t'make larger woundin'."

It was at this moment Arran realized, with a wonderful, delicious sense of shock, that he was looking across time toward an incredibly primitive era when, instead of the pure kinetic energy which thrustibles generated, weapons had been simple devices (simple in theory, anyway, he was still learning the difference between simplicity in principle and practice) for throwing tangible physical objects at people and animals and things. For him the contrast between this idea and tools of hand-knapped flint was less considerable than it might have been for someone of an earlier century.

Old Henry retrieved the original cartridge from the window of the spreighformer and replaced it in the pasteboard box among its venerable fellows. Now he took the fresh cartridge and, retracting a spring-loaded follower with his thumb, slid the shiny object into place in the top of the magazine he had removed from the walther-weapon.

"Now we'll just be seein' how successful we been," Old Henry told the wide-eyed boy. "Nor brass nor lead be hard part, but what be inside, primin' an' propellant powder.

Lotsa complicated organic mollycules they be made of. Also we'll be after seein' why this toy, as dangerous as it may be under certain circumstances, be no more than toy, compared t'thrustibles, why them as had wieldin' alesser weapons lost t'ye dread Hanoverians."

He slammed the magazine into the grip, pulled back its upper half, let it return under spring-pressure with a metallic, ringing snap. With a nod at Arran, he flicked a lever upward, pulled another down and backward, and turned the thing upon himself, its muzzle resting light against his solar plexus.

Something *flashed!* This time it was not from the lightning outside.

An impossible roar—not thunder—filled the room.

CHAPTER V:
NATURAL SELECTION

Old Henry Martyn had thrust himself!

Arran's ears sang with the room-filling roar of the walther-discharge. His mind reverberated with shock. Lightning glared outside the workshop's grimy windows, drowning shadows, searing images upon his brain in hard-edged black and white. A crack of thunder followed in an instant, not a decibel louder than the pistol, which seemed to mock the frightened boy.

"Henry!" To all appearances unharmed, Old Henry puckered his face into an evil and self-satisfied grin. Adding a wink for Arran, and casting his wrinkle-shrouded eyes down, toward his midsection, he laid the walther-weapon aside—the top half was locked back again—upon the oil-stained bench. A thin curl of bluish smoke drifted from its muzzle and the window in its side.

"'Twas after bein' some louder'n I expected."

An unfamiliar, and, it seemed to Arran, pleasant tang filled the air as Old Henry began picking with scientific preoccupation at a small, dark button-shape of distorted metal which, centered in a scorched patch of his tunic front, seemed to cling to the fibers there. The old man shook his head, waggling his jaw and swallowing as if to clear his ears. He freed the spent projectile from his clothing, upturned Arran's wrist, and placed the bit of lead, still hot to the touch, upon the boy's damp palm, where it danced from line to line in time to the shaking of his hand.

Residual noise in Arran's ears had by now become a thin, steady whine. It would haunt him for several days, heterodyning when he essayed to whistle, until it seemed to fade and vanish. In certain frequencies, in particular in the ear he'd had turned toward Old Henry at the crucial moment, he would never hear as well as he had again. Outside, a great exhalation of damp wind blew wet leaves and shreds of nondescript debris across the window, presaging violent change in the already unpleasant weather. The heretofore unnoticed hiss of raindrops upon the courtyard flags dropped in pitch and rose to a roar as the summer storm became a torrent, whipped by their impact into a froth which seethed across the stones.

Still stunned by what had happened, Arran nodded at his mentor with a certain absence of awareness. Thoughts foamed odd-shaped across his mind like the rain outside upon the flags. He stared in disbelief at the distorted object in his hand. To him, it presented the appearance of a miniature bog shroom, complete with broad, rounded cap and a short, hollow-bottomed stem. The cap, the portion which had struck Old Henry, was imprinted with the coarse texture of the fabric whereupon it had come to a sudden stop.

Old Henry winked again, seized the abused material of his peasant's tunic (the same sort Arran wore, speaking volumes of the Islay family) between both thumbs and forefingers, working it until the blemish, a stretching of the warp and weft where the projectile had struck, disappeared. The garment would require washing to remove the powder stain. Grinning, he pulled the tunic up and inspected his naked abdomen with mild curiosity. Upon his belly—with its thin covering of snow-white hair, yet smoother and firmer than Arran might have expected in one of so advanced an age—a thumb-sized reddening, scarce more than a rash, had already begun to fade.

"I mighta tried yon toy against my unprotected flesh," he observed, "but ye never know. Still, 'tis everything an' all I expected. I'll ha' ye know, lad, though 'twas after bein' very least of ancient weapons, this *twennytoo* 'twas still considered lethal instrument in proper circumstances."

Confused, Arran placed the expanded projectile beside the weapon upon the bench. He glanced outside. The courtyard had become a temporary, shallow, boiling lake, cratered by giant drops and what might be hail. He wondered for an anxious minute where Waenzi had got himself to. It failed to occur to him that, long before the coming of mankind to Skye, a million generations of the animals had proven capable of seeing to themselves.

"I understand. That is, I believe I do. Those old charges in their box were too far gone for replication. Or did the spreighformer fail—"

"No, young master, it didna fail. Yon cartridge worked just as it was supposed to. Yon ancients—bigger they were than us, their children, b'more'n head-height. Still, they were that mooch softer."

"What?" That his ancestors might have been different in their material beings, from himself and people he knew, was something Arran had never heard in his history lessons. He absorbed it as a metaphysical blow, much in its effect like having watched Old Henry thrust himself. "You mean to say what failed even to harm you would have killed one of them?"

"That it likely would." The old man shook his silver-thatched head. "In fairness, we might allow that our clothin' be some better. Common kefflar'll stiffen itself 'gainst any blow, but it was after bein' expensive drygood, used for armorin' warriors in yoredays. Now we dinna use nothin' else for togs, an' some say 'twas kefflar an' nothin' else put end to ancient art of weaponry called *ipsic* b'some practitioners, and be others *gundo.*" Arran nodded in the beginnings of comprehension, but offered nothing in reply, for he knew Old Henry well enough to understand that more was in the offing. He was right: "Even had I unleashed weapon 'pon me bare old ribs, without tunic t'stint blow, likeliest I'da drawn drap ablood or two an' no much more."

They paused, noticing as the light in the room brightened. Outside, the sky was purple-gray and dark as night. Inside, not for the first time since Old Henry had "adopted" him, Arran's grasp upon the universe had been shaken to its foundations. Satisfied with the effect, for he believed shaking anyone's foundations was healthy exercise for all concerned, Old Henry shifted where he sat and gave Arran a light punch upon the upper arm.

"We're *harder,* lad, perhaps from nothin' more'n centuries athrustin' one another for personal reasons an' in service t'Ceo, Monopolity, an' Empery-Cirot. Them as be goin' t'die of such, they die. Them as survives makes babies. Tougher do we get, though bitter may we regret selectin' process. Thus upon firmer flesh do bullets, blades, even lasers, have less effect than mighta been expected be our ancestors. Their weapons canna be called useless—I s'pose bullet in eye'd reach brain—but close as may be."

Arran nodded again. "Presumably our medical art is better, too."

Old Henry shook his head. "Such things dinna always improve with time. Had I used methods approved b'latest poison-peddlers, bone-breakers, an' ray-burners at 'Droom, ye'd be ailin' still, for all that they work miracles in other ways. Take this Morven fellow, friend of your father's. No reason for him t'be all bundled up in wheelie-chair if he didna want t'be, down deep inside. But cancer—I used what I had of ancient knowledge, an' here y'be."

Thunder roared. Somewhere beyond the margin of the Holdings an everblue fell in the forest, barkless and steaming. No one had heard it fall, but it would be lying there in the morning, just the same. The torrent hammered upon the workshop rooftop. Hearing the old man was difficult enough. Old Henry shifted again, as if uncomfortable with what he would say next.

"Any case, medical art works for individuals, against species. N'bad, ye understand, save soft survive t'breed. When they've time, mind ye. Men came blazin' up from Airth-a-Legend, thrustin' his way off mother planet, and've never knew moment's peace after. Hanover's been fightin' at intervals with Jendyne Empery-Cirot more'n thousand years. Bad for individuals, good for species. Horrible as may be to contemplate, 'tis what's made us tougher'n forebears." The old man narrowed his eyes, looked this way and that before continuing, caught himself in this precaution, and winked at Arran. "One way medicarts might've helped, aside from sometimes slaughterin' weak as easy as any beam or bullet. Could be a few errant chromysomes, be accident or design, sneaked outa labs where dreaded Oplytes rumor t'be born or bred."

Oplytes. Again Arran found his head whirling as the parts inside seemed to rearrange themselves. He knew next to nothing about the giant, unkillable warriors created by the Monopolity and the Empery-Cirot, among others. He was not alone in his ignorance, nor was it just that of a small boy upon an isolated world. It was claimed no one knew much about them. What was known was whispered or spoken not at all, although his father had commanded a battalion of them in the most recent flare-up of the Thousand Years' War. He caught Old Henry grinning that teacher's grin of his, and, for the briefest moment, wanted to kick him in his skinny shins. Why, he had always believed his civilization to be the most advanced, the most humane, the most . . .

The Skyan watched as confusion wrote itself across the boy's features. "Why, ye ask, does Old Henry bother himself tellin' ye these things? Dinna deny it, I see it upon your face. 'Tis your heritage an' birthright, Arran m'lad, for blood of conqueror an' rebel alike flows through your veins, child that ye be of Robret Islay an' Glynnaughfern Fair Mistress Woodgate teaches Hanoverian part of ye, an' Old Henry part that's Skyan."

"But—"

"Because, in memory of your mother, outa respect for those with whom he once made Great Bargain, your father asked me."

Arran blinked, surprised to the bone for the third time this rainy afternoon. Old Henry always acted as if things he passed along were secrets of the imperium-conglomerate, information suppressed by the Monopolity as treasonable, in any case lending the most mundane fact a delicious feeling of sedition. Now, to be informed that he was told these things at his father's specific bidding . . . the thought tapered off unconcluded and unsatisfying, as thoughts often did when Old Henry had provoked them.

As far as what Old Henry had asserted—Arran shifted his thoughts (unaware of the potential vice it represented) to a more comfortable and less-confusing subject, the fabled art of *ipsic*. The personal weapon of the present age, Arran knew, was the self-collimating kinergic thrustible. Utilizing §-physics—the same forces harnessed in the estate's power generator, and, indeed, which allowed starships to ply the Deep between the systems—the thrustible generated a focused pulse of pure, recoilless energy, rated in measure-keys of destructive force per square siemme.

Strapped to the upper surface of the forearm, with its dangerous end out past the knuckles, such a weapon had a thin "yoke"—grip-safety and thumb-trigger—which lay in the user's palm, connected by a bridge between the first and second fingers to the "axis": what another age would have called the barrel. The power supply was an ergonomic cluster located near the elbow. Sighting was accomplished by means of a built-in, low-power laser.

Possession of thrustibles was forbidden to all but members and retainers of the elite. They were expensive and, upon this account as well as others, rare by comparison with other artifacts. Most bore the mark, rather than the brandname of a mass-producer like this walther-weapon he'd found, of famous artisans. Despite the fact that he was entitled by virtue of his birth, Arran had examined such weapons only once or twice at his father's indulgence.

Unaware he was now eschewing the same vice of evasion which he had earlier begun to embrace, he resolved of a sudden to think the rest through—the part about his father and his mother—when he was alone. As good teachers do, Old Henry had an idea of what was happening within the boy's mind and let him alone to puzzle over it. When time came for more information, more foundation-shaking, Arran would come and ask. He always did.

Now, thoughtful and gazing into the obsidian darkness, Arran noticed a flicker of motion. Lightning burned onto his retinas the jerky movements and human angularities of what had been a mere shadow staggering across the storm-lashed space between the Holding Hall and the outbuilding.

In a moment, a disorganized clatter manifested itself, a dust-stirring freshet of damp cold. Arran's brother Donol stood shivering in the doorway, thin hair slicked down upon his scalp and water sluicing from his clothing.

"Arran, my boy!" he gasped, slamming the door against the storm and wiping his streaming face. He grinned, and excitement—a passing rare thing with him—filled his voice. "We'll sit this hurricane out a few more minutes, until it abates. You're wanted at the house. We've just received word. Father's ship's within the system! He's come back a few days early so he might help prepare for Robret and Lia's wedding!"

Arran's face lit up in a manner even Donol could be certain of.

"It's true, little brother! And by all accounts he's fetched back clowns, musicians, sages, mages, half the fools, professional and otherwise, of the Hanoverian 'Droom!"

PART TWO: THE OUTLAWS
YEARDAY 142, 3009 A.D.
SECUNDUS 12, 1567 OLDSKYAN
IRSSE 30, 509 HANOVERIAN

THE LOT DID IT FALL UPON HENRY MARTYN,
THE YOUNGEST OF ALL THE THREE,
THAT HE A STAR-PILLAGING ROVER SHOULD BE,
  SHOULD BE,
  SHOULD BE,
FOR TO MAINTAIN HIS TWO BROTHERS AND HE.

CHAPTER VI:
THE GOLDEN WHERRY

Hovering silent at her rest, a measure and a half above the ground, the estate's draywherry never failed to remind Arran of somebody's hasty, crosshatched sketch of a twenty-five-measure-long sweetmelon seed.

In construction and appearance she was a utilitarian, undecorated, and nonreflective gray where not open or transparent, the heavy wire mesh she had been fashioned from tarnished by the harsh sun and the crueller Skyan cold. In form she was as flat as a woodland tick, smooth-contoured, plump, round at her blunt stern, tapering to a flattened, slender point toward her bow.

Her design, if so formal a word were justified, had been laid down by unknown geniuses in dim antiquity, intended more for hauling cargo—farm and forest produce here upon Skye —than for transporting passengers. She herself had been fabricated—"woven" might have been a word of better choice—upon this estate for as much speed as the twin cones of her electrostatic impellers (wrought of somewhat finer mesh and powered by a modest §-field annihilator, the only features interrupting the clean flow of her lines) were capable of pushing her to. This for the most practical purposes, as she had never been meant as the object of anyone's exhilaration. She contained not a single moving part. Arran thought her an uncommonly beautiful sight for the unglamorous, old-fashioned means of transportation that she was. His opinion in this regard may have had to do with the fact she had been the first article of the Holdings' large machinery he had ever been entrusted by his father or Old Henry to operate, albeit under the most stringent supervision.

However humble the purpose she was meant to serve, she

was being scrubbed clean of hay, manure, any bucolic remnant she had recently accumulated, in preparation for a brief, happy voyage to equatorial Alysabethport. This was an unpeopled cluster of *ulsic*-automated buildings a few hundred klommes south of the Holdings, renamed not long ago in honor of the planet's newest mistress, now returning with her husband from their honeymoon. The task of readying the draywherry had not been made easier by the previous day's storm which had littered her from bow to stern—and, since she had lain unpowered all of yesternight, through and through—with the same bits of windblown, rain-driven dirt and vegetation which Arran had first noticed clinging to the workshop windows. Anyone, he thought, who believed rain to be a cleansing phenomenon had lived all his life indoors, with the curtains drawn.

"That'll do! Dry her off, boys!" Old Henry shut the nozzle off and dropped the soapy, long-handled brush with which he had been directing, rather than contributing to, the cleaning effort. Two younger Skyans, half-shadowed beneath her open-work fuselage, were finishing with rags along each section of the broad, curved, finger-width roddery which comprised most of the draywherry's underside. This extra heavy meshwork took the entire vehicle's weight upon those rare occasions when she rested her length upon the ground. At present, they dripped with rinse water and fugitive suds. Meanwhile, a fourth individual unwound the workshop's hot-air blower from its reel.

Abaft, at the location of her annihilator, the vehicle was screened more solidly than elsewhere, the better to protect passengers from errant radiation (for the most part, imaginary) and disguise the workings cultured visitors might find unsightly. So close was this narrower mesh, skip-woven to produce dense, decorative whorls and swirls, that she came close to being opaque. Arran remembered (the memory was dim, for he had been ill) that Old Henry had run off klommes of the finer wire to replace more utilitarian sheathing when the draywherry had served to take her master and mistress off to Alysabethport in the first place. Anticipating their return, she had been left as she had been. Never again would she be the same gray, mundane work machine.

Now he purposed a grander embellishment. As the last drop of rinse water rolled off her glistening wirework onto the muddy ground, Old Henry brought forth a vial, unscrewed the cap, and tipped its contents onto the draywherry's woven surface. A sizzling noise and peculiar odor issued forth as a blush of color began to spread. In moments, from the complex framing at her bow to the conical metallic cages of her electrostatic impellers, the entire vessel gleamed as if she had been sculpted of purest gold.

The old man turned and winked at the boy. "Polymerizer spreighformed up last night after y'left. Wish I'd thought of it at weddin'." He lifted a hand to caress the fabulous coating, which had cured in an instant. "'Tis but single mollycule deep, but that pretty? Practical, too. 'Spect yer father'll want it left for summer. She always did get a mite hot, sittin' in sun."

As he spoke, a giggling servant girl, assisted at the elbow by one of the male fuselage-polishers, clambered up the short hatch-ladder into the belly of the hovering machine, her arms laden with fresh-cut flowers. Others behind her were supervised by Mistress Lia. When they were through, the draywherry would be filled, stem to stern, with a more colorful (and more aromatic) cargo than had ever burdened her before.

"All aboard!" Robret *fils* shouted, striding across sun-dried flags hosed clean before the draywherry had been attended to. He was fastening a jacket quilted from a shimmering keflar brocade, the latest vogue to sweep the capital, which appeared in some lights a deep, heartbreaking blue, in others a dark, mysterious red. He disparaged it as his "peacock jacket" and never wore it without being persuaded by someone else. More and more, that someone else was Mistress Lia. His brother Donol followed in his wake, less exuberant of attire. As seemed consistent with his personality (or perhaps because he had no one to persuade him), he preferred to set sartorial tones more somber, affecting styles a trifle better tested by time and hues which remained, in any light, faithful to whatever they had looked like to begin with. As was fitting for the occasion, Arran, too,

had donned his second-best, which he had been at pains to protect from the muddy fun of preparing the draywherry. The best he had, trews and tunic of the same fabric as Robret's jacket, he saved for that event to which all this fuss was but preliminary. After all, he had *two* wedding ceremonies to dress for, one of them retroactive.

Ducking beneath the machine, Robret ascended the short ladder, kissed Mistress Lia upon her freckled forehead in open mock of genteel custom which forbade him more than that, and handed her down laughing. Donol and Arran trooped aboard after him. Only the brothers were along for this excursion, as was proper, Mistress Lia had explained to the boy, to greet their father and his bride. For the moment, these, and as yet none else, comprised the family Islay. Arran winked at her who would soon become his sister. She returned the wink in smiles and blushes, a picture so pretty even a child of twelve could well appreciate her. That this particular child was more precocious than anybody guessed as yet, and, at that magic moment, set his standards for the years to come, no one would ever know, not even he who set them.

In any case, Robret had added in his characteristic practical way, they would need space aboard to accommodate the returning party, consisting, as it would, of Robret Senior, the Lady Alysabeth, their baggage and servants, the baggage, servants, bodyguard, and person of Tarbert Morven, the Lady Alysabeth's father, and similar impedimenta of whomever else they had seen fit to bring back from the capital for the younger Robret's wedding. Most likely, the draywherry would be called upon to make several such voyages.

Thus for once was Arran without Old Henry's amusing company and sage advice. As chiefmost among the family retainers, he and Mistress Lia (by Hanoverian custom it would be presumptuous and unseemly for the bride-to-be to greet those soon to be her in-laws, as if she had already married into the family; in addition, until she was thus married, she was still in technicality a servant) would stay behind to manage things for the few hours the brothers would be absent. The youngest of the Islay scions must do without Waenzi, as well, a speeding draywherry being no place, in either of the elder brothers' opinion, for the curious and unpredictable triskel.

As those who must remain removed themselves from proximity to the idling machine, Donol pulled a lever which allowed the hatch-ladder to regain the form it best remembered, returning to its nest in the draywherry's underside. He found a seat, one of several installed in recent days in what had been cargo space, sat, and let the seat-restrainers close about his waist. Seated further forward, with a nod from Robret close beside him, Arran wiped nervous fingers upon a trouser leg, reached past the tiller bar, and passed his hand over a sensitive area of the steering pedestal. Aft, the draywherry's annihilator stirred from a partial somnolence which was never sleep in its entirety.

Lights upon the pedestal changed color. The glowing §-field built up along the woven surface of the vehicle, allowing light through the broad mesh quite unhindered—Arran could see Old Henry shooing the younger servants out of the way—but stifling sound from the outside, giving those inside a sudden shut-in feeling. With a gentle sigh passing through her fabric, the draywherry rose upon her pressor-fields another half measure above the wash-water dampness of her temporary berth, swung her narrow-pointed prow in a southerly direction, and began moving forward.

Inboard, seated behind a pressure-tiller and other simple controls which he knew in harshest truth to be redundant, Arran nonetheless felt a thrill radiate through his body, echoing stresses singing along the vehicle's length. Perhaps this was not the noblest of vessels, nothing to rival the great ships of the interstellar Deep. But she was here (as those great ships were not), operated upon the same principles, and, at least for the moment, responded to his command, however superfluous and well-supervised it might be.

Feeling the tiller vibrate of its own accord (it did not swing from side to side, but answered, without moving, to pressure put upon it by controlling hands) he watched the draywherry lift her sleek nose, surge forward, and gather speed with such ponderous deliberation that her acceleration was all but unnoticeable, even without the all-enveloping, inertia-less §-field. Noticeable or not, her headway was sufficient that, in a few score heartbeats, the broad and close-cropped meadow before the Holdings had given way to heavy forest, and the forest, in its turn—upon either side of the greenway unrolling before them—had soon melted into a solid, indistinguishable blur.

Quite unlike a proper road was the greenway to Alysa-bethport. It seemed to open before him like cloven waters, but this was an illusion. Much like the draywherry herself, it had been constructed by a simple method; only a flying craft (unknown upon Skye) might have traveled over a road less well prepared. An open, grassy bed had been cut, by men and by machinery, upon a direct line southward across field and forest, only the grosser tree stumps and upthrust boulders cleared away. Now the former lay in bleaching clawlike tangles at the edges, amongst piles of the latter. Die-straight and indifferent to the way the land lay, the greenway, fifty measures wide, might have been no more than a forester's firebreak—indeed, it served the purpose well—except whenever it intersected a line of hills where ridges had been furrowed by deep land-cuts, only to disappear again when the hills did.

Having been created by so laborious a method, the pathway required a minimum of further concern. The shockblast which accompanied passage of the draywherry at full speed, less than three measures above the ground, was sufficient to discourage any new vegetation from overgrowing it, all save the sparsest weedery from which the road derived its naming.

Soon the draywherry was boring through the countryside at the greatest speed of which she was capable, just below that of sound, almost twelve hundred klommes per metric hour. Softened by the streamlined protective §-field, the wind of her passage shrieked about her and was gone.

Extending invisible fingers, the draywherry's §-field groped ahead for klommes along the terrain flowing toward her, matching her thunderous progress to the gentle contours of the land so that she always stayed the same distance from the ground. As she felt her way, she kept watch for the unexpected: landslide, rockfall, upthrust tentacles of a wind-killed tree, some pedestrian beast or human crossing the greenway. If given sufficient warning, the draywherry could leap such obstructions, perhaps to the startled discomfort of those riding inside—and the certain consternation of pedestrians—preserving all in greater safety than might otherwise have been imagined.

Had too high or abrupt an obstacle presented itself, the field would give alarm, transfer its lifting energies against the motion induced by the conical impellers, shut the impellers off, and slow the draywherry to a halt, spilling kinetic energy into the meshwork as waste heat, or, failing that, into the fabric of unoccupied portions of the vehicle itself. These might flash into incandescence, or vanish altogether in the white heat of vaporization. The vehicle might sacrifice her very existence, yet the passengers survive to build and ride in others. It was not a perfect system, but it was a simple one and in most cases worked—or so Arran had been told. He had never experienced an emergency himself—it being an axiom that nothing interesting ever happens in the presence of a bored twelve-year-old—and wished in secret, at least just once, that he could.

Time passed with a swiftness which another axiom, not limited to twelve-year-olds, about life's few good moments, describes but does not explain. In due course, their passage brought them to a geographical feature a trifle more spectacular than a mere string of hills. These were real mountains, bordering the equator of the planet in this region, rising to a height at which an unprotected man would need to carry oxygen. The draywherry would climb them, but at an angle less steep than that of the slopes which rose before Arran's eyes. For the first time the greenway departed from its plumbline, swung in a long, gradual curve toward an easier approach, as it deepened into a roadcut first carved, from orbit at no small expense, by the mighty weapons of the great ship which had brought the Islays' predecessors to this planet.

As the draywherry plunged into the shadow of the roadcut, lifted her prow, and began to climb, a sudden noise shook her and her passengers. The blue-white of Skye's thin overcast, visible through the notch ahead, turned black as the sides of the cut erupted outward. Under an onslaught of forces she was not designed to withstand, she swayed, fish-tailed, ground her starboard bow against the riven hillside, throwing sparks, turning end-for-end before resuming something like a straight and level course. The mesh of which she had been fashioned groaned in one part, screamed in another, as acceleration stresses and the §-field fought to see which would control her destiny.

Reaching out both hands to steady his younger brother, Robret was torn from the deceptive safety of his chair and tossed aside as if he weighed nothing. Donol screamed, wide-mouthed and open-lunged. Somehow Arran clung to the tiller post, battered upon face and shoulders by his involuntary motion against the handle of the steering mechanism, as the inbuilt *ulsic* attempted—in desperation, it seemed to the boy—to stabilize the draywherry.

The vehicle struck the hillside again, raising a cock's tail of spark-punctuated dust behind her, shot onto the tableland beyond, spun end for end a final time, and stabilized. She did not stop. She had been designed never to stop in circumstances such as this.

To stop was death.

CHAPTER VII:
THE LANDING PENTAGRAM

Woodsrunners!

The word first ran through Arran's mind as he disentangled himself from the inconvenient solicitude of his chair. The draywherry was stable now, moving at perhaps half her normal speed. This suited the boy. He ached in every corner of his body and could only manage half his normal speed, himself.

Woodsrunners. Such an outrage was impossible! All of

that now-legendary sound and fury had come to a final ending some thirty or forty years ago. His warrior father, already weary from the interstellar war which won him land and title, had subdued the rebels. A glad agreement had been consummated in his marriage to Glynnaughfern Briartonson, daughter of the Skyan leader, Ianmichael Briartonson. More than just a marriage of two loving individuals— although they had been that as well, to credit the romantic tales which everyone, including Old Henry Martyn, told of them—it had brought unprecedented peace and happiness to Skye.

Nevertheless, from hoary and suspicious habit, woods-runner attacks were the reason why, even today, no convey-ance such as this could be induced to stop once damaged, even by her occupants, unless she first arrived where she was going or had been altogether ruined. Too many Hanoverians had been murdered in ambuscade, too many captives tor-tured or held hostage.

Free to rise at last, Arran looked round him. His eldest brother lay quiet, slumped upon his tailbone against the upcurved openwork of the portside wall, his pale face asheen with clotted blood. Suppressing panic and an urge to void himself, Arran knelt beside him, saw that all this gore stemmed from but one small gash above Robret's left eye-brow. Head wounds, Arran knew from his own experience of them, were like that. Robret was unconscious but unclammy, breathing deep and steady. To the boy's unknowing touch, he seemed not otherwise injured. Glancing over his shoulder to assure himself that the draywherry's course continued straight and level (they had left the mountains and were at this moment passing over a high, empty plain where an ambush would have been impossible), he limped aftward in search of his other brother.

"Donol!"

In answer came a groan. "Here I am, Arran. How is Robret?"

Donol was where Arran had last seen him, in one of sever-al passenger seats toward the rear of the compartment. From his tone and expression, it appeared that his dignity alone had suffered the worst injuries. As he spoke, he fumbled with impatience at the belt which had held him to

the chair throughout the draywherry's unconventional maneuvers.

"Safety belting is a mixed blessing, brother," Donol observed with a lopsided grin, "this thing kept me from
bouncing round like a bean in a box," he paused, shamefaced,
"but it hit me hard, and, uh . . . emptied me as well."

Too well could Arran see his brother spoke the truth. The
chair, his legs, and a deal of the decking were splattered.
The sweet-sour stench cut into Arran's consciousness, and, in
the aftermath of fear and shock, he had a difficult time for a
moment not following his brother's recent example.

"By the Ceo, an unlooked-for adventure!" With many a
grunt and groan, Robret, brushing flakes of drying blood
from his face, climbed to his feet. He gave a swift glance at the
lights and indicators upon the pedestal, felt about his person
for additional injuries, and looked out through the fabric of
the draywherry to ascertain whether all was as well as it might
be. He turned his attention to his brothers. "You are a nice
mess, Donol. Makes me want to do the same myself. What do
you suppose that was all about?"

With difficulty, Arran kept his peace. If by process of
reasoning Robret and Donol arrived at the conclusion which
his own mind had leapt to in the first wild instant after the
explosion, perhaps there was something in it.

"I would not care to guess," Donol answered without
answering, adding a word which Arran had once been pad-
dled by his father for using in Mistress Lia's presence.
Echoing the noises his brother had made, Donol held his
arms stiff, away from his bespattered body, and walked in an
odd manner. Perhaps he had let go at both ends. Arran was
not contemptuous, but wondering and grateful that the same
embarrassment had not befallen him. A simple sanitary
facility lay aft. The middle Islay brother made his awkward
way in that direction now. "I was not paying attention,"
Donol tossed back over his shoulder as he shut the door
behind him, "but thinking, instead, upon an error I had
found this morning in the accounts."

Robret winked at Arran. "How like him. We have some
excitement such as Skye has not seen in decades, and all he
thinks about are the accounts."

"I heard that!" The voice came muffled from the small

compartment Donol had just entered. "With father and stepmother gone, younger brother sick abed, and the elder fluttery-jittery over a pertpretty face, somebody must!"

Robret smiled, raising his voice. "Aye, there is justice in that."

Arran seated himself in one of the chairs. "Is that what it was?"

His brother glanced down at him. "What?"

"You think it might have been woodsrunners? Because if you do—"

"I cannot think, Arran, with nothing to think about. Not with this head upon me." Robret put a hand to his brow, for the first time showing signs of being in real pain. Perhaps, thought Arran, the shock was wearing off. "I do not know what it was, little brother, and, for the single fact we own, neither do you." His expression changed. He pulled his hand from his battered face and clenched it into a fist. "But by the Ceo, I swear I shall find out!"

Outside, it had begun to grow dark.

In the remaining hours the wherry required to limp into Alysabethport at reduced speed, the brothers learned more of what had happened to them, but not enough to justify conclusions. In places the heavy mesh of the vessel had been rent—broken wire-ends reminded the boy of his unruly hair when he awoke—despite her protective §-fields. Strewn through the compartment they found dirt, soil-covered roots, broken rock from the roadcut, and surmised that some kind of expanding §-field, perhaps even chemenergic explosives, had been used in an attempt to bury them under a mountain of sundered earth.

Peering through the broken fabric at a single star winking back from the overcast, Arran hefted one such fragment, tossing it from palm to palm while keeping an eye upon the greenway. He had ridden to the port upon excursions meant to keep the road from becoming overgrown, but had never traveled this way after dark. Bereft of light from the moonring, the night absorbed the beam of the emergency headlamp his brothers had rigged in the bow long before it could shed light upon much of the surface ahead. Robret and Donol labored over the shattered remains of the drawwherry's antique comlaser, although the arcane ceremony they attempted proved more funeral than resurrection. The object in Arran's hand had pierced the cabinet from end to end, lodging beneath its skin which it had dented outward from inside.

"It is no use!" Donol confessed at last.

Robret rose stiff-legged from where he had knelt for an hour beside the dismantled apparatus, dusted his hands off against one another, and nodded. "As I thought," he agreed with his brother, "the poor abused, elderly thing was never meant to be repaired at all, but, in the unlikely event of its failure, to be replaced by a fresh replica from the spreighformer."

Sitting full upon the deck, Donol stretched his long, thin legs before him and massaged his knees before he attempted, with a certain prudence, to imitate his brother and stand up. "Aye, that was time wasted, was it not?"

Robret took in the view Arran had from behind the pedestal. "Scarcely," he laughed. "Fiddling with it passed many a weary and vexatious hour for us upon this altogether too-protracted journey, which we might otherwise have occupied chewing our fingernails to the armpit. And here, in consequence—" In triumph, he pointed through the damaged hull toward a series of bright lights which had, without warning, appeared in the darkness before them. "—is Alysabethport, long before we might have looked for it."

The planet's one interstellar landing place lacked the glamor which anyone unfamiliar with the realities of thirty-first century life might have awaited, consisting, as it did, of no more than a collection of large, upright plastic cylinders and horizontal half cylinders, gleaming like abandoned bones, stark white, upon the high, dry, equatorial plain. Here and there gleamed the odd colored light. Most of Alysabethport's lumitory embellishment, however, was intended to be visible only from above. The oscillating receptor of an *ulsic*-automated instrument broke the simple lines of one building. Another sprouted thermocouples and a cluster of firefighting nozzles directed toward the landing-point. For most of the year, no human attention was required for maintenance of the place, which was well, for the population upon Skye was sparse and only a few possessed the requisite skills.

The draywherry had begun slowing her already balky pace even as Robret spied the starport. *Ulsic* systems had drawbacks, one being that the damaged vehicle's program called for speed reductions in percentages of the maximum of which she was capable. Despite the fact they were traveling at half speed, the machine reduced that by half, the resultant by another half, and so forth, until, although they were still several klommes from the port buildings, they might have walked faster than the draywherry carried them.

"Robret! Donol! Look!" Arran it was who first saw unmistakable signs that a great star-sailing ship had arrived in the system. In the quiet backwater which was Skye (the youngest of the Islays might have substituted "moribund," had he but known the word), few such wondrous occurrences had come to pass during his short life. The last time he had been too sick to care, let alone come see. Now he pointed with excitement to a feature of the miniature man-deserted village which was not cylindrical. A huge five-cornered platform of the same cast plastic as the buildings, perhaps five hundred paces in extent, had been laid out at the precise location of the planet's equator, and (as Arran well knew) the point highest in altitude which that imaginary demarcation crossed. More than anything else, this point had determined placement of the Holdings, situated northward in the planet's more comfortable and productive temperate zone. Countersunk in the center of the pentagram, a great shackle the thickness of a man's waist sent chrome-titanium roots half a klomme into the plateau's bedrock.

Unused 229 ordinary days of the 230-day Skyan year (Arran's age, those of his brothers, and the dates of other events including many important to the natives were reckoned not in Skyan years, but by a standard interval decreed by the Hanoverian Monopolity), now it tethered an alien, upright object, larger than the draywherry, hexagonal in section, taller than it was wide, and windowed from the middle upward.

This peculiar object, however, was not what had caught

the young boy's attention. From the roof-point of the object upward, far as the eye could see, stretched a fine, brilliant line of fire. The evening overcast was thin. Arran believed he could discern an ending to that fiery cabelle which represented more than an ultimate dwindling of perspective. A faint knob seemed visible to him at its uppermost reach, although this may have been an artifact of enthusiastic self-deception. To be certain, he understood that his older, wiser, less-imaginative (and, in his opinion, vastly duller) brothers would deny him any satisfaction of it, as well they might. The knob, if knob there be, would be sailing, ever above the same spot upon the planet's surface, some 35,680 klommes aloft, upon Skye's equatorial plane. Without a doubt the object he believed he saw might be as much as several klommes across (he had handmade two models of such things and knew the specifications well), lit full and well by a glare of sunlight undiminished by the damp, thick atmosphere of Skye.

Still, at this distance it might be too small to make out with the unassisted eye. Nonetheless, Arran thought he could. Whether or not he was correct, he understood how the odd, windowed object resting upon the center of the great pentagram (about its doorway he could, without any question, discern half a dozen human figures as, at her infuriating pace, the draywherry drew nearer) had been lowered with laborious pain upon that bright-blazed cabelle from synchronous orbit all the way down to Alysabethport.

A "lubberlift" he knew the thing was named, although the hardiest star-sailors used it (and in point of fact, were always the first to test it at each orbitfall), right along with dirt-kissing passengers grateful to be shut of it after a nervous and protracted voyage to the ground. The annihilation-powered steam-launches that starships carried were too expensive of operation to be grounded, save in the direst emergency, and the keel had yet to be laid of a starsailing ship which could reach the surface of a full-sized world in any but the tiniest charred and tattered pieces.

Vibrating now with the damage done her, the draywherry drew up beside the landing pentagram and halted. Cleaned up as best they could manage, Robret and Donol lowered the hatch-ladder and descended to the ground, waiting for Arran to catch up. They strode across the pentagram, their boots making gritting noises upon the smooth, hard, dusty surface, toward those who had arrived by lubberlift.

They were met halfway by their father.

CHAPTER VIII:
ROBRET "THE" ISLAY

Watching his sons descend the hatch-ladder of the damaged wherry and scuttle from beneath the low-hovering machine with every manifestation of good health, the senior Robret Islay relaxed his grip upon the yoke of the worn kinergic thrustible which was at all times strapped to his right forearm.

Inset upon the weapon's axis, over the back of his hand, a minuscule pilot lamp which informed him that the sighting laser stood ready winked out. Another warning pilot, indicative of the weapon's potential kinergic capabilities, would have burned with equal brightness had he squeezed the flat kidney-shaped yoke where it crossed his palm, eliminating safety circuitry and bringing the laser into play. He had not had reason to see it alight this day. He knew now that he might yet.

At the moment, however, seeing his sons safe, more important matters occupied his mind. Above all what he must remember not to say was "You are late," or ask them why. They would tell him. Young Robret was a grown man, hard though it was to think of him as such, late marrying, like his father. He, his father, must grant him the adult courtesy of assuming a good reason existed for the delay. It was his great fortune, as far as Robret *fils* was concerned, that the courtesy was appropriate.

Movement flickered in the corner of his eye. This annoyed the warrior in him, in especial contrast to the respect he felt for his eldest son's judgment. He had spoken to the hopeless twit responsible with as much sharpness as was decent, if not altogether 'droomly. Yet already the Drector-Honorary Nasai-Ulness' pair of Oplytes—cut-rate models to begin with, and in false economy purchased past their prime—were fanning out upon either side, attempting in an obvious and artless way to flank the draywherry.

Ceo, he swore to himself, he had not wanted their over-dressed, stupid owners along, let alone these useless, danger-ous, disgusting creatures! Yet the Drector-Honorary and Lady Witsable Nasai-Ulness were "dear, dear chums" of Alysabeth's, old and honored friends—and intimate business associates—of her father's as well. It was said they were quite popular in the Hanoverian 'Droom, although for what reason he himself could never guess. The Nasai-Ulness struck him as at best a halfwit and genetic cull. The idiot fellow's wife was worse, if anything. He had encountered camp-followers with better manners, breeding, and taste than this so-called Lady could lay claim to.

Ah, well, of all individuals whose acquaintance he could boast, who was he to judge manners and breeding in another? He himself lacked those qualities of refinement which might have made him better, or at least more civilized, company, and to which Alysabeth, reared as she had been upon the capital world, was accustomed. He must strive to accommo-date himself as much as was tolerable to the wishes of his young and painfully lovely bride.

At least the Nasai-Ulness knew better (or, as appeared more likely, was too much the craven) than to play at soldiering himself. Keeping a tactical eye upon that one—intoxicated as he always seemed to be, upon occasion waving weaponry about, as well as upon his ill-trained animals—would have constituted one temptation too many for the Islay's trigger-thumb.

Indeed, it had been for purposes of despatching the two Oplytes, if need arose, as much as for any imagined threat from the draywherry, that he had warmed his thrustible. Oplytes were unpredictable, never, nor at any price, pos-sessed of overmuch intelligence. This far gone into the senescence which swept over them like a sudden storm, they could be as dangerous to those they purported to protect as to whatever they protected them from. Out of long habit and bitter experience, the Islay preferred defending those he loved, or was responsible for, himself. He would not, in good grace, have accepted even human bodyguards, and he had taught his sons this preference, as well.

Hovering at an angled edge of the landing pentagram, the draywherry had a bedraggled, sheepish look about her, as if she knew she had failed in her responsibilities. For one thing, she no longer rested level upon her §-pressors, but listed toward the starboard bow, as if she somehow shared the Nasai-Ulness' inebriation. Her wire-woven fuselage was in places rent, as he had earlier observed, by terrible energies. How it could be, and yet his sons be still alive and hale, he did not know, although, as soon as possible, he meant to find it out.

And something else . . . yes, that was it: she was the wrong color! For a moment the warrior's eyes crinkled in his weathered face as he realized Old Henry Redshirt had kept his promise—or had it been a threat?—to decorate the homely vessel by some means he had latterly devised. The golden color must be something subtle and active, for, as he approached the machine, the Islay could see it had flowed over onto the damaged portions, giving a contradictory impression of splendid disarray.

"Father!" Robret *fils* approached wearing a crooked grin, young enough in outlook to be pleased by whatever misadventure he and his brothers had survived. As etiquette required, he locked his left forearm along that of his father, avoiding a potential clash between the thrustible his father wore and that which he did not, but might have. The elder Islay recalled a conversation he had overheard in the capital, among amateur scholars and antiquarians, to the effect that this greeting-gesture had, upon a time, been performed with the right arm, indicating that the hand was empty and the greeter unarmed and harmless. Odd people, ancestors. What value lay in the friendly regard of a harmless individual?

Now, at last, he could wave these thrusted Oplytes aside. Others aboard the lubberlift had seen the boys descend and were venturing from within the hexagonal conveyance. He hoped they would have the sense to give him a moment with his sons. Accepting the gesture of greeting, whatever its origin, he added to it, clapping his eldest son and heir upon the shoulder. He noticed that the boy winced, as if bruised.

"Father!" Hardly had the Islay opened his mouth to ask about Robret's injury, when he was greeted with the same most-welcome word by his youngest. Arran hurtled toward him. How good it was to see the boy up and about after his illness! But first came an awkward moment. Arran was twelve, perhaps too young for warriors' forearm clasps, perhaps too old for a father's—

Ceo take it! The Islay reached down (not quite as far as he had used to, he noticed with a mortal pang all fathers share), seized the boy and lifted him into his arms, squeezing him until they both squeaked. By the time this was accomplished, along with a ducking of the head which was not quite a kiss, and the boy set back upon his feet, his brother Donol's casual pace had brought him to his father's side, although so far without a word of greeting.

The Islay nodded at his middle son and clasped his arm. Donol made him feel a touch of guilt. In honesty, he had never been as fond of the boy as of the others. It was bound to be that he would love one more or one the less. He had striven to prevent Donol seeing it, but such deception was, the warrior knew, at the close range family life afforded and over a lifetime's risk of betrayal, all but impossible. It grieved him such deceit seemed necessary, as it must have grieved his not-altogether unloved nor unperceptive middle son. Thus it was Donol he first spoke to: "I trust, good steward, I shall discover affairs at home to be in somewhat better array than here."

Donol blinked, wordless and hurt-looking. *Ceo's eyes,* he had not intended to put it thus, a paternal and, even worse, sarcastic rebuke. It had been no more than comradely humor, commiseration over whatever circumstances had damaged the draywherry, and, more, an excuse to praise the careful administration of the Holdings into which young Donol of late, and upon his own initiative, had thrown his most passionate and concentrated effort.

Young Robret blinked as well, but for another reason. An unsettling thought occurred to him which, until now, had not crossed his mind. He was as disturbed at its lateness in arriving as he was at the thought itself. "Ceo's ghost, Father, I am inexcusably remiss! Are your communicators in working order? I believe we were attacked upon the way here, and have only just realized that something similar may have taken place at home!"

Lacking better means of retraction, the Islay took Donol by the shoulder and looked him in the eye, but it was to his eldest he answered: "Be not alarmed, son. When you were overdue, I used the lasercom here. It and its relays are in fine repair. The one thing they worry about at home is your well-being, concerning which we shall soon put their minds at ease." He winked, inviting his middle son to share a mild joke at the expense of the eldest. "In particular the mind of Mistress Lia Woodgate."

"How pehfectly *dweadful!*"

Witsable Nasai-Ulness was Drector-Honorary of a "planet Ulness" which did not in fact exist. This sometimes useful legal fiction, unique to the imperia-conglomerate, was no less peculiar, nor less useful, than the legal fictions of a thousand other civilizations, both before and after the thirty-first century. He peered over the top of his masque—a chartreuse buckley with protruding front teeth, a single arched eyebrow, and an insolent sneer which he himself was not quite up to—at the damage done the fabric of the draywherry. A pale man, with watery, weak-looking eyes, a narrow nose, and thin, purplish lips, his sparse carroty-colored hair jutted out over his ears.

It would have been more pleasing to the Islay's sense of the acceptable to assume the man feigned uselessness and stupidity for some sinister or cynical purpose of his own. Folk literature from a myriad of worlds abounded with such ironic conceits. But folk literature was not life, and the Islay had encountered enough of this disgusting kind at the 'Droom to resign himself that the Nasai-Ulness was exactly what he appeared to be.

It was not, thought the senior Robret, that the man was in any degree effeminate. That was not the word. The woman was rare who could exhibit such effete mannerisms and turns of phrase as he did and hold her head up. (No handy world like "wanque" came to mind for the few women who did.) Nor was it that he was a member of a decadent and inbred aristocracy. His family had been elevated to the Drectorhood only in his father's time, like many among the peasantry of a million worlds who were much like him. The Islay dismissed the fellow as a natural-born nonentity. It bothered him, wondering why a bright, aggressive, powerful, unstoppable individual like Morven should have known who he was, let alone have stooped to befriend him. What use was he to Morven? Something more was here than met the eye. Or perhaps something less.

Crowded beside the Nasai-Ulness, squeezed tight as they were between the pair of Oplyte guards, the Lady Nasai-Ulness (the Islay could never remember her first name, nor had he any wish to) followed her husband's intoxicated gaze toward the wire-ends shining golden in the starport floodlights. Anyone else from the 'Droom of the Monopolity of Hanover would have offered an urbane comment, or at least evinced a delicate, civilized shudder. Lady Nasai-Ulness shrugged and scratched at her ribs where her traveling dress bound her.

"Like the old days, eh, Robbie?" As the Drector-Honorary and his Lady gathered their voluminous clothing about them, ducked with a measure of awkwardness beneath the draywherry's belly, and climbed the hatch-ladder, passing beyond their host's immediate responsibility to those he had delegated aboard the vehicle, the Islay turned toward the only individual who ever called him by nickname. Pushed along by yet another Oplyte, one of the rare domestic conversions (more reliable, it was claimed, less prone to turning ugly, it bore a thrustible upon its forearm in at least the semblance of its owner's defense), Tarbert Morven leaned back in his chair as far as his paralysis would permit, gazing upward at the damaged hull. "Wreck and ruination! Perverse as it may be, I find it almost stimulating—do you not find it likewise?—I suppose because it reminds me of my lost . . . youth."

The Islay, occupied with his own thoughts and having felt no such emotion, gave the question a vague shrug. Lifting him from the chair, which would soon be useless in any case, and carrying the crippled Shandeen up the ladder in its heavy-muscled arms, the unlucky Oplyte stumbled, almost spilling Morven. A soldier's expletive followed, evoked, no doubt, by these reminders of the crippled man's youth, after which the Islay heard Morven add something to the Nasai-Ulness about repenting of having brought the creature, having intended soon to replace it. Having suffered considerable experience with Oplytes in his own youth (and less anxious than Morven to be reminded of it), the Islay was not certain he would risk saying such a thing in front of it.

Làst to enter, the Islay followed his bride. Ever practical, after her own impractical fashion, the Lady Alysabeth had consented to forgo the presence of servants during the brief trip to the planet's surface and what they had all assumed would be an even briefer voyage to the Holdings. The lubberlift of the vessel which had brought them to Skye, a mere carrack of fifteen projectibles' prowess, had scarce afforded sufficient room for those who had come, although he supposed the servants might have shared a perilous ride down with the sailors who had piloted the thing to its shackle. Alysabeth's servants—half a dozen of them, all human—and the considerable baggage their mistress brought with her would follow upon successive journeys from synchronous orbit, which would also bring other illustrious guests accompanying them from Hanover.

As the hatch-ladder was allowed to raise itself and the passenger-guests seen safe to their seats—Morven's wheelchair lay folded upon the deck nearby its owner—the Islay took his eldest son aside. "Open the panel upon the forward surface of the steering pedestal." Young Robret raised his eyebrows, but did not as yet offer a reply. The Islay continued: "Within, you will discover an old-fashioned keypad I installed myself, in secret and by hand, forty years ago. Push out the sequence T-457902." He repeated the digits. "This will allow us to override the safeties and halt this vehicle whenever and wherever we wish."

"And will we wish to?" Robret asked his father.

"If we have an uprising upon our hands—I find that hard to credit, but must proceed upon the evidence—it is best to deal with it without delay."

"Yes, sir. You will want me to pilot the wherry?"

"That we shall leave to Donol. Had you thought to bring a thrustible?"

"Why, no, Father, I never anticipated—"

"It is my fault, this oversight. We shall speak of it again. Sometimes, Robret, things must change if anything is to remain the same. Meanwhile, I shall speak to the Nasai-Ulness about borrowing his thrustible. He will not likely want to join us ahunting." The warrior grinned. "I cannot say how good a weapon it will prove, but you may rest assured it will be pretty."

The loan was arranged with Drector-Honorary Nasai-Ulness as the elder Robret had desired. The thrustible, indeed, proved pretty as he had predicted. As far as the Islay knew, this was the second time young Robret had ever strapped a thrustible upon his arm, the previous occasion being picnic practice at the Holdings when Glynnaughfern yet lived. He knew that his eldest son, a peaceable man within his heart (as his father and mother had brought him up), with a peaceable man's interests, cared little for the things and had less experience with them.

Still, he was confident Robret would follow where led. Even now, with the thrustible's power supply locked out at the elbow, the boy was familiarizing himself with the much-embellished weapon (if anything, his father's guess had fallen short of the reality), aiming the designator at an empty portion of the hull aft of where the passengers had been seated, squeezing the yoke, thumbing the trigger to see where the still-brighter flash of the thrust-simulating beam struck.

The senior Islay relaxed. Robret would acquit himself, did it come to a fight, as well as any. This was what counted, after all. The virtues and skills of soldiery were overrated. Ask anyone who had done some soldiering.

This settled, the Islay glanced about to make what disposition in his mind he might of the meager forces available to him: himself there was; young Robret, an amateur; likewise Donol, piloting; the three Oplytes—the Nasai-Ulness' aged pair and Morven's—for what they were worth. The rest, including his wife and youngest son, sat as safe as they might be (which, to judge from all appearances about him now, was not much) within the draywherry. Only when he had accomplished what he could, did he pause in his thoughts to wonder again.

Woodsrunners?

CHAPTER IX:
REMISE ET REDOUBLEMENT

They had arrived.

The nighttime sky was preternaturally clear. Stars shone, each encircled by an individual frosty halo. The mist-gauzed Skyan moonring spilt its milky light upon the greenway as the wounded wherry slowed to a weary halt at a prudent distance from newfallen rock which darkened the ring-silvered sward before the roadcut where the machine had earlier been ambushed.

Even so, they were anticipated. For the briefest moment, those inside the damaged machine found themselves bathed in the tepid, scattered scarlet of someone's faraway designator. A dull *thump!* vibrated the hull. The fabric of the wherry began singing with the energies of thrustibles directed toward it at the furthest extremity of their useful range.

Issuing terse instructions, Robret the Islay levered the hatch-ladder to the ground and preceded those he had chosen—if such word was accurate, given millions he might have picked before depending upon three aging Oplytes and two untried lads—to assist him. He knew he had small hope of finding those responsible for this villainy, but even less choice about trying, not only as a man whose family had been assaulted, but as the planet's Drector-Hereditary, representative and enforcer of the Ceo's law.

At the Islay's direction (given with a trepidation which, if the father were lucky, the boy would never know of), Robret *fils,* armed with a borrowed thrustible as untried as himself, departed for the left side of the tumbled roadcut with Morven's erstwhile wheelchair-pushing servant. The Nasai-

Ulness bodyguards, specialized to the task assigned them, newer but of inferior quality, went with his younger, unarmed, and less-experienced brother Donol through the menacing shadows down the center of the cut. The Islay himself would take the right, whence he believed the thrusts had originated.

His own well-worn thrustible, although he bore it all his waking hours, felt odd to him (it was always thus before a fight too long anticipated) where it lay along the back of his forearm. Its curved powerpack was warm, strapped to his elbow. Its cooler axis lay hard against his flesh, fastened about his wrist. Its lensed beam-end projected a siemme or two beyond his knuckles, and the yoke, two siemmes from front to back, palm-wide and kidney-shaped, was no more than a tenth that thickness, lifetime-tested, ready in his hand.

The Islay took deep breaths, thinking. He had never been one of those joyous warriors he had fought beside in the Ceo's wars. He no longer hunted, although he had aplenty in his youth, also in his first days upon Skye, and still encouraged his sons in the enthusiasm. Now he raised meat for slaughter at the Holdings and owned neither time nor energy to hunt for more. The killing of men or other thinking things such as he had encountered war-voyaging among the stars filled him with no delight. Yet never had he shrunk from the necessity, nor from the ruthlessness it required, when need was clear. Nor would he do so now. Cursing, he stumbled over an exposed and upturned rock.

It was passing strange, he thought to himself, to be seeing bare soil and barren rock, almost obscene after decades of his life spent upon this moist, rich world where everything soon acquired a layering of green, be it the grassy covering of meadow, the darker, heavier foliage of the forest, or the simple lawn of moss high in the mountain passes. It was like seeing the skeleton of a world.

He had long observed, upon every planet his feet had touched (and they were many), the manner in which his sense of smell became keener at night, be it upon account of vapors arising in the absence of sunlight to drive them away, or owing to the fact that, when eyesight was diminished by the darkness, one came to lean without volition or awareness upon other senses. Now, an alien scent intruded among those of soil and broken vegetation, heavy upon the damp and earthy night air despite time's passage, which he could not at once identify. It grew stronger as he left the violated earth and climbed higher up the steep slope beside the roadcut. Sharp it was, pungent, in some way even pleasant, yet it belonged neither to Skye nor anything he knew as Skyan.

A nightbird called in the silence. Disturbed by the sound, he sensed something wrong, something missing. That was it: at this time of night, this time of the year, insects should have made a greater racket than any bird!

Taking his time, he ascended, watching, sniffing, listening each cautious step of the way until at last he stood just below the violated summit of the right-hand ridge of the roadcut. What he saw stretched his sensibilities near to breaking between awe and anger. With the sky clearer moment by moment, ringlight there was enough by now to see what had been done here. It looked as if some titan had cut a giant cake. Over an undetermined period—time would have abounded upon this neglected thoroughfare—a long row of vertical holes had been drilled deep into the rock. He could see the grooving which was all that was left of them; the odor he had noticed issued from here. Explosives had been tamped into the holes. He presumed the same had been accomplished upon the other side. Young Robret would let him know in due course.

He knew the smell now for what it was: sulfur. The machine-drilled holes had been packed with the most ancient and primitive explosive known to man's part of the galaxy, which accounted for their number. Of a sudden he was filled with suspicion. If someone who did not know the planet, who had only read about woodsrunners from a datathille, had wished, for some unfathomable reason, to imitate the rebellious pattern of many years ago, they might think to stir things up with a political potion of charcoal corned with yellow sulfur and potassium nitrate, both abundant upon Skye, kneaded with water and alcohol and let desiccate, then ground coarse with cautious patience.

They might. And they would be dead wrong, because

woodsrunners, for all they pursued a rustic existence, were far from primitive, fashioning their own machinery, generating their own power (or stealing it from Islay conductiles and beamcasts, which was easier). They would make and use explosives not a whit less sophisticated than any found within the sky-wide Monopolity. The only mechanic arts they lacked were those which he, as Drector-Hereditary and representative of the Monopolitan Ceo upon Skye, was obliged by Hanoverian law to deny them. Likely such were practiced secretly in any case. Stooping, he ran a finger along one dew-damp groove, feeling chatter-marks of whatever tool had cut it into the stubborn mountain rock. This was a second betrayal of the same sort: woodsrunners would have used lasers.

Whatever fool was responsible for them, fused them together and set them off at once, the crude landmines had worked, hurling the entire face of the cut, a volume of two measures' depth by a hundred by another two, outward and downward onto the greenway. Had they been a fraction of a second better timed, he would have lost all his sons, buried alive in one ugly stroke.

The nightbird trilled again. This time something seemed as alien about the noise as the cloying odor filling the air about him. Without thinking, out of long years of warrior-training and near-fatal mistakes, the Islay had taken care not to silhouette himself against a sky which, filled with water vapor and backlit by the hazy moonring, glowed faintly to the night-adjusted eye. Now he was aware of what he had done, and grateful. Crouching low, he crept as silent as he could, feeling his way past slipping rock and brittle windfallen branches, toward the counterfeit bird-noise, an obvious signal, which came to him once again as he counted out his fifth and sixth paces.

A deeper silence followed, the Islay thought, upon the sudden awareness that he was not the individual for whom the signal had been intended and with whom a meeting was anticipated. A different sound came, of someone less woodswise than the Islay making his way toward him in intended stealth. Thinking thoughts about professional assassins accustomed to city-work, the Islay drifted left, hurried low along the ground, his progress rapid as stalking would allow, to get behind whomever was approaching. The flash of a bit of metal or a careless, unplanned movement caught his eye.

The Islay stood and shouted, "Stop, fellow!"

Standing as well, the stranger whirled to face him, kicking up dead leaves about his ankles in the effort. A wild, fearful expression widened his mouth and eyes, distorting his features. It was the look, the senior Robret thought, of a surprised and hunted creature. Yet, if the fool were still here in this place of ambush, metric hours after his intended victims and their vehicle had escaped the manmade avalanche, if he were the one who had thrust upon the draywherry only minutes ago, why should he be surprised?

Without delay, the Islay raised right forearm to left shoulder in a diagonal gesture termed, in sporting circles, the "salute." More practical than courteous, it covered the torso with the weak, secondary pressor-field surrounding the long axis of his thrustible. A deep breath calmed him. He meant to take this unaccountable incompetent alive, if such was possible.

"In the Ceo's name, surrender now to me and live!"

"Die, slutspawn!" The shout was weaker than the ugly words it carried, desperate, high, and strained. Ragged and dirty in the ringlight, his foe mirrored the salute with little grace, straightening his weapon-bearing arm in preemptory attack. Where the Islay stood, seven paces off, he could hear the fellow's breath rasp, frantic, observe his knuckles whiten where they wrapped about his thrustible's yoke, and knew he faced a villain frightened badly or worse schooled. In a vague way he was aware—these thoughts occupying less than a heartbeat—of the scarlet designator beam where it splashed upon his chest, wavering as the man's arm trembled from terror or exhaustion.

Disdaining the protective field about it, the Islay, too, straightened his arm before his opponent's thumb could twitch, gave the safety a squeeze across the yokefront, saw the spot of his own laser spring to life where he had known it would, upon those whitened knuckles, and, without awaiting this confirmation, thumbed the trigger. Great energies, invisible in themselves, flared harsh in the meeting. The air between the men roared protest, sparked with ionization, as thrust met thrust, canceling in a blinding flash.

"Again I say, surrender in the Ceo's name!"

"*And I say—!*" The assassin's voice chopped off. Again kinergic beams annihilated one another. The Islay's almost instinctive blink saved him from the dancing blue afterspot in his eyes which is the beginning of the end for a thrustiblist. The merest instant passed which seemed to him an hour. Before he was aware of having made the decision, he turned his wrist inward, downward, heedless of the designator as before, and thumbed the trigger.

Dealt a glancing blow upon the right hip, the bandit spun, responded by loosing a kinergic bolt even as he staggered backward against the bole of a tree, and fell with a thump upon a bed of dead leaves. He followed with yet another bolt as he struck the ground.

The Islay caught the first thrust in midair with an answering burst, the second upon the field of his upturned axis as he rotated his arm for another thrust. Downed or not, the fellow was better than he had guessed, becoming more so as he calmed himself and gained more confidence thereby.

Crimson filled the Islay's eyes a moment. Headthrust coming, something inside him warned. He ducked, hair ruffled by disrupted air about his head.

Suffering disadvantage, since he wanted the man alive, while the man labored under no such constraint, the Islay let loose a third time, almost in the same instant as before, anticipating another thrust from the supine bandit. He thrust at the foot the fellow was attempting to get under himself. The foot whipped out from under the man and in that moment he lost what self-control he had regained, answering with random windmill thrusts at the Islay while attempting to scrabble backward for the cover of a fallen tree.

"*Die! Die! Die! Die!*"

Hurried by a thing the practiced fighter fears most, an unlearned, flailing, desperate, and therefore unpredictable opponent, the Islay was pressed to defend himself: block in fourth, parry and reply from sixth.

A thunderclap! Pain sang the length of the Islay's left arm as bark exploded from a tree beside him. The standing remnants of its trunk steamed in the ringlight. *Riposte, riposte, riposte.* The tortured air between the men smelt of ozone and of §-field-scorched leaves. One hellish, invisible beam at a time, one desperate burst after another, the Islay met and canceled the flurry of red-fringed energies the bandit threw at him.

From a distance, voices shouted. His foot slipped, putting him upon his back like his opponent. He had been distracted by flashes from across the roadcut. Young Robret had found prey upon the opposite slope. This was no moment to be worrying about his son, who would acquit himself or not.

He felt a shocking blow to his upraised, vulnerable knee, heard a shout of triumph from his enemy. Attempting to raise his thrustible to ward off a killing thrust, he found he could not move his arm. His sleeve was entangled in an upthrust tree root. Scarlet flashed before his eyes once more.

As he struggled to free his arm, something within Robret the Islay began to prepare itself for death.

CHAPTER X:
AT THE PRECIPICE

The night was black and splashed with crimson.

Lacking other illumination—nothing in this dark wild place existed for a lampwand to give glowing to, even had one been stowed by providence aboard the wherry, which it had not—young Robret had discovered he might pick a path along the crumbling edge of the roadcut by squeezing, from time to time, the safety-bar at the yoke's edge of his borrowed and unfamiliar thrustible.

"This way, I think." The young man pushed between two thick and thistled bushes, his tone somewhat uncertain, for although he had been born and bred to issue orders, he had never before commanded something which was not quite human. Morven's grim, nameless Oplyte servant plodded wordless behind him, never acknowledging his orders (although obeying them without fail), contributing nothing to the task they shared in theory except the noise of ragged breathing and the thump and gravel-clatter of occasional stumbling.

To be fair to the unfortunate creature (Robret was in no position to appreciate how only a son raised by his father might have thought such a thing), it was a steep way they followed, never intended for the passage of human, or semi-human, feet. The soil had been turned by whatever energies had brought the roadcut down upon them and was still loose in places, threatening to slide at a footstep, even, he thought, at a sneeze. Rocks and boulders which long ago had found a kind of neutral buoyancy within the earthy medium they floated in now lay upon the surface, ready to trip the night-blind and unwary passerby. Not for the first time did Robret wish for something other than the ankle-length dress boots which might have seen their proper milieu at some play-party of Lia's, but by no means here, upon a broken trail thousands of klommes from the light and warmth of home.

Somehow, Robret wondering how to manage even as they managed it, he and his companion made it to the top, stood at the edge and looked down. He might have been looking into a well of ink. He knew his younger brother and the Nasai-Ulness bodyguards were down there, as he knew his father was upon the other side, but he could neither see nor hear them. Now what should he do? His father had been unspecific instructing him, saying it was an unspecific task they had before them. They were to look for traces of whoever had conceived this deed. Their greatest fortune (and much the most unlikely, considering the amount of time since the attack suffered by the draywherry) would be to find one of the culprits and bring him back alive to be interrogated.

Another designator flash told him nothing. He had hoped, in truth expected, to discover footprints in damp soil or other indication of recent human presence. In this he was disappointed. Save for the grooves left at the summit by whatever tool had drilled the rock for explosives, he had found nothing to indicate any thinking being had been here since the planet had first coalesced from interstellar gases. Even without conversation over it, he knew his father, having himself hammered out the Bargain which had given Skye four decades of tranquility, lent small credit to the notion that woodsrunners, with no reason anyone could offer in support, had risen again to harry their conquerors. But who else would have done such a thing?

Of a sudden he sensed motion in the low trees a few measures to his left, away from the roadcut. Unused to carrying a weapon or thinking about using one, he shone the designator toward the spot—and cursed himself for betraying his position. In answer, the bizarre, dizzying sensation of a near-miss passed round and through him as he flung himself upon the ground.

The Oplyte behind him was less lucky. Robret heard a grunt, accompanied by an uglier implosion as the beam struck the creature full in the torso. A child of his culture, Robret knew it was like being upon the receiving end of a huge timber sluicing downstream in white water from the Islay logging fields. A revolting gurgling noise—the sound of death, he somehow knew—was followed by a silence even more terrible. The metallic scent of blood fresh-spilled came sharp to the younger Robret Islay. He discovered that his stomach was in rebellion and, with some difficulty, quelled it.

With only sound to guide him, a sense he had never before used in this manner, Robret pointed his forearm in what he imagined was the correct direction and tensed both thumb and fingers at the same time, not waiting for the glow of his designator to give him away. He heard a crash, as if the trees had taken the brunt of his thrust. He rolled, in order not to be where his enemy now knew he was, and unleashed the energies of his weapon once again. A hoarse scream echoed across the mountaintop, twisting something deep and vulnerable within him. Was this what it felt like to do injury to another being? A form, no more than silhouetted in the mist-lit darkness, crashed from the foliage, staggering as if it could neither see nor think. Before Robret could catch the fellow's trouser leg (this close did he pass by Robret's face) he felt the fabric slip through weapon-encumbered fingers and heard, more than saw, his wounded assailant pitch over the precipice and, with another scream, hurl himself into the depth of the roadcut. Perhaps he only imagined the dull thud of the impact far below.

All at once no time was left for imagining. Another series of crashes, more purposeful, headed toward him. Wishing he could suppress the designator altogether (such a contingency had been provided for in the weapon's design, but Robret's sketchy lesson had not included this usage), he thrust again and again at the noise coming toward him, rolling, ducking unseen and perhaps unreal energies being thrown at him in return.

Another squirm and nothing remained to squirm upon. Having heeded not where his rolling and dodging carried him, Robret discovered with a start that he lay across the soft, broken lip of the roadcut, ankles hanging in dark empty space over a drop of hundreds of measures. Sweat sprang with the odd sensation of a million pinpricks over every siemme of his skin. If his life had afterward depended upon it, he could never have decided whether it was the sweat of fear or of relief. He began to crawl forward.

Sudden impact lifted his body from the damp ground where he lay near the perilous edge, and dropped it back again. Behind agony-hazed eyes, he had the fleeting thought it had been like being struck by a pillow traveling several hundred klommes per hour. Yet this, too, was a near miss, else he would not have been able to think at all. He heard the sound of running feet. With the greatest effort, against a mass of bone and muscle moving all too slowly for his racing fears, he raised an aching, injured arm and squeezed the yoke.

In the air before him, brightness seared the night as beam met destructive beam in mutual cancellation. Robret had the presence of mind to make a second thrust quickly. Again annihilation flared.

Upon his third squeeze, darkness reigned. He heard a muffled groan, a crash, rose to his knees and thrust in the same direction again. This time his opponent's answering blow seemed to catch him square in the chest. He was thrown backward, over the edge, somehow twisted his body in midair and slammed both arms and elbows against the yielding, near-vertical surface before him. Soil and gravel sleeted by his face as he clawed in the dark for a hold in crumbling earth. Dirt ripped through his fingers as he fell.

Angry and frustrated, Arran ground his teeth. At that, it was better than crying, which was what, in truth, he wanted to do and dare not. Instead, he slumped behind the steering pedestal, keeping a sullen back to unwelcome others, his father's and stepmother's guests, and stared into the featureless ring-lit night through the damaged and now inert fabric of the draywherry. The guests—in this despairing moment he discovered himself thinking of Morven and the others as "Greasylocks and the Three Bores"—were blabbering among themselves and paying him no attention. After all, he was only a child.

Only a child! Perhaps he was the youngest of his father's sons, a mere twelve, but had he been assaulted, insulted, thrust at, as Robret and Donol had been, any the less than they in the attack upon the draywherry? Would he have died less dead? Did he not also share a right—a duty—to take part in the defense of his father's position upon this planet?

"Stay you here." His brothers had each taken him aside— the command had not even come from his father!—adding, as a patronizing afterthought, "Watch over our stepmother and the Drector and Lady Nasai-Ulness."

Very well, (his demand was silent, of no one in particular), *with what?* He had not even thought to bring his almost-useless walther-weapon, although he could blame this oversight upon no one but himself. Live and learn, Old Henry always said. He would never make such an idiot mistake again!

For a long while Arran gazed in unseeing resentment into the darkness surrounding them. Curious, he thought as he began to calm down, how neither his father nor his brothers had mentioned watching over Morven, paralyzed though the Shandeen was. Somehow he did not seem the sort who required it of anyone. The grotesque entity which pushed him about in his chair seemed more a decoration—in poor taste, Arran thought—than a necessity.

In similar circumstances, a simple matter of unconscious reflex, Arran's idle thoughts would have turned his head round to look upon their object. He experienced no such reflex now. And noticed it. What was it seemed so dire about his new stepmother's father? The fellow was an utter cripple in an age of limb and nerve regeneration which witnessed few such, and upon this account, Arran thought, to be presumed quite harmless. Not wanting to be watched watching, Arran did observe the man now, but by courtesy of a reflective dial-cover upon the pedestal.

Morven hunched where he had earlier been seated by his inhuman servant, now gone with the younger Robret, dark eyes agleam as he related some esoteric and theoretically amusing item of Monopolitan palace plottery to the others. His wheeled chair depended upon so many—what was the word Old Henry used?—*electromagnetical* devices, it would not function within the draywherry's enveloping §-field, and had been folded upon itself and set to one side.

Animated as it may have sounded, the adult discussion was conducted, at least by one participant, without the usual gestures and gesticulations enthusiasm might have been expected to engender. Morven's useless arms had been crossed for him at the thin white wrists which lay before him in his lap. Beneath the light blanket upon which his hands rested, his ankles were not crossed, yet the feet dangling at their ends lay upon the deck in an angular, uncomfortable-looking position, almost as if they had been.

Oddest of all was the man's face, which added much to the mystery of his menace, for Morven possessed altogether the fairest male countenance upon which Arran had ever looked, in drama or in real life. Pomade-tressed he might have been, the boy thought (with broader generosity of spirit than he had earlier exercised), following fashions presently in vogue within the imperium-conglomerate. Still, the man was no sick-sallow, sunk-eyed, thin-lipped, pinch-nosed creature of indeterminate gender such as disgusted Arran of late in Mistress Lia's dramathilles, or like this chronic inebriate Nasai-Ulness. That he was sire to the beautiful Alysabeth was no mere guessing matter. After his own sinister manner, he was quite as beautiful as she was.

And beautiful she was, albeit somehow like an ancient ceramic doll. Arran shifted in his chair to observe her in his makeshift mirror. Hers was a distant and intimidating aspect. He felt unbalanced, awkward in her presence, cold-sweaty, tongue-tied, stammering if not altogether speechless. He always sensed that he was being judged. And convicted.

This was a different sensation from the grinning self-consciousness Mistress Lia sometimes evoked in him. That feeling warmed his cheeks, the back of his neck, his ears. While it, too, was embarrassing (although he somehow understood, in his precocious sophistication, that embarrassment in the female presence is a natural state for boys his age), at the same it was, beyond question, pleasant, even exhilarating. Although he was in essence a farm child, long since acquainted with the biological facts of life, he wondered now if this warm feeling was what his brother Robret felt about Lia and why he was going to marry her. Arran could think of many worse reasons.

Aware that his thoughts had wandered, Arran realized in the same moment that he had answered the question which he had earlier asked himself. Whatever it was he felt in Alysabeth Morven Islay's presence, whatever dampened his hands, made the blood stream cold within him, it was this which kept him from looking direct upon her father. Of a sudden, Morven stared straight at him—rather, at the dial-face where he must have known his own to be reflected—and sent a leering wink at the boy. Arran looked away, his heart pounding with unnameable terror.

At about the same instant that Robret *fils* and Morven's Oplyte achieved the violated crest of the roadcut, Donol and the creatures borrowed from the Nasai-Ulness found themselves picking a careful path through rubble in the silent darkness halfway along that portion of the greenway sliced through the mountain ridge. With startling abruptness, the hazy, ring-lit, star-filled sky was filled with annihilative flashes upon both sides, and with the gut-clenching sound of screaming. Before Donol or his inhuman companions could react, the hiss of falling earth came rushing, growing louder, lower every second, until it was a bass roar with undertones more felt than heard. It was punctuated by a nearby thump. And another. The roar became a hiss again, afterward a trickle, until about them only silence remained.

One of the Oplytes raised an arm, squeezing upon the

yoke of its thrustible, directing the designator beam ahead. Upon a black-brown slant of new-fallen earth, they saw a form rise from under a light covering of soil. Shaking, spitting, brushing dirt from its eyes, it seemed not to know it stood over a pair of similar bodies which would never raise themselves again.

"I say, s-stop there, you!" Donol found himself too confused to think of anything more forceful. Both Oplytes had their thrustibles aimed at the man who, for all he could tell, might have been his brother or his father. The slow-moving dirty figure turned, glancing at the bodies lying nearby as if seeing them for the first time, and raised an arm in gesture of surrender.

"T'other's broke, methinks." It was a gravel voice, an unmistakable peasant accent, although nothing born among the mountains and forests of Skye. "Don't y'be killin' me, sonny, givin' up as I plainly be." Donol felt himself relax a trifle, he and the Oplytes stepping forward a few paces. In the relief washing through his body at not having to subdue the man, it did not occur to him to wonder about the other fallen figures. He opened his mouth to speak, but was interrupted. "Ye'd be ain of Islay, ben't ye?"

"Yes," Donol replied, "I would." He had the discomfiting sense of being inspected. The cornered man's gaze went up and down his body, from one Oplyte to the other where they stood with weapons ready to strike or deflect.

"Meguess that's that, then." Of a sudden, the wretch before them nodded, grinned, fisted his weapon hand, and shoved it beneath his chin. The scarlet beam underlit his face in a hideous manner—just before that face disappeared in an up-blasted cloud of blood and disrupted flesh.

CHAPTER XI:
DEATH AT DAWNING

Even as he prepared himself for death—continuing, nevertheless, the struggle to free his arm from whatever entangled it—something within the warrior heart which was Robret the Islay's decided to *deal* death instead.

"Desist, bandit!" The Hanoverian cried out the words with an earnestness which, had his opponent but known what to listen for, bordered close upon an odd sort of desperation. "Desist and live, I tell you!"

Only the Islay's decades of training and inborn indomitable pride kept him from making it, "I beg you!" It had not been, in truth, so much a shout of offered mercy, although the desire he held dearest was not to add another life to his account, as the direst of warnings. Irresistible forces, deep-grained and dormant within him, were seeking release. Yet the only answer he received was another burst of §-field energy, thrust in mortal fear and murderous anger at the lawful Drector-Hereditary of Skye.

Even so, it is one thing to give offers and another to make delivery upon them. For all his fears and merciful intentions, the Islay was discovering (as before, upon countless occasions) that he could neither resign himself to oblivion, either his own or that of his enemy, nor yet prevent an unlooked-for but inexorable killing. It was, he knew, an ancient conflict within him, deadly in potential to anyone for whom survival hung upon decisive action. Still, the wordless argument was worn smooth as a river stone with the passage of years and the letting of much blood. And experience speaking—as it must—louder than intentions, the conflict could be resolved in one manner only.

Thus, despite any charitable limits he had set himself—firstly because he had never in his life delivered a mortal blow with a light heart, also because he desired an informative word with this would-be assassin—through no choice of his own, he began to bear harder upon the man, working him faster, watching his vain struggle to regain the initiative, while he, the Islay, tried in simple to save the idiot from himself. Still, if need be, it was the other fellow who would die this starry evening.

Round they danced through darkness upon dew-damp grass, in and out of churned soil which came close to being mud. The elder Islay, no longer a young man, found himself beginning to tire. This did not frighten him as it might many another, but served as a sign, bidding him realize the moment had arrived, all best wishes to the contrary, to put an end to folly. Nor breath had he remaining to warn the other fellow further, nor time to speak again in offer of charity or quarter. Reflex followed stimulus.

"Ceo!" he groaned with disappointment, seeing, almost as a detached witness to the exercise of his own deadly skill, the spectacle peculiar to a fight with thrustibles between two talented opponents. Adroit with counterthrust and secondary field as both combatants were, no blow could tell between them unless placed as this one had been. It appeared, he thought, as if the other had stumbled, full-faced, upon the gruesome stub of an invisible tree branch, or been struck upon the bridge of the nose by a well-centered hammer. Reflex demanded a successful coup be followed with another for effect.

It appeared, he thought, continuing to seek metaphors less terrible than the grim reality before him, as if one of the fragile masques popular upon Hanover had been crushed in from the nose by careless packing in a sailing chest. To the Islay, his perceptions speeded by adrenaline pumping in his arteries, it seemed he could see his weapon's §-wavefront sinking deeper until, no longer able to bear the titanic pressures imposed upon it, the bandit's head exploded in a night-blackened fog of blood and pureed brains. He let his arm drop to his side. The fight was over and, with it, his hope of unraveling the mystery of the ambush upon the wherry which had borne his sons—*his sons*—(safe, as it had turned out, did they survive this evening's mischief) to him.

The bandit's truncated body, streaming blood, dead before it had stopped thrusting at him, pitched over with a splash onto the muddy ground.

Heart hammering, lungs heaving, the Islay, far gone in pain and conscious at the moment of his years, would have given much to follow its example, to throw himself upon the cool, soggy grass until vision cleared and ears stopped ringing. Yet he could not allow himself the briefest respite. Minutes ago (it seemed like hours to him), he had been distracted by annihilative flares upon the other side of the roadcut, and, he believed, one other far below. He must somehow drag himself onward in case young Robret needed help.

Sweat broke from his hairline, blinding him further, and poured down the back of his neck. Heat radiated from his face as if he had been sunburnt. Summoning every particle of energy and moral strength remaining to him, he rose from the half slump he had assumed, and took a first step forward.

Robbie, lad, you are not getting a bit younger, thought one isolated corner of his mind which at all times remained detached and amused. He took a second step. A third. *Farcing about is for the young men,* he lectured himself. *If you intend dying in bed, you must give up this nonsense. You are a responsible married man again, already past the proper age to settle down*—a fourth step found his strength beginning to return—*and by the Ceo's privates, before this evening I had reason to believe I had done!*

Now, his blood still singing from exertion, still chiding himself for what he deemed a foolish weakness for adventure, the Islay knew only his duty. Growing stronger with each step, he staggered the short distance to the bandit's smoking corpse, knelt with a heartfelt groan which spoke for every muscle in his body, and stripped the thrustible off its already-cooling arm. Too dangerous and powerful were these things to be left lying round. Rising with the same eloquent noise, he seized the dripping carcass by the heel-cuff and began dragging it down the slope into the bed of the roadcut where it could be watched over by others. It was, he was grateful to realize, less difficult a task than he had anticipated. He was quicker to regain his breath and composure than he had expected. *It paid,* he thought, *to stay in shape.*

Finding none to meet him at the bottom, he left the body upon a heap of stones, crossed the cut, and had taken the first leg-straining, reluctant step upward, when he heard a familiar voice below him and to one side.

"Father?"

He stopped. "Donol, is it?"

"Aye, Father. No need to climb, unless more bodies you wish to collect."

Without thinking, Islay tossed the extra thrustible to his son and stepped down to meet him. "I see. How fares your brother?" Donol was quiet a long moment, as if wrestling with conflicting thoughts. *"Well?"*

"Father, I greatly fear that something terrible has happened . . ."

Flare and noise of canceling thrusts came to the draywherry across the klomme separating it from the roadcut. Those aboard ceased their chatter, glancing with varying apprehension at one another. They remained seated at the rear—perhaps in deference to Morven who could not take himself toward the bow as it was clear his daughter and their two guests wished to do—and peered forward into the glare-illumined night, straining to make out what was happening with the Islays who had left them behind. Annihilative light flared harsh again, this time upon the opposing promontory, followed in a heartbeat by the booming, echo-chased, which was all the muffling dampness of the night permitted passage of.

Left behind with the others, as if he were as useless as they, and no son to his father, Arran was furious. Even his patience, unusual in depth and span for a boy his age, had exhausted itself. Trusting the preoccupied adults (so-called, he thought with a mental sneer) to continue ignoring him, he arose from the chair he had so long occupied behind the inert steering pedestal, grateful that the draywherry had been powered down. The resulting darkness served his purpose well.

Sidling to the left, out of the others' field of view, remaining close beside the starboard wall rather than walking down the center aisle toward them, he ambled with a painstaking indifference aftward, toward the open hatch-ladder. Against the small chance he should be noticed, he played the part of the bored and restless little boy which, to a degree, he was, the difference being that most bored and restless little boys would have lacked the purpose which the darkness and distraction served.

He reached a point abaft of the cluster of grown-ups and crossed to the center where the hatch-ladder yawned, its free end resting a measure and a half below upon the ground. Here, he thought without pausing in his progress, was a case in point and vindication, and why he thought of grown-ups as "so-called." Had he been in charge, with his guests, his father-in-law, his bride aboard to worry over, unarmed and unprotected (except, he snorted, by a twelve-year-old to whom the task had been delegated as a sop to keep him from underfoot), this access would have been secured before he went achasing bandits. Arran meant no conscious criticism of his father. He suspected such instruction had been issued, only to be neglected by his brothers, their blood up for the hunt.

Now he squatted, as if in a trench, within the well formed by the open ramp, eyes level with the wherry's deck. With a final glance at the passengers, grateful for their preoccupation, and for the virtual invisibility which adult minds could be relied upon to lend a child of twelve, he crept the rest of the way down the ladder and into the night.

Outside, it was quiet. Beneath the smooth-curved wirewoven belly of the craft, the air was damp—his second-best tunic stuck to his skin like a workshirt—wrapped in the stillness anticipatory of dawn. Arran was not surprised to discover it felt no different once he had made his shuffling, hunched-over way from under the damaged vehicle and stood up to his modest but more comfortable full height in the greenway.

Yet, as his father was relearning at this moment, anticipation is never quite the same as realization. Insufficient light filtered down from haze-masked stars and moonring to see by, even had he known where he was going and what he intended once he got there. Even this faint aid failed him before long. Not far from the wherry, he caught a toe and stumbled over something in his path. He fell hard, desperate to stifle a cry of surprise and pain. Lying quiet a moment, feeling foolish and ashamed, he struggled to hold back tears, biting his lower lip as he had heard was useful in the effort. This proved not to be the case, but only added to the pain of abraded knees and elbows, although several deep breaths regained for him a measure of composure.

Another moment passed. Arran picked himself up, invulnerable to injury as boys are wont to be, and upon this account mostly unhurt. He discovered he had his right hand wrapped about a stout stick, half his height in length and almost as big as his wrist, with peeling bark and jagged ends where it had broken off. It was not from the earlier explosion, for the wood was dry, horn-hard, weather-seasoned to his touch. Perhaps, he thought, he had misgauged his luck. Although dried by the elements, the object in his hand had a certain encouraging heft. He swung it a couple of times to get the feel, making it *whoosh* with menace through the air, and remained satisfied with his find. What was even better, he thought with boyish viciousness, several projections where smaller branches had been stubbed off gave it teeth of a sort. It was a better weapon than the empty hands he had started with.

This time, he gave the places where he put his feet more than casual consideration, and had soon reached the spot where the greenway plunged into the utter blackness of the roadcut, the sides of which swooped toward twin crests where small, fierce battles had just been fought. By this time his eyes had adjusted to all but the darkness of the cut itself. As he heard voices coming to him from a fair distance to one side, he ducked backward into the dew-damp and scratchy but concealing embrace of a nearby bush.

"Bother!" At least Arran believed that was the word he had heard uttered. It seemed a niggardly sort of epithet for a woodsrunning bandit, hissed between clenched teeth and tinged with considerable fear. A pause, and it was answered by a second voice, further away, unrecognizable in the distance, colored with fatigue and caution, rather than fear.

"Trouble, is it?"

"I say bother! No need to climb, 'less more bodies you wish to collect."

Panic swept through Arran. He heard the clatter of metal tossed from one of the speakers to the other. Loot, perhaps, something which had belonged to his father or one of his brothers? Perhaps one of their thrustibles?

"I see," the second voice responded in a rumbling whisper Arran could scarce make out, although he began to discern shadows in the direction it came from. They were between him and the road, his only avenue back to the draywherry. "How fare the others?"

Quiet reigned a long moment. Arran did not wait for a reply which, with proper understanding, might have allayed his apprehension, but crept from the bush toward the right-hand crest. Perhaps they would not look for him there if everyone, as the first voice had implied, was dead. He had to make sure of that before anything else. But how to get back and warn the draywherry?

Arran's concern increased with each measure he climbed from the greenway. With every step he imagined greater terrors following upon his heels. Gone from his mind was every thought of caution. By the time he reached the summit, he was running, leaping, by chance or some remnant survival instinct missing every obstacle in his path. A moment arrived when he discovered he had left his wind-fallen weapon behind in the bush. He sobered, stopped his hysterical, dangerous plunge through the dark, and threw himself upon the ground so as not to present an inviting, silhouetted target.

He gasped in shock: his run had brought him to the brink. One foot hung in space and he could hear the fall of dislodged gravel. Also a voice: "Father?" It was his brother, below and to one side where only empty space should be, sounding weak and injured, or perhaps just waking up.

"Robret!" Arran's reply was a whisper in unconscious imitation of the voices he had heard below.

"Arran? Is it you, Arran? What—"

"Quiet!" the younger ordered and in contradiction, "Where are you?"

Robret took a while replying. "I have fallen over a cliff.

Not far, judging by your voice. I have been hanging for the longest time from a tree root. I believe I was unconscious, although how I managed to hang—"

"Quiet!" Again the issued order, his older brother's obedience instantaneous and unquestioning. "Someone is behind me," cautioned the youngest of the Islay brothers, "at the least, two of them. I do not know how, Robret, but I shall get you up somehow."

Thinking that a large stick like the one he had abandoned might be useful in pulling his brother up the face of the roadcut and to safety—he gave no thought as to where he would acquire the strength to use it, although he ought to have, Robret outweighing him as he did by twenty keys—Arran rose, cautious as could be, intending to creep into the trees which stood a dozen paces away. The boy's knees had not quite straightened when, in a heart-stopping instant, he felt a broad, powerful hand descend upon his shoulder.

"Arran!" As if by a miracle, the voice was his father's. "What in the name of the Ceo," it demanded, "are you doing up here?"

CHAPTER XII:
A FIERY SALUTE

A logfire of common hardpine and rarer spicewood roared in the room-sized hearth of the Great Hall of the Holdings. It cast but scant additional light upon a colorful and crowded scene already well lit by great curve-topped windows which had constituted Robret the Islay's—rather his late wife Glynnaughfern's—first and only major alteration to the building.

At the opposite side of the gigantic, high-beamed chamber, across what seemed hectares of parqueted and mirror-polished floor, broad trestle tables creaked under a glittering load of wedding presents with which they had been heaped.

Gold Arran saw, and silver, plates and goblets, services and samovars, contributed by less wealthy (or less pretentious) well-wishers. Richer gifts were here as well, of gleaming platinum and rhodium and osmium, beaten, spun, turned, cast, carven into a myriad of artifacts of varying beauty and utility. All bore, somewhere upon their elaborated forms, the modified arms of the family Islay.

The tables were not enough. Clustered about them were gifts too large to place upon them with the others, in several instances too large for anyone to lift. Among these, Arran eyed an idle, hovering pair of personal §-field riders, similar in operating principle to the draywherry, but more resembling legless mechanical versions of the riding-beasts Old Henry—at present supervising preparations in the kitchens—had told him of. The upswept airshield and sensor-pod might well be an animal's head. The wirewoven fuselage behind was, like an animal's body, contoured for the benefit and comfort of whoever sat astride the thing.

Left of the great fireplace, sweating even in expensive finery containing its own temperature-regulating devices, awaited His Manifold Eminence, the Archregistrar of Hanover, whose dignifying presence upon Skye was itself a kind of gift, one of many from the Monopolitan Ceo, Leupould IX, to the eldest son and daughter-in-law-to-be of one of the imperium-conglomerate's greatest (and, more important, publicly best-remembered) heroes.

Servitors, family servants Arran had known all his life and thought of as his friends, passed round and through the Great Hall with trays of drinks and flavorsome tidbits. Acting with exaggerated formality—many were dressed, if not in better clothing, then at least with greater care and exercise of taste—they refused him personal acknowledgement. Arran was not certain he liked this. It made him feel lonely. He wished Old Henry were here beside him, instead of busying himself with maintaining some kind of order amidst all this festivity. Even Waenzi might have helped, but Old Henry and Mistress Lia had both insisted, and Arran had conceded they were right, that this was no place for a triskel.

Nonetheless, Arran felt special pride in himself this day. Not only was he well enough to attend this wedding, unlike his father's, but, in addition to his finest tunic, matching

knee-stockings, platinum-buckled slippers spreighformed for
the occasion, he wore a grown man's loose-fitting trousers of a
colorful pattern which, except when he took a deep stride,
had been fashioned to resemble the *kelt* of ancient tradition
or the *srong* of an even older heritage. About his waist a broad
sash, its embroidery picked out in rhodium thread, bore a
fastener matching those upon his shoes.

Against his right side, the sash passed through the back-
loop of a special pocket, fashioned from a hard-surfaced
species of kefflar, which Old Henry called a "holdster." This
had been sewn by hand that Arran might carry the walther-
weapon, butt reversed in venerable military fashion, and
afterward present it with a ceremonial flourish to his brother's bride. It was, as weapons ought to be, clean and lubri-
cated, fully loaded with eleven tiny lead-tipped charges
manufactured for it. Under Old Henry's supervision, the
weapon had been restored, rust-pits filled with fresh,
untarnishable metal, its substance infused with ions which
prevented more corrosion, and finished in such a manner that
its deep and liquid-looking blue-black exterior would never
again scratch or wear or fade to gray.

Owing to the importance of Robret the Islay, father of the
groom, no less to that of his principal and honored guest the
wheelchair-bound Tarbert Morven, father of the groom's
stepmother, hundreds of visitors to the planet Skye had by
this time arrived in splendor from the Hanoverian 'Droom.
Each small group had descended in its turn to the landing
pentagram, making the voyage hence aboard a draywherry
hastily repaired. Military honors were supplied by Morven's
dread imposing household Oplytes which had followed their
master down from orbit upon the next trip of the lubberlift,
too late to assist in dealing with the roadcut bandits. The
Islay, naturally enough, had intended that it be so, never
wishing it asserted of him that he could not defend his
Holdings without help.

Each Oplyte stood two and a half measures tall, with
close-cropped hair and ashy, waxen complexion. Arran had
heard his father say that no Oplyte feared death, for he was
dead already. What the boy saw in the unreflective eyes of the
warrior-slaves confirmed his father's words. He wondered
how it must feel to be an Oplyte. Something sympa-

thetic within him strove to see the world from the perspective afforded by those metallic-looking eyes. Something even stronger deep inside him made him shy from
the effort.

It was rumored—this was a thing he had never asked his
father nor expected him to answer—that in the field, Oplytes
were never provisioned, but were expected to feed upon
fallen foemen as a grisly incentive to uncompromising victory. That they owned other appetites, which they satisfied
with equal savagery at the expense of women, children, and
other men, was, even to one as young and uninformed as
Arran, rather more than rumor. It had become, by shrewd
design, no less than an abomination of legendary scale. Little
expense was spared by the crafty Ceo of Hanover in assisting
potential enemies within and without the Monopolity to
appreciate what horror they faced did they oppose their will
to that of the imperium-conglomerate.

Arran shook his head, cleared his mind of unsubstantiated
surmise, continuing the surreptitious inspection of these
dread warriors which his sense of objectivity preferred. Each
was as broad at the shoulder as two ordinary men. Each wore
a tough, tight-fitting uniform which, upon command,
changed color and pattern to blend with any environment. At
present, what they wore was as bright as Hanoverian colors
ever were, light gray trimmed in silver. Silver, as well, were
the outsized thrustibles strapped to each arm of every Oplyte.
Ordinary men would want a hand free to do other things than
fighting. Oplytes, it was said, had a free hand anywhere they
wanted.

No doubt, Arran thought back to the roadcut incident,
their human officers had regretted this lost opportunity for an
outing. He knew the troops did not. Oplytes were not
equipped by their nature (if, in origin and character, they
could be regarded as natural) for regretting anything.

With effort, he tore his horrified attention from the deadly
beings, turning instead toward a host which appeared anything but deadly. Mistress Woodgate, soon to be his sister and
therefore "Lia," had told the truth (he never expected otherwise): each of the guests from the capital, dazzling enough in
costumes they brought with them, affected a masque. No two

were alike. Much clever maneuver and an elaborate protocol assured this was always the case. It seemed no two were even of the same color. From his studies, Arran recognized an alliupe, a moses, xander, kaisar, cleopaetre, all from the mists of half history; galileo, shakespeare, newton, faraday, holmes, einstein, and velikovsky from a better-known era. A scowling nietzsche argued with an even fiercer-looking rand. Lewis jested with cosby. A cordial schweitzer rolled among them upon pneumoplastic wheels.

The boy was of a sudden grateful he had thought (with some aid from his mentors) to confine Waenzi to the tower bedroom. In this confusing press, the triskel could be trampled underfoot. Arran hoped in earnest that the animal would remain confined. He craved companionship and hated being locked up, abandoned and alone. Upon occasion, locks or no locks, he was altogether too clever, getting in and out of places where he did not belong.

With disappointment, Arran in vain searched among the horde of Monopolitans for one of the fabulous intelligences who visited the Hanoverian 'Droom upon occasion, having arrived from out-of-the-way places and strange, alien civilizations located beyond the borders of the imperium-conglomerate in the black reaches of the unexplored Deep.

His Eminence raised jewel-bedecked arms, capturing the attention of all within the Holding Hall amidst a flourish of enthilled drums, pipes, and claxons—more, Arran thought as hair prickled at the back of his neck, like wailing battle calls than wedding marches—provided by Old Henry at an ancient, battered thille player which had always, in Arran's memory, stood against that wall. The old man caught Arran's eye and winked. They might have had an orchestra today, Arran thought. His father could with ease have brought symphonia entire from Hanover. Yet something about this music felt warm and goodly to him, traditional in the Islay family as it was and issuing from a well-traveled heirloom.

Young Robret followed behind the Archregistrar, through the door by which the elderly dignitary had earlier entered. Next came Robret's father and a heartbeat later the other of his brothers, both of whom, just moments ago, had been circulating among the guests as Arran was in theory doing now.

In accordance with tradition, and as if in echo to their own, earlier ceremony, the Lady Alysabeth awaited her husband beside the Archregistrar, her friends the Drector and Lady Nasai-Ulness nearby. To Arran, it was cold courtesy that moved Alysabeth Morven—*Islay,* he reminded himself, although he had known of her for longer by her earlier name—to avoid, in her calculated manner, taking attention from the bride. By any standard, she was the more beautiful of the two young women. Had this consideration, mechanical as it seemed, not been exercised, Lia Woodgate (also soon to become "Islay" which in Arran's mind served as a sort of compensation) would have stood in peril of taking second place upon that day, of all days, when, by rights and every maidenly expectation, she ought to have stood first.

In any case, this nuptial diplomacy had met with only limited success. The Lady Alysabeth had dressed herself in a plain gown of so pale a gray it might have been called silver had the fabric betrayed the slightest metallic sheen. The absence upon her person of any jewelry, save a bracelet indicative of her status as a married woman, lent—whatever her intention to the contrary—such stark severity to her attire that it accentuated her flawless beauty. Arran caught her eye upon him and felt a chill run through his body. It was like being examined by some dark, lithe, sharp-fanged predator. He wondered what his father felt in similar circumstances.

Realizing with a start that Old Henry's wink had constituted something of a summons, Arran hurried to catch them up and join the family party. The room—rather, those within it—reoriented itself from chaos toward the Hall's great hearth as the Archregistrar and the Islays took their places. A hush descended upon the crowd, along with a feeling of impatient expectation, rewarded before too many more moments had passed by the entrance of the bride.

To most of those invited to this place, what she wore would be—already had been—a subject of some interest. Even Arran could see why this was so. Although he had always appreciated his tutor's pretty face and figure, he had never looked upon quite so beautiful a woman as Mistress Lia had become. She had arrayed herself, from the tiara upon her brow to her hidden toes, in traditional pale green (it was claimed that for some perverse reason, Jendyne brides preferred white, the ancient color of mourning), symbolizing purity, fertility, that eager willingness which was the quality most prized in a new wife among all the imperia-conglomerate. The skirting of her dress was more voluminous than any Arran had ever seen, while the bodice, tight to an impossibly cruel degree, conforming to her precise contours as if it had been painted upon her, cut so low in the back, and in particular at the front, that it vanished into the waistline of her skirt, exposed more of Mistress Lia's pale flesh than he had ever before seen.

He experienced an uncomfortable tightness in his throat which swallowing did nothing to improve. To make matters worse, he was compelled to concentrate upon his breathing which had become difficult and unnatural.

This color and cut was not a scheme which suited every woman. It tended to make blondes sallow, while a redhead's complexion borrowed the hue of her attire so that she appeared ill. Upon Mistress Lia, it accentuated her eyes in a charming manner, was kind to her fair, freckled skin, and highlit her otherwise undistinguished tresses ("mousey," she was wont to say in self-deprecation) in a manner ordinary clothing never did.

For this occasion Lia affected no masque, although Arran understood they were sometimes worn at weddings upon the capital world, elaborate sculptures with wide, dark, artificial eyes and sullen, swollen, parted lips, attempting to convey both innocence and its opposite at the same time. With a warm thrill chasing through his body—the sensation was not new to him, manifesting itself, as it did, with increasing and embarrassing frequency—he wondered whether such a combination were possible in real, unmasqued life. It was certain Lia's own eyes were wide enough, whether with innocence or something else, Arran was in no position to guess. Her lips—that feeling came upon him again, and although it was pleasant enough to experience by himself in his own room, this was neither the place nor the time. He found himself speculating about what his brother— A deep breath, a hard swallow, and again he focused upon the ceremony.

One stately, unhurried step at a time, Lia came forward, concentration upon her face, holding the folds of her enormous skirt so as not to tread upon them. She had chosen, as a Hanoverian bride will, to underline her bridal willingness with a pair of wide silver bracelets, joined at purchase with a fine chain so as to comprise fetters. By tradition, the chain was broken in a laughing ceremony among the bride and her maids so that a short, glittering length now hung from each of the bands encircling her wrists. About her throat, and, it would seem this was Lia's innovation, at her temples, she wore matching silver bands, each disjointed in its center, ends pinked in a zigzag pattern, also representing broken bonds. Beneath her long, full skirts, Lia would be barefoot— bushels of petals had been strewn in her path to preserve her delicate soles from the chill floor—as a token of wifely humility.

Angry with himself, and attempting to regain control, Arran rehearsed in his mind the ceremony about to take place. His brother and Lia would meet (he had seen many weddings take place in dramathilles) just before the spot where the fat old Archregistrar stood beside the great fireplace. The music would come to a halt, for preference just as the bride did. After a moment of awkward, anticipatory silence, the Archregistrar would begin asking of the couple questions older in their origin than any antiquarian could calculate. In due course and in turn, Robret and Lia would offer their replies.

He would announce that what they told him suited him, whether or not it did. Struggling with self-consciousness and her awkward garments, they would embrace, kiss as Arran had never seen them do when they believed themselves in the presence of others, turn to face the gathering, and begin their future as husband and wife. They would be married. The boring part would be over with.

Now would come the moment which Arran, suspended between enthusiastic boyhood and dawning manhood, had in truth looked forward to most. Arrayed along the aisle-space where bride and groom would soon pass were two imposing rows of Oplytes, mighty weapons at the ready, set, Old Henry had told him yesterday, upon the twelfth-charge. At a signal from their officers, they would raise their thrustibles and thumb the yokes. Overhead, kinergic beam would meet kinergic beam in a fiery salute of annihilation.

Lia reached the Archregistrar where Robret stood waiting in a state of nervous impatience. Arran tensed. The music stopped. Robret and Lia stepped forward amidst beaming expressions and welcoming gestures offered them by the family Islay, even including the Lady Alysabeth who smiled and, with a certain shyness it seemed to Arran, ventured to touch Lia's hand. Silence fell as Arran had known it would. The Archregistrar opened his froglike mouth. Robret and Lia martialed their responses.

Of a sudden, out of sequence, a shouted order cracked, shattering the silence. The giant Oplytes raised their mighty, weapon-bearing arms. Half of them, every other warrior in each row, turned in the same instant upon his armored heel. All brought their weapons to the level, so that every person in the Great Hall was threatened.

CHAPTER XIII:
DUE PROCESS OF LAW

A collective murmur of astonishment swept the Holdings Hall, punctuated by indignant gasps and mutterings denoting a variety of reactions.

At the less-crowded rear of the great room, toward the Hall's great double doors which, so large and unaccustomed a number of perspiring bodies being present, had been propped half-open for the sake of ventilation, toward the scatter-cluttered edges of the gathering, a thin, shrill scream was audible. With a flurry of motion, one of the guesting women fainted. Others, overwhelming in their solicitude, crowded round to attend her.

A minute passed which seemed to the frightened Arran like a day in fullness, dawn to dusk. The Oplytes, through this timeless interval, stood like effigies of carven stone and, it seemed no less than a miracle of discipline to the boy, held their thrust. It was characteristic of the time and place that it occurred to not a single person among the gathering that this might be some kind of joke.

At last, amidst a high-pitched mechanical whine and an accompanying hiss of pneumoplastic tires rolling along the spotless translucent paving blocks, Tarbert Morven—his schweitzer done away with and the ugly scarlet face of hammurabi ribboned into its accustomed place—wheeled his inexorable way along the aisle which had been cleared in courtesy for bride and groom.

He stopped. The noise of his passage stopped with him. He had reached the feet of Robret *fils* and Lia Woodgate, standing frozen, much like each of the others in this place, paralyzed with shock, their faces white, their mouths agape. Morven turned in his chair and faced the elder Islay.

It was one of those rare moments in the destinies of men which would alter all that had preceded it, likewise determining everything which was afterward to follow. The look the two exchanged was hard and cold—all present felt it so—more tangible a thing than the destructive energies which the Oplytes' upraised thrustibles were capable of generating. It could not have been more visible had it been fashioned from a bar of steel. Alysabeth stood beside her husband, an unfathomable expression upon her inhumanly beautiful face.

The crippled Morven placed both useless, withered, motionless hands upon the armrests of his chair. With a grunt of expenditure, he pressed his weight upon them, elevating himself a few siemmes from his seat. By slow degrees, his awkward, atrophied feet slid like the unliving things everyone believed them to be from the treaded metal tray upon which they had so long rested, placed themselves before the chair, and, stirring to life, planted themselves firm upon the key-locked blocks of the floor. Shifting his weight, Morven rose to take a stance upon those feet, separate from the chair which, to all who knew him, had always seemed a part of his very being.

"You have speculated," Morven spoke as if addressing the crowd about him, yet never took his gaze from the shocked face of Robret the Islay, "why a man might choose, if choose he did, in a civilization capable of nerve- and limb-regeneration, to remain helpless, useless, trapped in and dependent upon an obsolete, noisy monstrosity such as I have just surprised you by abandoning." Now at last, although he trembled with the effort, he turned his head, scanning the breadth of the Hall, taking them all in, one, as it seemed, by one. "I have been aware from the first how this marked me in the estimation of many as a sort of freak, perhaps physically, genetically incapable of such regeneration, or, far worse, a psychotic, some kind of mystical fanatic."

In a sudden, furious gesture, he stripped the masque of the ancient judge from his face, revealing handsome, hate-contorted features. Gathering composure, he shook his head as if in sorrow and turned back to the Islay. "As you know . . . as each and every one of you is all too well aware for the sake of my privacy and self-esteem, I was, in my long-ago youth, a warrior in service to my family Shandish, my beloved Ceo, my revered imperium-conglomerate. I was, as yet, entirely undistinguished, but destined, at least within my own fancy—as many a boy-soldier is in his dreams—to remarkable and valorous achievements." He shrugged. "As the fortune of war would have it, I fell wounded in the first battle ever that I fought, rent almost beyond redemption. It was the selfsame shockingly bloodsoaked incident wherein my comrade-in-arms and closest friend—"

From intonations of reverie and closeness to tears, Morven's voice assumed a sarcastic timbre, the sheer malevolence of which made Arran shiver where he stood, lost in the astonished crowd. It fell almost to a whisper with the repetition of the last phrase, before it rose again. "—my comrade-in-arms and closest friend, the erstwhile classless, penniless, futureless, *peasant* Robret Islay, became the hero of the day and of the Monopolity by virtue of saving what was left of poor unlucky Tarbert!"

The last few words were shouted. Now silence fell once more. Morven stopped speaking as abruptly as he had begun. No one present thought to fill the oppressive silence with a word or question, even the noise of movement. Stunned, as he would never have been in physical combat, taken aback by the injustice of the accusation, its unexpectedness, by his closest friend's treachery, the Islay stood pale and silent as his son.

The Oplytes remained rigid. Their human officers imitated them, watching with minutest attention every gesture Morven made—when, from strictly tactical considerations, they ought to have been watching the accused—hanging upon his every word.

At last: "Poor Tarbert remained helpless, at least took measures to convey such an impression, in consequence of a secret, sacred vow of determination. Cruel chance, nothing more, had elevated this unworthy nobody who stands before you, caught out in his misdeeds, to the peerage. Yet, owing to the intimacy of wartime friendship and the advantage afforded by casual conversation in such circumstances, for some time before my personal misfortune, I had come to suspect both his loyalties and his intentions." Showing the strain of standing for so long, Morven inhaled and exhaled. "Yet it was I who, unwillingly to be sure, was ultimately responsible for the fame, the wealth, the power he won. Thus I vowed to set affairs aright myself, remaining in this chair where chance had placed me, until my suspicions be confirmed and I could expunge the evil I had unintentionally accomplished, while others, including this upstart himself, gossiped among themselves about me and were wrong."

The speaker allowed another pause, as if gathering himself for a final effort. "Robret Islay," he rolled the syllables across his tongue as if they were at once distasteful and savory to him, "having fraudulently arrogated yourself to the title Drector: in the name, and upon authority of his Wisdom and Sagacity, Leupould IX, Ceo of that august and terrible imperium-conglomerate we know as the Monopolity of Hanover . . ." He paused, enjoying the moment, searching faces about him for signs that the ritual was being performed to the letter of correctness. "I arrest you and your renegade, half-bred spawn under due and established process, in the presence and sight of numerous disinterested and distinguished guests, for the high crime of treason, in that you have held and acted upon an overtolerant attitude toward rebellious 'holdouts' upon the Ceo's dominion of Skye, and given ship-haven to his enemies, world-spoilers, picaroons, and brigands of the Deep!"

Of a sudden, space appeared about the elder Islay, evaporate of humanity, as if all who had been at his side now wished to be disassociated from him. It seemed natural that the Drector-Honorary and Lady Nasai-Ulness were nowhere to be seen. Arran spotted them at last. Somehow they had reappeared like thille-projected images behind Morven, that individual being, if not the true voice of Hanoverian righteousness, at least the obvious commander of the scene. The Lady Alysabeth, as well—and for some reason this did not surprise the boy—had taken several steps backward from her husband, leaving him alone to confront her father's dire accusation. The wry smile upon her lips left no doubt as to the position she would take in this affair.

Not aware he had acted, and even less of what he intended to accomplish thereby, Arran alone in all the room stepped forward to his father's defense. Scarce had the boy taken three short-legged paces when he was halted from behind. A hand descended upon the collar at the back of his neck, seized him, swept him up, all in a single unbroken gesture, into the steel embrace of a slave-warrior at the end of the row of Oplytes. As the breath was squeezed from his body, his struggles went unnoticed by the inhuman creature.

Almost the last thing Arran remembered, as a sparkling red haze descended before his eyes (poor substitute, he thought with the inanity of hypoxia, for the salute he had so looked forward to) was the gray-green, immobile, merciless expression of the Oplyte, the rotten stench of its cannibal breath. What wrenched him from the brink, saving his life, was the sound of a scream. One of the officers had fallen upon his face, a *bayonette*—a stout tubular knife affixed about the axis of an otherwise unworkable *Effen Effayal*, seized from a wall as the first weapon which came to hand—thrust through the back of his neck and upward into his brain.

Grinning down at his grim handiwork, Old Henry took fresh hold upon the corroded *Effen Effayal*, lurched toward the Oplyte holding Arran, and, with the slight weight of his body augmenting whatever power his muscles could bring to the task, jammed the bloody rust-toothed point into the creature's rippled back, where kefflar uniform and thick-fleshed ribs covered the kidneys. The blade penetrated no more than a couple of siemmes, leaving the weapon to stand out from the inhuman soldier's body like the solid limb of a tree.

More from curiosity than pain or anger, the Oplyte turned, dragging Old Henry and the weapon round, pawed with one hand at its back, wrenched the *Effen Effayal* free of the bloodless wound, and seized the old man by the face, covering his agony-distorted features with the span of its gray-green palm. The fingers closed, blood pooling about their tips, until, with a gruesome noise Arran would carry in his memory the remainder of his life, the skull fractured at the crown and burst, spewing brains in every direction. The Oplyte tossed what was left of its assailant at a wall, measures away, where the body struck, sliding down a broad scarlet smear onto the graniplastic floor, no longer recognizable as anything which had ever been human.

Arran was allowed scant time to mourn the death of his old friend, scarce enough for it to register upon his mind. Jostled by the Oplyte, he was reminded of the walther-weapon at his side. The Oplyte's crushing hold had forced the sash about his waist upward, jamming the pistol into his armpit. With only one of the Oplyte's arms wrapped about him, Arran's own arms were free. Wrenching himself round, Arran seized the steel and plastic handle of the weapon, jerked it from its holdster, shoved it into one of the Oplyte's soulless eyes, and pulled the trigger as fast and as many times as he could. Blood spurted from the ruined eye. The Oplyte staggered, its body shuddering.

The crashing multiple reports of the ancient chemenergic

pistol filled the great room as no humming thrustible could, breaking the spell of startled inactivity which held everyone in as firm a grip as the Oplyte had held Arran. Many things took place at once.

The Oplyte released Arran and fell dead upon its face, almost crushing the boy a second time. Arran scrambled from beneath the fallen giant, the weapon smoking in his hand. All about him, people screamed and backed away, disminded and fearful of any unknown, alien device which could overcome a warrior they had supposed invulnerable.

"*Arran!*" Robret *fils* and his brother Donol dashed through the open space the crowd had cleared for himself and Lia, later for Morven, afterward for Arran, leaping upon the glittering new riding machines which hovered upon their dormant §-fields beside the overloaded gift-tables. The vehicles leapt forward, engendering a kind of panic of their own among a crowd which had this day suffered too many surprises, clearing a path. Donol swept Arran up into the saddle-seat in front of him as Robret steered toward Lia, having hesitated a moment, thinking first to rescue his father.

"Seize me that man!" Morven's order was obeyed. Two Oplytes fell at once upon the Islay, taking him by the arms, the crack of broken bone audible to all within the room, forcing him to his knees and holding him there.

"Go!" he shouted to his sons. "You can do nothing but avenge me!"

This fortuitous distraction lent precious moments to the sons' attempted escape. As Robret *fils'* machine roared past Mistress Lia—the young man's split-second hesitation had not occurred without cost—she, too, was seized with cruel force by an Oplyte who, controlling the struggling woman with one great, gray-green, knobbly hand, struck out with the other at the eldest son, fetching him a glancing blow upon the forehead which sprang scarlet.

"Run!" Lia cried. The room began vibrating with unleashed §-energies. The Oplytes thrust after the brothers, unmindful of innocent spectators who fell like sheaves of harvested grain. Robret had no choice but to obey.

"Lia! I shall come back for you!" Thus he shouted over his

shoulder as both vehicles smashed through the half-open doors and were gone across the meadow before the Oplytes could act further. Arran's last thought within his father's house was of his pet triskel, Waenzi, locked up and forgotten in the tower bedroom, and of what might now become of him.

Within the Hall, a squad was shouted together, Oplytes being capable of speeds afoot which seldom failed to astound the most sanguine advocates of machine warfare, and commanded by Morven to pursue the fleeing brothers to the ends of Skye if necessary. As their surviving officer conveyed this in hysterical terms to his gigantic underlings, he emphasized each order with a heavy-booted kick which sank deep into the unresisting torso of Old Henry Martyn lying upon the floor before him. Other Oplytes would follow in the squad's wake once transport could be commandeered. The brothers would not become aware until some time afterward how, from this logistical delay, proceeded an infamous and general slaughter of the household retainers and their families, leaving behind one individual in fifty who managed to escape into the surrounding forest, thence into those mountains in which they themselves would soon lay hiding.

Blotting out Morven's voice and the screaming of the officer, Robret's words echoed within Lia's mind: *"I shall come back for you!"*

"I know you will, my love," she sobbed to herself, watching the machines dwindle in the distance, unmindful of the hard hand crushing her wrists. "I know you will."

CHAPTER XIV:
A FAIR HEARING

Spreighformed wheels of pneumoplastic hissed along the gritty corridor beneath a drapery of cobwebs hanging from the block-formed ceiling.

Nor, upon either side of the corridor, did the many dull-eyed Oplyte warriors, searching by twos and threes for escaped Islay retainers in the basement's dozens of twists and turns, bother to look up as the wheels passed. They would come to be a familiar presence in this place.

The man conveyed upon the wheels was equally oblivious to the warriors, deep as he was within the warm, dark embrace of his own familiar thoughts. Although he hoped this might be among his last rides in the uncomfortable contrivance, it was a necessary one. He had tired himself, straining to stand as he had in the Holdings Hall, standing as he never had in decades. It had been worth it, thus to confront his lifelong enemy. Still, the regenerative enzymes he had begun administering to himself during the long Deep-voyage here would require many months, perhaps even years, to manifest their powers to the fullest degree. Now, naturally enough, would follow an endless, agonizing period of daily exercises —therapy, his scientific staff would term it, astounded at being commanded to heal someone for a change—a time for reteaching blunted nerves and withered muscles too long allowed to grow forgetful of their duties.

Yet this fledgling effort, even the subsequent exhaustion it had engendered, had been worth the toll it was taking. It was a matter of pure chance, he repeated a sort of litany to himself, which of the two, he or Robret—no longer "the"— Islay, had become a celebrated hero and which a cripple, pitied and laughed about behind his back. Rather than feeling the gratitude toward Islay everyone always expected, and which he himself had simulated for his own purposes, Morven had burned with resentment of the man for thirty years. How dare that nameless social-climber overreach himself to an expectation of gratitude, when he had only been acting as any decent servant ought to!

Morven shook his head. He had already thought those thoughts a million times. He had even—at long last—spoken them aloud in denunciation of his tormentor. What was happening to him? He halted his chair and sat a long while in even deeper thought than was usual for him.

To his dismay, he discovered he was angry all over again, as if he had not just completed his revenge, as if Islay were not a helpless captive whose survival depended upon his captor's merest whim. With something resembling horror, Morven found his thoughts traveling the same, slow, smoldering circle which had burned into his brain for three decades. He wondered if a moment would ever come when he did not starve, did not feel parched, was not consumed altogether by a need for the revenge he had already accomplished.

No! No such moment could ever come! Not until Islay himself, his entire misbegotten half-bred family, every one of his lickspittle retainers, and the very memory of his vile name were erased from the galaxy! Not even a snippet of DNA must remain which could call itself Islay! Morven sat quivering, locked in the murderous throes of blackest fury. Passing his way, Oplytes and their officers—more had arrived from the starship in orbit—trod quiet as they could about him. He regained control of his thoughts and feelings, set his chair in motion once again, and, with it, his thoughts.

Now he, himself, had truly arisen from humble beginnings, as the second (and, upon that account, he felt, disenfranchised) son of a powerful family which ruled the faraway mining planet Shandish. To his eternal humiliation, unlike the battle-wounded Tarbert himself, his family *had been* grateful to young Robret—at that time not yet "the" Islay—for saving their son's life. Upon Tarbert's account, therefore, and this was what had rankled most, this nameless nobody, this *soldier,* had been elevated in a twinkling to the peerage and given outright grant of Skye, an independent Holding the likes of which Tarbert himself, as second son, could never hope for. Thus Morven's secret resentment had grown deeper, although it had required ten thousand bitter days and nights to reach full flower from the seed planted within him by mere circumstance.

They had not been empty days and nights. Ruined in body and spirit by wounds from which, by all rights, he should have died, he had come to owe Islay another debt, one which even now evoked real gratitude, and which he was about to pay in full. Robret had given what was left of him reason to continue living, to martial his resources, along with what he could accumulate of his now-indulgent family's, to rise upon his merit within the Monopolitan 'Droom of Ceo Leupould IX.

In some ways it had been childishly easy. Whatever was asked of him, he simply did superbly. Perhaps after all he could have been a hero but for terrible mischance. Perhaps, upon the other hand, only terrible mischance had made it possible to concentrate himself without distractions—those of love and merely mundane hatred—which ordinary men fall victim to. It mattered not. In either event, he had, over a long, steady course, acquired vaster power and wealth than even he might have awaited once upon a time, for no other reason than to obtain the revenge he ached after in body and spirit. Perhaps now, he thought (and it was not displeasing), with the inevitable return of his health, he, too, could occasionally be distracted by sensual diversions which other—

Of a sudden, flushed by the Oplytes from a branching side corridor, a small, fast-moving creature bounded across his path. One of the local vermin, Morven thought, about the size of a man's head, covered with short, stiff brownish-gray fur. Three legs, no more than pseudopods, sprouted from its underside, a matching number of eyestalks from its rounded top. With a swirling motion and a grateful noise, it ran to him, as if discovering long-sought refuge, and appeared ready to jump into his lap.

Morven shuddered. With a jerk of his head at its sensors, he swerved the chair. The creature struck an arm-support and fell, dazed, to the floor. His left wheel caught the fallen animal in a direct line over its center. No resistance, the man thought, disappointed. It had no bones. As the wheel crushed it, the thing gave a whimper and lay silent, dark fluid oozing from beneath it into the dust atop the paving blocks. Pneumoplastic wheels rolled down the corridor, one of them staining the floor behind it with a series of successively lighter, dryer spots.

For some unidentifiable reason Morven began to feel better, more aware of his surroundings. As his chair passed crossing corridors, screaming came to his ears of Islay servants being tortured. Nothing at all delicate was there in this rough, pragmatic procedure. It was quite unlike his careful, artful, pleasurable experiments at home, but motivated by a practical desire upon his part to gain as much information he could, with whatever alacrity was possible, as to the most likely destination of the three escaping Islay sons.

He was annoyed. What a pity he might not attend to that old man himself, who had killed his officer, making the escape possible. Morven resolved not to let his regret over a messy detail spoil his overwhelming triumph. He had accomplished what he had set out to do. Be pleased with that a while.

He must speak to his commanders, however, and soon—unless it was too late already—about sparing sufficient servants to maintain his comfort in this place. Damage or kill too many (the officers were fond of seeing how much they could remove, yet leave the remainder living, a crude sort of art, but one even he, a patron of higher aesthetics, could appreciate) and they would have the nuisance of enslaving or importing more to do their work.

Also that tidbit—what was her name?—the bride, Lia Woodgate. Not to his personal taste. He had enjoyed scant appetite of that sort the last three decades, although of late he had contrived adequate arrangement against the likelihood of increasing interest. But she would make a decorative gift. That was, unless Alysabeth, who had expressed some interest in her, desired her as a playtoy. Judging from Alysabeth's more creative childhood experiments, the Woodgate girl would not be of much use to anyone else, afterward.

Upon second thought, once his brilliant aesthetists and surgeons had arrived . . . At last his musings brought him to the end of the corridor, to a broad, thick, stout-barred door which opened for him without his having to command it. *That* was real power, he thought. He was in charge here, and no one to doubt it. A slender feminine figure standing at the door beside the Oplyte guard who had opened it reminded him that satisfactions remained yet to be wrung from the prisoner within. Morven nodded to his daughter. Smiling, Alysabeth nodded back.

Across the chamber, Robret Islay stood with his hands in the air, although he had no need to exert himself to keep them aloft. Titanium staples had been thrust through the bones of each wrist—any bleeding, swelling, or pain this might have engendered having been suppressed in a manner neat and humane—fastening him to the blocks of which the walls were constructed. Without help and proper tools, the man would stand there, hang there, in the end, for as long as he continued to draw the breath of life. And for a long time afterward, were it the whim of his captors.

Morven opened his mouth, but it was Islay who had the first word. "Black Usurper, you will be ruined when the Ceo hears what you have done!"

Morven's laugh, he knew, was not the most attractive of sounds, but it continued a long time while Islay hung before him helpless, just as he had visualized for so many years. It was obvious that the staples through his limbs, the grinding ends of broken bones in his wrist, were beginning to pain him as the treatment afforded earlier wore off. At last, Morven's laughter tapered away like the drugs in Islay's body. Servomotors reacting more from thirty years of habit than from any remaining necessity, the mechanisms within his chair wiped tears of laughter from his eyes.

"The Ceo?" he demanded with a mirthful, choking noise. "The august and terrible Leupould IX, you mean to say? We speak of the same man?" Exhausted of laughter, at least for the moment, he shook his head in mockery of sadness. "You know better, Robbie. I beg you dear fellow, do not compound disingenuous innocence with your manifold other failings." Even to someone who knew him as Morven did, Islay's expression was a peculiar one. Morven paused, puzzled, peering into his victim's face as if he could determine in this manner whether the man meant what he said. "Do you fail to understand even yet? This is too good for belief!

Even I do not deserve such a round, rich reward for my labors!" Of a sudden, Morven's tone changed from one of disbelieving amusement to something colder. "You utter fool! You stupid, hapless dolt! The Ceo is my *sponsor!* Yes, even in this insignificant and personal affair of Skye! I cannot believe —but I see it is true. As he ever has, our Sovereign continues to underwrite *all* my undertakings—an appropriate word, I think me—for the most ancient and obvious of reasons. Like any other sane being, he desires power and profit above all things."

Morven awaited further reaction from the Islay, perhaps indicating soul-breaking disillusionment. He did not receive it, although within his own soul he believed it was only a matter of time. The Shandeen sat a moment musing, an expression of irony painted across his features.

"And, too, I suppose in his sagacity the Ceo deems it prudent to keep an eye"—here, the chairbound figure lifted a hand, in modest gesture of self-indication—"upon what he perhaps conceives an overly ambitious young—for this, believe it or not, dear Robbie, is what I am in politics, which has always been an old man's game—upon an overly ambitious young protégé." Morven's face twisted into a grin. "It is a delicate matter of protocol, you understand—perhaps I should say 'etiquette'—in which timing is everything. Leupould would never object should I aspire to his position *after* he had enjoyed it to the fullest and passed away in his natural time. Indeed, a responsible ruler always gives considerable thought to his successor."

Still neither fury nor despair. Perhaps Alysabeth's presence —although Islay did not seem to notice she was here.

"I am certain the question in the Ceo's mind is whether I possess patience enough to wait him out, or would imprudently cut short whatever time he has remaining. I believe this affair, which you will admit required a certain superhuman patience, served a number of purposes for a number of individuals at one and the same time. From the Ceo's point of view, it was a kind of examination, which I believe I have passed." Morven nodded at the sensors. His chair backed him away from Islay. He continued speaking, but it was almost as if he spoke, now, to himself. "And patience,

Robbie, was only one—albeit admittedly the most potent—
of my many weapons. I needed to acquire others along the
long, tortuous way. For example—insofar as maintaining
your interest in our relationship was concerned—a beautiful,
talented, intelligent daughter—"

"Fully evil as yourself!" For the first time Islay acknowledged his treacherous bride. She offered no verbal response,
but stepped forward and stroked him where it would produce
the most humiliating reaction.

Her father shrugged, "As you will—fully as evil as myself
—whom I could train and use as . . . how shall I put it?"

"As bait!" Islay spat this in more than a figurative sense.
Alysabeth again said nothing, but her contemplative
expression—how might she most painfully return her husband's discourtesy?—was more terrifying than any words she
might have spoken.

"Indeed," her father answered for her. "See you how
agreeable I become when I have my own way in everything?
Where were we? Oh, yes. We mentioned my lovely daughter.
As you may well appreciate, my plan required certain connections, as well." Morven paused, thinking again how it had
rankled to be a second son, deprived by merest chance of the
power and prestige he deserved. Perhaps this was a fate he
had been born to. He shook his head. "Eventually I came to
be in overall charge of the imperium-conglomerate's efforts
to increase wartime manpower, being granted the title 'Military Procuror.' "

Even in his pain and indignation, Islay managed a small,
cynical chuckle. "Procuror you say? Morven, if what you
have told me of the Monopolity's part in this illegal outrage
be correct, you deserve what you are called everywhere
within it—everywhere, until now, excepting here, where
courtesy of lifelong friendship moved me to forbid it—the
Ceo's pimp!"

It was Morven's turn to chuckle. As a man in his position
could afford, he otherwise ignored the epithet. "Naturally my
duty to Ceo and imperium-conglomerate included overseeing
contracts with, shall we say, *manufacturers* of Oplytes. Where
others were too fastidious, I made manifest a willingness to
engage myself intimately in the sordid business, winning the

esteem of more pragmatic power wielders. Yet it may surprise you to learn that, as far as my personal plans were concerned, my most valuable—and secretest—alliances were with thieves, pressgangers, and freebooters, the very dregs I have accused you of dealing with. Does this not especially rankle?"

Islay disdained to reply. Morven turned to an attending Oplyte. "I desire an answer. You may strike him."

The Oplyte's first crushing blow fell backfisted upon Islay's cheekbone. At the sound of it Alysabeth inhaled, licked her lush, full lips, and made a noise, a whimper or a sigh, as if she were being caressed by a lover. Into the stoic silence which the man, stapled to the wall and helpless though he was, had somehow managed to maintain, came again the sound of breaking bones. His face colored and began to swell where it had been struck.

"Have a care!" Morven hissed at the slave, his eyes ecstatic with the long-awaited sight which filled them. "Do not end this before Robbie and I have had time fully to enjoy it!" Morven turned to address his daughter. "Islay shall endure a series of severe but essentially futile beatings," he observed, as if discussing a recipe or dramathille, "in service to the Ceo somewhat extreme, yet, this being a case of treason, under-standable, excusable by everyone, and ostensibly meant to extract a confession."

Alysabeth smiled an odd, crooked, eager smile and nodded agreement. "In point of fact, they shall serve no more than ceremony's sake, ceremony I have anticipated longer, my dear, than you have been alive. He shall expire be-fore anything useful can be learned, a conviction upon all counts brought in against him posthumously. Much the safest way for all concerned." Morven appeared to start of a sudden, although the gesture was dramatic and arti-ficial. "But what can I be thinking?" he asked his victim. "What sort of host have I become, to omit your guests from the primary event to which they were invited, to deprive you of the many pleasures which I myself so eagerly anti-cipate?" He turned to his daughter. "Kindly advise the guards to begin admitting those witnesses I have summoned and who, by this time, ought to be gathering outside in the passageway."

Alysabeth obeyed, returning with three individuals Islay

recognized through a haze of pain. "The Director and Lady Witsable Nasai-Ulness you know, Robbie. I brought them, not as the wedding guests you believed, but to observe and testify that you cannot keep peace upon the planet with which you were entrusted. Either this, or, as may prove consistent with necessity, that you engaged in an alliance with the forces of disorder, conspiring with them to assassinate certain members of the Hanoverian elite upon the greenway."

Nasai-Ulness offered a polite nod to Islay, as if the latter were not stapled to a wall. The Lady Nasai-Ulness curtsied. Alysabeth clapped her hands with delighted laughter.

"More than a hundred other such," her father continued, "known to you, can be called upon to swear to whatever they are told they saw. Likewise, no need to introduce Captain Ballygrant Bowmore, master-murchan and owner-in-command of the selfsame vessel by which we came to this unhappy world, at present still in orbit. For today's purpose he is a self-confessed Deep-rover, testifying under perpetual and unlimited grant of amnesty that you have had frequent dealings with him over the years, a capital offense. Should corroboration prove desirable, three of his officers—whom you may consider present in spirit—will be shown by thille to have been here in the flesh."

Bowmore was a short, broad, swarthy individual, wearing a pair of thrustibles like an Oplyte, arrayed in the outlandish getup affected by those following his trade. As a passenger aboard the man's carrack, even the egalitarian Robret Islay had thought him uncouth and avoided his company. All this was to the Deep-captain no more than a business transaction, for he gave Morven an impatient look and turned his back.

"We are somewhat hurried. The captain has schedules to keep. Finally, I, Tarbert Morven, shall not only be your judge, but another witness against you. My corroboration shall be the testimony of your own wife. Against us will stand none but the mute corpse you are soon to become!" Morven addressed the Oplyte. "Now hit him again—and do it correctly this time!"

The Oplyte gave its master a sidewise glance which, in a human, might have meant reproach. It said nothing. Being what it was, it was no longer capable of speech. Instead, it tucked its elbow into its side and unleashed its fist again, which sank deep into Islay's solar plexus. This time, Islay made a noise, involuntary exhalation as his body imploded. He gasped afterward for breath. Before he could recover, another blow took him in the midsection and he vomited upon the floor.

Morven backed his chair away from the stinking mess while his guests made comments upon the Oplyte's technique with the expertise of interested amateurs. And his daughter shrieked with laughter.

Chapter XV:
Three Brothers in Hiding

Arran's knees were wet. Again. Here in the deep, untenanted forest, the ground was carpeted, as everywhere within a hundred klommes of this man-forsaken place, with a thick, moist, springy covering of moss. Nowhere could naked soil be seen except among the upturned roots of an occasional windfallen tree, and that would not last long.

Without a doubt, the warm yellow sun of Skye shone bright somewhere overhead. Between the eternal overcast which dragged drizzling skirt hems over the forest, and the lichen-encrusted trunks and black-needled foliage of the close-spaced everblues themselves, it seemed to Arran, where he crouched in the miserable shelter afforded by those upturned roots, as twilit as a sickroom in which thick curtains had been drawn.

For the tenth time that misty morning, Arran exhaled, expecting to see the pale vapor of his breath hanging cloudlike before his frozen face. That he did not continued to surprise him. It felt cold enough. For the hundredth time he wished he and his brothers could risk lighting a fire. The dense, damp forest, the rain (if one could dignify it thus) tormenting him, the thickness of gravel-studded clay lining the underside of the fallen forest giant which made a half cave about him, all of these together ought to provide ample shielding against the instruments by means of which, the three of them believed, they were being searched for.

Still, Arran decided with a shrug which, despite his firmest intention, transmuted itself into a shiver, he was warm enough. If truth were told, he suffered no real peril of freezing to death, no matter how it felt. That his hands were stiff and awkward, his nose red and sore, were trials he could endure because, at the moment, no likely alternative presented itself.

Behind him, huddled into the rearmost corner of the shallow cavity beneath the roots, Donol emitted the first syllable of a snore and was awakened by it. In the few days which had passed—less than a week, Arran realized with astonishment (it seemed like much longer to him)—changes had swept through their lives like the winds of a great storm.

For the first time in his brief memory, Arran had failed to get a single decent night's sleep. This deprivation had by now begun manifesting itself as a peculiar, tranquil, detached feeling, engendering clumsiness, forgetfulness, sudden temper, nervous tics, odd aches and itches, brief visual hallucinations, chills and hot flashes. It was much like suffering a mild viral infection, something he feared inevitable in any case.

Yet another change, somehow even less welcome, was that he had discovered he could fall asleep anytime, anywhere, in any contortion of the body, as fatigue-tortured flesh attempted to make up in brief, unsatisfying snatches at oblivion what it could no longer depend upon receiving in unbroken intervals at night. The border between reality and unreality had blurred. Like Donol, like their eldest brother Robret, at present foraging for food not far away, the slightest sound, even the cessation of normal noise, could snap him out of deep sleep into terrified alertness. Arran was ungrateful for the education.

These and many other things learned hard in recent days were skills he had never thought to acquire. The edification was worth far less to him than what he had given up for it. The trouble with trouble, he was beginning to realize, noting the redundancy without humor, was that it sought you out whatever you preferred, and never asked you for your feelings or opinions.

Arran shifted where he sat to a less uncomfortable position, and balanced his antique pistol across his knee. Since he had used it to buy their escape, neither of his older brothers had ventured to take it from him nor so much as dispute his possession of it. Of the ten small cartridges in the magazine, he had used five upon the Oplyte—he had killed a man, he thought with wonder again, or at least a sort of man— pumping every one of the lead projectiles into the creature's eye-socket which had funneled them to its brain. With one more in the chamber, this left six, until he took precaution of changing over to the spare. Its half-depleted counterpart now rested in a left trouser pocket of his tattered wedding finery— this thought led him to one which, at last, he did find humorous. If fugitives they were, his brothers and he, home- less, friendless, futureless, they were the best-dressed fugitives he had ever heard of.

Rustling in the nearby undergrowth brought the blade-sight of his pistol up without a conscious thought upon his part, while his index finger, living its own life, rested light upon the fine-grooved curve of the trigger-face.

"Peace!" came a harsh whisper. "Do not thrust, little brother!" Robret emerged from between a pair of greenberry bushes, head-high and regrettably out-of-season, arms laden with what he had found deeper in the forest.

Arran had been in hiding long enough to understand something important. Who found himself lost among the endless everblues of Skye—and this sort of pointless tragedy had been reported more than once in his brief lifetime, oftenest when village-living peasants wandered off upon picnics—and was afterward discovered dead of hypothermia (more frequent in summertime than otherwise) or starvation, such a hapless individual had to be a prize-winning fool. Life was easy in untraveled and uncultivated places, as long as one took caution to stay warm and was unparticular how the many things which could sustain him tasted. As Robret approached the cavelet where his brothers awaited him, Arran observed that the greater part of his burden consisted, as he had anticipated it would, of wild shrooms which grew in abundance everywhere upon the planet but its antipodes. This variety, as he recalled, felt, smelt, and tasted like fried bacon.

In this, he was compelled to admit, they were lucky fugitives as well as well-dressed. Moisture-rich Skye afforded home to hundreds of thousands, perhaps millions, of varieties of edible fungus, constituting the sole profitable item among the Holdings' exportables. Some—valued elsewhere for pharmaceutical properties, and which they believed they had thus far avoided—had strange effects upon the mind, yet not a solitary species was toxic to man or any tame beast, offworld or domestic. Arran knew this was not the case upon other worlds, although he had heard of places where no poisonous reptiloids or insects lived. This was not so upon Skye. Whatever cornucopia of textures and flavors was available, their good fortune—as is fortune's habit—was limited. Shrooms consisted of little more than water, carbohydrates, and minerals. They could not live long upon them, did they consume keys of the things every day.

Where fortune failed them, intelligence sufficed. As Robret knelt and spread his discoveries upon the moss a measure from where his youngest brother sat, it became apparent he had not limited himself to shrooms. Several multicolored handsful of berries—greenberries being just one species in the great forest—Arran recognized. They were tart, sweet, and doubtless carried within them disease-preventing vitamins they all needed. At this thought, his ears began itching somewhere deep inside, and he sneezed.

Robret had used a cunning tool from one of the §-riders' kits to cut and peel the inner bark of an everblue. As long as they were among trees they would not starve, no matter how jaded their palates. The white, stretchy stuff he had harvested was tart like the berries, bitter but filling. It would soon dry, even in this climate, to a light, crumbly, self-preserving food, heavy in complex sugars, the boy guessed. Arran's mouth watered at the sight, and, catching himself, he shook his head in wonder and mild self-pity.

Protein continued to represent a problem. The youngest Islay, at least—still growing, and, to a certain extent, still recuperating—was beginning to feel the effects of deprivation. None of the brothers was desperate enough as yet to essay the bill of fare available beneath any rotting, phospho-

rescent log or largish stone they might care to turn over.
However, in the baffling absence of large animals—which, at
their father's insistence, Robret and Donol had hunted, but
never without appropriate weapons, guides, and beaters—
Arran never entertained the slightest doubt they would come
to it. Having been raised upon domestic meat, with a bit of
wild game as an infrequent variation in their diet, the
brothers had no knowledge about methods of trapping smaller animals, or even that it could be done. Nor did it occur to
them that their very presence here was what had driven off
the larger animals.

Earlier, Arran had considered expending some of his
remaining precious cartridges. Old Henry had proved in the
most graphic manner that they possessed small value for
self-protection except in a rare, unrepeatable instance such as
had recently preserved their lives and liberty. However, the
boy appreciated all too well that he and his brothers were
hunted animals themselves, and one of many instruments
bent to the purpose would be sensitive to noises far less
conspicuous than the ear-stabbing roar of a pistol-thrust.
Arran pondered what had happened to Old Henry. With
effort now becoming reflex, he suppressed a thousand
answerless questions about life and death, along with the pain
they evoked. Without consciousness or volition, he transferred his curiosity to a safer topic, wondering whether the
kinergic thrustible might have been invented for no better
reason than to eliminate inconvenient noise.

He felt his other brother stir behind him. "Leave it to
Donol," Robret's grin belied his words, "to sleep until the
prospect of eating arises."

The jest, they all knew, was unfair. Donol had kept watch
throughout the rainy night while the other two slept. What
Robret and Arran did not know was that it was also inaccur-
ate. The truth was that, curled up in his burrow all morning,
Donol had been feigning sleep while his mind raced. Now,
sliding from his muddy, makeshift bed, he yawned, brushed
at his torn and soiled attire, and, kneeling, began picking at
the products of Robret's foraging.

"Aye," he answered Robret. "Lucky one among us understands life's priorities, which I refrain from listing for fear of
embarrassing an elder brother with my erudition and a

younger with knowledge he is unready for. This is terrible
stuff you have brought; what have you been up to, besides?
Do they still talk about us at home?" He nodded toward the
brush in which the §-riders, their charges nearing exhaustion
by the flight to this place, had been concealed to replenish
themselves. After the lengthy, high-velocity escape, they
would be at it a while. Still, they were not altogether useless:
each possessed a low-powered transceiver similar to the 'com
damaged aboard the draywherry. This was somehow known,
for the whirling mirror of the Holdings' emergency laser-
caster had been active every moment since they had left, by
turns gloating upon Morven's behalf, screaming demands of
them and the rest of the planet, and offering bribes.

Robret shook his head. "It took most of the morning
finding something to eat—I wonder if we get back from our
food what we put in looking for it—and did not listen.
Why?"

Donol arose from his crouch. "Let us do it now." It cost
him a moment's effort to clear the brush away, the better to
receive glimmerings of the invisible coherent light they knew
permeated the air they breathed. In one respect, the §-riders
represented a danger, since all three thought it likely that
metal detectors would be used to search for them. Once
recharged, they would provide means for swift flight. In the
meantime, they offered certain conveniences. This one lay
upon its side, no longer able to maintain an upright position,
thanks to switches thrown once they had arrived in this
place. Thus Robret had conserved power in order to keep a
figurative ear pointed backward whence they had fled.
Donol's brothers arose and joined him beside the disabled
machine.

"—outlaws in hiding, cold, friendless, hunted, and miserable," it began at once, with uncanny accuracy describing
their condition as it had for uncounted repetitions since it
was first enthilled and lasercast, "Give no thought to what
you once believed was your inheritance. You are foredoomed,
the same as the Old Islay, to be hunted and put to death,
unless, in return for your prompt public acceptance of the
legitimacy of—"

"His usurpation!" Arran now knew that his father, whom
the smug, vile 'casts named "Old Islay," as was customary

with the passing of a Drector, had been dragged off in power-restraints and had died, he suspected, more of anger and humiliation than any torture he had suffered at Morven's hands. Through bribery transparent even at this remove, through blackmail, lies, and outright threats, the Islay had been convicted, in the convenient absence afforded by his death, of crimes which the brothers were confident Morven himself was guilty. This turnabout must have given the second son of Shandish immense satisfaction. He had had his revenge, and at the same time enhanced his already-great power and wealth, all in a daring swoop. Even now, although the lasercast voice was his, he must be cackling over it with his evil daughter.

Donol waved Arran to silence. "But—" Both his brothers hushed him.

"*—necessity of the actions of the designated representative of the Monopolity of Hanover, and thereby earn an amnesty, full freedom, and immunity—and, of course, your lives— which I, your lawful ruler, Tarbert Morven, Drector- Protempore of Skye, promise you.*" The lasercast ended. It would begin repeating itself within five minutes' time.

Excitement filled Donol's voice. "I have been thinking on this!"

"You have been thinking, this morning," Robret growled, "of nothing but the insides of your eyelids!"

Realizing that his enthusiasm had almost betrayed him, the middle brother took caution. Life, as he had lived it, had taught Donol never to let anyone see into his thoughts or feelings. For a moment he had believed, not altogether consciously, that this tragedy sweeping into their lives might have changed things between his brothers and himself, but now he saw he had been mistaken. The old, unruf- flable shrewdness crept back into his voice. His brothers, although they realized it not, had been disturbed by the alteration of his character, however positive and healthy it might have been. They were calmed now, just as subtly and unconsciously, by a return to the familiar in him, however sinister.

"Go easy with him, Robret."

"What?" Of all the changes he had witnessed in the past days, this, in Arran, was most amazing to Robret. That it was not a change at all was something he had never been in a position to appreciate, the difference in their ages being so great and he having been preoccupied with his own affairs.

"I told you, go easy. Between bad food and worse sleep, we are all in a failing way. Perhaps he has been thinking the same thing I am."

"And what," Donol asked, peering with suspicion and alarm at one who claimed to know his thoughts, "might that be, baby brother?" Had Arran's kind and spirited defense come but seconds earlier, at Donol's unguarded moment, it might have fostered yet another change in their lives—something none of them, not even Donol, was ever to know.

Arran turned to Donol first and afterward to Robret. "We must take the rapespawn's offer."

CHAPTER XVI:
THE SHORTEST TWIG

"One among us," Arran hurried before his brothers could discover they were taking counsel with a twelve-year-old, "must return to the Holdings—"

"Shamefaced," Robret interrupted, a bitter expression writing itself across his features, "affecting the humiliated manner of a whipped triskel."

Arran bit his lip. "Better a whipped triskel than a dead one."

The three still squatted over the down-powered §-rider, Morven's appeal from the Holdings all but ignored. Donol agreed with what he could anticipate of Arran's plan. It was, he believed, and only differing in detail, the very notion which had excited him moments before.

"You must—" Thinking better of it, and with a new idea forming, Arran began again. Neither of his brothers ever learned which he had intended by the word you. "Whichever of us is chosen, by whatever means, he must accept the risk of Morven's amnesty, surrendering against the likelihood of yet another treachery, with the idea of getting back into the graces of what passes in these evil days for law upon the planet Skye."

Donol made a noise of shrewd consideration at the back of his throat. "I feel—and believe I can persuade you to my point of view—that less risk may be involved in this course than might first appear to be the case." Both brothers looked at him as he ticked off points upon his upraised fingers. "In the first instance, did not our father keep the peace here for three long decades, never by the threatened force of weaponry alone, but through an agreement which all concerned felt was bound by love?"

"Yes," Arran answered.

"Yes," his eldest brother agreed.

Indeed they all believed the Bargain to be more than political. Robret "the" Islay—Old Robret as he was now called, even in their own minds—had been wont to refer to peace between Hanoverians and Skyan woodsrunner as "kept by ties of blood, nor streams of it." Old Henry had used the phrase, as well.

"In the second instance," Donol continued, "Morven must face, is already facing, the severest difficulties consolidating his rule of our birth planet, since he had no part in the history which all upon it share."

"The speculation," Robret agreed, for once following a line of political reasoning, with the most urgent incentive, and fascinated by it, "is likely." Arran remained silent, having accomplished what he intended. His brothers were making his argument for him, and with a measure of eloquence.

"In aid of consolidation," Donol suggested, "the apparent assent, even of one Islay brother, would be received with gratitude, would it not?" It was clear Robret had not considered this possibility. A look of amazement—and renewed hope—came over him. He began to nod his head with considerable vigor. "This agreed upon," Donol rushed on, not giving Robret time to interrupt in a first blush of new and unaccustomed insight, "with one of us at the Holdings, another must remain in hiding, his purpose being to rally those faithful retainers who have fled, and recruit woodsrunners from among our mother's old friends—our father's old enemies—who would assist us in prevailing against this black usurper."

"Yes," Robret answered, "I agree."

"Now, brothers," Donol prepared to make his final point, "while none of our family possessed—indeed ever sought—close acquaintance with political intrigue, eschewing involvement in the peril-laden intricacies of the Ceo's 'Droom, our father was a genuine, much-admired hero of the Thousand Years' War. In addition, as the three of us know well, he was a man graced with an open, winning way." Arran suppressed a sudden urge to tears at the remembrance of his father. His eldest brother gulped in a similar effort. Donol, however, was still moved by practical necessity. "Moreover, even did our father not have friends, it is an ancient, essential fact of politics, appreciated by the most naive observer—present company excepted—that, for every party in predominance, at least one (and, in common practice, more than one) displaced and malcontented faction considers its subordinate position no more than a galling temporary circumstance, a merely ephemeral obstacle to inevitable victory, vindication, and vengeance."

"In arts of warfare, politics, or love," Robret stared past them into empty space, quoting the sweetheart who now seemed lost to him forever, "nothing is ever settled or to be taken for granted."

Donol blinked. "Well spoken, brother! You have unplumbed depths I had not anticipated." Robret gave him a look of irritation but offered not another word. "In consequence, we surviving Islays cannot be without influence of our own, at least potentially, within the Monopolity."

The discussion continued a long while. For the most part the brothers agreed—Arran sitting quiet, keeping counsel with himself as long as conversation flowed in the direction he thought wisest—that aid were likeliest enlisted among many of their recent visitors, wedding guests now embarking, it was presumed, for the capital and other worlds.

"Therefore," Donol concluded, having run out of fingers to make points upon, "with one of us surrendered at the Holdings and one in hiding with the woodsrunners, the third must somehow find his swift and surreptitious way aboard one of the starships still in orbit awaiting propitious circumstances—" Time was a factor, as well as ever-changing subatomic currents. "—for departure from the vicinity of Skye. None of us being destined to sail the Deep, we were never schooled in the relevant observations and calculations. More than a possibility exists that whoever undertakes this task will find himself at . . . at Alysabethport too late to accomplish his mission. Nonetheless, I, for one, believe it worth an attempt."

"Stow away?" Robret demanded.

"All the way to Hanover?" Arran finished for him.

"Upon the contrary," Donol replied. "Whoever the unlucky fellow may be, he would not attempt to reach the capital himself, but seek converse with those powerful individuals who still hold our family in esteem—"

"Or," Arran interrupted, still a boy in spite of his precocity and no longer able to resist displaying his powers of reasoning, "and this may be more to the point, individuals representing interests in the 'Droom at odds with those to which the Black Usurper is allied."

Donol chuckled, whether at his younger brother's broadening enlightenment or his elder's density he could not have attested. A period of silence followed.

"Well enough," Robret vowed at last, determination filling his voice. "Nothing can bring our father back. Yet perhaps we can begin unmaking some small portion of the many injustices Morven has wrought."

"Done," his middle brother answered him.

"And done," Arran confirmed.

Thus it came to pass that the three brothers cast lots. With solemnity revealing not the slightest trace of his accustomed sarcasm, Donol took it upon himself to arise from where they sat and snap three twigs of differing lengths from the bush which concealed them and the §-field rider whose transceiver they had been listening to when the conversation first began.

All else was quickly decided among them. The longest of the three twigs would determine which of the brothers would surrender himself to Morven. The middle-sized twig would be drawn by he who would remain fugitive and counterrevolutionary. Who drew the shortest twig would make his way south to the landing pentagram—Donol's reference to "Alysabethport" had earned him sour looks—and attempt to gain audience with potential friends and allies.

Donol held up both grubby fists, having arranged the twigs in such a manner that no difference could be perceived among them. He rolled his palms against one another, saying not even he should be able to declare which twig was which. At his brothers' impatient insistence, he closed one hand while the other drew out the first twig for himself.

It was longest. Donol would return to possible torture and execution, but also the hope of deceiving their enemy. Despite the risk, this suited him, as it did his younger brother. Both felt—and explained by turns to Robret—Donol to be the most sophisticated of the three, the closest match for Morven's treacherous talent, and (Arran meant no insult by it, even Donol had to agree) better equipped for the required dissimulation.

His younger brother's judgment suited Donol for another reason, one he kept to himself, for he had come to realize during this brief fugitive period that at heart he was a bit like Morven himself. Without realizing it fully before now, he had always been envious, with some justification, of the advantages he felt the other two had over him. A middle brother always got the worst of everything. Now, among the myriad possible outcomes he saw before him, a goodly number pointed toward his someday becoming "the" Islay under circumstances which no observer could afterward claim to be his fault.

He held his fist up. Robret drew the middle twig. He would remain in hiding. This, too, his brothers asserted, was proper, as if blind chance were acting to confirm their judgment. Now himself become, however reluctantly, head of the family Islay—and, in a universe more just than this one appeared at present, rightful heir to the Skyan Drectorhood—who among them was likelier to win allegiances they needed to combat the evil Morven?

Only Robret harbored doubt of this blithe estimate. For his own reasons, although they would be obvious to anyone who thought about them, he had hoped to draw the long twig.

He no longer recalled the exact words, shouted overshoulder in panic, haste, and flight, but knew what he had meant by them at the time. He had promised Lia he would return for her. He entertained no question in his otherwise troubled mind that she had misunderstood.

Donol and Arran—little Arran!—were mistaken. The eldest and heir was most valuable to Morven and belonged at the Holdings. In a sense, he had less to lose than they, for already he felt himself half tortured to death by uncertainty. However, and more like his middle brother than himself in this, he concealed his disappointment at the outcome of the draw. It was less difficult, under the circumstances, than it might have been. A thousand hideous probabilities assailed him. Not being Skyan, one of the lifelong Islay retainers, but an unbound Hanoverian employee, and upon this account either more or less than a family retainer, Lia was either more immune to official persecution, or less. Robret could not— dare not—calculate which.

Lia he knew well. Until persuaded he was dead, she would wait where he had seen her last while they both grew old and died, unless they dragged her from the planet. He ached to place himself beside her, touch her, feel her lips upon his, and to assure himself of her safety. Whereas his hereditary duty—and the foul luck of the draw—had now determined for him otherwise.

Lost in despair, it was some time before the eldest of the brothers Islay realized that, by elimination, the shortest twig, the final task, the long, dangerous journey to the equator, had fallen upon Arran.

Chapter XVII:
The Shroom Crate

"'Twas a trackless time she wallowed,
And a timeless track she followed."

The melancholy lyric of the star-sailor's ancient lament left something resembling consciousness—unasked for and unwanted—in its wake.

Naked and befouled, bleeding from a dozen insults, Arran Islay, shattered inside and out by what had happened to him, sprawled where he had been thrown upon the flesh-cutting gundeck floor-mesh, hard against the heavy caliprette of one of the carrack *Gyrfalcon's* great kinergic projectiles. For the time being, he had been left to himself. What further, after all, could be done to him or taken from him? The injured boy had no way of knowing, although by now the knowledge would not have surprised him, that this place where he lay in pain and anguish was considered the least-comfortable, least-desirable spot in all the vessel to sleep. The weakling dregs among her crewbeings gravitated here, where he had been tossed as human garbage, used up and discarded—although too well he realized he would be used again, and soon.

Despite all that had happened to him and would doubtless happen again, it was a kind of sleep he slept, although it also bore resemblance to the drug-induced delirium he had suffered in his own warm, safe bed, what seemed to him centuries ago. In his pain-fringed and fitful periods of waking, the major effort his mind made was to blot out every memory it ever had contained, for not one remained among the lot, no matter how bright and colorful, no matter how inspiring and cheerful, no matter how filled with love and warmth, no matter how long ago, which had not been rent and soiled like himself.

Given what he considered the greater sufferings of his

dead father, his brothers, and his friends, it would have shamed him to be caught in the belief that he had been singled out for persecution. It was not within the compass of Arran's character to count his losses, yet they weighed upon him, wearing away his resistance to despair. Already half-orphaned with the loss of his mother, Glynnaughfern Briartonson Islay, he had, in a briefer and more recent span, been deprived of his hero-father, the legendary warrior Robret "the" Islay; also his two kindest friends, Mistress Lia Woodgate, tutor and sister-to-be, and Old Henry Martyn, mentor and partner-in-mischief. He had lost his lifelong home, the Holdings upon Skye, and his beloved pet Waenzi. His brothers, Robret and Donol, had been taken from him by the exigencies of what amounted to war. Moreover, through a heinous act of betrayal, he had lost his name and his inheritance. Had anyone demanded of him yesterday what else he had left to lose, he would have answered "nothing." Now he knew better.

Despite himself, he did remember. His clearest, cleanest memories were most recent, days spent in the wood which he had thought terrible to live. Casting lots with his brothers, he had come to an hour he had believed the beginning of adventure. Instead, it had been a doorway into hell.

Having decided upon their separate, complementary courses of action, Robret and Donol had helped him drain the remaining power from one of the exhausted §-riders into the other. The elder brothers would depart upon foot, one for the nearby rebel hills, the other for the Islay Holdings. He had bidden them farewell, waved with a reckless gaiety feigned only in part for the sake of their mutual and desperate resolve, and ridden out of the forest, leaving them to their own fates.

Evading Morven's Oplyte searching parties had proven easier than expected. Too few had been assigned for the task. He suspected, or at least hoped, that to some degree their energies were being occupied by his mother's people—the beginnings of violent persecution had been another tale told between the lines of the repeated, demanding lasercasts— now that the Great Bargain wrought by his father was abrogated. Neither the Oplytes nor their officers had seemed much gifted with intellectual acuity to begin with. Knowing they had means of detecting the heat of his rider and his own body, Arran had risked traveling by day. For whatever reason, the risk had worked.

During the long, cold, lonely nights Arran forced himself to sleep under the soft light of the moonring in nightmare-ridden intervals while his machine soaked up the ambient radiation which powered it. The chief cleverness of its irreproducible design lay not in the energies it could absorb —infrared, ultraviolet, visible light, solar radio, cosmic rays, even stray neutrinos—but in the use to which it put such subtle fluxes and potentials, bending and altering them so that each particle somehow sought its metaphysical opposite and was consumed in annihilation which drove the craft's suspending and propelling fields. The §-field rider was neither as efficient nor as powerful as the larger draywherry. The latter could absorb as much power, each moment, as it used. In part, this was a measure of nothing more than the relative surface areas the two exposed. For each hour's travel, Arran was required to give his machine another of rest, which, in truth, he needed himself.

The climate changed by gradual increment. Temperatures rose and fell again. One sort of bird or animal was replaced by another better able to prosper in each area he entered and, with all possible rapidity, left behind. All about him, stage by imperceptible stage, the deep blues and greens of the temperate zone began to pale as he crossed invisible lines of latitude and began to climb into the equatorial mountains, retracing the earlier, eventful voyage of the draywherry until at last, and without incident, he passed through the roadcut in the highlands, still unrepaired after the dual avalanche which had occurred there, and emerged onto the bleak plateau beyond.

In all, it had required another week to reach the unmanned, isolated cluster of *ulsic*-automated fabrications which he, at least, would never again refer to as Alysabethport. Having arrived, he discovered evidence that many starships had called here and departed. Each of the farflung corners of the landing pentagram, with its own heavy tackle, metal bright with unaccustomed wear, had been employed not once but often. The soulless townlet was left littered by the comings and goings of hundreds of wedding guests, their servants and guards, invited to visit Skye to witness happier events than had proven the case. Now all that remained, aside from litter, was a single thrumming lubberlift cabelle, anchored to the center of the pentagram, as it had been when he and his brothers had first come to meet their father. Somehow, Arran must get aboard the starship it was connected with and see whether any help was to be found among its passengers.

The plain stretched endless before him. No bird sang. A chilled and arid prairie wind riffled the sea of gray-yellow mosses which, even in this sere, lifeless place, kept the naked soil of Skye from being seen. Examining, in the lucky absence of the lubberlift, each service shed in turn, Arran found one of the answers he sought. Morven had not been altogether preoccupied with consolidating his political and military position. This was a farm world, a working world, but not a rich one. Continuous, concentrated effort must be expended to wrest even a modest profit from it. Arran now knew how to get aboard whatever starship hung above his head and the equator at the end of the long cabelle which vanished into the zenith. The largest of the utility buildings had been stacked to its ribbed, translucent ceiling with huge crates of native Skyan shrooms. The lubberlift could not carry all this bulky cargo in one load. In probability it had been used watch-and-watch since the departure of the other starships, and might return at any moment.

It was the work of but a frantic few minutes, employing the toolkit from his §-rider, to prise open one of the sturdy plastic crates and hollow out a hiding place among the musty produce for himself. The rider he concealed—sore, in certain places, as constant riding had made him, he patted its mesh-metal flank in a gesture of regretted farewell—in a building which had been emptied already and might not be inspected when the lubberlift rode down again like a giant legless web-spinner. Securing the hinged top of the crate, once he had crawled deep inside, was a more difficult matter. Knowing it would be handled gently, he had no fear it would open by accident. The shrooms he lay among were perishable, fragile, an expensive delicacy offplanet.

Wrapped in the overpowering musky odors of his native world, drained in body and spirit by weeks of anger, effort, and terror, Arran slept within the crate, not waking until, an uncalculated time later, he felt it being shuffled and rocked toward the pentagram. Comments and curses, shouted orders, muffled by the crate and its contents, came to his ears without meaning. For a while after the movement stopped, he could not sleep, suspended as he was between the fear of being discovered and the excitement of traveling into the Deep as he had so long dreamed of doing. How he wished he could see out! No such provision had been made, however, and the smooth, cabelle-guided voyage in the lubberlift, prolonged and anticlimactic, the profound humming of the cabelle itself, lulled him back into a deep and healing state of unconsciousness.

"Well, well! What have we here?"

Arran leapt from dreamless stupor into panic and pain. The voice shouting into his upturned face was rough-timbred and raucous. Someone had him by the hair, prying his head backward against protesting muscles in his neck. He was blinded, or almost so, by the agony of it. The only light, an eerie shadow-flickering of blue, emanated from the §-field, playing at reduced power along the interlocking mesh which constituted the fabric of the vessel.

"Harhar!" Another ugly voice laughed at him, milder only by comparison, its source invisible, and with even less pity in its lower-class tone than the first. "Meguess somebody thoughtful has sent us a treat, Jimbeau!"

Arran's head swam. He felt like throwing up, a reaction to intoxicating vapors exuded by the fungus he had concealed himself in. He had fallen asleep with his walther-weapon in both hands, wrists locked between his knees. Now, hands tingling and limp, he tried to bring the pistol up, to point it at the first voice, but it was snatched away, tearing his fingers. Hearing it clatter, far away, against some meshed metallic surface, he reached for the hand entangled in his hair, prying at the fingers. The knuckles were like knots upon a tree limb.

"None athat, now, sweetie!" The first voice admonished him in a terrifying mockery of tenderness, ignoring his most energetic efforts to break free as insignificant. "Fry me, Paddy, if it ain't so!"

The volume of the voice changed, as if the speaker's head turned aside. "Whaddya say, Stewie old pal, can me and Paddy take a rest-break here?"

From a far corner of whatever place they were in, a third voice called to the others. "'Pon condition you'll share this unlooked-for bounty, Jimbeau. Finders keepers, share and share alike, I always say. Hmm . . . wait a moment while I square this list away. What have you and Paddy found for us?"

The sound of angry exhalation came now, carrying to Arran's outraged nostrils the smell of something rotted. Between the darkness and the pain the frightened boy still could not see, but he could hear. The banter was gone from Jimbeau's tone as he called back. "As you will, *Mister* Van Merrivine—field take your eyes!" The second phrase was spoken under the breath. "But y'better hurry 'fore I throw this here d'licious titbit to the gundeckers!"

Pain transcending anything which had preceded it seared through Arran's scalp as he was hauled from the crate by his hair and dashed to the deck. Something hot and heavy landed atop him, knocking the breath out of him. A weight upon him squirmed, settled itself, and the nightmare began in earnest.

Hurried, cruel hands stripped him of his clothing. Excepting the antique weapon taken from him and cast aside, Arran carried nothing valuable about his person. Upon Skye, currency was exchanged by village Skyans in market-trade. A Drector's son had no use for it. Nor, unlike inhabitants of other planets, in particular the capital world Hanover, had he ever worn jewelry. This angered the men, for their usage of him grew more violent with the discovery.

Things were done to him, the unlikeliest of outrages, obscene acts forced upon him which he had not known possible to human bodies. Afterward, had he been inclined to tell another of it, words would have failed him. It seemed to last forever.

When the three were through with him—at least for the moment, they kept telling him with laughter, threatening even as they used him to use him again—his body had no secrets left for them. No part, no square siemme, no fold of skin, no opening, remained to himself, unviolated. At the time he thought it ludicrous, given the searing torment he suffered, the indignities they put him to, that the most objectionable thing about them were the noxious smells which told him they had not washed themselves for a long time, if ever. He had never known, had never been told, neither by Lia nor Old Henry, that men did these things to one another. Or did they reserve them to young boys?

Some analytical portion of his mind which had remained sane—or become more insane than the rest—was turning this question over when he lost consciousness at last.

It would be a different Arran Islay who awoke.

Part Three: The *Gyrfalcon*
Yearday 205, 3009 A.D.
Mayye 34, 509 Hanoverian
Quintus 6, 1567 Oldskyan

There was a lofty ship
And she wandered wide and free,
'Til she saw that she was followed by the Jendyne enemy,
And she feared the course she sailed upon was never
   meant to be,
As she came beneath the Jendyne,
  Jendyne,
  Jendyne,
She came beneath the Jendyne lee.

Chapter XVIII:
The Gundeck

"'Pon deck, ye rapespawn—an' look lively!"

A savage kick to his already-battered ribs awakened Arran from his stupor. Before he could so much as groan or turn over, a slashing blow from a whip or light club cut across his naked back. By the time he had climbed to his feet, hand over hand up the cold, hard side of the massive caliprette, or projectile mounting, where he had the previous night collapsed, whoever had struck him thus, the same one yelling at him—in fact, at all of the grimy, sleep-stupid denizens of the gundeck—had passed along to his next victim.

Grumbling, staggering, and scratching, the gundeck crew—a sorry lot of both genders, all colors, sizes, and ages—hunched beneath the low ceiling. Arran was lucky to be of so small a stature, else he would have struck his head upon it. As it was, he might as well have taken such a blow, even with all that had happened to him of late, for he was stunned and revolted at the sight of many women—gentle creatures he had been brought up to believe should be respected, sheltered, somehow set apart from the sordid, pragmatic, masculine world—who appeared as naked as himself, and every bit as dirty.

With the men, some hundred seventy-five or eighty altogether, the women filed without spirit toward a heavy-gasketed door set in an in-curved wall, pausing several at a time to further shock Arran's preadolescent sensibilities by relieving themselves before the others, no different in their demeanor than their male counterparts, into a pair of steaming troughs upon either side of the hatch. The air was already thick with the odors of sleep, the crowding of too many unwashed bodies, and a hundred exotic vices. Individuals in this time and place inhaled the weedsmoke, chewed or brewed the leaves, seeds, roots, or stems, of plantlike species from a million planets. Now the place began to take upon itself yet another stench, emanating from the troughs, before Arran—gulping to control his stomach, retched dry the night before—had used one himself, whatever his reluctance, and passed in turn through the hatch which swung shut from the inside, closing with ear-popping pressure.

Arran found himself standing upon a mesh-constructed spiral stair, lit by §-glow and built round the inner circumference of what seemed, looking down, a bottomless circular well. Above his head, it appeared to soar without limit. Of a sudden, jets of scalding, chemical-saturated water sprang from the walls. All round him as they climbed, people began awakening, scrubbing, shouting and laughing at one another. Unacquainted with the conditions responsible, Arran wondered how they had come to look and smell so filthy. He later learned that this rude bath was a luxury occurring once every hundred watches.

He began to imitate their motions, if not their bawdy enthusiasm, rediscovering many bruises and other injuries. Much of what washed off him onto the treads was dried blood. The rest, the residue of countless indignities, scarcely bore thinking of. In too few moments, before he had finished, the water turned frigid, shut off, and drained into the glowing depths.

The stair—termed with astronautic correctness the "ladder," a nicety of which Arran was presently ignorant—brought them to another hatch which swung open before them. Dripping men and women filed out, every one, he observed, bearing long, thin, ragged scars across their backs, arms, and shoulders. Many limped as if from ill-healed injuries. More than a few were missing ears, toes, or fingers.

An interstellar vessel, Arran knew, having constructed models of such ships, consisted in the main of a hull, in this instance some thirty measures in diameter and half again that length, fashioned, to a greater or lesser degree, after the unprepossessing proportions of a peasant's water bucket, and containing within its volume space for crewbeings and cargo. This, the area corresponding to the surface of the water within the bucket, was the maindeck.

No clue was to be had whether it be day or night upon deck. This was the merest matter of convention aboard even the most luxurious of passenger vessels. Nothing but the continuous multicolored flickering, tending toward blues and greens, of the §-field illuminated the scene Arran saw before him as it performed the dual tasks of suspending the effects of inertia within the starship and keeping out the vacuum and cold of the surrounding Deep.

At the ladderwell exit, two fat women sat upon stools behind makeshift tables. In the uncertain light they appeared, if such were possible, even older than Old Henry. Arran remembered his friend and mentor with a heartsick pang. One woman fingered folds of rough greyish fabric piled upon her table. As Arran passed, some of this was thrown at him and struck him in the face.

"Look lively, lad! Fresh meat, eh?" In quick appraisal, the larger of the women eyed recent injuries which, in addition to his expression of confusion, made his status obvious. "Did a right thorough job, they did."

The women looked at one another, the big fat one frowning in what looked like anger, the small fat one shaking her head. The big one spoke again. "Looks like our old friend Jimbeau's style. Best get into them togs, 'fore you tempt him further. Or any of our other lads."

Even had he been inclined, Arran was given no chance to reply. Pushed by the slow-moving queue, chilled and impatient to exchange their scarred and thin-ribbed nakedness for clothing, he stumbled into what proved a crude, ill-laundered coverall. Still damp and barefoot, he wiped his hand down the front of the garment, closing the seal—already it had begun to chafe his damaged flesh—and staggered forward to discover what would happen to him next.

A few shuffling paces, and Arran had arrived at the other table, upon which were stacked dozens of small, white foam-plastic boxes. An odd aroma, savory but revolting, arose as they were handed out by the second and smaller of the fat women, merciful in her silence, one box to a crewbeing. As he passed the table, Arran accepted the box offered to him. It was snatched by the man ahead of him, who added it to the one he had been given.

"Hey!" Arran reached for the box. The man, twice Arran's weight, struck him backhand across the mouth. He stumbled into a knot of crewbeings and almost fell. They shoved him back at the man, and, of a sudden, Arran recognized him. It was Paddy, one of the three who had assaulted him.

"Keep your whiny mouthings to yourself, chicken, or you'll get another!"

Shaking with fear and rage, Arran started forward, reaching for the box again. "Give me that, or I'll—"

"Silence upon queue!" Another voice joined the shouting, somehow to Arran dreadful and familiar. "Ye there, newboy! 'Nother breach, I'll have y'lashed t'hatch cover for yer first dozen!"

Arran turned. The man shouting at him wore a uniform, baggy pantaloons which might have been the bottom half of a coverall such as he himself had been issued, and a frayed, dirty, stiff-collared tunic. He carried a peculiar object in his hand, nothing more than a short section, forearm-length, of wire-reinforced kefflar cabelle, such as was used in heavy farming operations at the Holdings—another pang beset him—with big, tight knots worked into its end. Of a sudden, the boy understood the scarred flesh all about him.

Sufficient reason there was for him to recognize the voice. It belonged to the man his other tormentors had called "Stewie." Nevertheless, Arran pointed out the crewman who had deprived him of his food. "But he—"

The uniformed figure swung the cabelle's end, slapping its knots into a palm hardened by years of such demonstration. "Two chances for fresh meat, by Ceo's naddies, more'n most get. This ain't no lady's pleasure charter where figure-headin's worst y'can expect, outa sight from refined sensibilities!"

The man placed his accent upon the first, elongated syllable of "refined." As Arran was to learn, punishment was a constant topic of conversation aboard the vessel. He had already discovered, unable to avoid overhearing the bathing crew, that one of the mildest forms, sometimes reserved for officers, was "figureheading." The victim was tied to the sculptured mascot at the forward tip of the mast, where fluctuations in the §-field singed skin, hair, eyebrows, or—

providing opportunity for wagers—seared eyeballs to opacity with a rare flicker or devoured half an individual's face. For crewbeings, this was too gentle and private. Their punishments occurred in public, where they served as examples to others.

"Along now, faggot," he was commanded, "or 'tis *dead* meat ye'll be!"

Without a word, Arran turned and began moving once again. Ahead of him, Paddy swiveled, held one of the precious boxes out, and leered at him. "I'll give back half, chicken," the obscene whisper issued from one corner of his mouth, "'pon condition y'pay later, 'pon gundeck, after watch."

Still shambling along, Arran looked up at the man towering over him, and also spoke without moving his lips. "I will pay you back, right enough, with interest, in my own time. Keep looking over your shoulder. You are going to be the sorriest turd who ever lived."

The man raised a work-hardened hand, then hesitated, whether because of the boy's determined scowl or the ludicrousness of his threat, Arran could not tell. The villain looked down at the undersized, beaten-up twelve-year-old, lowered his fist, and laughed. Something of a nervous edge spoiled the menace of it. He turned his back and moved along. Thus passed Arran's first and second conversations aboard the starship he had stowed away upon.

As he shuffled forward again, his thoughts, as they ever would in evil circumstances, buried his immediate fears of their own accord and focused upon practical points. Overhead, seen vaguely by the half-powered §-field, the ship's single mast stretched into apparent infinity. Here and there along its great length, a full klomme in extent, a blob of color presented itself.

In a sense, Arran was finding that his education as a sailor had begun before he set foot aboard this unhappy vessel, before tragedy had overtaken the life he had earlier known. What he had learned at the behest of Mistress Lia began to serve him as he struggled to survive. Arran knew something of ship-handling (like all boys he had thought to take it up, although never to begin in precisely this manner), enough to realize what the faint glow of the deckmesh—and the fact the deck remained beneath his feet—implied.

In this, the thirty-first century (commemorating what event not even scholars were certain), starvoyages were undertaken at velocities greater than that of light, through the application of §-physics, in essence a matter of employing the manifold and subtle aspects of ordinary matter and energy. As any object might, during a less-sophisticated era, have been rendered "weightless"—by removing it from gravitic influences or manipulating it properly within them—so, upon account of §-physics, an object might analogously be rendered *inertialess* by enveloping it within a §-field. Thus, no longer subject to what were termed "einsteinian effects," starsailing vessels traveling from system to system depended upon the tachyon winds, streams and currents of massless, faster-than-light particles which, like cosmic rays, were and are a feature of the natural fluxes present within the galaxy.

Therefore, Arran reasoned, although still orbiting the planet—his beautiful moonringed Skye, now doubly lost to him—and not yet under weigh, the ship had a sufficient number of tachyon-filled starsails set aloft to maintain a small but appreciable spiraling headway against a springline angled to the anchoring cabelle of the lubberlift from the upper hull, establishing the illusion (and, illusion or not, useful and welcome) of gravity underfoot.

All of this, however, and more that he knew in some lost corner of his mind, was only empty theorizing, of less practical significance than certain barbarous everyday facts. This being a first watch during planetfall, new and untried crewbeings were assumed to have made their way aboard in one manner or another. A third pause now was made before tasks were assigned the group of which Arran found himself a disoriented and reluctant part. Crewmen and women of the watch were ordered to face away from a back-slanting wall two measures and a half in height encircling the deck they stood upon, pierced by windows with drawn curtains and topped by a rail. Arran knew the upper area to be the quarterdeck, whence the starship was commanded. Beneath it lay officers' quarters and caliprettes for the bow chasers, projectibles of lesser power than those upon the gundeck. All hands faced inward toward the mast, through the base of which they had arrived upon deck, round which, at two man-heights, hung a platform. At its rail stood a uniformed individual who held his hands behind his back examining with contempt the specimens of humanity before him. He was gigantic, broad as he was tall, and, except for his coloring and animation, might have passed for an Oplyte.

"I be Phoebus Krumm!" he announced in a voice which matched his stature and would have been audible above the planet's most violent thunderstorm. "First officer and navigator of the carrack *Gyrfalcon*. Ye'd best mark me well, for this be the onliest warning ye'll receive."

With this introduction, he hefted an object—ridiculous as it seemed, it appeared to the hungry Arran to be a loaf of bread burnt black upon one end; a basketful stood beside the man—and hurled it from the platform, across the deck where they were ranked, and over the railed wall surrounding it. As it crossed the starship's outer circumference, it exploded with a flash and crack like lightning. Not a crumb or wisp of smoke remained of it.

"It be lethal bodily to intersect the field margin." Another loaf was hurled with the same result. "Settle quarrels amongst yerselves any way ye like, so long as it don't interfere with ship's routine, but to strike an officer be death."

A long list followed of additional items—failure to obey an order, cowardice, stealing ship's property (as with fighting, no prohibition existed against stealing from another crewbeing) —most, it seemed, ending with the same phrase and the same impressive demonstration of what that meant aboard a starship. Arran had known starsailing to be hazardous; it now appeared the greatest hazard lay in the last three words of each rule being read.

At last, having emptied his basket, First Officer Krumm brushed his hands against one another. Arran's mouth had watered as he watched each loaf arc to spectacular destruction. He wondered what the exhibit was when the baker had not burnt several dozen loaves. His body sagged with disappointment at the waste and his stomach growled. The entertainment portion having come and gone, the crewbeings queued up a final time to file before another table. Each was asked what name he—or she—went by, what his position was aboard the starship, and had he heard and understood the articles.

"Arran Islay," he answered sullenly as he reached the table, wasting no thought on evading commitment to the ship and a new life, however terrible; he was a stowaway, and far worse awaited him on Skye. For those who could barquode or make other symbols a ledger was provided. With second thoughts about identifying himself as a hunted criminal, he put down in ancient letter-writing the first name that came to him. No one could read it, anyway. His attention was fastened upon a thille recorder taking down his every gesture. In the event he should appeal some punishment of the officers, he would confront his own voice and likeness consenting to their authority. It was likelier, before it came to that, he would confront a cabelle's end.

"I've no position I know of—" Several bawdy suggestions from crewbeings crowding round him were ignored by Arran and the man behind the table. "—except, I guess, stowaway. Yes, I heard and understood the articles." He looked up. The man behind the table was Jimbeau.

He laughed. "Ye're signed up, chicken, move along!"

Without further ceremony, the watch was set to its tasks. Many of the men and women were sent up, riding Krumm's steam-powered platform the first half klomme into the mainyards, where they would continue aloft and forward on their own hands and feet. Not long afterward, a protracted, horrifying scream came from above. One soul returned, plummeting to silence upon the mesh, not a measure from the Skyan stowaway. Before he looked away and gulped back a sour taste, he had time to see injuries other than a crushed skull and broken neck. The man was a mass of fresh blood from waist to knees. In this manner Arran learned the fate of those manifesting fear of heights. Seized and taken up, as this one had been, they were forced to balance the whole watch, hands tied behind them, with the organ which made them male tethered to the yard. Did they lose their balance, this was the result.

For Arran's part, someone threw a clutch of dirty rags and brushes at him, pointed to a section of deckmesh, and gave

him to understand that the rags and brushes were to be
rendered even dirtier. Through that long, painful watch, he
labored at the most menial tasks imaginable, all with a light
head and growling stomach. It was the first time in his life,
even as a forest refugee, or afterward upon the greenway
where he foraged for himself, that he had ever been hungry.
This, in addition to the injuries and indignities previously
inflicted upon him, made him slow to absorb what he must
learn, awkward in its execution, and earned him many blows
until, had he been keeping track, which he was not, he would
have lost count of them. He drew small comfort from
observing that he was not being singled out, that these
attentions were lavished upon one and all, without discrimi-
nation.

According to the first officer's dissertation, sickness among
crewbeings, while not a capital offense like so many other
transgressions, was punishable as disobedience; hard work
and sweat being considered sovereign remedies for every
laborer's malady. Complaining of work could be—often
was—rewarded by having a wrist bound to an ankle and
being required to work anyway, even if it meant going aloft.
Those suffering rupture or broken bones (both epidemic
aboard starsailing vessels) were compelled to continue their
labors. Did they collapse, a common form of resuscitation
was "striping," the soles of the feet being lashed until they
bled. Individuals thus treated were slower for a time, but
thought upon their work and nothing else. Malingerers might
be fined their ration of food and water, even if they happened
to be dead.

In the beginning, no one save task-masters assigned to
his instruction told him anything, not even what he must
know to do his duty. In this, he soon found, all aboard
had the advantage of him, for gossip had spread through
the *Gyrfalcon*. None among his fellow sufferers had not endured similar ordeals, nor remained ignorant of what he had
experienced in his first hours aboard. Common affliction
failed to render them more sympathetic to his plight. In
fact, as he discovered, much the contrary was true. Men
and women alike—save one—deemed it a precious opportunity, choosing moments when officers were not watching to taunt him by mock endearment, foremost among them

"newboy," which was plain enough, also "faggot" and "chicken," whatever they meant. He dare not bend over without bracing himself for a pinch or probing hand. Even the one—the boy was never certain who he was; he had appeared as no more than a looming shadow as Arran, who had learned better than to look up, devoted his attention to the deck—did not seem much help at first, for he only whispered enigmatically and moved on.

"Did y'know, newboy, that the knee be the weakest part of the body?" Arran pondered this odd lecture in anatomy for hours, believing it applied to his own knees, bruised and bleeding from deckwork. None saw fit to inform him that, according to their view, it had been his free choice to sneak aboard. That he must pay (however ill-informed his choice, whatever consequence fell due, however dear the coin he paid in) seemed to one and all no less natural—perhaps more so—than breathing. Thus, in the first hours which determined his survival, before he could move again with relative ease (a condition he was encouraged to with many a kick and cuff—and worse—through that first endless watch), self-education was a matter of sink or swim, work or starve, and starve in all probability in any case. Foremost, he was expected to learn to perform at the bidding of another or to perish.

Many vital data of this kind Arran absorbed while scraping, brushing, scrubbing, and—enveloped, ill-protected though he was, in the noxious fumes of solvents—helping refinish the resin coating of the mesh of which every square siemme of the *Gyrfalcon* had been fabricated. He was inspired, in aid of this pragmatic education, by the curses, threats, feet, fists, and knotted cabelles' ends of those placed over him. By the time the watch had ended, he had learned his lessons well, in particular the one about knees, which he had at last seen the sense of. Hands aloft were called down—"aft" was the word—and with those from the maindeck were formed into a queue again, at the terminus of which a table had been piled high with white plastic boxes.

It was an offense to complain of the food, punishable in various manners from simple starvation to being forced, if it amused the officers, to eat the plastic packaging or waste from the troughs. The cruelest discipline is inconsistency. As Arran had expected, Paddy soon materialized, this time behind him. As they shuffled along, the man leaned down and whispered, "Y'can't hold out forever, Chicken Little, not unless y'wants t'starve."

Arran ignored him until they reached the table, took the offered box and stepped forward. Collecting his own ration, Paddy also snatched the box from Arran's hands. "See what I mean, chicken?"

Stepping back as if frightened, Arran leapt, bringing both feet up to kick Paddy's left knee with every fiber of his strength. The joint gave way with the sound of breaking celery. As the man slumped, Arran steadied himself, twisted and smashed his elbow into the man's right eye. Paddy fell to the deck, his hands to his face, screaming. Blood streamed between his fingers. With the ball of his left foot, Arran rolled the ruined knee experimentally. Paddy screamed louder and shifted his hands to his leg. Arran lifted a foot and brought his heel down upon the man's throat with another sickening crunch. Paddy gurgled and ceased breathing.

Expecting all the while to be struck by a cabelle's end, lashed to the rigging and flogged to death, or picked up and hurled into the §-field margin, Arran forced himself to inhuman calmness, collected both boxes from the deck, and glared his defiance round. All eyes were upon him. No word was spoken.

At the behest of an officer, hands bent to Paddy's body and dragged it off. Recalling the words, *settle quarrels among yourselves in any manner you wish as long as it doesn't interfere with ship's routine,* Arran neither knew nor cared. The queue shuffled onward. He went to find a safe place to eat against the broad base of the mast. No one ever touched him against his will again, save officers who struck one and all alike with rough egalitarianism, or called him "chicken."

He was learning.

CHAPTER XIX:
THE FOOTCABELLE

"Islay?"

It seemed to Arran, huddled blanketless again beside the caliprette belowdecks, that he had scarcely slept a minute when he was aroused—albeit in a manner gentler than yesterwatch—by a hand upon his shoulder and a shyly spoken word.

"Islay?" Arran startled awake nonetheless, heart hammering. He would have been unsurprised to learn it could be heard by all sharing the gundeck. His inarticulate grunt and sudden movement must have been as startling to the one who awakened him, a thin, ragged boy his own age whom Arran had not seen before. The boy jumped back, out of what he believed was Arran's reach, and swallowed. Word of what the stowaway had done the previous watch must have gotten round to all hands.

"What is it you want?"

"Beg pardon . . ." The words tapered off before an unspoken "sir" as the boy realized he had addressed Arran as a person of rank. "I mean, Second Officer Van Merrivine's passed word he'll see you straightaway 'pon maindeck."

Well, Arran thought, here it comes. He wondered—not for a moment did he anticipate justice or extenuation—what would be done with fresh meat that killed a crewbeing. Perhaps he would be crisped upon the §-field like one of the first officer's loaves after all. Perhaps they had something worse in mind, although he could scarcely imagine what it might be. Likewise, he wondered why the punishment in store for him had not taken place before now.

Thus preoccupied, Arran nodded to the boy, never realizing it was the reflexive, impatient, condescending gesture of a born aristocrat toward an unfamiliar servant. Nor did the boy, at least nominally Arran's superior (like everyone aboard the *Gyrfalcon),* understand, in surrendering to Arran's casual superiority, how he betrayed his own unconscious estimate of their relative positions and volumes more, besides. Had Arran been prepared to understand, he was being informed of the manner in which recent events were viewed by those who had witnessed or heard of them. The sleepy crewbeings all about them (disposed—yet another indication—a discreet distance from Arran's chosen place) were roused from fatigue-induced torpor by more than curiosity, although the fact was lost upon both boys.

Instead, as Arran seized the caliprette to pull himself to his feet, a shock of pain washed through him, every muscle—overworked by unfamiliar tasks, strained further by the fight, stiffened by what seemed less than an hour's sleep—screaming in dire complaint. Arran, who had thought himself fit, was torn between the urge to scream along and a more powerful compulsion to void his stomach. He did neither, maintaining silence by force of character, another unconscious aristocratic act. He found himself awakening to greater alertness than he was accustomed to. Whether this was attributable to the uncertainty of his circumstances, or the difference between physical labor and sedentary lessons, he was not in a position to say. Biting his lower lip and inhaling, he brushed shaking hands down the soiled surfaces of the clothing he had slept in, and—with a gesture similar in tone and meaning to the one he had earlier given—bade the messenger precede him, and followed.

Some, here upon the gundeck, were idlers, supposed neither to be working nor sleeping during this period. They remained below out of the way of the working watch or to avoid being assigned extra labor. A majority dozed in silence, catching—or accumulating—extra sleep, as was ever the practice of those under discipline, but some were active, telling tales or gambling. At the latrine, Arran and his companion watched four crewmen drag a young girl, screaming in a language neither understood but obvious in her pleading, from where she had been sleeping, to be gang-raped before the dull, uncaring eyes of any individual upon the deck too apathetic to look away. Despite every cruel lesson he had learned thus far, Arran started forward.

The boy beside him seized his sleeve. "Here, what y'think yer doin'?"

"Why, I—"

"She's propmarked, can't y'see?" The urchin pointed a bony finger at the girl, her screaming now stifled, held by three of the men as a fourth took a turn between her legs. Peering into the gloom for something he did not in all truth wish to see, Arran, numb and horrified, discerned a mark upon her flank.

"'Propmarked'?" For a second time, he fought the urge to vomit.

"Aye, biggest, toughest crew-quarters bosses'll burn or cut favorites, girls, faggots, all accordin' t'taste. Likeliest her prop's a noncom, loanin' her out. She'll learn soon enough: crewwomen as cause trouble gets chained t'maindeck hatch a watch or two, spread t'be used by anybody."

Arran gulped. "For refusing intercourse, they are given by their . . ."

"Their prop."

"Proprietor? They are forced to . . . they are given over to anyone unashamed to take his pleasure in public from an unwilling victim?"

The boy shrugged as if the rising and setting of the sun were being brought into question. "There be some as considers it an honor—bein' propmarked, not hatch-spread—a measure of protection from all comers, if ye'll pardon my expression. If I hadn't stopped ye, ye'd been hatch-spread in her place. Ain't no end t'be desired, since it's a deal harder upon us men."

Across the deck, the rapists stood joking with one another, straightening their filthy clothing, and abandoned their sobbing, disheveled victim. Arran looked at his companion, discovering he detested sight of the complacent boy as much as he had detested watching what had happened. Almost as much as he detested himself for having watched without taking action.

"Upon us men, you say?" he asked at long last. The question was rhetorical. He was recalling what had happened to him his first hour aboard the carrack. "I wonder." With no further word upon the subject, he headed for the ladderwell.

Despite the general disinclination to educate "fresh meat," Arran had been neither too busy nor too unobservant during his first watch to have learned something of the circumstances he shared with them. Even now, despite his worries and the horror he had just witnessed, Arran had more time and composure than heretofore to look about him and absorb the significance of what he had thus far seen.

A starship typical of the period, *Gyrfalcon* was a carrack, a small, swift passenger-freighter of fifteen projectibles' strength, capable of reaching any destination within the explored galaxy, defending herself against predators, or, were it her wont, practicing predation herself. Penetrating all levels, integral with the great length of her mast, were inlaid traceries of metal and silica. The system was ancient and devoid of moving parts. The starsails, impermeable to tachyons which drove her through the Deep, were sieves for other energies. Like the §-field rider, they trapped quanta, channeling them through the yards to the mast circuitry, which altered them in curious ways to produce power beyond comprehension of an earlier age. *Gyrfalcon* boasted nothing resembling batteries or generators, having minimal need to store energy accumulated from the Deep. Her circuitry required scant attention from her crewbeings, the possibility of malfunction—save from damage so massive the entire starship would be destroyed in the process—being unheard of.

Divided into levels, *Gyrfalcon* afforded room for passengers, officers, and crew, the working of her defenses, and the stowage of cargo. The gundeck Arran knew: less fortunate crewbeings, without status, slung hammocks between nine primary projectibles and cargo partitions, for this level was, despite its belligerent name, in principal a hold. Also upon this deck, by the circumference of the ladderwell which was also the foot of the mast, was the galley, at most times padlocked, source of the boxes which had cost Paddy his life. (Arran discovered within himself no qualm concerning the older crewman; it might as easily have been Arran's life which was forfeit.) The two boys, alike and yet so different, entered the well within the mast, a hollow structure of strong, lightweight material spanning six measures at its foot, whence it tapered to but finger's width a klomme forward.

Above the gundeck lay the boatdeck, named for six small annihilation-powered steam-rockets swung outside the *Gyrfalcon*'s hull. She reserved her boats—more expensive to operate than the lubberlift and less reliable—for ship-to-ship travel, hull inspection, repairs, and emergencies. Upon this deck as upon others, ample stowage could be found. Here also were junior officers and less-pampered passengers quartered. Arran noticed, as they climbed past this level, no sign of a hatch. Access was through the commanddeck alone, a provision to protect passengers (in particular, female passengers) and boats from pressganged crewbeings given to mutiny and desertion. Under different circumstances, Arran knew he might approve this arrangement. As it was, he understood it, and this seemed sufficient for the time being.

In due course, they reached the level above the inaccessible boatdeck and left the ladderwell. The maindeck they stepped out upon was "outdoors," atop—forward of—the hull. Crewbeings labored here, protected from rigors of the Deep by the all-enveloping §-field, in what forever had been called a "shirtsleeve environment." When conditions permitted, informal cooking was done here, and it served the secondary purposes of exercise and recreation. The maindeck's prime importance was as anchorage and workspace for thousands of cabelles, standing and running, by means of which sails were supported and manipulated. Rising to the foremost extreme of the §-field, the mast boasted three tiers of yardarms radiating outward in as many directions. Starships were oftentimes depicted bearing vast triangular expanses sometimes compared romantically to the wings of birds. *Gyrfalcon*'s rigging was at the moment nearly naked, giving her greater resemblance to a winter-barren forest giant.

Had Arran expected special reception (beyond question of punishment, the thought never occurred to him), he would have been disappointed. The incident of the previous watch, although not forgotten—nor was it likely to be—was by now relegated to history, no more than another disbelievable item of crewlore. Practical considerations held sway: *Gyrfalcon* still lay above Skye, the moonring forming a dusty halo about the planet. Much remained to be accomplished by officers and crewbeings before she got under weigh.

As the boys emerged, the messenger glanced about until he spied the officer who had sent him. Gesturing Arran to follow, he made a winding way across the busy deck. Mr. Van Merrivine, the second officer, was the individual certain others called "Stewie," probably, Arran reasoned, because his duties included those of cargo steward, a task which, aboard a larger murchan-frigate with two decks of projectibles or a military dreadnought with a splendid and intimidating four, would likely be performed by a separate officer. They found him supervising the coiling of cabelles using a disciplinary aid of the same material. The boy halted—just outside reach of the improvised weapon, a cynical Arran observed—announcing completion of his mission. Van Merrivine eyed the boy as if searching for an excuse to stride forward and strike him. Finding none, with a disappointed expression souring his thin-lipped, arrogant face, Van Merrivine dismissed him.

"Islay." Arran's name, as uttered, carried not the slightest intonation indicating what the man meant by it. Arran had yet to learn that this was a species of cruel art, practiced to refinement by officers of this and other ships. A word thus spoken might encourage a guilty crewbeing (even one who was not guilty) into reading too much into it and betraying himself.

"Sir." This courteous appellation was delivered with equal —albeit unwitting and reflexive—neutrality, as none but one reared as an aristocrat might manage. The bodily attitude which the deliverer assumed, of stiffened attention, was something Arran had in recent days learned for himself.

"Islay, against my better judgment, I am ordered to elevate you from the sewer where you rightfully belong, and attempt —in vain, I assure you it will be—to make more of you than you'll ever make of yourself."

"Sir?"

"Do not take an innocent tone with me, you murderous prick-teasing little faggot! You are qualified for one duty alone, as far as I can see, one which, however grudgingly, you have already performed. Were it left to me, which, to my deep regret it is not, you would be safely disposed of and forgotten. Yet you are to become a ship's boy—at the behest of Mr. Krumm—like the one who brought you here. Is that plain enough for you?"

Arran tried to straighten his tired body, to stand more at attention than he was. He sensed this as an urgent necessity. Although his words were delivered in a harsh whisper—a bellow only by intent—and Van Merrivine's expression was coldly superior, what Arran saw, deep within his eyes, was disbelieving terror. Men, he had learned from his father, capable of such disminded fear, were dangerous. Something even more dangerous—deep within Arran—chuckled to itself.

"'Ware the margin!"

"Idlers below!"

"Riggin' hands aloft!"

Shouting seized the attention both of boy and man. Despite what he had suffered aboard her, Arran held *Gyrfalcon* to be a wonderous thing. He had once, before reality imposed the choice, imagined any starship a better place than planetside. Now, standing at the foot of the quarterdeck still undismissed by her distracted second officer—and upon this account not technically among the idlers ordered belowdecks—he beheld a spectacle to make all previous pale by comparison.

Devices employing electromagnetism—the motors driving Morven's chair—could not operate within a §-field. It was expected by those like Arran, whose education allowed them to speculate without engendering sufficient cynicism to damage their belief in progress, that someday §-motors might be invented. Some visionaries (this, too, included Arran) believed that §-fields themselves might be used as starsails. Meanwhile, working a ship such as the *Gyrfalcon* remained labor-intensive. Uneducated and unspeculative sailors placed faith in the steam-winch (in sparing usage, as it consumed precious water) and in high-advantage hoists upon the maindeck, along mast and yards, and in their own impressive courage, strength, and skill.

Amidst shouted incomprehensibilities, dozens of men

and women scampered aloft with a semblance of enthusiasm.
Some climbed the rigging, which seemed to stretch from
every portion of the maindeck into the complicated webbery
of cabelles overhead. Others scurried to the platform where
Mr. Krumm had stood. In an instant they were whisked
up the mast, outdistancing the climbers, until they
and the platform seemed to dwindle in the distance and
disappear.

More commands were issued, relayed by high-voiced jun-
iors stationed at intervals along the mast. With a titanic
crack! the first of the voluminous triangles unfurled between
two long yards at the mizzentier. Another opened thunder-
ously, and another. Higher aloft, crewbeings spread the triple
suite of the maintier and the foretier, while others manned
curved staysails which stretched in a staggered spiral from
tier to tier. Arran felt his weight, unnoticed until now, press
down upon the deck, the pressure growing, stage by gradual
stage, upon open blisters with which the previous watch had
decorated his bare soles. The pain increased as well, but, for
the moment, Arran was unaware. Beneath his feet, the
starship herself began to throb with pent-up forces as her
widespread starsails performed the double task of drawing
her out of orbit and feeding her fresh and enormous appetite
for energy.

Hove to, her modest requirements had been provided by a
few smallsail, all but invisible from the maindeck, which kept
her upon even keel and fed her galley. The lubberlift, regaining in the downward voyage most of what it consumed in the
upward, required little to make up losses all machinery
suffered. Now, §-fields heretofore maintained in somnolence
roared and flared where they encircled the quarterdeck
taffrail, dazzling Arran, making his eyes water. Augmented
brilliance crept like a living thing, measure by inexorable
measure, up the rigging, forward along the mast, into each of
the sailtiers in turn. The carrack *Gyrfalcon* was cast off under
all plain sail.

Arran glanced back at Mr. Van Merrivine. The man gave
him a speculative eye. "I can, upon the other hand, select the
manner and condition of your training, Islay. And I believe I
know what is in the best interest of the ship." Whistling

between his teeth, he summoned the boy who had brought Arran to the maindeck. "Pass word to Mr. Shwarts. I wish to speak with him before he takes trainees aloft. Tell him I have another for his practice squad."

Hardened as the ship's boy may have thought himself, he glanced at Arran, pity written in his eyes. He had seen crewbeings ordered aloft in a neutrino storm, when wild undulations along the mast and unpredictable vibrations in the yards threw them off into the §-field, and, in precaution, double the number were sent aloft to replace them. Once, as part of a handful being punished for an offense committed by one of its members (when blame could not be assigned— sometimes even when it could—such punishment was ordered to weaken mutual support among the crew), he had been required to report upon the maindeck every hour for forty watches.

The second officer seemed gratified when his victim grinned in agreement, for the man was deceived by what he took for naive enthusiasm. It had always been a mystery to him why an individual, pressed into this terrible vocation, would prefer the miserable and perilous estate of a humble crewbeing upon a starsailing vessel to an alternative which, however desperate and final, was, given the multitude of means at hand, easier and more comforting to contemplate. Perhaps a solution lay in the very peril which characterized life aboard a starship, for attrition among new crewbeings was enormous, leaving only those behind who loved life well enough to endure its agonies.

Arran may have been one such, although for him the greatest hardship he anticipated, aside from what had befallen him upon what he now knew as the liftdeck, was the utter impossibility of sleep. Not only had he other members of the crew to fear, he and others might be turned out at any time for drills or extra duty. Perhaps the boy labored beneath a burden of what he looked upon as unfinished business, to be honorably disposed of before he might, in decent conscience, consider easier, more comforting alternatives. In any event, ordered aloft despite muscles aching from the previous watch (as well as his fight with Paddy), he went to it with an outward exultation which might have surprised anyone interested

enough to be aware of it. That his attitude actually owed its
existence to the identity of one going aloft with him escaped
Merrivine, despite the fact that he had sent Arran (nor was
Arran unaware of it) to die. Heading the practice squad was
Gyrfalcon's third officer, Mr. Schwarts—better known as
"Jimbeau."

For Arran it was a quick, easy climb up the ratlines,
ladderlike contrivances anchored at their after ends to the
maindeck. No crewbeing was ever sent far aloft the first
time—the three great yards of the mizzentier were closest to
the maindeck, not more than several dozen measures above
it—intended, as the exercise was, to provide them with basic
instruction in the working of the ship. Yet it was safer only in
a relative sense. A fall from this height would kill with the
same finality as any from the foretier, two thirds of a klomme
higher.

High in the mizzentier, Arran and other neophytes were
ordered to space themselves along the yards, each of three
squads supervised by a seasoned hand. It was intended that
they should practice furling and unfurling the starsails, and to
this purpose some worn expanses had earlier been set upon
this tier, great volumes of mesh sheerer and more flexible
than that of which the hull was fashioned. In this they were
assisted by the footcabelle, of several gleaming strands, not
unlike that from which the lubberlift depended, running
through stout eyes attached at intervals to the after surface of
the mizzenyard, and upon which, as might be imagined from
its name, they placed their feet as they hung their arms over
the yard and shuffled crabwise along its intimidating length.
Veteran crewbeings eschewed this artifice of amateurs, preferring to run barefoot along the smooth upper surface of the
yard. With equal spirit, they scorned the ratlines and scaled
instead the cabelles like vine-climbing arboreals in some
storythille jungle of Arran's childhood fancy. The boy believed a long time would pass before he would count himself
among their number voluntarily.

No sooner had this passed through Arran's mind when
the third officer made it plain that "voluntarily" would never
be a word in currency aboard any ship for which he was responsible. With a sadistic chuckle, he inspected the green

countenances of the dozen crewbeings allotted him for the drill. Strung along the mizzenyard, they clung with a loving dedication never demonstrated at their mothers' breasts. The cabelle danced beneath their unpracticed feet. None— including Arran, who, save Jimbeau, had taken the position closest to the mast (suiting the third officer's preference as much as his own)—was capable of contemplating anything except the blessed moment when they might be allowed to return to the comparative comfort and safety of the maindeck below.

"Here, timorous tartlets," he laughed, "is where we separates live ones from corpses-t'be!" Swinging his right leg over the mizzenyard, Jimbeau let his left foot—bare as that of any crewbeing, long-toed, with spurred and hardened heels—slip from the cabelle. Holding the yard with his right arm, he leaned down, undid the shackle, attaching the inboard end of the cabelle to a turnbolt upon the mast and began jerking at it.

Arran was alert, fear forgotten in a wash of something hotter, cleaner than the terror which, seconds before, had dominated his being. Man and boy were blocked from sight of the others, not just by the uncontrolled flapping of the practice-sail, but by the crewbeings' fear, not a whit better controlled. Arran watched and listened, calculating. Jimbeau opened his mouth to speak, Arran could hear the preliminary catch of the third officer's indrawn breath. Before it could be completed, Arran jumped hard upon the cabelle, letting it take his weight, all but letting go of the mizzenyard.

The cabelle, no longer shackled, screamed outboard, taking Jimbeau with it. Its turnings whistling with friction, it ran through the eye between the two of them, dropping Arran his full height and whipping Jimbeau round, tearing his arm free of the yard. He hung for but a moment by the callused spur of his right heel. His own arms pained by past effort, straining with what was demanded of them now, Arran scurried up the cabelle, regaining purchase upon the yard. It was an instant which seemed to last forever: Jimbeau still held the free end of the cabelle in his right hand; his trembling left reached toward Arran; a pleading expression was upon his face.

"Help me!" Another lifelong moment passed.

Arran whispered, "None of that, now, sweetie!" and let Jimbeau's whitened fingertips slip through the air a siemme from his own. Jimbeau's heel left the yard, his face yanked from Arran's view. Once his desperate appeal had escaped the doomed man's lips, he was silent. Accelerating as he fell—for some reason he continued holding the cabelle—his course deviated, becoming a steep curve as the cabelle, stopped at the bolt nearest Arran, shrieked as it reeled slack from the yard and altered his fall. Instead of plummeting to the deck, he swung toward the §-field. As he struck the limit of the cabelle's slack, the shackle was torn from his hand. He continued onward, outward, and—with a huge, dull *pop!* and a flash of light—the *Gyrfalcon's* third officer vanished, vaporized like one of Mr. Krumm's loaves.

Right, Jimbeau, Arran thought. Inside, he was empty, experiencing nothing he could have named save for the mildest sense of satisfaction. *Here is where we separate the living from the corpses-to-be!*

It was a philosopher of crime, renowned for intelligence guided by experience, who observed that killing is best accomplished spontaneously, when means and opportunity are present by fortuity. Never having heard this advice, Arran had nonetheless acted in a manner consonant with its sagacity.

And thus became a wolf among sheep.

CHAPTER XX:
KRUMM THE BAKER

This watch, First Officer Krumm had chosen a stout ring-bollard upon which to rest his enormous fundament.

He sat at the break of the commanddeck, the annular structure built upon a level with the maindeck. Overhanging the circumference of the hull (providing a scenic gallery for the privileged as well as some protection for the boats) the commanddeck housed the captain, a few of his officers, and the more important passengers. Here, officers and passengers dined, in comparison to less-fortunate others, amidst formal splendor. The commanddeck lay below the quarterdeck, a railed area like the maindeck open to the stars, from which ship's operations were ordinarily supervised. Here, however, Krumm could gather about him all of the ship's boys—including the new one—for the day's lesson, and still keep an eye out.

"Now, bravos, mark me. Whatever its manifold other intricacies, interstellar navigation's the most meticulous of arts, requirin' detailed charts——" He thumbed over his shoulder, indicating the commanddeck behind him where the all-important documents, the captain's log, and instruments were kept. "——seasoned judgment, an' a knowledge of abstruse mathematics."

He was answered by a general groan of boyish distaste which a greater disciplinarian, and lesser teacher, might have punished them for. Krumm, with nothing academic in his background, harboring similar feelings upon the subject, let it pass. Properly motivated, young minds could master any subject, once they knew it stood between them and whatever it was they wanted.

"Travelers aboard a starsailin' ship——" He raised a hairy right arm to point forward, while pointing aft with his left. No blacksmith could boast muscles to match those of a man who had spent his youth mixing and kneading bread-dough in hundred-kilo batches. "—are as unable t'see where they're goin', as where they've been."

One or two younger boys appeared puzzled. The new one just looked miserable, and with reason. Lacking a more useful aptitude, he had, the previous watch, been set to hunting clots of fangmold in the aftmost recess of the ladderwell. A carnivorous vegetable pest encountered early in humankind's exploration of the Deep, fangmold was so hardy and ferocious it had rendered even shipboard rats a relic of the past. It could be dealt with only by searching out individual clumps, pulping them before they scurried away with a cabelle's end wrapped in barbed steel wool, and soaking the remains with something noxious enough to destroy the spores, seeds, cuttings, and runners it was capable of reproducing itself from. Combating the stuff was a matter of endless losing warfare, yet it was essential, for the stuff ate anything. Without the effort expended, vain as it was, to expunge it, it would have draped the starship, mastfoot to figurehead, in loathsome, dangerous festoons. The new boy was bedraggled, his coverall shredded in a dozen places, countless smears of blood upon it and his skin. Fangmold did not bleed.

"Bear with me, lads." Krumm cleared his throat. "Even were they able, seein', in the end, proves t'be of less than no help, owin' to the laggard speed of light which lends a picture of a universe, for'ard an' aft, thousands of years outa date."

Spreading broad hands and raising his eyebrows, he looked among his students for sign of enlightenment. His explanation did not seem to have helped. Despite the simplicity of the concept, it was, at first—in particular by children of untutored farmers and planetbound fisherfolk—only grasped with difficulty. Converting his hand-spread gesture to a shrug, Krumm sighed. Taken in his youth by a raid upon his port-city home, he had killed fourteen slavers (or fifteen, the count varied in the telling) with a "peel," an outsized, razor-sharp oven spatula. Neither farmer nor fisher, at heart the mighty Krumm remained a peasant, nonetheless. He still baked, between drills, landfalls, and battles, assisted by his pair of stout, merry wives. Krumm was a patient man, with all the time in the galaxy. Although they came to him by differing pathways, all the boys (save this latest with his snotty accent and murderous habits) were as humble in origin as himself. Allowance must be made (it did not occur to him that allowance had never been made for him) for none possessed the advantage of education. In Krumm's experience, vast and long, all would come right in the end.

"Be brave, lads, it gets worse. The degree of visual obsolescence varies with the distance. Also, some destinations an' departures are too small, dim, occluded by intervenin' gases, brighter stars or clusters, or far away t'be seen at all!" By their expressions, Krumm could tell this made more sense to the boys. They ceased their squirming and waited with what even resembled patience for him to get to something else they could understand. "Upon the face of the known Deep, an' along the more common routes 'twixt those long-settled an' more densely populated systems considered 'civilized'—"

"Beg pardon, Mr. Krumm," this from one of the older boys, less forward than he appeared, for it was not yet clear what the day's topic was to be. "Considered civilized by whom?"

"Why," Krumm answered, laughing, "by their inhabitants, naturally!" He had sympathy for the boy who had asked, both coming, as they did, from planets derided by Hanover as backwaters. "Where was I? Ah: upon more commonly traveled routes, currents of subatomic particles—tachyons benevolent, neutrinos malevolent, an' everything relevant between—and their fluctuations have long since been mapped by generations of careful (or lucky) explorers." Krumm leaned forward, elbows upon knees, whispering in a conspiratorial tone. "In the Deep as yet unknown, mappin' these anomalies constitutes the first an' most important task. The uncareful (or unlucky) wayfarer leaves nothin' behind as a guide to his successors."

This time, their reaction was a shudder. Each had heard tales from the older hands of starships disappearing. Arran, too, from Old Henry, dramathilles, and Mistress Lia's histories. They assumed new meaning, and new terror, when he could glance up as he chose and gaze out through the §-field

—dangerous in itself, as he well knew, although designed as a protection against eternal night—into the uncaring, deadly face of the galactic Deep.

Mr. Krumm laughed. Arran had not been surprised to learn the *Gyrfalcon's* second-in-command was a pastrier. He appreciated Krumm as a gigantic, good-natured, somewhat barbarous lout, this almost comical first officer whom all the crew called "The Baker." He was one whose laughter came easy and deep—Arran liked this about him—and the warmth and power of it was such as to dispel any terror ever a young boy lost sleep over. At present, although neither was aware of it, he constituted the only bright spot in the boy's life, all that preserved a remnant of his humanity. Arran's prospects for advancement may have brightened (had he cared), but, as his companions in suffering began to note, it was a special wrath which brought the misspent days of Paddy, and perhaps *Gyrfalcon's* third officer, to an end. Arran, they came to see, was by no means superhuman in his savagery. He, in turn, found that promotion did not relieve him of a necessity for conspicuous readiness to fight for food and a safe place to sleep.

Krumm laughed again. "Nothin' behind," he repeated, shuddering himself. "Upon happier occasions, involvin' sufficient care, aye, an' luck, vast fortunes, indeed, entire gavagin' empires, have come to owe their sovereignty, prosperity, their very existence t'this kind of esoterica. A greater treasure it is, though ye'll not believe me till you're frosty-templed like meself, than ever was hoarded by ceo or brigand!" He watched their eyes. Some lessons could never be taught, but only learned, oftentimes over and over, the hard way. To young minds, treasure was treasure. It would require years, and no small experience of life, before they came to believe him upon this point—the value of information—or even that he had been serious about it.

"Excuse me, sir," Arran, having to a degree recuperated from his labors, and emboldened by the boy who had spoken, indicated the view-distorting field which enwrapped their starship. "How is such information safely gathered?"

Narrowing his eyes, Krumm inspected the newcomer, wondering, as ever in such a circumstance, whether the question, undistracted as it seemed by the candy-word "treasure," confirmed his judgment that granting this particular boy special attention might pay dividends.

"Sometimes, when a vessel's in the perilous process of feelin' her way through new territory upon her figurative tippy-toes—" He made a spidery finger-gesture. All, save one, laughed at the funny little phrase coming out of this giant. Arran looked impatient, even a bit insulted. A warm feeling spread through Krumm; he was beginning to believe the boy might be something special after all, killer though he was. "Or more often," he continued, "in the known Deep, when she's been swept off her intended course in a storm—" He paused to chuckle, as if at a vivid memory. "Or when the man responsible for her management's a bad navigator—ahem!—a starsailin' ship might at intervals be brought below lightspeed for corrective sightin's."

This engendered an expression of curiosity upon the faces of more than one. Good lads, Krumm thought with satisfaction, or none would be here listening to him. He ought to know, who had handpicked them. Mustn't overlook a one. Young Islay might be a prize, but they were all good lads.

"You're way ahead of me. She'll heave-to, all save smallsails furled, field damped to a necessary minimum, inertia thereby increased to its normal, speed-inhibitin' quality. Her captain, if he's desperate, may even run out the lubberlift, the better to achieve maximum parallax for sightings, or to let the length of its cabelle taste the winds of the Deep."

The *Gyrfalcon,* like two-decked frigates and other vessels her size and larger, was too fragile to make planetfall, instead lowering passengers and cargo from synchronous orbit. As with other decks of specialized function, the liftdeck, in addition to housing beneath the mastfoot the lubberlift and kiloklommes of cabelle, held cargo and crew quarters. Krumm observed each of the boys imagining the loneliness of a starship brought to a complete halt in the heartless bosom of the Deep, without planet or even nearby sun in sight. How much worse might it be all alone—swinging at the end of a cabelle tens of thousands of klommes from the only source of warmth, light, and companionship—he was certain they dare not imagine.

"After our next port—" he chuckled, "—when our esteemed second officer's finished his overhaul, p'rhaps we can persuade the captain t'run the lift out as exercise. In emergencies, this is needful, as Mr. Islay has indirectly pointed out. Above lightspeed, outside the influence of the §-field, the universe appears t'those onboard t'shrink—aye, as you've already learned, philosophers an' superstitious starsailors will gleefully agree it actually does—to a blindin' hot blue light infinitely far for'ard, an' a duller red one aft." He pointed aloft—forward. As each of the boys knew without following the line of his finger, it was as he described it. "All else is blackness—till one starship comes within §-field range of another."

A stir went through them as they sensed the exciting part arriving.

"The effects of fields intersectin' are detectable by instrument at over a hundred klommes, increasin'ly discernible from vivid color an' pattern changes as the range closes." None of the boys had found occasion to confirm this for himself, although they looked forward to it with greater enthusiasm than their officers. The Deep was, at the best of times, a savage place. The §-fields of passing vessels coalesced into a large all-encompassing envelope (as soap bubbles will) making it possible for attackers to board. It imposed asymmetric stresses upon both §-field and hull structure, in particular when the vessels were upon differing courses. Experienced starsailors felt the chance meeting of two ships, even of the same imperium-conglomerate, seldom brought good fortune. "An old deck hand'll claim—an' often demonstrate—that he can sense an approachin' vessel before the captain's instruments." No one disputed it for, despite the lying and bragging which took place onboard, each had begun to learn the amazing things some hands were capable of. "He'll offer estimable guesses as to her course, condition, class, an'—"

"Idlers below! Riggin' hands to the maindeck!" Whistles shrilled about them as change of watches commenced. The spell was broken, the day's lesson at an end. As they arose from where they sat at Krumm's feet, dispersing to various responsibilities, Krumm held one of them back. "Mr. Islay."

"Sir."

"I see a many a question still alurk behind those eyes."

"Sir?"

"Come along, then. We'll see if we can't answer 'em." Arran nodded as the first officer arose from his improvised seat with a mighty grunt, and followed the man's broad back, winding across the crew-crowded maindeck and its ordered clutter, to the man's quarters, opposite the captain's. Krumm grinned as he turned the knob and entered the cabin. "Afternoon, medcars! How's the batch I started this mornin' comin' along?" The aromas of fresh, yeasty dough, a hot and well-used oven, of a thousand seasonings and spices, some familiar, some exotic, rolled about Arran like a thick, hypnotizing fog as he passed through the door and closed it behind him. Krumm lowered his voice a trifle. "And by the by, I've brought a guest for tea!"

"How nice, Phoebus dear!" A familiar female voice was audible to Arran from somewhere in front of the giant. "Your dough seems perfectly normal to me. That yeast you brought up from that ringed planet will do nicely. Will you ask our guest—wherever he might be—whether he'd like to wash up?"

Arran stepped round the first officer. Smiling at him, Tula Krumm's eyes crinkled shut above her round, red cheeks. She was seated beside one of Krumm's ovens—Arran could count four in the room, all of different sizes—peering over the tops of wire-rimmed spectacles as her plump fingers performed some sort of cleverwork with thick, fuzzy thread and flexible needles. This was one of the women he had first seen handing out coveralls and food boxes. Traces of a glower had passed across Krumm's face as his wife spoke his given name. Arran surmised he was embarrassed by it, and that one in so lowly a position as himself would be ill-advised to repeat it in the hearing of the crew. Krumm bent to kiss his wife upon the cheek and went straight to a huge crock covered with a damp cloth. Lifting this aside, he peered into the container, sniffed its contents, nodded to himself, and covered it again.

"Ask him yourself. I'll tidy up a mite. Where's Tillie off to?"

Her ample form filling the door, Krumm's other wife entered from another room. "Here, husband. What's this you've dragged in off the deck?"

Greeting his second wife as he had greeted the first, Krumm grinned down at the boy. "It followed me home. Can I keep it?"

"I don't know, Phoebus," answered Tillie, "is it housebroken?" In her corner by the oven, Tula Krumm emitted a pleasant chuckle, lifted a thick strand of her cleverwork over another, and did something to it with a needle.

"A good question, Mathilde medear. One more I think we'll be findin' an answer to this afternoon." Both wives nodded. Tillie put water to boil for tea, Tula continued her work. Wondering what the man had meant, Arran washed his hands at the tap he was shown, sat where he was told in a handcarven chair, and stared at a platter of biscuits, cookies, tarts, and other sweets the like of which he had never seen, even at the Holdings.

The boy was aware he had not known what to expect concerning the first officer's private arrangements. For that matter, being invited to see firsthand had been the least of his expectations. Perhaps he had awaited variations upon the dismal, dangerous surroundings he himself occupied, earlier upon the gundeck and now, a level higher, upon the boatdeck where, since his promotion, he slept in a hammock used by two other boys during watches when he was busy elsewhere. Perhaps, knowing Krumm's avocation, he had expected everything to smell of rancid lard, covered under a dusting of stale flour. In any event, the bright, spotless home Krumm's wives made for him, with its gingerbread furniture, its sparkling, many-paned windows overlooking the maindeck, and its books—the Krumms had real books, like the one Old Henry had given him!—now seemed much to Arran like the storythille den of a family of giant, cheerful animals. At once he was upon his guard.

". . . perhaps," Krumm was saying, "after our young friend has delivered himself of the question or twenty I brought him to ask and have answered in private." Like an absurd insect buzzing from blossom to blossom, Krumm had been flitting about, if that was an appropriate word, inspecting first an oven, next a crock, checking bins and boxes, sniffing, tasting, and adjusting. Now he stopped. Arran looked straight up into the giant's big face.

"Sir, I should like to know why you chose to make me a ship's boy."

Sounding like his shorter wife, Krumm chuckled. If his peasant accent seemed to fade a trifle, betraying a searching and powerful, if self-educated, intelligence, neither he nor the boy seemed to notice. "Learned that much, have you, that in some languages the word 'gift' means 'poison'? And always count your change? Loss of innocence: a pity I suppose it is, but the better part of growin' up. It's this simple, Arran Islay. I've watched you, as I watch everything and everybody aboard this carrack. It is my job. And, by default, the job is mine, as well—for the captain, as owner-in-command, has other matters to occupy his attention—of findin' her new officers." Krumm sat at the table, his chair groaning beneath his weight. "You meet certain standards, lad. My standards, which each of your new messmates likewise met. You're agile, quick-witted, a survivor—though ye'll hafta be learnin' a more versatile form of hand-t'hand. Never depend upon trickery which works the once, leaving the user helpless against an informed adversary."

Arran nodded, wishing to understand. Over what now seemed a lifetime, despite the improved circumstances in which he found himself, he had seen incredible brutality. He had witnessed theft and extortion as everyday fact among crewbeings less able than he, or for some reason less willing, to defend themselves. He had seen torture disguised as discipline. He had more than witnessed murder. Rape he knew upon an intimate basis. These were violent times, Lia had told him, life being held cheap even by those who lived it.

"Also, however well deserved their grim comeuppances, you've cost me a crewbeing who'll be missed, and an officer—don't deny it!—than whom I've had a number worse. I'm curious t'see if you can replace both."

Again Arran only nodded, his ruminations elsewhere than upon the man's words or perhaps extracting different meaning from them than intended. The rest of the visit was spent eating, and afterward exploring the facilities which had produced what they had eaten. With proprietary pride,

Krumm had shown off his ovens and explained the steps involved in baking. Despite circumstances calculated to produce self-consciousness, Arran had taken in everything. If not fascinated, his questions were at least intelligent.

Now, Krumm shook his shaggy head as he watched the thin, tense figure of the boy recede across the maindeck. He had been uncertain whether to tell him he met the standards mentioned earlier better than any he had seen during his long, colorful career. In the end, he had decided not to, for the present. The decision had been emotional. Decades aboard all types of starships, in every position—he, too, having begun as a virtual slave—had taught the man to trust his feelings, doubts in particular. Potential greatness loomed about this child, he thought, but something else, as well.

As an apparent result of the boy's example, several rapists —not men alone—had died or were so injured at the hands of their intended victims that rape was becoming a rarity aboard *Gyrfalcon*. Food-stealing—interfered with only when it threatened, through starvation, to deprive the starship of able crewbeings—had become a thing of the past.

In Krumm's experience, as a voyage progressed, and with each shower interval, the pressure seemed to drop. Intended for issue to all crewbeings, for purposes of washing and drinking, water was withheld and sold to them. Since they possessed little or no money, the accepted currency was sexual, pain endured for the enjoyment of sadists, or, most valuable of all, tales identifying individuals likely to resist authority. Now the body of the noncommissioned officer who sold the crewbeings' own water to them had been discovered, facedown in a shallow pan, drowned in no more than two siemmes, and the first officer was having difficulty keeping it quiet.

Sickness and injury, always a problem upon voyages, were falling off, efficiency increasing. More time for music and dancing upon the maindeck had been found. Without prompting from officers who never cared to exert themselves, while it was never altogether pleasant belowdecks, it was becoming cleaner. Crewbeings took more pride in personal appearance.

Arran might be more than just an officer, someday. He

might be a mighty captain Krumm himself would be proud to
serve. Or he might fail, winding up a cruel negligent or a
red-handed slaughterer like—the big man throttled the insubordinate thought. Time would tell, which was why
Krumm had withheld something which belonged to the boy
by rights, taken from him by force, and which, in truth, the
big man had intended acknowledging—by regulation, it
could not yet be returned—during this visit. He went to a
bureau beneath one window and opened a drawer. He did not
remove the chemenergic pistol lying there, nor touch it, but
looked down at it for a long while, thinking.

For his own part, Arran was uncertain whether to feel
relief. Krumm had accepted the killing of Paddy as motivated
by cause and arrived at in justice. The kindly giant had even
expressed a willingness to take the third officer's death upon
much the same terms. But would he accept what had yet to be
discovered with similar equanimity? In his first hour aboard
Gyrfalcon, Arran had suffered the cruelty of three men, not
the two whose executions Krumm had forgiven. Somehow,
the resolution Arran had just the previous watch contrived
seemed fitting. Since the second officer had been occupied
inspecting every siemme of the liftcabelle, a painstaking task
he would entrust to no one, this was the first watch Mr. Van
Merrivine—"Stewie"—would be missed.

Pity, the way the man had struck his head, becoming
entangled in a length of rejected cabelle. Too bad his screams
were stifled by a clump of some squirming gray-green substance which had fallen into his open mouth, nostrils, and
eyes. Arran only hoped that Stewie and the fangmold had
enjoyed their last meal half as much as he had enjoyed serving
it.

Chapter XXI:
Flatsies and Rollerballers

As it is inclined to do whether one wills it or not, and for good or ill, time passed.

Another series of watches came and went, and another. Days, fleeing unmarked into the black depths of the changeless Deep, accumulated into weeks, likewise unmarked. These accumulated into months, and with each second he survived, Arran harbored fewer illusions, in particular about people.

Even a kindly sort like Krumm was too complacent—he did not appear intimidated even by the captain's authority— to attempt changing an unhappy vessel like *Gyrfalcon*. All things being compensated for in an uncaring universe, a disappointing awareness dawned upon the boy (where dawn is never seen) that Krumm made up for his kindness, wisdom, size, and greater strength by lacking, insofar as Arran could discern, any initiative or ambition beyond whatever had brought him to his present estate. The boy could imagine him asking himself what else he might aspire to, when already he possessed all he wished: his women, his commission, his ovens (an appreciative, albeit captive, market relied upon his bread and cakes and pies), and an audience for his tales. Arran believed Krumm rather fancied the life he led as half startrader, half explorer (and sometimes, Arran suspected, half brigand). The man even appeared grateful to those who had forced it upon him long ago.

While perhaps the first officer sympathized with Arran's plight, he, like all men, suffered limitations. He was far from omnipotent (Arran told himself in hope of avoiding final disillusionment) and could not be counted upon—*would* not be, perhaps—to do anything to ameliorate it. Krumm's plump, merry wives were even more sympathetic, and less able than their husband to do more than give Arran an encouraging word and an occasional sweet. Upon his own, lacking other choices in the matter, Arran discovered himself growing strong upon the bitter nourishment of adversity, surviving by expedient of learning to become more brutal than anybody else aboard.

At no time since stowing away had he caught a glimpse of the captain. He had no way of knowing it was not uncommon. Aloof invisibility was practiced by captains self-perceptive enough to understand that they possessed none of the rare power of personality which commands a willing and unquestioning obedience. In its absence, they preferred to let lieutenants hand their edicts down, as if issued from some ineffable but undeniable source.

From Krumm and the others, upon the other hand, Arran experienced guarded acceptance as one among crewbeings, self-initiated by his killing of Paddy and the suspicious circumstances (which deceived no one) of Jimbeau's death. In due course, Arran learned many useful skills from them. Unknown to the boy, the first officer suffered greater difficulty grappling with what had befallen Van Merrivine, whom he had regarded as fundamentally decent, and—more important—competent. His cruel fate discovered at last, nothing tangible had remained of "Stewie" save buttons from his uniform and a scattering of polished teeth. Being devoured alive by fangmold was an unusual, yet not unheard-of, manner of dying by accident aboard a starship. The first officer was never uncertain about the truth of the matter, but no way presented itself of proving that Van Merrivine's demise—in this respect the boy seemed to improve with practice—had been anything but the misadventure it resembled. Although he dispensed, in the captain's name, absolute authority aboard the carrack, and was not required to produce evidence in support of life-and-death decisions, Krumm was persuaded that, having consumed those who had ravaged him, the full, furious measure of Arran's vengeance had been exacted.

It had been their own blasted fault, Deep take their eyes and whatever else was left! While what they had done may have been customary for ten thousand years aboard ships and among sailors, it possessed nothing in common with ordinary, healthy horn. In the first officer's lengthy and disheartening experience, rape, gang-rape in particular, never did. They were by no means man-lovers, those three. He ought to know who, long before taking to wives, had wenched with them in many a starport brothel. For that matter, Krumm's thoughts digressed, his two best, bravest topmen *were* man-lovers; a more decent, upright, dedicated couple he never hoped to see. It had been a matter of power, nothing more. They had done it because they thought they could.

Well, they had been proven wrong. Arran's drive and intelligence were rare. Valuable. In absence of further action upon his own part, Krumm believed—which might, in actuality, make things worse—the boy represented no threat to *Gyrfalcon* or anyone aboard her. Thus, where a failing grade meant death or worse, without being aware of it, Arran was evaluated, his patent of scholarship extended, and soon began to command a modicum of respect from his tutors and coworkers.

Like each of the ship's boys, he was instructed in starship-handling, and to manage cargo and accounts, these constituting the essence of survival for the *Gyrfalcon,* the reason for her existence. A trifle too mundane to suit the average adventure-thirsty youth, they nonetheless interested Arran, justifying in this respect alone Krumm's growing partiality toward him. However the discipline which Arran came to love best (in this, Krumm forgave him, sharing the same preference), learned most about in consequence, and which, at this moment, occupied the better part of his mind, owing to a practice exercise he anticipated during the next watch, was weapons-operation.

The expression applied to the starship's kinergic projectibles, fifteen all told, and nothing else. Although an arsenal of small-arms was hoarded in the captain's quarters, none of the officers was about to encourage any pressed crewbeing to better himself in a facility with personal thrustibles until it was certain he would become one of their number.

Arran descended the ladderwell to the lowest level of the

vessel. Although he owed his attention to a different errand, as he prepared to perform it, he reviewed what he knew about the starship's weaponry. The first officer had certain expectations of him, after all. Over the course of the Thousand Years' War, the armaments of starsailing ships had passed through many generations of improvement. The first, Arran knew from his studies at home, had consisted of rockets laden with the atomic explosives humankind had carried from the dim mists of antiquity. However, like the pistol he had restored and used to gratifying effect upon Skye, atomic weapons were by now so obsolete they had been all but forgotten by practical-minded beings, thanks to the phenomenon of "fratricide," in which a flux of subatomic particles prevented a nearby chain reaction, which fortuitous capability was inherent in the second generation of shipboard defenses, particle beam weapons.

Arran reached the bottom of the well and broke his ruminations to open the hatch. Among his multitude of duties as the newest ship's boy, a task which both fascinated and revolted him, was a collection of chores which, at intervals, brought him into contact with *Gyrfalcon's* "cargo."

Under a mandate issued by a long-dead Hanoverian Ceo who purposed preventing isolation of—and ensuring adequate service to—the imperium-conglomerate's millions of colonial starports, spreighformers (excepting as disassembled cargo in transport to specific destinations) were forbidden aboard any Monopolitan vessel, truncating its potential range and duration and necessitating frequent stops for refitting and replenishment. As other ceos, of other imperiaconglomerate, came to appreciate the murchantilist wisdom of the prohibition, it was extended to all starships plying the galactic Deep. With spreighformers in use everywhere else, colonies and capitals required, sought, and fought over raw materials to feed the protean devices. Ores and other minerals constituted tradable cargo, for spreighformers could not fabricate elements. Rare or heretofore unheard-of items, for which no duplicating programs yet existed, were also valued. Exotic organics, too complex for economical synthesis, had been a speciality of Arran's ring-encircled Skye. One more commodity existed which, unsuited to multiplication in spreighformers, had become a staple of interstellar traffic: slaves.

Closing the hatch behind him, Arran dogged it shut. Where had his thoughts been? Yes: known of old with a sailor's familiarity as "peebies," particle beam weapons were employed, before invention of the §-field, aboard starships, and, capable of rendering atomics inoperable, to defend fortifications. With the advent of §-physics, the tactical and strategic usefulness of peebies was reduced to negligibility, owing to the nature of the inertia-canceling fields surrounding vessels. It must have been astounding, he thought, the first time it happened. Employed by ground installations against an inertialess marauder, peebies wafted her away, unharmed, like a dry leaf upon the wind. Worse, an inertialess starship attempting to employ peebies was whisked off under impulse of her own weapons. (It was an indication of Arran's growth and state of mind that he already calculated ways to make surprise use of this phenomenon in battle.) For a time, "tactics" had consisted of no more than waiting for an enemy to drop his shields in order to thrust—"shoot," the word was—hoping to beat him to the punch.

This time, Arran's nose distracted him. Whoever last had duty here had done a thorough job—of doing nothing! Noxious odors assailed him and he was hard put to control his stomach. Although the expression "crewbeing" circulated aboard every ship, and it was not unusual for captains to fill their complements with members of half a hundred sapient species, that of the *Gyrfalcon,* and every other vessel plying her trade, was human in its entirety, this, too, by edict of the Monopolity, promulgated for the best of reasons. It was her *cargo* that was alien.

Human slavery was by no means rare within a culture which otherwise considered itself civilized, mostly referred to by less discomfiting names—polite usage it was felt, constituting the one discernible difference between civilization and barbarism. *Gyrfalcon's* unwilling passengers, upon the other hand, were non-human captives, labeled slaves without a qualm (when they were not called livestock), and, as such, inheritors of indescribable misery, subject to eventual fates which no one, not even their self-styled proprietors, could predict with accuracy.

This watch it was Arran's task to provide what comfort was now and again afforded the unfortunate creatures pent upon the liftdeck and elsewhere. Arran had not been surprised to learn that the *Gyrfalcon* trafficked in little besides slavery. Her dark holds reeked with the stench of it, echoed with the terror and agony of its victims. Perhaps, after all, worse fates than death existed; worse fates, indeed, than many often held to be worse than death.

Slavery was one such. Somehow it made Arran feel filthier than the huddled, miserable beings he attempted to care for. Bizarre in manner and appearance though they were to the unsophisticated boy, their intelligence was undeniable. Upon this account he believed them worthy of a happier destiny. In many ways, he reflected during introspective moments of increasing rarity, he had been worse affected by exposure to the practice than by any of the other depravities he had witnessed, which had befallen him, or with which he—unwilling, at first—had become acquainted with to a point of terrible intimacy, his first day aboard the starship, or at any time afterward.

Each of *Gyrfalcon's* several levels was partitioned—with the same §-field-reinforced mesh the remainder of the ship was fabricated from—into wedge-shaped compartments extending from the mastfoot to the hull. Some of these afforded room for what inanimate stowage she carried, equipment, and supplies. A larger number housed crewbeings. The majority had been given over to her most profitable lading. Each wedge holding living cargo was separated from its neighbors by a double wall of mesh, forming a narrow corridor accessible from an annular walkspace circumferential to the ladderwell.

Into this space Arran now emerged, attempting for another few seconds to ignore the terrible noises, the unbearable odors, the hideous sights which, in essence, had brought him here. He opened a utility compartment and unrolled a length of hose. Intended to control fire, it was already fastened to a valve inside the compartment. He had only to make certain the nozzle was closed before he turned the wall-mounted handle, felt the hose stiffen with pressure, and, his thoughts defensively centered upon the next watch and the antici- pated drill, plodded outboard with it until he reached the hull.

Time had had its way with peebies, just as with atomic rockets. In due course §-field weapons were invented, and, by the time of Arran's tenure aboard the *Gyrfalcon,* all of the more ancient weaponry was centuries obsolete. More impor- tant, in view of what was to come, it had faded from human memory.

So efficient were §-fields (he detected an analogy to what he had learned of modern flesh and fabric from Old Henry's shocking experiment) they could protect the ship they rigidi- fied even from atomic explosion. It was ironic that §-physics could also initiate such explosions by squeezing fissionables in a collapsing field. This was generally known, but, save one application, regarded as a useless parlor-trick, albeit upon a spectacular scale. Crewbeings belowdecks believed that a "Doomsday" bomb constructed upon the principle was se- creted in the officers' quarters of every Hanoverian starship, and could, as a last resort, be set off in case of mutiny. Be this as it may, it had occurred to Arran's facile intelligence that such a device might make an effective secret weapon. The principle was forgotten or dismissed, offering those who remembered, and could arrive at a method of applying it, the advantage of surprise. In the majority of minds, only projectibles availed against starships. Arran had learned to take nothing for granted.

Within horribly crowded pens either side of him, Arran was recognized. The captives, alien as they seemed (some measure, he understood, of how alien he must seem to them), had come to see that, unlike other keepers, this one took no delight in cruelty. Those healthy enough moved forward against the press of their sicklier fellows to the mesh which limited their freedom, taking advantage of the service he was about to perform. Arran opened the nozzle, directing a blast of water into one of the pens. Characteristic of him—this, too, the pens' inhabitants appreciated—he aimed the poten- tially injurious torrent at a snubbing-post, presently unoccupied, reserved for the restraint of violent specimens. This kindly precaution broke the stream's force, allowing the captives to shower in its gentler reflection.

Two nonhuman races were represented upon this voyage. As a security measure, the idea being to reduce communication among them and any resistance it might engender, they had been divided and the much-different species alternated about the circumference of the deck. Arran was scornful. He had witnessed the creatures signing to one another without regard to species, and believed they had already worked out a rough pidgin among themselves.

In the pen to his left, facing the mast, resided the compact creatures whom the crew, somewhat redundantly, referred to as "rollerballers." Arran had no idea what it was proper to call them, nor where they came from. They, in all probability from a primitive civilization, were in no position to tell him, even had he possessed mastery of whatever they used for language. The new cargo steward's manifest, which Arran had perused in the course of his lessons, stated their system coordinates—meaningless to him, astrogational neophyte that he remained—their quantity at loading-time (they had already suffered an attrition exceeding forty percent, although they were still jammed together so that, had they been human beings and one among them fainted or died, he would not have been able to fall), and a taxonomical number.

This rate of attrition brought to mind a tale told by another of the ship's boys. During a long, stormy watch before the *Gyrfalcon's* arrival at Skye, with the first officer occupied shiphandling and the captain reputedly ailing, several slaves not rollerballers but the others, and only the cleanest, healthiest looking specimens—had been dragged out of a pen and slaughtered for food. Casting about for a precedent by which certain limits customarily imposed upon his authority might be exceeded, the captain had recalled a time during his own apprenticeship when some variety of insectile vermin were discovered nibbling at the inanimate cargo. The individual held responsible had refused the ordained punishment, eating the pests in place of the foodstuffs they had consumed, and was instead trussed up and the vermin inserted into various of his bodily orifices until he died. Of what, Arran was uncertain and the storyteller had not ventured an opinion.

By the captain's order, the culprits in the latter instance were punished not for murder, but for theft of ship's property, a more serious offense, by having their ears and noses cut off, loss of these being unlikely to affect their performance as laborers, and being compelled to watch as their flesh was pulped into the feed given the slaves. At that, Arran's informant had been bland, it might have been worse. The guilty parties might have lost certain other appendages of no use to ship or captain. It might have been their fellow crewbeings who wound up, knowingly or otherwise, consuming what they had been deprived of, rather than alien slaves.

The largest of these came no higher than the boy's waist. In form, he thought, it was as if someone had upholstered a three-legged stool in purple leather, having placed another like it, up-ended, atop the first. From between the padded, upthrust "legs" of the upper "stool" arose a fat, furry, golden worm-thing, boasting three huge, protruding eyes spaced at equal distances from one another. These disturbed Arran with their human appearance and their color, a penetrating and appealing blue. No additional sensory appendage nor, indeed, any other orifice or protuberance adorned the knobbish head (assuming it was what it appeared), nor was a mouth visible anywhere. Arran's watchmate had informed him that individual fibers of the golden fur were thought to be organs of smell or hearing. As he had learned to do with all other sailors' opinions, Arran had reserved judgment.

Uncounted measure-long transparent tendrils, half the diameter of Arran's smallest finger, arose about the base of the worm-part, as well as from underneath the three lower "legs." These were mobile but not strong, as he had learned by approaching—at his messmate's invitation, which proved to be an ugly practical joke—too close during his first watch assigned to this duty. Two or three tendrils had torn loose during his panic-stricken struggle to free himself, but the creature who had seized him (or caressed him, how could he tell?) had shown no sign of pain. In the end, Arran had concluded that the appendages were expendable, regenerating with wear or breakage. As for his messmate, Arran had broken one of his appendages—his nose—presumably less capable of regeneration and likely to heal crooked.

Grinning at the memory, Arran let his thoughts turn back to matters of consequence. In addition to nine projectibles upon the gundeck, the commanddeck boasted three vertical bow chasers of middling power, aimed parallel with her mast, the vessel's starsails tuned transparent to their energies. Here upon the liftdeck, three similar stern chasers were aimed aft against pursuers. Thus was *Gyrfalcon* defended about her perimeter, aft, and along her direction of travel. It cost something, from what the tachyon sails collected, to employ fifteen projectibles, for they were the most power-greedy mechanisms aboard. As with intersecting §-fields of two approaching vessels, their residual kinergics—a kind of recoil—imposed considerable strain upon the starship's fabric. A stout, new ship could thrust with every projectible at the same time (although this was seldom done), but older, weaker vessels might rattle themselves apart doing so.

As Arran washed the pen, taking care not to strike the aliens with the direct stream, he saw several who had assumed a different shape, retracted their inner bodies and rolled their outer legs until they resembled two-lobed balls a measure through. Before an uncordial parting, Arran's informant had claimed rollerballers came from a planet too hot, too cold, or bathed in too much radiation, to which they had evolved a natural barrier. They were valued because they could enter a dangerous facility—ancestral reactors, which new construction upon the capital world seemed always to be digging up—extend short-lived tendrils through seams in their armor, and perform tasks in an environment which would kill other sapients. Arran remained skeptical of such claims, yet they made sense. An unmistakable metallic sheen characterized their purple skins and a sharp odor of heated iron. Perhaps they absorbed shielding substances from their nutriment, depositing them in their circumference. He had been cautioned, by Mr. Krumm, not some ignorant gossip, never to ingest their feed, nor permit it to linger on his own skin.

The rollerballers' bite and touch were also rumored

poisonous. Other than a moment's terror, he had suffered no
ill effect from the latter. He was curious to know what they
would bite him with. They appeared to absorb the evil-
smelling mash he fed them through their tendrils and possessed no mouths to speak of. Or with. If they communicated,
it was by means of their tendrils, although he believed they
displayed emotion with their great, sad eyes; the texture of
their golden fur; and by the expedient—whenever they
seemed threatened or despondent, which (given their unhappy situation) was often—of rolling into the ball-shape which
gave them their name, and, with greater and greater frequency, of dying in this universe-rejecting posture.

Having done what he could, Arran directed his attention to
the right-hand pen. If rollerballers were strange and incomprehensible, their companions in misery, creatures the crew
dubbed "flatsies," might have appeared ridiculous in differing circumstances. Arran was uncertain, had he stumbled
across them upon their own world, that he would have
recognized them as people, although had they not been
intelligent beings, they would never have found themselves
imprisoned within the stifling holds of the *Gyrfalcon*. Neither
her officers nor crewbeings would stoop to hauling domesticated animals about the galaxy, a resort which they one and
all—without much logic, considering their principal
occupation—felt was beneath them. Intelligence being the
chief prerequisite to slavery, that institution was, Arran felt,
if not the ultimate depravity, then by all means the lowest,
most pitiable (and, to both parties alike, degrading) variety of
parasitism conceivable.

Perhaps the captain knew where flatsies came from. No one
else did, nor how many times this consignment had changed
hands. The manifest offered nothing more illuminating than
a repetitive string of N/A barquode symbols. Perhaps the
captain even knew what flatsies were good for, whether they
possessed some special aptitude as was alleged of
rollerballers. Possibly they had been captured upon a speculative basis, in hope they would sometime, somewhere, prove
to be of value.

Stretched full length upon the deckmesh, as they never
were unless ill or already dead, the average flatsy spanned half
again Arran's height, half a measure wide, and no more

than two siemmes' thickness. Both ends were rounded, one folded to support the creature's erect stance, the other sporting eyes at the height of Arran's own, but—unlike those of the rollerballers—without the faintest resemblance to anything human. Each seemed to consist of no more than a bright red spot a couple of siemmes in diameter with a bright red circle round it. Overall, the flatsies were a pale, milky white. Arran thought, sometimes, that he could see through them. Horizontal rows of short lines or grooves marched down their bodies like uncrossed tally marks. When clean and healthy, they gave off a neutral, not unpleasant smell, and flowed along the deck without effort, like garden snails, although they left no slimy track. They possessed no visible appendages and communicated, if that was what they did, by means of soft hooting and a low, complicated, inharmonious whistling which prickled the hair at the back of Arran's neck.

They, too, recognized Arran. Each time he arrived, they approached the partition to greet him, as if they understood that nothing within his power could alter their unfortunate circumstances—did they know he was helpless to alter his own?—yet appreciated his attentions nonetheless. He had never touched one of the things, and was never to know, until much later, how, in their own way, they had touched him. As far as the boy was concerned, he was finished with an onerous task and now at liberty to ascend to the gundeck, where, in his view, something interesting was about to happen.

General Quarters shrilled while Arran was in the ladderwell.

CHAPTER XXII:
THE JENDYNE CORSAIR

Bells rang, lights the color of blood flashed within the well as Arran dodged the hurtling forms of crewbeings hurrying to battle stations.

The alarm was deafening, voices of bell and siren stirring themselves into those of the crew scattering to take their places. By the time he emerged onto the gundeck, the drill he had looked forward to, thoughts of which had preoccupied him belowdecks, was transformed, by wayfarer's fortune, into a matter of survival.

"Belay that racket!" Beside a projectile with a huge "01" stenciled upon its curved back, Krumm was in command, his voice carrying above all others. Dressed in little besides worn trousers torn off at the knees—even with his belly overhanging their waist he cut an imposing figure—strapped to his muscle-corded forearms as if he were an Oplyte, he affected a pair of thrustibles heavy enough to have been taken from one of the giants, if such were possible. Someone behind him lunged for switches, silencing the shrill. Crewbeings ceased their top-of-the-lungs chatter to hear what he would tell them. Arran was at his appointed place, that of projecteur's helper and third alternate at the fifth projectile. Three deep about the ladderwell, where they would be out of the way unless needed as a desperate resort, dozens of untrained, nervous replacements stood by as a reserve.

Krumm spoke again. "Medears, here be little *Gyrfalcon* mindin' her own business in the black heart of the Deep. Now, as a reward for her virtue, she finds herself pursued by a corsair of the Jendyne Empery-Cirot!"

A buzz arose among the crew. Krumm permitted it. Had they not been thus occupied, they would have had too much to think upon. Arran knew a corsair carried the same number of yardtiers as a carrack, the same count of starsail, but of greater area, spaced further apart, upon a mast half again as long. Their enemy was a sleek, swift hunter-vessel commissioned by a rival imperium-conglomerate which, for centuries, had been at times inimical to the Monopolity—whenever the two were not at truce, allied against some third.

One thrustible glittering, Krumm raised an arm, motioning them to silence again. "Findin' ourselves unable to outhaul the Jenny killer, we're obliged t'trade broadsides with her in self-defense. We'll test her legs, then heave to with all rags aback an' deliver our surprise!" At this, someone a couple of stations from Arran started a cheer. He, like the murchanman whose fate they shared, was alone. The solitary cheer tapered off and seemed to die of embarrassment. "That sounded like a Navy man," Krumm snorted, "anxious t'be killed as t'be killin'. When you so hastily abandoned Ceo's bed and board, ye shoulda left such crap behind ye 'pon the pentagram!" Laughter followed all round, nervous, but hearty with relieved tension. "But he's right, messmates! We'll get through this, by hook or crook, t'lie an' swear we're heroes afterward! Somebody hand me a darthelm 'fore I hand 'em their head!" He had not given them time to cheer his words. A hiss of indrawn breath replaced the buzz of speculation which had not diminished altogether. All conjecture was done with. The battle for survival was about to begin.

The ship's fifteen projectibles did not resemble the personal weapons whose basic principle they shared. Each of the nine disposed at intervals about the gundeck, directed toward an oval "window" (differing from the rest of *Gyrfalcon's* fabric in that, woven in concentric ellipses, it was transparent to the energies of her weaponry), stood two measures tall and consisted of the axis itself—an enormous cone, its apex pointed outboard, capped at the back with a massive hemisphere—and its caliprette. This was a pair of trapezoidal slabs, thick as Arran's waist, among few artifacts aboard not mesh-constructed, between which the cone was trunnioned. Armored conductiles from a boss in the center of the hemisphere disappeared between the uprights into a run beneath the deck. Upon the outside of each caliprette-half, a chair and neckrest were bolted for the backward-facing projecteurs, along with a "glove box" from which a smaller conductile ran to the sighting helmet or darthelm, referred to with typical irreverance as the "head box." One of these contrivances was doffed by a projecteur at the 01 projectible and handed to Krumm. The first officer placed it over his head.

"There she be for a fact!" he exclaimed, glancing about helm-blinded and intent. "Hard astern an' comin' up as fast as every measure squared can carry her, stunsails in the bargain. Brace yourselves, for I believe—"

A titanic *thump!* lifted the deck beneath Arran's naked feet, tumbling the startled boy onto his back. Mesh imprinted a grid pattern into his flesh but did not break skin. The air about him darkened with raised dust. He coughed, staring openmouthed and empty-minded. The carrack groaned and shuddered as her §-field soaked up punishment inflicted upon them. Did she survive the ordeal, this energy would be flung back at the foe. The vessel slewed, or perhaps her inertia-canceling fields faltered, and steadied. From underfoot to overhead, the gundeck filled with curses. Arran climbed to his feet.

"Stand by your projectibles!" Krumm grinned like a skull, his big feet—he had stayed upon them—splayed over the deck, toes dug into the mesh. *"Numbers four, five, six! Look sharp, projecteurs, make each thrust count! They've the legs of us, and a stern chase is to their advantage!"* This time knowing what to expect, Arran braced himself at the caliprette awaiting the next thrust whether issued by carrack or corsair. He watched his projectible and its starboard operator, trying to anticipate the needs of machine and man, for the darthelmed projecteur was as blind to events within the murchanman as Krumm, and for the same reason. All upon the gundeck tensed.

Each projectible consisted of three subsystems for which projecteurs' helpers were responsible. At its heart, deep within the hemispheric shield, lay a bundle, larger than the boy's head, of four half-twisted coils, each wound at right angles to the others. Tachyonic currents flowing through the tortured microcontinuum they created were required by an insane geometry to do impossible things in impossible directions. They protested by emitting pseudoquanta of kinetic energy. The thruster core, a transparent, wrist-slender cylinder, ran through the coil bundle, down the center of the mechanism to its pointed tip. A single crystal of rare elements, it was here that energies extorted from the moebius coils—finding no other avenue of release within the interlapping fields—were collimated into a narrow beam.

Encircling the length of the core was the equivalent of a thrustible's designator. Similar in operating principle—in an earlier era, against a less-defended foe, it might have been an effective weapon itself—the age which had invented it, preferring the counterfeit profundity of acronyms, had dubbed it "DARTACEP": "Detection and Ranging through Tachyon Amplification by Coerced Emission of Pseudo-uanta." Now it was referred to as the "dartjacket" which, through the darthelm, gave the projecteur eyes outside the ship.

The final component, an internal, torroidal cryopacket, helped make up, after the fact, for inefficiencies arising in the alteration of scale from thrustible to projectible. Without it, residual "recoil," transmuted into heat, would soon have converted the system into shimmering slag. It was the most vital—and most failure-prone—of the subsystems.

Arran's task was to replace failed components, including the projecteur himself if need be. In the boy's hands, damp and trembling with what he hoped was anticipation rather than terror, he clutched a sheaf of spare conductiles, fabricated below specification in order to serve as fuses, ready to tear old ones loose and socket new ones in. Bins within reach about him contained half a dozen crystalline thruster cores, parts for the cryopacket, replacement modules for the dartjacket, and one spare precious coil assembly.

Oily sweat streaming the visible portion of his face, Krumm shouted another warning. *Gyrfalcon* staggered again. As she yawed, he bellowed *"Thrust!"* Projectiles four, five, and six discharged as they bore, slewing within their caliprettes to prolong engagement with the enemy. Valiant helpers hopped back and forth, trying to stand close by their projecteurs and at the same time leap out of the way of the heavy, quick-moving machinery.

"And thrust again!" The noise was such that the ears disbelieved it, a throbbing echo of the energies they hurled forth as the carrack's projectibles discharged, the residuum more felt than heard, experienced in each cell of the body as a kind of anguish fundamental, as if the stuff of space itself were being stretched toward some catastrophic limit, and at any moment might be torn asunder. To Arran, his hair soaked with perspiration running into eyes already watering and half-blind with smoke and dust, the sensation was—

"Belay thrusting!" The vessel straightened, taking the full-powered projectibles upon her gundeck out of play, an unfortunate necessity brought about by equally necessary ship-design. It was a situation often commented upon, but about which, it seemed, nothing could be done save the obvious ploy Krumm had described. Elsewhere, the higher, less painful thrumming of *Gyrfalcon*'s stern chasers could be sensed through her fabric like the prickling, Arran thought, of restored circulation in a limb.

"Stand by your projectibles, three, four, five!" To Arran this meant the ship had begun rolling, perhaps to spell some of her weapons or—perish the thought—distribute whatever damage the corsair was inflicting. By setting her fore-and-aft rigged staysails astagger, she could be induced to spiral about the axis of her mast. Even through her §-field damping, the boy could feel a slight pull, away from the deck beneath him, outboard toward the hull.

He braced himself again, watching his projectile. A thin, bluish wisp issued from the boss upon the hemisphere which, in part, acted as a heat sink. This phenomenon was normal, it was the conductiles he concerned himself with. At present, in his estimation, they showed scant sign of—

The carrack stumbled, this time without warning. Alarms clanged. Men and metalloid fabric shrieked as an enormous section of the hull bulged inward a full measure, glowing with kinetic energy it could not shed. For the first time in his life, Arran smelt the odor of burning human flesh. A crewwoman at the second projectile had ventured too close to the hull. Arms flung wide, she screamed and staggered backward to lie smoking upon the deck, jerking in pain-induced convulsions, branded bone-deep with the pattern of the mesh. She was far from the only individual injured thus. Arran saw many forms writhing upon the deck, lifeblood streaming into the thirsty mesh to be filtered and recirculated, he supposed, as drinking water. Horrified, he could not tear his eyes away. It seemed impossible, yet the dinted hull-section, visible to his adrenaline-tunneled vision dulled by stages in color and brightness, pulled back into shape by inforged memory and powerful hull-fields. *"Thrust three, four, five!"* Krumm bellowed. *"Stand by two, three, and four!"*

Siemmes from Arran's unprotected face, something popped and sizzled. Compulsion broken, he watched one of the flexible conductiles at the hemispheric breech of his projectible flare into pyrotechnic life and burn through its shielding. Not stopping to think, he whipped at the conductile with the spares in his hand, snapped it from the boss, bent and jerked it from its socket in the caliprette, and replaced it. Above him, something heavy or fast-traveling struck the hemisphere a blow he felt through the deck, showering his back with searing fragments.

Jumping up, he whistled at the glittering powder splashed upon the hemisphere. Peering into smoke which, reeking with excrement and smoldering pungency, now filled the deck, he calculated that the hot debris had been hurled across a long chord from the eighth projectible, whose thrusting he had not heard ordered. All of the machine's conductiles had volatilized upon the first attempted thrust, this minor and foreseeable disaster being far from the worst. The heavy boss now flapped from stop to stop upon its thick, invisible hinge like the storm-ravaged door of a flimsy building. Behind it, the thruster core had failed, as they were inclined to do, unpredictably obedient to the complex laws of §-probability, having upon this occasion shivered into useless powder, dangerous because it occupied hundreds of times the volume of the solid core, exploding through the rear of the weapon killing both helpers, one of their projecteurs, and coming close to settling Arran's prospects. His own projecteur was dead, jeweled with a lethal and prismatic encrustation.

At the same moment, operators at the next projectible screamed and jittered, spewing malodorous fluids from every orifice as their sphincters failed. A microfracture in the core of their weapon had allowed a fraction of its energies to seep into the DARTACEP circuitry. As helpers struggled to free them, a pair of dull explosions inside their helms preceded a gush about their shoulders of superheated blood, boiling spinal liquid, and pureed brains. Arran vomited into the deckmesh until he was emptied and aching.

The second alternate projecteur, the helper at the other side of Arran's projectible, stepped round the caliprette. Sharing the boy's grim silence, she assisted him in pulling the dead projecteur's smoking corpse from its place, took up his scorched but functional darthelm, and strapped herself in where, seconds earlier, her fellow crewbeing had been roasted alive. As the remaining projecteur's helper, it was up to Arran, now, to do the work of two. About him, the ship began to flail and vibrate like a tortured thing. The weakening fabric of the *Gyrfalcon,* bludgeoned again and again with increasing accuracy and effect by the swiftly approaching Jendyne foe, shrieked a funeral dirge to the fallen among her crewbeings. She did not keen without accompaniment. Rising to the overhead, the moaning of Arran's burned and mutilated comrades returned the compliment to the dying vessel.

"Stand by all projectibles!" Krumm bellowed. *"Thrust the rapespawn as y'bear!"*

Even so, Arran felt lucky, given the grisly alternatives represented by his wounded and dying messmates. At the same time, he was astonished, realizing that he was no longer frightened. Perhaps—his thoughts were analytical and cold —because he had been willing to consider death, since his first hour aboard the *Gyrfalcon,* if not desirable in itself, then a reasonable alternative to life as it had become; what remained for him to be afraid of now? Incredibly, as had been the case while caring for the slaves below, his thoughts turned again to his lessons.

Early §-fields being less than perfect (Krumm was unaware he repeated Lia's teaching), lasers served following peebies until §-fields improved. Krumm held that their efficacy had always been exaggerated. Materials ancient when mankind leapt to the stars reflected or absorbed them, sacrificing themselves for the sake of whatever they protected. However, in all but the most moribund of cultures, when means fail, others await. The thrustible had for some time constituted the last word in personal weaponry. Now larger "projectiles" arose, suffering none of the limits of atomics, peebies, or lasers, working as they did upon a subtler level of reality. Projectiles were expensive and unreliable scaled to vessel-size. They required a deal of training and their appetite for power was voracious. Thus a principal mode of ship-to-ship combat even now consisted of maneuvering "to windward" of an enemy, robbing her of headway, and putting armed parties aboard.

It was this, more than the ceaseless battering, which experienced officers and crewbeings feared. According to a saying more ancient than starsailing, a stern chase is a long chase. Yet the Jendyne predator's steady reach upon her Hanoverian prey was inexorable, each of the latter's counter-moves proving futile. Despite armament and power sufficient to most contingencies, the carrack, klomme by bitter-fought klomme, had begun to fail those aboard her. A moment had arrived for the most desperate, unprecedented measure to be afforded serious consideration. Arran discovered himself deep in furious concentration upon all he had learned aboard the murchan vessel, everything Old Henry and Mistress Lia had ever taught him. Something nagged at the edge of his consciousness, something from his lessons which might be of use. Idea after idea surfaced in his inventive mind, only to be rejected.

What in Ceo's name was it? Boarding parties fit in some-where, he was certain. Intersecting §-fields, as well. Parties could not board until fields coalesced. Something else . . . something Mr. Krumm had shouted only minutes—Deep take him, it had been hours before—about "all her rags aback." What was it about parlor tricks, the possibility of initiating explosions by squeezing fissionables within a shrinking §-field? Arran was certain whatever idea was both-ering him was something promising and important, but, in all this noise and smoke, steeped in the odor of death and dying, he could not quite fit it all together.

The first officer tore his darthelm off and cast it aside, bringing the small fingers of both hands to his lips. Arran thought his eardrums might burst with the shrillness of Krumm's whistle. *"Belay thrusting! All hands stand to! Stow*

that noise and listen! Captain's belowdecks!" It was as if even
the pursuing corsair heard and obeyed. Silence settled over
the gundeck. Krumm had scarcely finished speaking when the
moan came of a hatch-dog, followed by the scream of
battle-stressed hinges. A stocky, cloak-swathed figure
emerged from the oval ladderwell entrance, straightened,
acknowledged the first officer's salute—Krumm's head
bowed until his chin touched his chest, both wrists out-
stretched, palms upward—and stepped onto the mesh.
Straining behind him, a pair of sinewy, sweating crewmen
dragged a metal-bound chest from the ladderwell and set it
upon the deck with a thud.

Since first coming aboard the *Gyrfalcon,* Arran had dealt—
in ways which would have astonished his family and teachers
—only with her first, second, and third officers, Krumm, Van
Merrivine, and Jimbeau. Neither he nor any other crewbeing
he knew had even glimpsed whoever commanded the vessel.
Thus, until now, they had been spared a singularly impressive
spectacle, after its own manner more alien in character than
any nonhuman aboard.

Master-murchan Ballygrant Bowmore, owner-in-command
of the *Gyrfalcon,* had seen as much of the known galaxy as
could be experienced firsthand in any one lifetime. Yet his
travels, wide adventure, and even greater wealth, had not
been without their price. One of the man's eyelids was
stitched shut over an empty socket, whence a deep-furrowed
scar curved along one dark cheek toward a pierced, ring-
bearing ear. The wound must have been terrible, for it was
not beyond the power of medicine to replace an eye, given
sufficient resources.

The other ear was missing altogether. Given other of his
features, this went almost unnoticed. His long gray hair hung
in more than a dozen stiff braids, stopped at the ends with
bands of polished metal. Each served as a setting for a row of
colored stones which, even in this age of spreighformers,
might be considered priceless for their brilliance and unpro-
grammed rarity. They swung, amidst their glittering companions, about his scarred and swarthy face, from time to time
alighting upon his shoulders like iridescent insects. His nose
had been broken so many times and so thoroughly that it now
spread twice as wide upon his cheeks—pocked with the

weather and disease of a hundred worlds—as it had in his youth. It, too, was pierced, through sidewall and septum, where a pair of baubles made it more grotesque. Beneath it, a moustache drooped from the corners of his full-fleshed, cruel mouth. Beneath his lower lip, a triangle of beardlet had been spared the raser.

Like Krumm, the captain wore a thrustible upon each arm, his being lighter of construction and more embellished. Their wristbands were jeweled bracelets, the hands beneath them much adorned with heavy rings. Unlike his near-naked first officer, he wore a billowing, shiny-surfaced blouse fastened with elaborate studs, ruffled at the throat as at the cuffs, the sleeves being rolled up to facilitate the use of thrustibles. His loose-fitting trousers ended at a pair of kneeboots, fashioned from the hide of some exotic animal. Over all, he had draped a deck-length, voluminous cloak of heavy texture, tailored with a hem and high collar of some long-haired, spotted fur.

"Get that trash cleared away!" Speaking to Krumm, he pointed a weapon-heavy hand at the ravaged bodies at the eighth and ninth projectibles. His voice was high, nasal, with a rasping edge that carried through the din. "I want replacement crews an' those machines returned to action in two minutes, or, by the last fifty ceos, I'll figurehead every officer 'pon the gundeck!"

Despite his outlandish appearance, Arran knew at once that this was not a man to laugh at. Bowmore was a man to fear.

Chapter XXIII:
The Night-Black Deep

The youngest projecteur's helper was not the only individual considering desperate, unprecedented measures.

Beneath their feet and everywhere round them, crewbeings felt the fabric of the vessel shudder with another

Jendyne volley. Upon the gundeck, the stench of burnt, sundered bodies was intolerable. Like his youngest projecteur's helper, his first officer, and everyone else aboard, Bowmore worried about his starship and the corsair pursuing her. That his worries differed in their particulars from those of the common crew was something he kept to himself, although he suspected Krumm was aware of his thoughts.

As *Gyrfalcon*'s stern-chasers howled their futility below, the tips of Bowmore's ring-laden fingers strayed for an instant over an unusual weight and thickness concealed in the double lining of his cloak. It was not often, he thought, peering about through blood-tanged smoke, that a man carried all his hopes and fears in a single pocket. Violating every advertised convention—a cynical usage in currency upon the capital worlds these days—he had in recent weeks, and at considerable expense, become the holder of letters of marque from the Ceos of *both* the Jendyne Empery-Cirot and the Monopolity of Hanover, granting him the privilege of despoiling vessels of that imperium-conglomerate over which, respectively, they did *not* rule.

A trickle of sweat ran down his neck into the elaborate collar of his blouse. Understandably, neither Ceo (nor, more to the point, certain among their deputies with whom he had done business) was informed in every detail of this double-ended arrangement. To his regret, he had not yet found time or opportunity to exercise the privilege. The *Gyrfalcon* was too frail a reed in which to go aplundering, and he had, to his annoyance, become diverted to serve the purpose of one who had discovered his secret and found means of exploiting it before a better ship and crewbeings could be acquired.

Above the racket of thrust and counterthrust, he could hear the burble of someone, likely one among the wounded, sobbing. It reflected his own mood. If he were captured and the documents discovered in his possession (having sacrificed so much to keep them, he could not, despite the dictates of prudence, bring himself to dispose of them), he would be punishable by each side as brigand and traitor. Unschooled as he may have been in any relevant precedent, he knew the character of both polities. Every diplomatic nicety would be exercised in his behalf to assure that he received a measure of retribution from each and that his death would be the last, least, and, in the end (to him), most welcome item upon the bill of reckoning.

In desperation, he had come below, into the savage, cloying death-stink of the gundeck (as he had never before ventured to do) and commanded Krumm to gather all hands about him. He had chosen them, in part, because the main-deck crew and those aloft were needed to purchase the extra hour his plan required and must neither be distracted nor diminished in number. Yet it was the presence, and the presumed understanding, of the giant first officer which, in the end, had decided him upon this course. Purposing to preserve their lives, that of the carrack which bore them, and, of course, his own neck, Captain Bowmore announced something of a tactical innovation. Their contribution, he informed the gundeck crew, would be a volunteer to execute it.

"A volunteer, sir?" Bowmore bent to hear better and came close to being knocked over by a sudden leap of the vessel. The rhetorical question had been asked by the first officer, who reached out a hand to steady his superior.

"A bloody pigeon, he means!" Krumm scowled through the thickening gloom. Who had yelled that before the captain could reply? He could not find the culprit. Arran, nursing a tactical innovation of his own, drifted as far toward the officers as the bounds of his station would permit, the better to see and hear. He was far from alone in this. With the gundeck projectibles out of play, a circle was growing about Krumm and the captain. As a newly-fledged ship's boy, now a blooded projecteur's helper, it was unquestionable that he had, with the first officer's assistance, made of himself much more than the lowliest crewmember he had begun as. Still—

"A pigeon save a falcon?" Someone at the front was encouraged by the previous insubordination committed without punishment. Bowmore, however, raised an arm. A crack sounded as §-wavefront met undefended flesh. The speaker fell to the mesh. A long silence followed. Someone behind Arran nudged him in the ribs. "No pigeon, then. More likely a chick—"

The voice broke off as its owner, too, slumped to the deck, alive (likely to his regret) and vomiting as he held both hands over his genitals. Arran rubbed the back of his fist and continued thinking. He had nothing to say about his own fate. Some among the crew (and elsewhere, in likely a majority of so-called sapient life) welcomed relief from responsibility for themselves or anything else. To a boy educated otherwise, it was the least tolerable feature of life aboard the *Gyrfalcon*. He discovered now, without surprise, that he was willing to do anything to alter his circumstances.

Among the crew about the smoky, stench-filled gundeck, undiscouraged by the lesson in deportment just given, considerable muttering arose over the captain's announcement, regarding—in short sentences and shorter words—the inadvisability of volunteering for anything. Possessing, as an oppressed class will, a nice judgment in such things, they deduced that the captain, in his hour of need, was (within limits just established) obliged to tolerate it. Proving them correct, he spoke again, more for their benefit than that of the man he ostensibly addressed. "Aye, Mr. Krumm, a volunteer, an' a handsomely rewarded one." Bowmore turned, looking as many crewbeings in the eye as he could. "He will, if a pressed man, provided he succeeds in this here undertakin', find his liberty restored to him, along with a document, issued under my authority as reserve officer of the imperium-conglomerate, grantin' him perpetual immunity from future conscription."

"Until next time!" Pressing the limits, someone had shouted from across the gundeck. Krumm scowled in that direction as the captain plowed on, to all appearances unperturbed. "He may remain onboard as a free crewbeing, perhaps trainin' as an officer, or be delivered dirtside at our next destination."

Muttering about the pair continued unabated. *"Prong everyfing as moves, swab everyfing as don't, an' nivver volunteer!"*

Bowmore cleared his throat. "In either event, there'll be other rewards. Me personal profit from this voyage, 'pon the order of two hundred thousand clavises. A not inconsiderable sum, I'm sure you'll agree? Also—"

A delighted buzz replaced the muttering, rising so rapidly

it became difficult to think, let alone hear or be heard. *"I still says nivver volunteer!"*

"Pipe down, you barrel-scrapings!" The first officer, although he most likely agreed with the advice, sounded furious. *"By the Core, I'll stripe the next man as speaks without leave!"* Silence fell like a weight. It was unusual for Krumm to threaten in so grim and serious a manner. When punishment was warranted, he struck without preliminaries. Now, he cleared his own throat. "You were sayin', sir?"

"Thank you, Mr. Krumm. I was about t'say, should our volunteer be male—female, for that matter; in the end what difference does it make?—and of appreciative inclination, I offer additional inducement, a rather old-fashioned one, the person of me beloved daughter." Reaching to his collar, Bowmore extracted from within the many overlapping frills a finely-wrought chain he wore about his neck, upon which depended a small, deep-graven, and bejeweled cylinder of less than a siemme's diameter and eight or nine siemmes' length. Turning the free end upward, he made manipulations with his fingers and an image sprang into the air above it, the miniature moving figure of a lovely girl. Arran stumbled forward.

It was an unpretentious remembrance. She stood upon a polished inlaid floor, a shaft of yellow sunlight falling upon her hair and shoulders from a pair of tall windows behind her. It was possible, he thought, that she had not known her image was being taken. In one small hand she held a fold of her voluminous velvet skirt. Her other—her eyes were half closed, lips half parted—made gentle motions to the beat of unheard music. A floor-to-ceiling mirror set between the windows conveyed another view of her as she turned, with an unhurried, flowing motion, upon her tiny feet, rising to her toes and down again, coming round at last to face the unseen eye before her image began fading, only to repeat itself.

The device in the captain's hand, Arran realized, was a rare, expensive autothille, something he had heard of and never seen, a self-playing record requiring no reader to release stored information. The image dancing before his face gave him pause. At first glance he had believed it—although he did not know how it could be so—that of his tutor. The girl shared something of Mistress Lia's coloring. Her hair, arranged after what he knew to be the current Hanoverian fashion, was the same brown-auburn. To the extent he could tell, from the minuscule full-length portrait, she was even freckled in a similar manner.

Upon closer examination, there were differences. She was younger, somewhat more delicate of face and form. Even this vignette conveyed a repose that touched the boy in places, buried within him, which, for the sake of survival, he had forgotten existed. A portion of his mind which, from habit longer than his servitude aboard the *Gyrfalcon,* stood apart, offering wry commentary, wondered how such a creature could be daughter to the vile Captain Bowmore. A portion of his heart which, despite everything, had never grown cynical, told him he had found the woman he might love for all his life. Something else, something he had seldom heard from before, stirred below his navel, sizzled through his blood, and gave his body an odd, strained feeling.

"Here, lad," grinned the captain, "keep it, if y'like." He removed the autothille and its chain from his own neck and placed it about Arran's.

"And what small task, sir . . ." It was one of the projecteurs who asked, a tall, clean, personable man with an educated accent, darthelm tucked beneath his arm. ". . . might a man perform to acquire all of this largesse?"

"Ah," replied the captain, "Mister . . ."

"Sarles," Krumm supplied, "first projectible."

"Mr. Sarles, the answer lies within yon chest." For the first time, Bowmore acknowledged the coffer he had caused two strong men to bring from his cabin. It sat upon the mesh, not quite producing a depression, its bearers standing guard beside it. Whatever tragedies and losses had befallen a child innocent and cheerful by inheritance, Arran's intellectual capacity was undiminished. Without being told, he knew what was inside the chest, for he had learned the lesson of the walther well and had been determined to apply it again if given a chance. Such a weapon as the captain now offered him, or anyone who volunteered, would be useless against a starship's protective §-envelope. However, when the fields merged—if, say, the *Gyrfalcon* hove to, pretending to surrender—such a device, releasing its fury inside the Jendyne's §-field would, at the least, kill every member of her crew and leave the vessel derelict. Never expecting half of what had been promised, and against the urging of comrades, Arran stepped forward.

The fact was that Bowmore's tactic had, until this moment, depended more upon what he could induce a volunteer to do than feasibility. The master-murchan was delighted to discover this ship's boy (in increasing optimism, he failed to catch the lad's surname, but he seemed familiar) had conceived the all-important final details. He would, as Bowmore suggested, don one of the carrack's half-dozen worksuits, a seldom-employed alternative to boats which attended to repairs that could be carried out traversing the Deep. He had refused, in the beginning, to strap onto his arm a thrustible Krumm offered, insisting he was not familiar enough with its operation to make good use of it, nor, he avowed, justify the loss to its owner. Krumm pressed until the boy conceded that one or more among the members of the Jendyne's crew might be quick-witted enough to ruin the plan, or spoil his escape.

In any case, the boy would venture overboard in a manner contrived between him and the first officer and—this was the boy's part of the plan—drift at the end of a cabelle past the pursuing vessel. The captain's contribution was that half-legendary weapon of last resort which caused a §-field to shrink about a core of heavy metal, becoming a small (and in ship-to-ship combat, he hoped unexpected) atomic explosive. *Gyrfalcon* would be prepared to make her getaway, separating fields from the Jendyne before the explosion. The carrack's thrustibles would, if necessary, accomplish the rest of the bloody job. Afterward, the boy would be picked up by lubberlift.

An hour's preparation passed like seconds. Alone save for the metal-bound chest, set with excessive caution a measure away, Arran rode the mastlift, where he had first seen Krumm holding forth, aloft into the yardtiers. The worst (he recognized the thought as irrelevant if not irrational) was not knowing what to do with his hands. The ride into the foreyards was long enough; circumstances made it seem longer. For the endless while it lasted, he attempted, without success, to affect casual demeanor, leaning, despite its inconvenient height, against the encircling rail. His arms—folded across his chest, hanging with fingers interlaced before him, bracing him from either side with hands spread upon the railtop—would not assume a natural position. He felt the autothille upon its chain where the suit pressed and wished he had kept it out to look at, or never accepted it to begin with. The awkward armor was filled with someone else's sweaty odor. Donning and adjusting it had offered something useful-appearing to do, but there were limits to how long that lasted. Now the lift carried him past each of the yards and stays, the curious eye of every topman inspecting him, wondering at his courage or his sanity. It was not a feeling he cared for.

He reached the limit of the lift's travel and must debark onto the yard. Little as he had enjoyed the ride, he looked forward to a climb aloft less, encumbered by a suit he was unaccustomed to, carrying the contents of the chest. Fortunately, owing to the plan he, Krumm, and Bowmore had devised, he did not have far to climb. The rest of his journey was not, as it might have been, horizontal, half a klomme outboard along the dorsal foreyard to stunsail booms extended in a desperate, futile attempt to provide *Gyrfalcon* with more legs than her pursuer. Swaying as they were in the currents of the Deep, swinging with her evasive maneuvers, jumping with each thrust, he would not have relished venturing onto them, despite what he was about to do instead.

He required use of bitts and cabelles at the inboard end of the foreyard, and leverage obtained from the distance between the point he now occupied and the outboard end of the dorsal mainyards far below. A staysail cabelle, stretching down and outward, was stripped of its expanse of sailmesh. The topmen who had helped him rig it and carry the chest this far retreated, possessing exaggerated notions of his weapon's deadliness at rest.

Arran unlatched four spring-loaded hasps—through his helmet he heard alarms ping at the intrusion—and opened the chest. A louder alarm within his helmet told him he was bathed in low-level radiation. Inside, as he had been told he would, he found, nested in rich quilting, another coffer, cubical in shape, thirty siemmes upon a side. No provision existed for opening this one; when time arrived, it would open itself. Judging from the condition of the liner, it had rested without attention some years longer, perhaps decades, than he had lived. He wondered whether it still worked. Stuffed beside it, a set of coveralls had been cut and sewn across the waist. He lifted the device, sealed it within this makeshift bag, and tied the arms about his neck so that it hung before his chest. Cords stitched in by whichever Mrs. Krumm had done the work allowed him to attach it about his waist.

Seizing a turnbuckle, he unfastened the cabelle and held it in his hands, feeling the impatient tug of its weight. He awaited a luff of starsail about him which would signal Krumm's part in the undertaking. *Gyrfalcon* would stop accelerating, allowing the corsair to overtake her. Before her master could help it (likely he would welcome it), the §-fields of both ships would merge. Before boarding parties might launch themselves across the bridge they had been provided, Arran would act.

He felt a mighty shudder through the mast which all but cost him footing and knew it for what it was, the vessel's protest at being taken aback. Not waiting to observe the starsails, he reached into his makeshift pack, flipped a cover, tipped a toggle beneath it, firmed his hold upon the turnbuckle, and leapt. For a timeless moment nothing happened, as if he were suspended above the foreyard and would stay there forever. Then, stomach complaining of being left behind, he descended in a swoop. The weight of cabelle and his burden carried him aft at a sickening rate. Starsails and spars streaked by in an undistinguished blur, punctuated by a staring eye or gaping mouth. Maintier, mizzentier, and deck rocketed toward him. The cabelle carried him outward—he was reminded of the path Jimbeau had followed, which had given him this idea—until, at a point he failed to notice, he crossed the line, no longer lethal, which marked the margin of the *Gyrfalcon's* field. Inertially, she was one with the enemy corsair, among whose mainyards he now found himself.

Likewise, among her defenders. Unlike those of the *Gyrfalcon,* these crewbeings—literal usage being necessary, given the inhuman horrors swarming her decks and yards—were trusted with personal weapons. Having achieved (as they believed) the §-field coalescence they desired, they were occupied with preparations for boarding. Had more of them observed Arran alighting halfway along the corsair's mainyard, he would have died in an instant, battered to jelly within his suit by a hundred thrustibles.

Something desperate in the boy's temperament worked now to his advantage. His footing, as he ran along the yard toward the mast, was confident. Nor did he miss a step when a being which seemed to consist of nothing but sinuous arms rose before him wielding an oddly shaped thrustible. Arran lay his own designator upon its center of mass and thumbed its life away. It splayed its limbs and died without falling, draped over the yard like laundry, so that he was obliged to step over its steaming bulk and continue inboard. His second killing was even easier. A glint upon a nearby staycabelle, caught by the corner of his eye, led him to aim and thrust without thought. The starsailor, human, screamed through the whole long fall to the deck.

By then it was too late for anyone who noticed to stop the intruder. He had armed the device lest he should die before planting it. Removing it from its sack, he held it against the mast, leaning with his full weight, and pushed a button. A tingling jolt like that produced in the hand by striking an anvil with a hammer told him it could no more be torn away now than it might be taken and tossed overboard by mutineers. As he turned to escape, a limbless entity slithered down a cabelle before him, attempting to bring a thrustible to bear. Both of their first thrusts missed, as well as their second, the range being closer than that at which thrusting is habitually practiced. "Nose to nose" would have described it, had the crewthing possessed such an organ. Arran aimed with his third thrust at the cabelle supporting it. This parted, carrying the climber to its death upon the mesh.

It had no sooner hit than he was forced to duck as a bolt dashed against the mast. Many thrusts were being aimed at him, although he was hidden by folds of starsail which, like those of the *Gyrfalcon,* were deprived of rigidity. He seized a turnbuckle identical to that he had begun with, wrenched it free, and swung outboard. The carrack had squared herself away, refilled her starsails, and departed from under the Jendyne lee. As agreed, he aimed himself at that portion of the double §-field which, as the vessels parted, grew more attenuated, trusting a suit constructed for such activity to protect him as he crossed the diluted margin. It had been Krumm's opinion that nothing could preserve his life if he crossed a full-strength boundary.

As he drifted further from his victim, the bomb exploded, contained, ironically, by her §-field, bathing all aboard in lethal radiation, and, as certain mechanisms were destroyed, exposing survivors to the Deep where they would die by suffocation, freezing, or decompression. The corsair herself remained in one piece, thanks to fields which, even as they failed, permeated her substance. He had succeeded. All that was left, before he claimed his reward, was to await the lubberlift, swinging at the end of its long tether.

Someone shouted, *"She blows!"* Bowmore required no darthelmed lookout to tell him his enemy was dead. He was wearing such a helmet, himself.

"Mr. Krumm, my compliments to all for a valiant fight. The gundeck may stand down." He had by this time recognized the child who had saved his ship, his cargo, and his life, from a thille once shown him, as the fugitive son of a disgraced Drector-Hereditary against whom, at Tarbert Morven's blackmailing insistence, he had offered perjurous testimony upon a moonringed world.

"Thankee, sir. Projecteurs, square away your weapons! Helpers, form squads for repairs! Idlers to another deck! Deploy the lubberlift—time t'look for our brave lad out there!"

Bowmore chuckled. Always the conscientious Krumm. What would he do, what would they all do, without him? He removed the darthelm and looked round. Krumm, the captain realized, would have to be handled with care. He was at heart a peasant, more like the crewbeings than the elite commanding them, while he—the captain—had never intended keeping any promises, whoever volunteered. It would not do to let any among them think to elevate themselves by a foolhardy act. Better they believe, as most already did, that no officer's word was to be trusted. He needed that two hundred thousand himself. And, to his knowledge, he had never had a daughter.

"Mr. Krumm, belay that last. Do not deploy the lubberlift." To settle past accounts and impose new debt upon Morven which might someday prove profitable, he would leave the boy to the same death as whoever among the corsair's crew had survived the blast. "Get us under weigh," he ordered, "with all deliberate speed."

PART FOUR: THE BLACK USURPER
YEARDAY 192, 3010 A.D.
DECIMUS 14, 1568 OLDSKYAN
NOVVE 33, 510 HANOVERIAN

"OH NO, OH NO," CRIED HENRY MARTYN,
"MY HOMEWORLD YOU NEVER SHALL HOLD,
FOR THOUGH I'VE TURNED SHIP-ROBBER OUT IN THE DEEP,
  IN THE DEEP,
  IN THE DEEP,
I SHALL TAKE BACK WHAT WAS ONCE MINE OF OLD."

CHAPTER XXIV:
THE AMBUSCADE

The new road, the guerilla commander thought, was like a long, open wound in the flesh of the planet.

Lying hidden with several dozen of his fighting comrades upon the grassy slope of a forested hillside, half a klomme distant from the furrow of fresh earth and upturned boulders—a few hundred measures above the place they knew the Monopolitan supply column must soon pass—he contemplated changes which the past several months had inflicted upon his world. They were not good changes. In his experience, changes of any kind seldom were.

There had been a day when such a project as this would have been contemplated a klomme—perhaps only a measure —at a time, laid where it would be least conspicuous, where it would least damage the natural landscape, leveled and replanted edge-to-edge by hundreds of careful retainers. No more. This hateful gash ran true as the terrain permitted from a series of new pentagrams lying east and west of the old facility to a grim fortification which the Black Usurper had caused to be constructed in the foothills, just north of the mountains, for the purpose of controlling access between the starport and the rolling plains below.

It had not worked. Rather, its principal effect had been to the Black Usurper's detriment, supplying his enemies, rather than his establishment: a low cluster of gray, wall-rimmed cubes moulded not from ancient, honorable graniplastic which this world's first settlers had built with, nor woven from the glowing §-reinforced mesh which was preferred by thirty-first-century Hanoverians, but slurped in a rude process out of some grainy liquid stone which hardened in a few hours between plastic forms over metal rods, and which, if damaged, could be repaired with great speed in the same haphazard manner.

About him, where he lay concealed, soil, leaves, and grass were slick with dew which had not burned off this morning and would not before nightfall. Moisture darkened his make-shift uniform, misassembled Hanoverian livery captured in previous actions and rough peasant clothing, adding to his camouflage. His feet, always a soldier's first concern, were warm and dry. Otherwise, he had grown accustomed to being wet and dirty all the time.

A scarlet flash at the corner of his eye told him a scout had spotted the anticipated enemy column. This clever method of communication had startled him at first, the gentle fisting which caused coherent light to be generated by a thrustible and the firmer thumb-pressure which would unleash a bolt of deadly kinergy being of small difference to an adrenalinated fighter. It made his spine itch to lie within its focus. Nonetheless, the system worked uninterceptibly, and he had, in the end, grown accustomed to it as well. Close beside him as was prudent lay one another age might have labeled aide or chief of staff, Fionaleigh Savage, an appropriately named woods-runner girl, dark of hair and fiery of eye. Just out of her teens, she possessed a wild, unaccountable genius for strategy which sometimes arises without antecedent among a people pressed by great necessity. Seeing the signal, she turned to grin at him and concentrated again upon the roadway.

Fionaleigh. Day by day it became more difficult to avoid confronting her ardent desire to be something more than his assistant. Nor was he altogether immune, himself, to the aphrodisiac quality of a shared cause. Yet he had scant time or energy to spare, and a previous obligation claimed him.

Soon, sounds of the column's arrival were unmistakable even to the commander's uneducated ear. His talent lay elsewhere. It had been difficult learning to overcome centuries-old distrust which Skyans felt toward their now-displaced colonial rulers, or roiling factional conflict among the independent-minded woodsrunners which he must con-trol while continuing to fight a war. Along the way he had learned much of politics (as well, to his dismay, of the more dismal side of human nature) and had, as much to his

surprise as anybody's, proven himself as capable a leader as
anyone had a right to expect. This stretch was a portion of the
new road which had not been laid die-straight, but looped
round a massive monolith of obdurate stone, upthrust from
the planet's core, standing in the bird-flight between the
Usurper's new pentagrams and his fort. It was not their first
ambuscade in these surroundings, but most had occurred
upon the bend itself. (The damages he and his partisans
inflicted in this manner had been expensive to the new
regime.) Still, the enemy had grown wary and would be upon
their guard. By the time they were past the curve and upon
the straight again, they would be relaxed and easier prey. So
did the commander hope.

Aside from the thrum and hiss of the oncoming foe, he and
his comrades lay in silence. Birds and animals were hushed,
in part by the prospect of inclement weather, in part with an
expectation which the enemy, unwise in the ways of this
world, would not be sharing. Nor were Monopolitan recruits
often given time to discover what was normal here. Mostly
they perished, replaced by what seemed an endless reserve of
newcomers, at the hands of woods-wise natives before they
could acquire enough experience—if they were not taken
before they could get here by Deep-rovers which reports
claimed were striking Hanoverian vessels with increasing
frequency and ferocity.

Among them was one with a curiously coincidental name.
Henry Martyn, it was rumored, was not only a terror to all
imperia-conglomerate within the black heart of the Deep, the
normal provenance of brigandry, but swooped down upon
ill-defended planetary installations—mines, refineries, mar-
shalling yards where levies like Morven's were gathered, given
minimal training, and sent to die for Ceo and Monopolity—
as if he were waging war, rather than raiding for booty. The
commander had entertained a notion that this Henry Martyn
might be the missing grandson over whom another Henry
Martyn had once grieved. He had dismissed it when it was
pointed out (by independent advisors, both female) that even
the crude census taken of this planet's natives every couple of
decades produced hundreds of Henry Martyns, just as it did
Robret Whytes and Donol Brownes. Well, he thought, may

Henry Martyn prosper, whoever he may be, as long as he keeps killing Hanoverians.

Freebooters of the star-roads aside, the rate of casualties upon both sides was dismaying. Supplies were never adequate. To the commander's consternation, his opponent anticipated his best-aimed blows. Even he could not have attested, at this point and over all, how well the resistance fared. Unlike the Ceos' celebrated interstellar conflicts—themselves mere episodes of a Thousand Years' War which threatened to become humanity's normal mode of existence—it was no matter of clear-cut victory and defeat, but of grinding attrition, not of destroying an enemy (which appeared impossible), but of dissuading the faraway and faceless entities who paid his bills.

This ambuscade, however, had been thought out long in advance, kept secret from almost everyone involved until the last minute, and appeared to have caught the Black Usurper's legions flat-footed. Between the hill where the commander lay and that from the flank of which the offending roadway had been cut, lay a creekbed, almost dry this time of the year, deep, but with climbable slopes upon both sides. The road appeared here as a shelf scraped from the hillside with projectibles calipretted upon the military equivalent of the Holdings' drawwherry. Fearful of attack, the builders had remained within their vehicles, never setting foot upon the ground. In consequence, it was neither as well planned nor well executed as it might have been, providing many opportunities and advantages to the woodsrunners.

The sky was an unbroken bowl of pearl-gray overcast. Upon the hill the air was clear, but a thin mist filled the creek and lapped over the road, sweetening the woodsrunners' chances for success. The commander took a deep breath, always conscious that it might be his last. The smells about him were those of the forest, seasoned by the lubricant with which his thrustible had been coated, as well as by the woodsmoke of a hundred campfires permeating his clothing and the odor of his own tension. Nearby, where he could not see them, which was as it ought to be, half a hundred other rebels lay, each in a pool of similar smells, and waited.

Forms moved upon the roadway. Scouts straddling their §-field riders hummed through the ambuscade unharmed. Without humor, the commander grinned to himself. They were traveling too fast to afford the countryside proper inspection. He was grateful for an incompetence upon their part which was the one thing he had discovered he could rely upon. War, he had come to realize, far from consisting of valorous deeds, of brilliant stroke and counterstroke, was simply a matter of not committing as many errors as the other fellow.

Soon the leading element of the column proper rumbled into view, a low-riding vehicle bristling with projectibles, pulsing with protective energies, pierced at such frequent intervals with thrustible ports that it looked like an openwork basket. This machine, like the unobservant scouts which had preceded it, would be permitted to pass unmolested. For the moment. It was followed by another like it. And another.

Upon the figurative heels of the ponderous, death-dealing escorts followed freighters, slowed by their own considerable weight of §-armor, full of frightened troops beginning to realize they were still unharmed after their danger-fraught passage of the blind curve. This, too, represented long-standing fortune to the commander and his woodsrunners. More often than not, in this backwater war, they faced human opposition instead of the dreaded Oplytes their enemy might have brought to bear. Even with the Ceo's active abetment, the Black Usurper's resources, it appeared, were limited. The near-invincible warriors were expensive to acquire and maintain.

The same was only by comparison less true of peasant conscripts drawn, unwilling, from nearby Monopolitan possessions, and ferried, shipload by brigand-vulnerable shipload, to a planet, in their view encircled by a funeral wreath, which it was the rebels' objective to make their graveyard. Nor could the Usurper count upon supplementing their numbers from the native population. In open countryside, the likeliest candidates for conscription melted into the woods. Morven's henchmen were afraid to venture forth in less than regimental strength. In more settled areas, less given to recalcitrant individualism, the people grew sullen under what they considered illegitimate rule, and through slow-downs and sabotage endeavored to cost more than they were worth. Pressgangs and tax-collectors returned to the Holdings and their master empty-handed or, for one reason or another, not at all. The commander was aware of half a dozen men among his companions who had not been born upon this planet, who had deserted rather than work the Usurper's will (or face the consequences of doing so or of failing). Some offworlders had even married rebel women. Others, more determined and courageous, remained as spies in their old jobs, at what was now designated (as it had never been) the world's capital.

This brought him back to present circumstances. His spies had chosen well. The column was of the correct length, an even dozen freighters laden with what must be valuable cargo. As the final elements—three more weapons carriers, a heavy complement, indeed—skim-floated onto the straight, the first were still within sight. No further signal among the waiting resistance fighters was required. A dull, muffled thud communicated itself to the commander through the ground. After a pause which, even after all his experience with such operations, stirred the beginnings of doubt within him, half the hillside above the road began to slip, like baker's flour piled too high, onto the three rear escort vehicles. Blocked by the column ahead, they could not accelerate from the path of the slide, however slow its journey downhill. Nor had they room or time to turn about.

Permeated by armoring fields insufficient to resist the titanic forces involved, the mesh from which the vehicles were fashioned flashed and sparkled, penetrated by falling stones, battered into shapes their fashioners would never have recognized. Doomed occupants bellowing in uncontrolled terror, the machines were pushed, almost gently, off the roadway by a smoke-crested wave of moving earth into the dry creekbed, where they were buried. Once crushed, they exploded, lifting the earth a final time before it settled with a dread finality upon their broken forms. The roadway was cut off.

At the same instant, a similar blast and earthslide destroyed the leading vehicles of the column, leaving the freighters stranded but untouched upon the now-isolated section of roadway. It appeared that the Hanoverians could not accustom themselves to this ancient method of chemenergic warfare, although the idea had been borrowed from assassins hired to destroy the Islay sons' draywherry, what now seemed years ago to the commander. If the scouts upon their §-riders exercised their usual foolishness, instead of running ahead to summon help—just one of three precious flying machines Morven had imported recently could reverse these so-far happy results—they would turn about to see what was wrong and be cut down by sharp-thrusters waiting for them.

Rising where they lay or thrusting from sparse cover, the woodsrunners launched their assault. Steam arose in trailing wisps where the energy they spent was absorbed by wet soil, mist-dampened clothing, and human tissue which was, for the most part, liquid itself. Where beam struck §-field, iridescent interference rings fled outward like ripples upon the surface of a pond. At the closest ranges—some fighters had been lying among the tumbled boulders of the creekbed —the less-attenuated power of their weapons was converted into even greater heat and their targets into expanding plasma. Smoke billowed. Flames danced and crackled. Trapped conscriptees screamed as their heated weapons burned their hands or their clothing and flesh began to crisp.

The surviving Hanoverians were desperate now, aware that their opponents could afford to take no prisoners. Blind thrusting began to plow the dirt all round the guerilla commander, scattering gravel and broken vegetation. A waist-thick tree beside him absorbed a direct thrust—its trunk shivered—spewing outraged bark in every direction and dropping leaves in a wide circle. The phenomenon was nothing new, and he allotted it scarce notice.

His own first thrust was a long one. It split the skull of a uniformed youth climbing from his vehicle to take refuge behind it. Pink haze above a stump of neck drifted and mingled with the mist. His second thrust caught another Hanoverian squarely in his soft-armored chest, slamming him against his machine where he dropped to the ground, legs straight, arms splayed at his sides. Among other travesties to which the commander grew accustomed of late, he was now a skilled slaughterer, capable of accomplishing the deaths of children in a casual mood, without hate, and at astounding ranges.

As moaning from the wounded filled the valley and a hundred thrustibles flash-canceled one another upon the ruined road, Robret "the" Islay, guerilla commander and legitimate heir to the Drectorhood of Skye, rose to a prudent crouch and started forward to see what Morven's suppliers had brought him. In his mind's eye, he was already witnessing—and to his disgust enjoying—the spectacle of the plundered vehicles being set afire and tipped over to join their buried escorts in the creekbed. He was aware that it was odd—how his enjoyment did not grow from hatred of the enemy. Months of fighting had stripped him of such feelings, if he had ever had them. It seemed he had never been motivated by any emotion—but had, from the beginning, regarded the Black Usurper as an unfortunate circumstance, like bad weather. If he hated anything, it was Alysabeth Morven Islay, for betraying his father's trust. Often, in the twilight between waking and sleep, he caught himself imagining her death at his own hands. When his mind was in control of his being, he believed she would receive her due through Donol.

The bloody work proceeded well enough without a seasoning of hatred. When spring floods arrived in a few months (unless Morven acted at once, incurring risk of further interference), these slides should act as dams, assuring that the roadway remained washed out and useless without additional effort upon the part of—

To his utter horror, a different spectacle unfolded as a deep thrumming, a great subsonic pounding, filled the canyon from one end to the other. The Usurper's "sky force," three §-suspended fliers, were skimming upon long kinergic legs up the creekbed from the direction of the Holdings. As they came, they showered destruction upon the woodsrunners who, with the collapse of resistance from the freighters, had hurried forward, all unheeding, to claim the fruits of easy victory.

The machines themselves were nothing more, in principle, than §-field vehicles written large. Their rarity and cost arose from a profligate consumption of power and the subtle *ulsic* circuitry necessary to keep them stable over varying terrain upon what amounted to a continuous thrust, often several klommes in length. If the enemy had not relearned the use of obsolete explosives, he wielded this newer, more hideous weapon to terrifying effect. Where they strode, the fliers each put down a "footprint," its width and depth dependent upon their size, weight, and altitude. At a klomme's height, it merely rippled the grass. Yet it was capable, when the machine was just overhead, of stamping turf, foliage, men, and machinery into smashed caricatures of what they had been, or of driving them into soft ground like nails under the descending face of a gigantic, invisible hammer.

A shadow passed over Robret. He threw himself to one side, out of the deadly track, only to watch a comrade beside him trampled—he felt a limb-weakening wash of gratitude it had not been Fionaleigh—and converted into pulp before his eyes. He raised his thrustible, discharging it into the §-armored underbelly of the passing machine, producing no effect aside from expanding interference rings and sparks. Everywhere it was his own men screaming now, fleeing as the fliers ran them down. Troopers at thrustible ports rained volleys upon them, widening the trail of death. Holding his ground and taking careful aim, Robret picked off several of these, forcing others to retreat inside the safety of the mesh where they could do no harm, even tumbling one through his port and over the edge. He fell to the ground and was crushed by the next machine to pass.

Seasoned warriors streaked for the nearest cover, the forest, or the comparative security afforded by proximity to the long embattled column, knowing their enemy would be reluctant to destroy the freighters and their contents. Robret and Fionaleigh were among these latter, thrusting as they climbed, side by side, hand over hand, up to the roadway. Scarcely had they made their painful way to the level, plowed strip of ground when the sides of the freighters opened outward, vomiting dozens—hundreds—of Oplytes.

The tables had been turned. The ambushers had become the ambushed.

CHAPTER XXV:
THE MAGIC LANTERN

Lia had kept her guilt, along with the pain it caused her, to herself.

Even now, perhaps especially now, the burden was more than she could bear. She knew she had made another mistake, climbing the long spiral flight of stairs to the tower room which had been Arran's in what had turned out (although, like people of every century everywhere, none living through them had realized it) to be happier times. Yet, just as her mind required respite from the calculations of survival, her heart required refuge, some fragment of the warm familiarity of a lifetime and a way of living, which, whatever happened now, was shattered and its pieces lost beyond recovery.

It was peculiar, she thought, and dismaying, how small a series of personal catastrophes it took to change everything beyond recognizability, to alter the appearance of everyday places and things—rather, her perception of them—until it was as if she had never seen them before. By any objective standard, this small room was much as it had always been, neither cramped nor grand, constructed from translucent plastic blocks which, not undertaking the load borne by identical blocks far below in the Holdings' foundations, displayed surfaces which were a bit concave. It had been a good room. The thinnest imaginable patina of dust, softening angles and edges all about her, was still almost invisible. Even so, the knowledge that the room's former occupant was missing, and presumed dead—in the field, even when instructed otherwise, Oplytes were unlikely to leave identifiable remnants of their victims—like the man who had helped keep it, permeated everything, from the shapes and textures of common objects to the color of the sunlight streaming now through the high-arched windows of stained glass and the ringlight which sifted through them every night.

Nevertheless, she had come here for a purpose. This chamber had been searched by tireless inhumans, like every cubic siemme of the Holdings, when the Black Usurper had seized power. Amidst more compelling preoccupations, it had been forgotten with a similar efficiency. No better sanctuary existed within these walls where she could do, in privacy and in safety—which these days amounted to the same thing—what she was about to do.

Lia wiped her eyes. They had, without her realizing it, become tear-filled and unfocusable. She took from the pocket of her skirt the slim, finger-length cylinder which had been handed her this morning by one of the groundskeepers, an elderly Skyan who, despite the fact that he had been with the family Islay for as long as they had been upon Skye, had somehow been passed over, just as she had been in Morven's grim series of housecleanings.

Acting as housekeeper—Morven had not brought a seneschal, and Old Henry, who had always seemed in charge of everything, was gone—Lia thus far enjoyed free run of the Holdings. She appeared (in this way, if in no other, the tower room suited her) almost to have been forgotten by the Usurper's minions, perhaps because she had been an employee rather than a retainer. In an age which euphemized chattel slavery away, the differences between the two were subtle, but real. Upon the other hand, it was her wedding to the eldest of the Islay sons which had been chosen for dramatic interruption. As a consequence, her precise legal status remained nebulous, although her intimate association with the family could not be so to any observer.

In the end, Lia could not have told why she was left to herself. It was among her greatest, most continuous fears that her freedom—not to consider her life—might come to an arbitrary end at any second. Never for a moment did it occur to her that she was innocent of any offense meriting such a state of apprehension. As an educated observer of history, she was too well aware that a common feature of all civilizations—anytime, anyplace, any protest to the contrary notwithstanding—is that an individual's innocence or guilt has nothing to do with the fate to which authority consigns him.

Finding Arran's reader, a child's model they had often used while she instructed him—she wondered what had become of Waenzi, the triskel who had been his shadow, and was afraid she knew—upon a cluttered shelf, she inserted the thille. The likeness of the man she loved, the face which filled her thoughts from her awakening each morning until she succumbed to trouble-tossed exhaustion every night, sprang into being above the reader.

"My dearest Lia . . ." She had been prepared for Robret to be strained and tired, not for the fact that he looked years older. How like his father he was. *"This enthiller was appropriated in one of our raids, so I thought I might finally undertake to send word to you. I can safely convey not much by way of facts, fearing this may be intercepted. I shudder at the risk it represents to what it is my fervent wish is your continued well-being."*

Behind the man who may or may not have been her lawful husband, she could make out something of his background, for the image was virtual, allowing her to focus where she would, rather than wherever some lens decided. Not that much existed to see. He sat upon the ground, legs folded beneath him, under an expanse of mottled brown-green kefflar, further camouflaged with leaves and branches whose shadows fell upon the fabric. Beyond the opening of this makeshift shelter, propped with a crooked stick not altogether stripped of smaller twigs, lay a woodland clearing which might have told a botanist Robret's latitude and altitude. It told Lia nothing. Skye was a world covered with trees, all of which looked alike to her.

"Nonetheless, it is possible that not hearing from me may be as trying an experience for you as not hearing from you has been for me. I would do what I can to ease that trial. In return, you must promise to erase or destroy this thille as soon as you have read it. Do not permit sentiment to compound the risk to which, in my emotional weakness, I subject you."

Between the nearby woods and the rough tent, Lia discerned half a dozen figures reclining round a smokeless fire, toasting something unidentifiable upon sharpened branches thrust at an angle into the ground. Now and again, someone leaned forward to turn what he—or she; it had not occurred to Lia that females might be rebels—was cooking and sit back again.

"It will not give anything away to say I am among friends and well as can be expected. I have found allies, and, by now, you will have heard something of our activities. You are in a better position to judge their effectiveness than I, which, I am given to understand, is usually the case in war."

A portion of the entrance flap was dragged aside. A woman—hardly more than a girl, but very beautiful, with glossy black hair and eyes as dark—bent to push her head and shoulders into the tent. Robret gave her a brief glance, nodded without a word having passed between them, and returned his attention, now divided, back to the enthiller. *"For war it is, in the event they have not seen fit to tell you. Let no doubt remain. We are waging it upon the Black Usurper as often and as ardently as we are able. We destroy his transports, burn his crops, sack his encampments and fortifications, harry and murder his minions. We do this not in any hope of destroying him, for he could, if he were so determined, reduce the planet to a cinder, but against the possibility that we can make Skye too expensive for him to hold without reaching some accommodation with us."*

Robret took a deep breath, again glancing aside at the black-eyed girl. Making unnecessary adjustments to the straps of the unadorned, businesslike thrustible she wore upon one slim forearm, she waited for him with an impatient, proprietary manner which set Lia's lonely and uncertain heart to aching with an unaccustomed variety of pain. *"Lia, dearest, Fionaleigh is telling me, in her subtle manner, that I am wanted elsewhere and must go. Among my fondest hopes is that you two will someday meet under more fortuitous circumstances. By the time you receive this, it will no longer matter whether I have told you that we are about to accomplish something they will not be able to keep you, or anybody else upon the planet, from hearing of. I know you are holding up bravely back home, and, if we ask your help, you will respond in a manner to make me proud. In the meantime, I remain your Robret, 'the' Islay, Drector-Hereditary-in-Exile of Skye."*

The image vanished. Had it been a trifle distant? Feeling

an unsortable disappointment grow within her, Lia struggled against a temptation to play the thille again. Or to jerk it from the reader and dash it to the floor. Where she had expected a love letter, it seemed, she had been subjected to a political lecture intended to augment her morale. Was anything of genuine affection to be discerned in it? Deeply in love with Robret, as she had found herself almost the moment she set eyes upon him, now that this incredible disaster had befallen them, now that little Arran (among many, many others) was dead, Robret had become her entire life. All she had left of him was the memory of their parting—and now this impersonal *military* correspondence. She sniffed back tears, caught herself at it, and, transferring the bitterness she felt to herself, shook her head in sudden anger.

No! This was her imagination playing petty tricks, colored by the well-deserved weight of her guilt, the pain of separation, the uncertainty of her status, her cowardly fear of . . . whatever she was afraid of. She was Robret Islay's woman. He was her man. Whatever she feared, he confronted every bit of that, and, she believed, worse every day. He was depending upon her. Had he not told her so just now—or whenever his message had been enthilled?

She would stifle these feminine flutterings and do whatever he needed of her. In absence of instruction, she could at least force her behavior into something resembling rational channels. Unless she learned to act as wisely and nobly as the man she loved, the family she had aspired to marry into, she was indeed no more than the social climbing snippet attempting to rise above her station, which, in her blackest moods, she accused herself of being.

Still, her guilt remained to be dealt with, omissions upon her part which had brought them to this unenviable estate, which had likeliest found direct result in the deaths, and worse, of those upon Skye whom she loved.

It was so simple. Morven, younger son of the Drector-Hereditary of Shandish and a personal favorite of Leupould IX, was not a name unknown upon Hanover, where she had been born and brought up. It seemed to Lia that she had heard it whispered, along with certain terrifying accusations, all her life, in particular after (being without family of her own, but possessing promising intellect) she had sought and won employment as a tutor among the capital's wealthiest, most influential families, whose money and power failed to prevent them shuddering at its mention. Even more responsible positions had exposed her to progressively more disturbing rumors regarding the crippled Shandeen. And, in the end, he had proven himself every bit the black and terrible presence of which her friends and employers had warned her.

Of course, Alysabeth had to be considered, as well— "Alysabeth Morven Islay" as she now styled herself. Lia's acquaintance with the Black Usurper's daughter was more recent. In Lia's view, Alysabeth had, with both hands, cast away everything which Lia herself had ever hoped for, and, with it, any right to bear so honorable a surname. Moreover, since, through her father's treachery, it had become attainted, why should she wish to? Without understanding Alysabeth in the slightest, without knowing the particulars of her life, Lia knew her, nonetheless. She represented everything that disgusted and terrified Lia in a human being.

Thus the unbearable guilt she felt for never having warned her kind employer, good friend, and father-in-law-to-be concerning his best friend, the man who had become, in what she had always privately thought a bizarre twist of events, his father-in-law. Never mind that it had not been her place to do so, even after she had become engaged to Robret's *fils*. Never mind that, without doubting her sincerity, he would have dismissed it all as idle capital-world gossip. Lia felt she should have found a way. And if she had everything would now be so different.

Who was that dark-eyed girl? What kind of name was Fionaleigh?

"Who do you suppose that young woman was?" Morven leaned back in his wheeled chair and spun the thille he had just pulled from the reader upon the polished surface of the desk before him. As a matter of course he had ordered a copy made before allowing the message to be passed along, but this was the first opportunity he had found to view it.

Standing with one hand upon her father's shoulder, Alysabeth shook her head. "Another sweaty, heavy-uddered peasant cow, who will doubtless sport a moustache and hips a measure wide before she sees thirty. It was the same with his father. These elevated colonial brutes do love their prolly cunts, even given a chance at something a cut or twenty better."

"Like pursues like," the Black Usurper chuckled. "Blood calls to blood. I wonder whether Mistress Lia will see what we saw, as it were, between the code-bars, and how she will react. Her usefulness could well depend upon how she feels about that girl-lieutenant of young Robret's."

Alysabeth's lips hardened into the implacable line which, without surgical attention, would spoil her looks long before Fionaleigh Savage was touched by time. "Mistress Lia Woodgate will make herself useful regardless of how she feels!" The words formed an unbroken hiss.

"I believe you mean that." Morven looked up at his daughter with the closest he would ever approach to a father's affectionate approval. Well conditioned to obedience, she was subservient to him in every way. Out of his presence and upon her own, he could rely upon her to exercise the precise mixture of ruthlessness and discretion in his behalf which he would. He was proud of Alysabeth, as proud as he was of anything he had ever built.

He touched the desk edge in a certain spot. A cube of the wood it was made of rose from the surface. Reaching to swing one side open, he revealed a space within which held a peculiar object. Removing it, he let the cube lower itself back into place. "However, my dear, this is the reason I wished to see you this morning. It arrived upon a carrack, *Desert Owl*, now orbiting Skye, in a small fibrous crate of alien construction bearing my name. Security has examined it. The master of the carrack could only tell me it was given him by a courier, human—with strict instruction that it be hand-delivered—when he was trading in the Massad Ayoob. Do you know where that is?"

Alysabeth frowned. "A long way away, Father, and a wild place. A neutral system, as I recall, between the Monopolity and the Empery-Cirot, near the outer borders of both imperia-conglomerate. A haven for picaroons and Deeppillagers at the edge of the unexplored."

Morven was proud of his daughter's education, as well as her ruthlessness and discretion. "As you say. The captain claimed he had, by the narrowest of margins, avoided being taken in that quarter by a star-rover of whom we hear with distressing and increasing frequency, upon his passage to Skye. Henry Martyn. Was a Henry Martyn not among the casualties here, the first day?"

Alysabeth nodded. "An old servant who ran the estate. Both the Skyan census and our intelligence reports are full of Henry Martyns, Harry Martyns, Hank Martyns, with a sprinkling of Henrietta Martyns, as well. I believe you had a technical subject by the same calling the last month we were upon Hanover. A peasant's name, among the most common in the Monopolity."

"So it is. In any event, my dear, the Massad Ayoob is most successful at playing one imperium-conglomerate against another. It is tolerated in its outlaw existence because it remains a reliable source of useful information and unheard-of artifacts such as this."

They both looked at the object in question, sitting upon the otherwise uncluttered surface of the desk which had once belonged to Robret Islay. An unprepossessing transparent cylinder eighteen siemmes in length, seven in diameter, it lay upon its side upon an integral rectangular foot. Each end, for a couple of siemmes, was metal, of reduced diameter, as if the object were a jar with screw-caps upon both ends. A heavy wire bail paralleled its length, originating at the caps. Despite its transparency, it was impossible to see through it, since it appeared to be filled with a fluorescent amber gas, pulsing and glowing. Short-lived sparks filled it with effervescence.

"Of obvious alien manufacture," Morven remarked, "a rather primitive culture, I would surmise, since this is supposed to be its equivalent of a datathille. In short, we have a letter from a secret admirer, my dear. One is instructed to place a hand upon the bail, and, if desired, another upon whomever one wishes to share the message with. Shall we see what it says?" Uncertain, Alysabeth nevertheless nodded. Taking his daughter's hand, Morven reached out and lay his other, palm-down, upon the heavy wire handle.

"Aaaaaaa!" A palpable heat blasted them. Light hammered their bodies like hurricane-borne hailstones. Noise threatened to tear their being into tatters. Unable to let go of the device, Morven felt himself convulse in agony. His daughter could not let go of his hand. All round them, the dim, cool, paneled study seemed to vanish, replaced in a blinding flash with a dazzling, alien spectacle which filled their helpless minds to overflowing.

"Customary acknowledgement of mutual existence and psychological visibility." It was like being transported into the searing depths of a Hell too bright for eyes to look upon, too hot for bodies to withstand. Only by comparison less excruciating to behold against the overwhelming brilliance of the background was the being communicating with them, a man-sized, multi-armed, soft-bodied mollusc fashioned of fire. The ambient noise was that of the inside of a waterfall, amplified a millionfold, yet the creature's voice stood above it all, each syllable a peal of thunder.

"I am a pseudoresponsive communicale, possessing artificial intelligence within limits capable of answering any question you may wish to ask, once my essential message has been transmitted. My outer envelope is necessitated by extremities existing between your natural environment and that within which I was enthilled. Without it, I would not survive exposure to your surroundings long enough to fulfill my function, nor would you survive exposure to me.

"Your inevitable questions will be: what personage is responsible for my enthillement; what is the nature of the place you experience with me now; why does my enthilleur seek communication? He is Zerushaa, authorized Thinker-Questioner to the Ordinators of the nation-state Aahnaash, of the Rii—as such might be rendered in terms meaningful to you—a sapience as yet unknown to your species. It is the voice-analog and physical aspect of Zerushaa you now experience. Thinker-Questioner Zerushaa has caused me to be enthilled in what would appear to you the central region of a medium-yellow sun, not unlike the primary of the stellar complex you inhabit. My first purpose is to convey knowledge of the existence of the Rii. My second is to propose a transaction of potential mutual benefit.

"It is essential that you understand how the concept of your

environment—the frozen surface of a gobbet forever circling beyond reasonable light and warmth—is as forbidding to my enthilleur as that of the Rii springing into existence, evolving to self-awareness, and creating a culture within the heart of a star must be to you. Ritual formula of request: permit me to convey how forbidding. Until recent history, the Rii were cognizant of three phases in which matter manifests itself— plasma, gas, and liquid—the lattermost of which was contemplated only by Thinker-Questioners authorized in scientific speculation. That a fourth phase might exist was not suspected, but something they learned—to their astonishment— when, by accident, they established contact with beings like yourself during a series of experiments.

"Among those values gained from this contact was a heretofore unsuspected fact of the existence of environments—other suns—suitable for settlement and exploitation by the Rii, of structures analogous to the nation-state of Aahnaash, and of concepts among beings like yourself analogous to trade. Following consideration, it was agreed among the Ordinators to pursue this possibility, that the appropriate structure to interact with toward this end was the imperium-conglomerate known as the Monopolity of Hanover, that the optimal being to approach was an Ordinator-analog known as Black Usurper Tarbert Morven, Second of Shandish, Drector-Administrative to Ceo Leupould IX, Drector-Interventionary and -Protempore of Skye . . .

"What the Rii desire is transport and title to an unlimited number of stellar habitats within the Monopolity and any territory falling within its influence. Riian occupation will in no manner alter the function these stars perform for beings of your kind. In return, the Rii offer Black Usurper Tarbert Morven technical means of reducing every sapient being within the Monopolity to a state of absolute, unquestioning obedience to his will."

CHAPTER XXVI:
A TOKEN OF PROMISE

Morven broke contact with the alien "communicale" in a burst of effort which hurled him, and his chair, against the paneled wall.

For an unmeasured time he sat, ears ringing, chest heaving, clothing soaked with acrid perspiration stimulated by an intolerable heat he had imagined suffering. Having experienced, however briefly, existence—he could not think of it as "life"—within the seething heart of a sun, this quiet study about him now seemed swathed in arctic silence, thick as a blanket of midwinter snow. He found the sensation agreeable and it was a long while before he attempted more than sitting with his dazzle-blinded eyes shut, soaking in the stillness, letting white-hot memories of the *Riian* radiate, as it seemed to him, out of his complaining tissues.

He took a final deep breath and opened his eyes. A timepiece built into his signet ring informed him six hours had passed. In a manner of speaking, he found himself alone. Alysabeth lay in the tumble of her skirts upon the floor beside the desk, insensible—"relaxed" was far too sentient a word —her face blanched, her eyes open, blank-white, the pupils rolled back into the sockets. She trembled, emitting an occasional whimper. A thin line of saliva trailed from one corner of her mouth across her pulsing throat. Her breathing was shallow. At some point over the last six hours, judging from the stain spreading through the fabric of her gown, she had wet herself. To his dismay and consternation, Morven discovered the same of himself, as well.

He had never been tolerant of frailty in others, yet in this moment, he came closer than he ever had—or ever would— to sympathetic understanding for another being. It was not a sensation he found comfortable. As with the terrifying after-images of the world of *Zerushaa* of *Aahnaash*, he pressed it away from himself as soon as he found strength. Nonetheless, for these betrayals of weakness he could neither blame his daughter nor himself. He was astonished to have been left living, and would not have been surprised if she remained in this shattered idiot state the rest of her life. He wondered—and was grateful—that he did not present the same humiliating spectacle.

In due course, Alysabeth shut her eyes. Her trembling ceased. As he watched, her natural color returned. The rise and fall of her breasts became even and vigorous. She seemed to drop, where she lay, into a normal, restful sleep which her father—demonstrating the fleeting remnants of an uncharacteristic kindness—refrained from disturbing.

Keeping his respiration deep and deliberate, Morven examined the *Rii*an communicale with circumspection appropriate to a poisonous reptile. It sat upon the polished surface of the desk as if nothing untoward had transpired. He doubted whether sufficient incentive existed to induce him to touch it again in his lifetime. He felt fortunate that it would not be necessary.

Before the message had played to conclusion, the authorized Thinker-Questioner to the Ordinators of the nation-state *Aahnaash*—rather the machine or program (Morven was uncertain which) speaking for *Zerushaa*—had added detail to its proposition, outlined specific procedures. It appeared (he discovered that he could not abandon a reflexive caution in this matter) that nothing they desired of him was beyond the bounds of accomplishment for an individual of his influence and resources. He wanted—needed—what they had to offer him in exchange for what amounted to his services. Skye was becoming an embarrassment to his wider ambitions offplanet. Furthermore, the creatures had somehow anticipated everything he had ever dreamed—even in his wildest flights of megalomaniacal fancy—of possessing or achieving.

A noise interrupted his thoughts. Beside him, Alysabeth moaned and began to stir. Turning in his chair—how delighted he had been at the first sign of this renewed capacity, a token of his returning physical powers—Morven reached down to his daughter, smoothed her hair, and, when she was ready, assisted her to her feet. It constituted, he thought

with satisfaction, a peculiar turnabout in the normal course
of their relationship. She found a chair beside the desk and
sat, not speaking, not even looking about, lost in the daze
which he himself had been such a long time coming out of. At
last, she spoke her first words. "I . . . I do not trust those
monsters, Father!"

Morven raised an eyebrow. "Oh?"

"I find . . ." She hesitated. "I am at a loss to explain,
Father. For some reason I do not understand, I find them vile
and . . . *loathsome.*" Again, she halted. Morven remained
silent as she composed her thoughts. *"Please,* Father, you
must listen! Promise me you will not undertake a bargain
with these entities! Whatever we gain from them over the
short term, in my heart, I believe they will destroy us in the
end!"

Astonished, he shook his head. It was the first he could
recall her attempting to move him to do, or refrain from
doing, anything. She had beheld—and accomplished—far
worse in her short, eventful life, yet she was, at a visceral level
beyond reach of conscious alteration, disgusted by the *Rii,* as
he became convinced after further discussion, experimental
upon his part, emotional upon hers. It was a case of prejudice
at first sight, analogous, although of greater magnitude, to
interspecific culture-shock, not uncommon in a galaxy populated by thousands of sapient species. He himself experienced
no such trepidation. Whatever else he may have been, the
Black Usurper never suffered the pangs of bigotry. Since
earliest childhood, it had been his way to assess everyone
upon a basis of strict equality, in cold, pragmatic terms
of the potential benefit they brought to his ambitions. He
had never looked for such an affliction to befall Alysabeth,
upon whose keen, and, in the main, self-interested judgment
he relied. She would be a poor advisor in this affair, as she
would doubtless prove in a related undertaking which, in
the unceasing nether recesses of his mind, he presently contemplated.

Morven sighed. *"Go tidy yourself up, my dear. You are a
sight."*

Her eyes glazed a moment under the onslaught of conditioning to which she had been subjected since infancy, a vocal
stimulus which compelled obedience.

"Yes, Father." She arose, steady upon her feet—a degree of bodily certainty being a benefit of working someone else's will—and started for the door to the outer office.

"No," Morven commanded. Halfway to the door, Alysabeth stopped as if she had run into an invisible wall. "Do not bother going all the way up to your suite, my dear," her father told her.

He was accustomed, from a certain measure of prudence, to employ command-cues with a sparing economy. They were, in fact, no longer necessary. The girl had been imbued not only with compliance, but with as wholehearted an enthusiasm to see her father's least desires (or his greatest, for that matter) translated into accomplished fact, as if they were her own. Which, by now, of course, was what they had become. She turned—calmly herself once again, fears and prejudices washed away, at least for the time being, by her father's indomitable will—and raised a single inquiring eyebrow, a genetically transmitted knack they shared.

"Use the small facility behind that panel," Morven continued, "for we have an urgent need of haste. I shall ring for staff to fetch you a fresh dress. Meantime, it will please your father greatly if you make of yourself the irresistibly attractive creature you always are." Alysabeth dimpled and curtsied. He was relieved at the transformation he had wrought in her. "When you have done, and I am making my own use of the facilities, I want you to find Donol, personally, and bring him here to me. And that servant, what was her name, the tutor, Lia Woodgate?"

Order being restored to the persons of Morven and Alysabeth, tea was laid by a house-servant, although none among the four present had touched it as yet, upon a small, wheeled table beside the desk. All was as it should be within the paneled walls of the study which had once belonged to Robret Islay.

Conversation began casually—news from Hanover, the weather, increasing problems with Deep-rovers, the crops, details of operating a great household—in which both Donol, a probationary member, and Lia, through some default, were encouraged to take part as if the Drectorhood had not changed hands. At Morven's request, Lia arose and, having poured, passed the fragile cups and saucers round, afterward sharing with the others a tray of crustless sandwiches and crumbly tidbits from the ovens. As Lia stood, tray in hand, the conversation took an ominous turn.

"Donol, my daughter this morning expressed her regret that your brother Robret, whom she regards as rather silly, continues his compulsion to obstruct her father's reforms upon this planet." Morven turned to Alysabeth. "Have I stated your view correctly, my dear?"

Had anyone thought to look up, he might have observed the rigid posture in which Lia held herself, the way her freckles stood against a paler countenance than had been the case a moment before. Something of significance was about to take place in the small room. She was afraid to predict, even to herself, what it might be.

In the esteem of father and daughter, she knew, Robret represented no more than an inferior imitation of his sire. They were infuriated more at the presumption represented by his continuing resistance, than at any of his manifold transgressions. The Black Usurper remained confident that Robret might be overcome, if not by more numerous and superior arms, then in good time, at the proper opportunity, by simple cunning, like his father.

Alysabeth seemed to blush and not quite stammer embarrassed affirmation. The intonation of command had not been employed. As a consequence, her response was spontaneous. These were her feelings, however childish the terms in which they had been rendered. They included, as he had calculated they would, a degree of awkwardness at having been asked this question in the presence of the son and daughter-in-law-by-betrothal of her own dead husband, whom she had helped betray. Enjoying the returning muscle and sensation which permitted a broad, expressive gesture, Morven spread his arms and gave forth with a hearty laugh, inviting all within hearing to share his viewpoint.

"You see, Donol my boy, how it is with us. We have grave problems upon Skye and enormous responsibilities to the Ceo Leupould. Powerful individuals, factionalists without our interests foremost in their hearts, are watching, judging how we prosper, waiting for us to make mistakes by which they might derive some benefit." Morven astonished the middle Islay brother—and terrified Lia—by winking at him. "Always it is politics," the man complained jovially, as one cosmopolitan to another. "As a consequence, Donol, in an effort to lighten our burden, transfer our energies and attentions where they are sorely needed, I have decided to promise you not just the amnesty you have earned and which is due you, but a full official pardon, in exchange for a demonstrated willingness upon your part to share some of those responsibilities and help us solve our problems."

Donol shut his eyes, took a deep breath through his nose, and let it out slowly. Lia felt her body tense again. She would never have expected to find herself hanging upon the reply of this particular individual. Silence filled the room. "You ask," his next words were as deliberate as he could make them, "my cooperation in quelling the rebellion my brother leads."

Morven nodded. "We shall not mince words. Believe me, your reward will be commensurate. To name one example, my lovely daughter already has her eye upon you. You did not know, boy? It would not be a bad thing, politically or otherwise, if, at some future time, our families reunited in some manner other than a protracted struggle to the death." If Morven awaited some word or gesture from Donol, he did not receive it. "You wish firmer assurances from me, before committing yourself? I can scarcely blame you. I should want them myself, in your place. Or perhaps you desire a more timely and tangible gesture of good faith between us, a down payment, as it were. A token of promise. Very well, permit me to be as open with you as I would."

Straightening in his chair, he cleared his throat and proceeded to tell Donol the substance of his message from *Zerushaa* of *Aahnaash*.

"In due course," Morven concluded, "with suitable precautions against freezing to death (or whatever happens), toasting us, or being taken by Henry Martyn and his peg-tentacled crew, our friend *Zerushaa* purposes to visit us in person—we cannot say 'in the flesh'—here upon Skye."

Donol sat back in dumb astonishment, not so much at the message—it was a wide, wondrous universe in which many bizarre things had proven possible—as the fact that Morven had seen fit to tell him of it. Had he wormed his way this far into the man's confidence, or, as seemed more probable, was this some elaborate test? Donol realized that for his own reasons, he was desperate to discover what the—how were they called, *Rii*?—had to offer.

Morven favored him with a self-satisfied smile. "I spoke of two families reunited, two great families, each after its fashion, yours newly-elevated by your late father's valor in the Ceo's service. Whatever his later failings, he was a warrior of prowess and daring, which run in your line as inheritable traits, judging from the surprising resistance you and your brothers mounted against us—" He raised a hand to stay interruption. "Pray do not demur my praise! Let understanding exist, even here. I never believed it was cowardice which brought you back to the Holdings. Rather, your loving concern for the welfare of the Skyan people conceived some scheme among the three of you—do not trouble to deny it, for you have won my admiration thereby—for subverting our rule, of which your part, dissimulation of surrender, required the greatest steadfastness of heart."

Morven reached for Alysabeth's hand. "Ours, by contrast, is a family steeped in ancient and sophisticated tradition. My daughter, I will have you understand, is a sensitive, intelligent girl of fine breeding, augmented by an education obtained at the center of the greatest civilization humanity has ever produced." He smiled up at the girl. "Whereas you, Donol, well, I intend no insult. Let us say that opportunities you might otherwise have enjoyed were denied you by circumstances of birth and upbringing. Let me hasten to add that this is nothing which cannot be overcome, with proper assistance, through personal application and the passage of sufficient time."

Listening horrified, Lia only now became aware that she had remained standing all this time with the sandwich tray in her hand. Nor did she move as Morven's calm, reptilian gaze flickered across her. He grinned at Donol. "I even suspect, with no offense intended, that certain of your aptitudes— except perhaps with the occasional help of some clumsy, overwilling peasant wench—have been neglected. I refer to those relating to . . . how shall I put it?" Again his eyes fell upon Lia. "I have it: here is a young woman without respectable or undeniable connection to either of our families, too well educated to be wasted as a servant, yet for whom we have no other use."

Donol turned to look at Lia with a peculiar, tentative expression. Never realizing it, she paled another shade and took a step backward.

"Her status among us," Morven continued, "is awkward. Even more so if by marriage she be considered Skyan. Those who preceded Hanover to this world, having for centuries resisted our preeminence, never having sworn submission to the Monopolity, cannot lay claim to any recognition of their existence, let alone legal rights." Lia took another step backward. If Morven noticed, he betrayed no sign. "Upon the contrary, if she is subject to the Monopolity, given her obvious sympathies, she has betrayed loyalties which, by virtue of the circumstances of her birth, it was her solemn obligation to observe. She is, after all, betrothed to a traitor, himself the son of a traitor. Although we remain uncertain, at present, whether she is legally married to him under any jurisprudence. The people call her his 'unwedded wife.' "

This time, when the Usurper cast his gaze upon her, she was left no room to doubt it. "There is less confusion here than meets the eye. I might have used the expression *proven* sympathies.' She was observed this morning receiving unauthorized communication from the outlaw leader himself. This, and the fact I have read the missive in question, settles her status and seals her fate." Another step backward. Lia felt her heel strike the baseboard of a wall. Morven was relentless. "Her life is forfeit. She no longer belongs to herself—if anyone can ever claim to do so—but to the Monopolity of Hanover, a sort of ultimate fine levied, if you will, by Ceo Leupould IX through his lawful representative. She is the property of the imperium-conglomerate, to use, under our authority, or cast aside, as we find helpful in performing our appointed tasks upon this unruly planet."

He reached for a control beneath the desk edge. The crackle of a fiber-guided lasercom which of late linked this room with the administrative office which had been the library preceded an interrogative noise. Morven raised his voice, assuring that all, within and without, might hear and obey. "Mistress Lia Woodgate is to be confined to the tower room whose isolation she appears to find amenable. A new lock is to be fitted upon its door immediately. When this is accomplished, send someone for her. Meanwhile, keep the doors to this room under watch." He released the switch and lowered his voice. "In her way, Donol, having been educated in the capital, I gather Mistress Lia shares traits in common with my daughter. You will be given the only keythille to that lock. Consider her body a gift from me. Overcome her reluctance by any means you find efficacious and diverting. Keep her as long as you wish. Make what use of her amuses you. Dispose of her afterward, as you will."

Donol gulped, looking from Morven, to Lia, to a grinning Alysabeth. Lia dropped the tray, closed her eyes, but remained upon her feet.

"And mark me well," Morven admonished him, "much that you may observe in the handling of this young woman, my own daughter may thank you for having learned." A knock came upon the door. "Is my meaning clear? See that you enjoy yourself. We shall speak further of your future before long."

With these words, he turned his chair, servos whining, wheeled it round the desk and out of the room, to speak with the guards he had sent for, leaving Donol with the two young women, one of whom was now his personal property. A long moment of silence ensued.

"A handsome gift." Alysabeth's smile was sweet. Rising, taking the chair next to him, she laid a soft hand upon his arm. Her voice was level, loud enough to carry to Lia. "My father was always a generous man. If you are generous as well, Donol, you will consider loaning your new toy to me from time to time. I need my pleasure, after all. Later, we can play with her together."

Donol gulped.

Chapter XXVII:
Luncheon with Alysabeth

Amnesty.

Clutching the all-important document behind his back—rolled into scroll-form and bedecked with elaborate seals and ribbons—Donol was content. For the moment. A degree of loneliness accompanied his satisfaction, no one being present to whom he might have declared the latter. No more nor less unused to speaking his feelings than any in this age of dissimulation, still, upon his part, it would have been a remarkable declaration, coming from one who normally felt he possessed so much justification for discontent.

He gazed through the many-paned windows of what had been the library, now the anteroom of Drector-Protempore Morven's office suite. What he saw beyond—in recent memory a grassy meadow surrounding the Holdings where peasants had stooped to gather lawn-herbs—had undergone a striking change over the past few months. At this edge now lay a sinuous, low fortification, festooned with ripmesh, beinged by Oplytes standing at tireless attention, thrustibles ever at the ready.

As always, when he looked upon the grotesque warriors, he wondered what had befallen his brother Arran, whether his death had been merciful. It was possible, he realized, given the jokes an ironic universe delighted in playing upon mortals, that his brother had met his fate at the hands of a brigand who bore the same name as the boy's beloved mentor. One heard more about the infamous Henry Martyn as time passed, and desired to hear less.

Beyond the fortification, clusters of unattractive, boxy fabrications, not unlike those at the starport, gridded by raw streets, comprised a town still under construction for offworld conscriptees and retainers, pressganged Skyan workers, along with a great number of volunteers and their families eager to earn Hanoverian currency and eagerer to spend it—too great a host to be quartered within the Holdings, even had this not represented the worst sort of security risk.

What the locals must think of the foreigners, he had no way of imagining. Both were, in their own way, victims of the imperium-conglomerate and its minions upon Skye and elsewhere. Yet, if Donol had been taught to extrapolate from history, they were unlikely to sympathize with one another upon that account. Pressed by lifelong unavoidable adversity —inflicted upon fifty generations trained like domestic animals to identify the source as beneficial—they would, with minimal excuse, visit the consequences of that millennium of pain and frustration upon one another.

Wood and charcoal smoke wafted upward, mingling with the dust and noise of the as-yet unpaved thoroughfares, most of it from cookfires, as other energy necessities were provided for from the estate's collectors. It was, Donol thought, a peculiarly volatile situation, which Morven—as he, himself, would not have done—had created, arguing that the populations regulated one another. It was claimed that, after sundown, even Oplytes could not travel without fear of molestation through the rutted, ring-lit, often muddy streets. Perhaps Morven knew what he was doing. Donol strove to learn from him, supplementing his studies elsewhere. Much waited to be discovered within the rough borders of the new town, toward which end he mustered courage with what rapidity he might. The offworlders had imported exotic tastes in food, liquor, a myriad of vices. Above all, it was rumored, they had brought women who knew secrets in the arts of twining flesh which a country boy, in essence if not by intention, might never dream of. All in all, the changes of the past few months, manifold and drastic though they be, suited him.

Donol turned—phantom caresses of a warmth unwelcome at the moment brushed across his cheeks and down his neck, trickling through his body to his loins, weakening his knees— and faced into the room. Some things never changed, not in *ten* thousand years. At a field secretary nearby, all hinges and mottled gray-green fabric as foreign to the splendid room it invaded as an insect upon a birthday cake, a smartbrush-wielding clerk produced thille after docuthille which he filed away—and made notes about upon another docuthille. A small fire burned in the grate, as it had at all times of the year since he had been a boy. Bodily sensations again under control, Donol turned back to the window.

That he lived at all, he knew, was entirely to Morven's credit. Yet he had applications in mind for what he had thus far learned—of which Morven likeliest would not have approved—and the time, Donol thought, was arriving when he might begin. It was, he reflected, a matter of hands. Into his hands he had this morning received, from the hands of one he must never think of as the Black Usurper, his long-promised pardon, barquoded in the exquisite hand of Ceo Leupould IX himself and delivered by the hands of the master of the latest vessel to arrive, somewhat worse for the wear, at the starport upon the equator. The document ended his probation, allowing him to set his own hands to the fulfillment of his plans.

Having been assured, some months ago, of achieving the amnesty he had sought with his surrender and paid for with his freedom, he had undertaken frequent expeditions into the growing townlet to minimize what it had cost of his reputation, encouraging an impression (true, to an extent) that, rather than collaborating with the enemy, he was a hostage in his family's name against the good behavior of a world. He had let slip hints that deeper works of retribution were under way. Upon either account, he was therefore not to be held responsible (and, indeed, was not in the Skyan quarter) for atrocities the Usurper's legions committed against the native population.

Officially, he denied—as might be expected of anyone in his position, even by the most sanguine intransigents—any part in his brother's rebellion. This device was winked at as a necessary deception—pretending to sophistication they did not, in his estimate, possess, Skyans told themselves, as Donol had believed they might, that, here at the Holdings, he seemed to be accomplishing more in pursuit of their cause than Robret in the field—while, at the same time, it ingratiated him with Morven. A delicate, dangerous task, remaining in the middle thus, but one to which Donol, agreeing with his brothers, felt himself suited.

Of late he had assumed additional risk by offering the Black—*Director-Protempore*, he reminded himself, *Tarbert Morven*—advice which, given his knowledge of Skye and its people, would produce short-term gains for Hanover, strengthening his own position, while in the long run weakening Morven's hold upon the planet. Donol and Robret had been educated in the same school, by the same teacher. (Again the ghostly fingers, the tightened breathing, the tingling in his loins.) Each of the brothers knew well, in schoolroom theory and, of late, in more established practice, the objective of any guerilla—

"Good morning, Donol Islay!" His ruminations were interrupted by a feminine voice and the rustling of velvet, coming from the doorway. He turned, noticing that the clerk had disappeared, in all probability for the midday meal, and watched as Morven's daughter entered the room.

"Good morning, Alysabeth."

The girl smiled, acknowledging without words that they were alone. "Rather good afternoon, or very nearly. Have you taken luncheon yet?"

"Why, no, Alysabeth." The words were delivered in a squeak. Donol was obliged to clear his throat. "I was conferring with your father until a few minutes ago, and had not given thought to eating." He believed he concealed a different hunger which this utterance, and the images it engendered, might otherwise have cast upon his face. With his eyes, he indicated the inner office where he had left the planet's new Drector. "Why do you ask?"

Half-promised to him as she was, Donol experienced even more difficulty than usual keeping his thoughts ordered in her presence. He had always found her breathtaking good looks —she had been described as "inhumanly beautiful"— intimidating. She approached him now, standing so near that he became aware of the scent of her hair, which was so fine that each strand, even this close, seemed invisible. It floated about her head in frothy curls, framing her features in a golden cloud. Donol was uncertain what "inhumanly beautiful" meant. Perhaps it meant her eyes, set against the surprising tawny color of her skin, large, luminous, of as pale and perfect a blue as the pale, perfect gold of her hair. Perhaps it meant smooth shoulders, sculpted collarbones, a seamless blended curve into full, rounded breasts, or the taut young belly beneath her bodice as the garment flared about her slender hips. Perhaps it meant no more than a glimpse of a cunning foot at her skirt hem or the expressive grace of her hands. Alysabeth knew of her effect upon men and enjoyed it. Donol only knew he felt embarrassed to look her fully in the face, or be discovered gazing upon her body, as if he were again a stammering adolescent confronting his first sly and knowing servant girl.

"I was given to understand," she replied, "that today is an occasion for you. I thought it would be pleasant if we took luncheon together to mark it. You have become a powerful figure in my father's esteem—" He held up both hands, protesting. Yet what she claimed was true enough. For her part, she continued, unrelenting. "Second son of an attainted Drector, at ruination's door only months ago. Who might have guessed how soon you would be at liberty to seek your own happiness, awarded new responsibility, with the prospect—" Maidenly modest, she dropped her eyes to the carpet. Donol noticed the length of her lashes, and was astonished he had noticed such a thing. "—of marriage into a rich connection, a Drectorhood in your own right, reestablishment of your dynasty? The tragic conflict of two great families is gratifyingly resolved to the satisfaction of all, and, heaping fortune upon fortune, to untold political advantage."

Donol stifled denials he had been about to deliver, smiling lopsidedly at the exquisite creature standing nearer than was comfortable. "I . . . would find that pleasant—I refer to luncheon. Er, where do you care to eat?"

Her mysterious smile communicated that she knew her father worked just the other side of the door, and that this made what she was about to say all the more enjoyable. If possible, she drew closer. "I suppose," she answered, arching her eyebrows, "we could have luncheon brought here." She inspected Donol's face, as if for a sign of relief or disappointment. "But that would be rather dreary, snapping up an office meal like some retainer."

She stood upon tiptoe, her breath upon his cheek, her

delicate features radiating warmth not a siemme from his own. Radiating a certain warmth of his own, Donol restrained a nervous finger from loosening his collar, somehow grown tight and irritating. Alysabeth placed a soft hand upon his arm. "Or we have the courtyard, although it now fronts upon a depressing view of the shabby town my father has put up. I suppose we could eat there."

Donol smiled back, weakly.

Placing her other hand upon the same arm, she wrapped her fingers about his bicep, as if she were unaware of what she did, pressing his arm against her breasts, the heated firmness of which he could feel through his tunic. Gathering his eye with hers, she glanced upward. "You are tense," she whispered, "in a way you would not be, were you availing yourself properly of Father's generosity. Pets are a responsibility, Donol. They grow lazy and ill-mannered when their owners neglect discipline and training. Have you not put yours over the jumps this morning? Perhaps it would serve two purposes to have luncheon served in the tower."

A log within the grate crackled, releasing sparks up the chimney where the tusk-jowled *thiss,* framed by *steyraugs* against a field of everblues—arms now in disgrace—had been replaced with the pick-axe and miner's lamp. Missing was the original assault rifle. Since Morven had taken power, since Arran's pistol had deprived him of an expensive Oplyte, weapons of any sort were forbidden to unauthorized hands. Peasants had been arrested, tried, and fed to the warriors for possessing harvesters' knives a siemme overlength.

"Then again," Alysabeth suggested, "my suite overlooks the forest. With chaperonage to preserve our reputations, we might enjoy a repast there."

The rooms had been his mother's. "Really, Mistress—"

"Fiancée, Donol. The difference is significant, especially when I am speaking of my bedchamber and sitting room. But you know what I would prefer, do you not?" She released his arm, reached down, ran a manicured nail from his knee to his thigh. In due course, it arrived at another place where he radiated heat, which she massaged in tantalizing circles with her fingertip until it swelled beneath her touch. "I think I should like to eat *there.*"

Before Donol could speak—or so much as take a breath—
Morven's office door flew open. The older man emerged,
rolling in his chair toward the outer, double doors. As he
spied Donol and Alysabeth, he slowed without stopping. She,
meanwhile, had stepped away from her victim. "Pray do not
let me interrupt you, children. Today is a signal day for our
friend, my dear. See that you find some way to help him
celebrate it, will you not?"

"I shall endeavor," she informed her father, "to think of
something."

He nodded, dismissed them from consciousness, and rolled
from the room. In the grate, the log settled in its irons,
scattering sparks and ashes.

Before another minute passed, the two were in Alysabeth's
chambers, in former times belonging to Glynnaughfern
Briartonson Islay, consort to a conqueror from the stars,
highborn hostage in an unwritten Bargain. They had lain
closed for a decade.

Luncheon was brought them where they were seated, thigh
to thigh, upon a small divan. The chaperonage Alysabeth had
alluded to, in the person of a homely Shandeen girl, her body
servant, appeared with the tray moments after it was ordered,
setting it upon a low table before them with a careless splash,
and abruptly disappeared. Alysabeth pulled at her skirts,
inspected them for spots—stunning Donol with a flash of calf
and thigh—and rearranged them to suit a modesty she did
not possess. She took his arm, ducked under it, and placed it
upon the narrow back of the divan where he had no choice
but to rest it about her shoulders.

"Pray do not think me forward, Donol. These are times of
crisis, for action. We do not enjoy sufficient leisure to observe
the formalities."

Donol gulped. "Formalities?"

"You must know that my father is pleased with this
amnesty you have earned, with how visibly you repent your
days of rebellion. If it would not distress you to hear it, it
pleases me, as well."

He took a deep breath, intending to say something intelligent. "Oh?"

"You failed to comment upon my observation that, because a title is attainted, this does not mean it always must be."

A thrill went through his body, for more reason than her tempting proximity. He warned himself that he must remain cautious. "I suppose," he answered, "in the abstract, this is true enough."

Alysabeth moved closer beneath the shelter of his arm. Lifting his free hand from the arm of the divan, she placed it upon her breast, half exposed by a low-cut bodice. With each breath she took, it swelled into the hollow of his palm. He could feel her heart beat, against the surging counterpoint of his own, beneath the full, firm flesh. She turned to look into his eyes.

"Remain in the abstract, if it makes you comfortable. You appreciate the, um, efficiencies of leaving a Drectorhood within the same family."

"I, er . . ." Ignoring his stammer, she pressed his hand against her, encouraging his fingertips, and gazed away, as if thinking. An awkward moment passed, during which Donol was afraid to move his hand. At last she made a gentle noise which, in one of her gender and breeding, denoted scorn.

"I should think it embarrassing when a Ceo grants a man title, praising his valor to the galaxy, then must revoke it upon charge of treason." At mention of his father, Donol's temper surged. As ever, caution restrained him. He played a risky game and did not know what the rules required of him. Alysabeth placed both hands over his before he could speak. "Forgive me, dearest. I only meant that some embarrassment might be saved, some confidence in the Ceo's judgment retained—if only his own—should the honor be restorable in the succeeding generation."

Donol dared offer nothing in reply. Upon occasion, regardless of the bargain with his brothers, this had been his very thought.

"Especially—" She seized his hand as if to press it the more chastely to her bosom and at the last instant turned it, so that his fingers slipped beneath the fabric, clasping the warm roundedness they discovered. His palm brushed a hardening nipple. Donol swallowed and was aware again of an uncomfortable heat rising within him. Alysabeth sighed and continued as if there had been no intervening period of silence—which there had been—as if their thoughts had not wandered—as they had done—but lingered upon the same subject. Which they did. "Especially when that confidence is reinforced by the opinion of the selfsame individual whom the Ceo was compelled to place in temporary charge of the Drectorhood."

Taking a rare risk, he firmed his hand upon her, looking into her eyes as he fumbled beneath her clothing. She shuddered, as if with passion. "Your father's good opinion?" As an afterthought: "I have not frightened you?"

Alysabeth smiled. Even Donol could not guess what feeling the expression was intended to convey. The corners of her eyes crinkled with delight, as if a dull-witted student had at last learned to recite his lessons. "It was your vehemence which moved me, darling. Yes, I mean my father's good opinion."

She pressed his hand the firmer to her body, released it, and let her own wander where it had earlier strayed in the office. "And what could constitute a more conspicuous testimonial—" her long-nailed fingers played over the fastening of his trousers, "—than that he offer the hand of his daughter to that individual possessed of sufficient virtue to step back into leadership?"

She plunged her hand into his clothing and it was his turn to shudder. As she leaned against his hand, he was compelled to bend his elbow, turning his forearm, which, intended or not, levered her gown from her shoulder. He caught a tantalizing glimpse of partial nakedness and knew a moment in which he burned to tear the rest of her clothing from her. She was almost lying in his lap. Her breath, hot and moist where he pulsed and hardened, was unbearably pleasurable. What it promised in the next few seconds—

A knock came at the door. Alysabeth was erect, clothing back in order, and standing beside the divan—while Donol fumbled with his trousers—when the door flew open. The servant girl had come to reclaim their untouched tray. Before she did, she turned and curtsied, casting her eyes to the floor as no Islay retainer had ever been required to do. "Begpardon, Mistress. Your father wishes t'see you quick as quick, in his offices."

"Oh dear, I must fly." Alysabeth dismissed the girl and turned to Donol, an expression of dismay wrinkling her otherwise flawless countenance. "It was a pleasant luncheon, Donol." Aching in every joint, he rose. She took his hand. "And we must do it again, soon."

Gritting his teeth, Donol bowed against the pressure of a dull throbbing he had begun to feel. "If you, er, wish it, dear lady . . ."

Alysabeth, out of sight of the departing bodyservant, winked at him. "Indeed, I do, I assure you most heartily. I shall be counting the hours."

"So shall I," his answer was grim. "Also." He followed as she left the room, both headed for the stairs. They turned from one another only at the last, she to descend to the office, he to ascend, the ache between his legs growing worse by the minute. Climbing stairs was difficult.

It was possible, he thought, that the price of all of these benefits Alysabeth and her father promised him might prove too dear. It would be worse when those formalities she had mentioned began to be observed. He was certain her father would insist. The Hanoverian custom—he had been so amused when Robret found it burdensome—held that what lovers had pursued with joy and vigor before their betrothal should, upon announcement of their engagement, be denied them until their wedding night. Thank the ironies of fate (he trembled with renewed anticipation) that he had a palliative close at hand, to which he had not earlier found recourse, but which he would now most likely seek—and use—with increasing frequency.

He hastened to claim his prisoner—his property—in the tower.

CHAPTER XXVIII:
A RENDEZVOUS IN NEWTOWN

"Newtown."

Lacking a better name or sufficient imagination, everyone called it that. "Thrown up" was an expression his informant had used, referring to its hasty construction, a phrase more descriptive than he had realized. How a place fresh-built could have such an aura of decay about it, Robret was uncertain. For all that it had been provided with the most efficient of waste disposal systems, it stank to the overclouded skies.

Clumping along a cheap meshwalk fronting flimsy buildings, he attempted to stamp away the mud his boots had acquired when he had crossed the unpaved street. All he achieved for his trouble were stares from passersby crowding him shoulder to shoulder. His impression was that they marked him for a dandy who would be easy prey once darkness fell. Well, he thought, comforted by the thrustible beneath the sleeve of his jacket, let them discover differently. Where, in the Ceo's dirty name, was the place he was supposed to find?

It was the noise, rather than the wordless placard over the door, which directed his steps. In garish daubs the latter depicted the drifting wreckage of a starvessel, putting a name to the establishment, *The Wasted Corsair,* while indicating the social stratum occupied by its habitués. The former was a nerve-despoiling mixture of coarse laughter, masculine and feminine, rattling serviceware, and unmelodic thill-blaring which, after his many days and nights in the deep silence of the forest, managed to sound obscene.

Taking a deep breath, and regretting it, he steeled himself to push the swinging doors aside. The scene within *The Wasted Corsair* was like a glimpse into some mythical repository of evil souls—or a parody of Hanoverian society. In the first place, it was dark. He could not, at first, make out a single human face, although, as his eyes adjusted, he observed that more light was available than he thought. Or desired. What made it seem so dark was a layer of smoke hanging at eye level. Voyaging through the galaxy, humankind had thus far discovered a hundred thousand things to set alight and inhale. Robret was conscious, as never before, that he was breathing air which, only moments earlier, filled the lungs of the disgusting creatures all about him. Through the haze, backlighting it, fuzzy globes of lanterns hanging from the rafters shed what illumination had been provided. The place would have been better off—and brighter—had they never been strung. Wherever he turned, he stared into the corona of one or another of them, other details in the room washed out by what could only be called their dim glare.

The Wasted Corsair was as crowded as the meshwalk outside. If possible, it smelled worse. In addition to the now almost friendly stenches of stagnant mud, animal excreta, and decaying garbage he had endured, to his revolted nostrils came effluvia of two hundred unwashed bodies, their physiologies—and resultant byproducts—altered by many kinds of smoke and drink, other drugs, an exotic mixture of foods. These last, with the vapor of many an upended beverage, added weight to the already overburdened atmosphere.

As his eyes adjusted, he looked round for the man with whom he had this meeting, despairing of success in a jungle of human forms. Although tricked out as a sailor's bar, this far from the port the tavern's male clientele affected farmers' and herdsmen's attire, along with the uniforms of soldiers from the Holdings. (How he longed for the day, forever lost, when this had been no more than a sweet, rain-washed meadow!) The women he divided into two categories, those who worked here and those with the men, distinguishable by the amount of clothing they wore—those belonging to the place wore cheap imitations of Hanoverian masques. At last he spied the one he was looking for, hunched at a small table close to the thille-player, dressed in well-worn *thiss* huntsman's leathers with a billed cap pulled over his eyes.

Robret pushed his way through the crowd. "Well, by the Ceo's septic sores, may they be fruitful and multiply, here I am."

"What is the password?" Donol grinned up at him from beneath the capbill, lowered his eyes again, and spoke to the dirty, drink-ringed tabletop. Robret sat upon the other chair, which threatened to dump him onto the floor before he reached down, straightened, and reseated a loose leg.

"How about 'I shall wring your pimply neck for you until you leave off playing children's games'?"

Across the table, Donol chuckled without looking up. He laid a hand upon his brother's forearm, felt the thrustible, and pulled his hand away. "I believe you mean it. You look the part of a woodsrunner, trim, hard as graniplastic. But a rude life has coarsened your sensibilities, old fellow."

This time Robret chuckled and began to relax. "It has coarsened a deal more, *old fellow*. Granting I ever had any. I have not slept in a bed in three months, nor had a hot bath in a week—though you could never tell it here—nor eaten since yesterday. I hate to be unsentimental about seeing my last remaining family member, but as soon as you have said what you have to say, I am for a bath, a meal, and a fortnight's sleep."

Donol shook his head. "The exigencies of history in the making. Let us have our council of war, after which you will be free to enjoy the fleshpots however you wish. I have grown rather to enjoy them, myself. It is not only your sensibilities which have been coarsened by current events. But would you care for something to drink? Whiskey? Klimstoag? Perhaps a beer?"

"That slop? I shall have a steaming cup of real caff, if they sell it."

Donol laughed. "I am informed that, upon certain planets, consumed by certain species, it is a narcotic. Extremely illegal, therefore guaranteed available in *The Wasted Corsair*. A moment, if you please—*barkeep!*"

As a serving-wench in a dirty apron brought their drinks, they heard a tinny crash. The smoke-filtered light within *The Wasted Corsair* did not flicker. Nor, save for the gong, did the noise rise or fall. Yet, within the tavern, the ambience changed as a flimsy curtain at the back was thrust aside and seven young girls in white, loose-fitting, high-necked garments, gathered at the wrists and ankles, issued past onto the stage, a mere hand's width above the filthy floor, and, unlike the building itself, constructed from metalloid mesh such as was to be found aboard starships.

The first girl turned to her right as she emerged, the second to her left. The third joined the first, and the fourth the second, until all six stood, perhaps two arms' lengths apart, in a well-formed row across the back. The seventh, and last, girl brushed past the curtain and appeared upon the stage without dramatic pause, without breaking the rhythm the previous six had established, a rhythm which existed, thus far, only in the minds of the men who watched, for, in the beginning, the girls had no accompanying music.

The seventh, too, dressed in white, one simple piece with voluminous sleeves and legs, cut from a fabric light in weight, yet not revealing. Nevertheless, Robret observed—nor could he have avoided feeling—an increasing tension among the men as she took her place at the center of the stage, forward of the others. They had rolled their hair or wore it short. She had wrenched her own dark tresses into a thick hank, held by a ring and cascading from it to the small of her back, leaving her long, graceful neck exposed. In her left hand she carried a small, cylindrical bundle, black, some twelve or thirteen siemmes in length, half that in diameter.

In what now seemed like the darkness offstage, a drum began to thump at a pace just slower than the beating of a sleeping heart. Moving to the beat, the girl at center stage bowed upon a straightened leg, arms spread, hair sweeping in a circle until it touched the floor. She rose and lifted her empty hand, gracefully indicating the others to her right, by way of silent introduction. They bent at the waist before she pivoted upon her toe and indicated those upon her left, who also bowed, although whether to acknowledge their audience or their fellow performer, Robret could not have attested.

The drum beat a trifle faster. Turning to her audience again, the girl held out the object she had with her for inspection.

Before Robret could tell what it was, she lifted her hand and poured its contents into her other hand. The cylinder had been a loose collection of thin nails or hair-needles, which gleamed and tinkled as they fell from one hand into the other. A low whisper, not quite a moan, swept through the audience. The drum beat faster. As before, the girl at center stage indicated the others who accompanied her. They, too, held bundles, smaller than hers, composed of fewer needlelike objects, which they transferred from hand to hand in glittering arcs.

Now the drum beat like a waking heart, alert, not quite yet frightened. Imitated by those behind her, the girl separated a needle from the bundle and held it in one hand, high above her head. Looking upward at its gleaming point, she danced in place beneath it, turning about as if as helpless to look away from it as Robret was to look away from her. The needle plunged, driven by her hand. She ducked at the last instant. The point entered her flesh at the hinge of her jaw, below the ear. When she took her hand away, only the shining head stood out from her skin like a bauble fastened to her lobe. The audience erupted with sympathetic groaning and wild applause which rose, stage by stage, to an unbearable volume of whistling, cheering, and stomping as she turned, bowing to display the bloodless self-inflicted wound.

"A terpsipuncturist," Donol whispered, his breath moist upon the sharper consonants, "from some backwater called Tannatham, and reputed to be a good one. Her apprentices are locals, I should reckon." Robret made a swatting motion at his younger brother, as at a buzzing insect, his eyes riveted to the figure upon the stage, fascinated and revolted by the spectacle before him.

With a graceful slide the terpsipuncturist removed herself to one side as her apprentices danced beneath their own gleaming needles. One by one, perhaps as each found the courage, they plunged the cruel implements home, standing for a moment as if surprised they had survived, afterward bowing to the delighted audience and their mistress, who pointed an accusing finger and shouted. Robret was aware of blood trickling down one girl's neck, a spreading stain in the white, absorbent fabric at her shoulder. Sobbing, the bleeding girl covered her face with her hands as the others stepped away from her. She pulled the needle from her flesh and scurried through the curtain.

"We'll not see her again," Donol asserted before he could be prevented.

The drum beat faster as a reed flute began twining itself like a sinuous reptile into the rhythm. The ritual was repeated, the dance beneath the deadly looking needle, the sudden plunge, the applause and cheering. The girl had stabbed herself in the nape of the neck, the needle sinking full length into her satiny flesh without shedding a drop of blood. Each of her remaining apprentices imitated her until the last fell, thrashing in convulsions, victim to a misplaced needle in her spine, hauled off—amidst hooting and jeering from the heartless crowd—with the rough, unhappy stage assistance of the establishment's peacekeepers. The drum beat faster, taunted by the flute.

This time, the crowd burst into applause at the veteran dancer's daring even before she placed the needle. She did, and stood back to give her four apprentices a chance. Imitating her mistress, the first placed a needle beside her eye, thrust, and, without a sound, pitched forward, dead. As she was being taken off, the terpsipuncturist waved the last three girls away, perhaps for further instruction, and faced the audience alone.

The drumbeat tripled its pace, leaving the flute confused and far behind. Leaping upon tiptoes, the dancer spun, whirling from one side of the stage to another, plunging needle after glistening needle into herself. Siemme by square siemme, the garment concealing her body yielded its secrets to her bizarre stitchery. As each bit was pinned to the girl's flesh, her voluptuous form emerged, to the enthusiasm of her audience, as the folds were tucked against her. No trace of blood could be discerned; to be certain, the fabric would have shown it. As the music reached an ear-shattering peak, it was as if she danced unclothed before them. Robret found himself unable to breathe. A glance at Donol caught him staring, openmouthed, although Robret gathered he had seen this all before. The drum continuous and the flute running ahead, the terpsipuncturist slapped furiously at herself. Robret cringed with each blow. She threw herself down and rolled about. Someone at a nearby table fainted. With the flute shrieking its final notes, she leapt up, snatched the needles out in handsful, and flung them aloft. The drum stopped. The needles pinged and clattered upon the planks. She was gone.

Robret thought the tavern might collapse about him as the men reacted, roaring, screaming, throwing food, drink, articles of clothing, pounding tables, stomping their feet. Coins of a thousand planets clattered upon the stage like hailstones upon a corrugated roof. Noise dwindled and he turned to his brother, almost failing to recognize the flushed, hungry face panting back at him. "I say, we have grown a bit primitive recently, have we not?"

Donol's feral expression dissolved as he regained control and transformed it into a cynical sneer. "You refer to me, brother?"

Robret sighed and looked about the room which had returned to whatever passed for normal. "I was making a more general observation, Donol. No personal slight intended. I must say, that was rather—impressive."

Donol's was not a pleasing expression. "Was it not, just? Well, I suppose one must get down to business, then."

"My plan is simple, brother," Donol spoke in low tones, more beneath the noise of the tavern than above it, "to reduce the esteem in which Hanover holds Morven, providing us an opportunity to replace the Usurper ourselves."

Robret nodded. "Yes, the plan is good—it always has been. And, whatever our failures, much has already been accomplished toward both ends."

"You believe," his brother asked, "Hanover will accept a *fait accompli?*"

"I did not risk all to come and discuss generalities, Donol. We must, in what time we have, exchange information and begin to cover contingencies."

"Sir, more respect." Donol made the protest with a crooked half smile. "You speak to the man about to marry the daughter of the Black Usurper!"

Robret gave him a sour look. "Anxious to legitimize himself in the eyes of the populace. He believes marrying her into the original ruling line will accomplish that." He paused, weighing his next words. "I fear this proposed marriage has produced mixed results. By some reckonings, Skyan among them, betrothal to one's father's widow is incestuous. It has angered people."

"What can I do?" Donol spread his hands in a helpless gesture. "At the Holdings, I am scarcely more than the prisoner I was to start. Forget the adolescent cynicism I displayed before hard circumstances taught me better. Any damage my reputation suffers as a result of our connivance is a welcome sacrifice to the cause of ridding Skye of the Black Usurper."

Robret gave his brother a look of inspection. His brother looked back and grinned. "Then we are agreed. I shall continue sending what material aid I can, and meet with you whenever needful, having established a pattern of habituating disreputable places such as this. Meantime, let me tell you what I have managed to learn of the Usurper's plans."

They ordered another round, caff for Robret, and settled to an account of Morven's contact with the *Rii,* their desire for new stars. The silence existed only between the brothers, *The Wasted Corsair* remained as noisy as before. As Robret attempted to absorb what Donol told him, of a sudden the younger of the two seemed to change the subject. "Father may have had his reasons. Perhaps he had wearied of a lifetime of politics and war—"

Robret sighed and rubbed his palms over his eyes, which were surrounded by black pits. "A weariness I well understand."

An impatient expression crossed his younger brother's face. "Still in all, we Islays have made a great mistake, isolating ourselves from the rest of the galaxy, a mistake we must remedy in future if the family is to survive."

Robret let his hands drop to the table. "For conversation's sake, how, at this late date, do you suggest we begin?"

"I have done. While you were among the mountains and forests, I studied our enemy and the landscape he moves in—a deal more, brother, than our father knew of his friend Morven." Robret nodded, growing interested. "The first thing," Donol offered, "is that, interminable and frequent as we know them to be, the Ceo's wars consume soldiers in quantities unimaginable to us. And Oplytes, who do the bulk of the Ceo's fighting, do not last long."

"So I have heard. And?"

"He whom we call 'Black Usurper' is called by another name within plush-paneled council chambers of the capital. 'The Ceo's pimp.' This is how he rose to prominence, finding soldiers for the Ceo. If he would maintain his position, he requires a supply of bodies. Skye, which otherwise possesses nothing of unique value to Morven, aside from opportunity to revenge himself upon our father, is in unparalleled legal position to provide bodies."

Robret shook his head in tired confusion. For him the freedom of Skye, the preeminence of his family and their reputation, were primaries. This was new to him, that events here had broader meaning beyond the battle for this world. He said nothing. Donol continued: "Now—and, I believe, unlooked-for by anyone upon Hanover—Morven has been promised by these *Rii*ans some device, substance, or process capable of enslaving an entire planet."

Robret sat up straight. *"What?"*

The younger brother nodded. "No more than I have said. It is his most cherished secret. Even exaggerated, it can only add to our sufferings. It not only offers to solve the imperium-conglomerate's manpower problem, but to resolve the Thousand Years' War or any future conflict in the Monopolity's favor. Or, as I believe, in favor of a more powerful Morven."

"This is fantasy, Donol, such technology has no antecedent in Mon—"

"In a manner of speaking"—Donol chuckled—"you are correct. Morven's secret is no outgrowth of human scientific endeavor, which falls, these days, into greater and greater neglect. I suspect not one original invention has been made in any of the imperia-conglomerate for centuries." This was something Lia had made much of in the years she had been their teacher.

"So?"

"So I have come to believe in this promised power he looks forward to, for the very reason that it is non-human in origin."

Although he remained skeptical—his brother's logic was not the best—Robret nodded. Human endeavor, in all respects save those of brutalizing, robbing, or enslaving other beings, was upon the wane. Moreover, heretofore unheard-of sapients were hardly novel within the boundaries of the Monopolity. Some, brought home as living souvenirs from voyages of exploration, traded through hundreds of hands in dozens of systems until no one might guess their origins, were known to appear in the capital and elsewhere, as carnival freaks, to enjoy dubious welcome as objects of curiosity and derision in the 'Droom, and later to become ordinary slaves, in the capital, upon subject worlds, or upon their own planets under Monopolitan "protection."

Some, the eerie "stiquemen," the enigmatic turnip-shaped *kooloon,* appeared from time to time upon their own exploratory voyages. These visitors hailed from powerful but unknown domains, bringing gifts to the 'Droom. A copious (if somewhat disorganized and mysterious) trade throve in odd artifacts and substances—even odder ideas had a way of showing up at unpredictable intervals—with more unknowns outside the ill-defined boundaries of the Monopolity. Sometimes outbound Hanoverian starships disappeared in stranger circumstances than was to be expected when privateers roamed the Deep, a Thousand Years' War raged, and unknown reaches were being explored. For the most part, however, human culture seemed to be the most advanced in portions of the galaxy so far explored. Those looking to others for secret powers or new technologies were more often disappointed than otherwise.

Robret ignored the surroundings and his brother to think, difficult when one was as weary as he felt. Donol was unsure what the Usurper had promised to pay for the alien technology. They guessed, knowing the man, that in the end someone else would be left to settle the bill. He was certain Morven did not actually possess it yet and would be anxious to test it. Both thought the test would be carried out upon Skye, with the intention of impressing the precolonial population, since their rights as subjects of the Monopolity were—this was as new to Robret as anything Donol had to tell him—a matter of legal debate. The brothers and their allies would be fools not to seize this opportunity. If the technology were real, they had no choice.

Returning to the world outside his thoughts, Robret settled down with his brother to forge a plan.

CHAPTER XXIX:
UPON THE SPIRAL STAIRWAY

He was late.

Fastening his trousers, Donol locked the door behind him and started down the staircase leading to the lower Holdings. What he thought of as "the Festivities" were beginning in the courtyard, and here he was, malodorous, sweaty with exertion, unkempt and disarrayed, having dallied overlong at what, by any objective estimate, should have been no more than a hobby.

Reflections danced upon a curving wall where light struck upward through an arch-topped window of the landing outside the door he had just secured: the glitter of polished military hardware, far below. Under the gaze of Morven and his administrators, nonentities to the last man, the Hanoverians were forming themselves into ranks, Oplytes in one long row, humans in another. Even high within the building, their booted clattering across the flags, the shouted commands of officers, could not be mistaken.

Running a hand over his face, Donol wondered how quickly he could change his clothes, bathe, and shave. Before he had descended three steps, he felt a tickling sensation and lifted the hand to his cheek again. It came away bloody. A small scratch, one he would obtain payment for the next occasion he came here, tonight or tomorrow. Events were beginning to pile up. He found he had little time these days for anything besides the complicated, dangerous game he played with Morven and his brother. He extracted a monoquoded handkerchief from his tunic pocket, dabbed at his cheek until the cloth came away dry and, putting it away, continued downstairs, sated for the nonce, the current of his thoughts rushing along channels other than the hot, black, churning of arousal, frustration—and desire, for the moment satisfied, to exact a toll from more than one individual at once—which had become of late a sort of background noise roaring in his mind.

He paused upon the next landing and through another window watched preparations for the arrival of the entity Morven was calling the *Rii*an ambassador. He had seen, as yet, no sign of an approaching vehicle, nor would he. The creature was not coming from Alysabethport. The story being handed about was that, although they could not travel among the stars without human assistance, *Rii*ans possessed means of overcoming gravity, at least within the minor influence of a planet, independent of such awkward contrivances as starports and lubberlifts. Given the delight with which his brother and the woodsrunners interrupted greenway traffic, Donol thought this just as well. He began to curse himself again for being late, when, with sudden insight, he realized it might not do any harm, being absent from what was about to happen.

Weeks had passed before Donol announced an opportunity to make good their plans. Robret was allowed to learn of Morven's arrangement for meeting with the *Rii* somewhere upon Skye, sometime in the near future. The guerillas would raid the meeting place, the Holdings itself, directed by Robret, operating upon information the elder brother could only obtain from Donol. The strike would be timed to embarrass the Usurper at a crucial, reputation-destroying juncture. More important, it had to occur before Morven could make use of the *Rii*an technology he awaited with greater anticipation every day.

Upon the next landing, halfway down the tower, Donol met a soldier, human rather than Oplyte (Alysabeth, he had learned, affected a horror of the latter and would not have them "in the house"), perhaps no more than nineteen years old. Seeing Donol sooner than expected, he halted and snapped to attention.

"Sir!"

Donol had found time to rearrange his clothing, run fingers through his sandy, thinning hair, and fasten his tunic to the throat. Standing several steps higher, he gave the boy his most supercilious expression.

"Sir, I have been sent to . . . to . . ."

"To hurry me? Speaking as aristocrat to peasant, we shall spare you embarrassment and consider your message delivered. Has the fighting begun?"

"Nossir, that it ha'n't. Have no fear, sir, 'twere never in doubt." At that moment a scream followed the thrum of thrustibles. Further off, came an explosion. Donol returned the boy's eager smile with one more cynical.

"You are commended for your prescience. I want you to remain here, where you are, and permit no one to pass. Do you think you can do that?"

"Yes . . . sir." Disappointment clouded his features. Donol was appalled. The boy *wanted* to go and risk his life! Could one ever account for another's taste? Perhaps this was the difference between classes, a willingness to fight, as opposed to a willingness to send others. To Donol, the latter seemed far more rational. The boy could learn something from this reprieve. In any case, he would not be the first unhappy soldier in history.

"See you do; they also serve who only stand and guard." Without awaiting reply, Donol hurried downstairs, thinking about this willingness to fight, and about his brother. They had met again upon several occasions, in *The Wasted Corsair* and other lower-class haunts, arranging transfer of supplies pilfered, although Robret was unaware of it, with the Usurper's permission, planning action after lesser action which consumed more resources than they won for the rebellion, seeing to the reproduction and distribution of subversive thilles intended to arouse the populace—but edited by subtle, clever Alysabeth, so that, by accumulation, they produced an attitude of despairing apathy—outlining various contingencies, and finalizing their overall plans.

In one respect, he had no further reason to envy Robret. Each time they had met, the latter had asked after Lia, once other business had been settled, and entrusted the former with some message which impressed even Donol as impersonal and perfunctory, considering that the two were lovers interrupted upon the brink of marriage. Mocking himself for it, Donol had felt almost indignant upon her account, although he had not hesitated to relay the cold communication at propitious moments, enjoying its disheartening effect.

Passing another window in his downward spiral, a deep shudder of gratitude—that he was up here watching instead of down there fighting—crept through Donol's body as the battle heated below. It had all been so sudden. The woodsrunners and Morven's legions were now engaged man-to-man, squads against individual Oplytes (the latter mosttimes victorious), puny humans attempting to defend themselves, without much effect, from skycraft whose walking beams crushed whatever in their path their thrusting failed to destroy. The plans he and Robret had made, over many weeks in many different taverns, were now betrayed. By evening, likeliest within the hour, Donol would become, as he had always intended, next to inherit the Drectorhood. Chuckling to himself, he resumed his twisting descent.

Robret had found it easiest to accept whatever his brother had seen fit to tell him of the well-being of the young woman who was, in fact, Donol's well-used property, occupied with no concern other than the chafing of her restraints, the confines of her kennel, the extent to which survival depended upon permitting her body to gratify his every demand, however intrusive or humiliating. So much for love stories and fairy tales. The sad reality appeared, even to Donol, that Lia was less important to Robret than Robret to her. In truth, the eldest of the brothers, in the estimate of the middle, had never seemed much motivated by any passion, let alone those attendant upon romance, sex, even the duties of Drector-Hereditary-in-Exile upon which he acted, but for which he demonstrated little visible enthusiasm.

Passing yet another window, Donol was distracted. Even this far from ground level, the screams of dying men, and of those killing them, were next to intolerable. More and more of the courtyard seemed covered with crimson splashes or the crude soot-stains of explosions. It was futile, Donol told himself, and stupid. Did no one recognize a fact of grim reality as he did? Could no one cut his losses, give in to the inevitable, instead of wasting what pittance he had left of his resources without hope of future recovery? As before upon the greenway, Robret's attack upon the Holdings had proved, as ordained from the beginning, a Hanoverian ambush. Why could people never—

Balloonlike, the window before him bulged inward, glowing with unnatural light, crazed over its surface like pottery gone wrong in a kiln. In a corner of his mind, Donol realized this was adrenaline, his perceptions heightened by the threat of death. He threw himself aside, out of the way of a window in process of being destroyed, and the spell broke, time resumed its normal flow. A primitive rocket grenade crashed through, filling the passageway with the smoke and flames of its exhaust, and splashed against the wall, dashing itself to pieces. The hand-shaped explosive charge had failed to detonate. As he picked himself up off the floor, inspected himself for injuries, and shook broken glass from his clothing, Donol discovered that he was indignant. What could Robret have been thinking of? His own brother might have been killed!

Upon the other hand, what led him to believe Robret could think? Already he had another lover in whom he found whatever solace he required, a hardy woodsrunner girl. Donol never doubted she had made all the moves in the direction of his brother, who always had other matters occupying his feeble mind and seemed to have forgotten Lia altogether at some level, visceral or lower. He had even brought his haughty peasant wench, scarcely more than a teenager, to their last rendezvous. In her presence, Robret had appeared more animated and at the same time more relaxed. Fionaleigh Savage: appropriate for the manner in which she radiated musky energy for measures in every direction, as well as for the fiercely proprietary manner in which she clung to Robret's side, devouring him with her dark, fire-filled eyes. Donol had withheld it all from Lia until the moment he could savor it best. He doubted that any female would ever look at him with quite the same—

At last, and perhaps just as well, he reached the stairfoot, feeling he had fallen into the barrel of a huge kaleidothille, filled with chaos churning for its own sake. A few rebels had breached the Holdings—it was amazing any had managed— but were being mopped up. Personnel poured from Morven's office to combat a blaze started when one had hurled some volatile against the wall, dousing himself as well. Before being extinguished, flames had crawled to the ceiling, consuming an ancient hanging from Shandish and scorching an expanse of graniplastic, although greater heat would have been required to melt it. Having died screaming, the arsonist was now a pile of blackened, grinning leather smoldering upon the floor, filling the place with the reek of petroleum fractions and cooked meat. Waiting for a clear avenue between him and his goal, Donol observed it all with detachment, his thoughts elsewhere.

Robret's new girl-woman. What a waste! Young she was as their dead brother Arran. Not as amply proportioned as Lia, but with a compensating dynamism. Tight-bodied, smooth-skinned, moist-mouthed. Quivering with pent-up heat entirely lost upon its principal object. How anyone could be so obtuse as Robret, Donol was at a loss to understand. He would believe anything any self-serving knave told him, so long as it was less bother than the truth. It annoyed Donol, even when the self-serving knave was himself. It had never occurred to Robret that Donol might be anything but what he represented himself to be, or might want anything but what he represented himself to want. Perhaps gullibility demanded less effort.

Donol crossed to the double doors. Inside, chaos was more bureaucratic than military. The suite was deserted. Maps, abandoned by those conscripted into firefighting, had been marked, erased, remarked as tactical actualities changed. Situation estimates elsewhere upon the moonringed planet were being updated, disposition made of the spoils as if already won. He peered at the largest map. Robret had put everything into this operation, as he and his future father-in-law had planned. The rest of Skye was quiescent. The majority of the rebels' hard-won equipment—vehicles, weapons, supplies—had been brought against the Holdings only to be destroyed or taken.

An aide appeared, looking for Donol to inform him that Morven had taken to the safety of the dungeons at the first sign of invasion. Now a prisoner had been identified who merited special questioning, Donol to assist in the process. Pulse quickening, Donol left the office, thoughts racing ahead of their own accord. He was, he told himself, the victim of no such illusions as his brother suffered. At least such was to be believed provisionally, wished for with some fervency. He knew what he was, a male Fionaleigh, no less savage for all that she bore the appropriate name, no less avid for satiation, no less desirous of power in all forms it might assume. Toward fulfilling his desires he had labored, conferring with his brother against Morven, with Morven against Robret, making visits to the tower often as he could, where he could discharge the tensions a double life engendered, in an ambience where the power he wielded, over a single life, at least, was absolute.

In the first weeks of her captivity, he had supplemented his visits with excursions into town, in part from a necessity to learn things he might apply during his sessions in the tower. His experience with Lia had been dangerous, exhausting, and left something to be desired in the way of compliance upon her part and satisfaction upon his own. Also, he had ventured out to establish a pattern accounting for his absences when meeting with his brother. In the end, out of loathing for the tawdriness of professional women, dissatisfaction with a submission they counterfeited in exchange for money, and fastidious fears he had not realized he owned of exotic, incurable maladies—new artifacts and ideas being not the only things these days imported from beyond the Monopolity —he had begun making fewer such trips.

More stairs, into the foundations. He paused at the top, watching order being restored, surrenders accepted, with shouts for quarter and reversed arms everywhere as the rebels realized their situation. Prisoners would be sorted, some fed to the Oplytes, others sedated and lifted offplanet in consignment to the Ceo. This, he reflected, shaking his head, was the inevitable return upon intransigence; the coin in which, throughout history, little men always paid for breasting currents set in motion by larger men. Integrity and bravery were not the irreducible primaries these defeated idiots believed. They were scarce commodities, luxuries no wise individual aspired to unless he could afford them. Like money, they were not ends in themselves, but instruments to be accumulated—and expended—with greater gain in mind. Why had these fools set so impossible a figure upon their honor that anyone wishing to deal with them was priced out of the market? What had they hoped to purchase with their courage? Freedom? What was that? Donol knew these people. Had they driven Morven offplanet, they would have turned the next moment and enslaved each other, calling the process "self-government."

He had never owned any bravery to expend. With that share of integrity which is inherited by every being, he had purchased something less illusory, less ephemeral than freedom: power. He had traded off a quality men call character, as he had traded off excursions into town, telling himself he obtained all he wanted within the confines of the Holdings. Events here, revolving about his brother and prospective father-in-law, merited more concern. Alysabeth also demanded attention, her promises, ever couched in the most provocative terms were always interrupted short of fulfillment, causing someone else, within as few minutes afterward as possible, to suffer the more. Someday he would make property of the Usurper's daughter, add her to his collection, as it were, and work his will upon her as he did Lia.

He reached the bottom of the steps. Even here, in the dusty dampness of the foundations, the air rang with shouted excitement. Its general import seemed to be that the war, to any extent the word applied, was over. The back of the rebellion was broken. Donol wondered idly what that woodsrunner bitch would be like to tame and add to his—so far—imaginary collection, then shied from the thought, recalling the casual grace with which a thrustible had rested upon her arm. His first act as Drector would forbid women to carry weapons. Feeling better, he pushed aside a grated door to confront the prisoner being held there for questioning. "Hullo, Robret," he addressed his brother, "how have they been treating you, old man?"

Threadbare coverlet about her, Lia folded the bit of conductile she had used to unlock the tower door, relocking it behind her in precaution. It might delay anyone who suspected she was missing. Otherwise unclothed, and barefoot, she hurried down the stairs toward the occupied floors of the Holdings, too aware of what was happening in the courtyard. She was also aware of the stench of fear clinging to her, mingled with the sweat of physical conflict and worse—and that her hair stuck out in all directions—but nothing could be done about it now. Spots of milling, multicolored light upon an inner wall reflected greater events below. Morven's minions were retreating from attacking rebels, shielding behind a wall of Oplytes advancing across the flagstones at the shouted command of their officers.

Lia ran a hand over her face, wishing for real clothing and a bath. She descended, each motion awakening bruises, scratches, strains, and other abuses which, until this moment, she had no choice but suffer. For too long survival had hung upon satisfying Donol's punitive appetites, hoping for opportunity to exact retribution. Now, tonight or tomorrow, unless his "helpless prisoner" prevented it, he would become next claimant to the Drectorhood. She had no time for the fury roiling within her, but paused upon a landing below only to glance out another window. Had she learned earlier of this meeting with an alien ambassador, she might have stopped it before it was planned. Donol's boasting had warned her of the event and the guerilla raid it was bait for. One look told her the rebellion was finished, all overt resistance to Morven crushed. Certain obligations remained to be discharged, one of them to determine whether these aliens in fact existed, along with their mysterious technology, and what use Morven hoped to make of it.

At the next landing, halfway down the tower, a young soldier jerked to attention as, lost in thought and—she realized too late—incautious, she halted, expecting the thrum of his thrustible to end her escape.

"Stand where you are!" His voice squeaked at the end of the sentence. Her smile was as sweet as she could manage, while, grateful he was not an Oplyte, she planned the next few seconds' action.

"Of course, Sergeant. Is it permissible to see the battle?"

He cleared his throat. "Trooper, ma'am, I got orders no one passes."

"Well," she smiled again, awaiting opportunity, "I would not wish you to disobey—" His attention distracted by an explosion and a scream, he let his eyes wander. This was all she required. Flipping the one weapon she had—a metal brace from the bedframe which she had, with great effort, removed and sharpened over the past weeks—from where it lay concealed by her palm and wrist, she drove it with her whole body, straight at his cheek. The makeshift knife slipped into his flesh, skipping along his cheekbone into the eye socket. Lia released her grip and drove it home with the heel of her hand. The trooper crumpled at her feet. Pausing to strip his thrustible from him, she hurried downstairs, tightening the straps about her arm.

Her descent, now, was more circumspect. At the next stop upon what had begun to feel like an interminable journey, she discovered a window shattered by one of the chemenergics— "arpeegee," Robret had called it, in one of his cool, mechanical messages—he had reintroduced to good effect into the art of thirty-first-century warfare. The hand-made contrivance was far from perfect. She found its unexploded cargo lying at the foot of the wall it had struck, amidst glass fragments and other debris, along with one of Donol's handkerchiefs with which it appeared he had wiped blood from some part of himself.

Pacing the limits of her cell, trying to evade a despair threatening to overwhelm her, Lia had told herself she did not blame her fiancé for conveying no warmth in messages entrusted to a third party, even a brother he falsely believed reliable. Donol, not content to torture her physically, had leapt at the chance to comment upon the sterility of Robret's communication, wallowing in the effect it produced upon her already devastated morale. Despite taunts, she had always known she loved Robret rather better than he loved her. As his bride-to-be she had resigned herself, mindful of the many preoccupations of a conscientious heir, admiring his unrufflable, undemonstrative nature—contrasted with what she felt to be her own unpredictable swings in temperament —for, although he had never been much given to passion's heights, neither was he a victim of the inevitable, compensating depths.

Lia shook her head, tears in her eyes, ashamed she had permitted her mind to wander. It was not that she avoided the grim facts of reality. She had focused upon one at the expense of others with better claim upon her. Through the broken window she observed the courtyard, stained with the blood of those whose dying screams already ceased to echo. It had been over with so soon. Man against man, woodsrunner against trooper—even given the Oplytes—it might have been a match. But humans, protected only by their courage, against flyers! She could see the trail they had left, spelled out in broken flesh.

It would not change what Lia had to do. Although she sometimes served interests at conflict with her beliefs—or made greater sacrifices—she was guided by what she felt were certain self-evident (or at least fundamental) principles. Liberty, for all the word had fallen out of fashion, was the inheritance of every individual. One thing was efficacious in defending it (no guarantee being given even then): uncompromising courage. If Robret's counter-stroke had failed, if he himself were killed or taken, even if he had taken this Skyan girl as his lover, as Donol gloated, and forgotten his "unwedded wife," she must continue his effort. If her role in life was to keep promises made by others, so be it. She would keep promises of her own at a better place and time, once the other was accomplished.

At the stairfoot, which she reached at long last, the clamor had not altogether died. Upon the contrary, the ground floor seethed with movement at cross-purposes, yelling and killing. Somehow the rebels had broken through, or perhaps had been within the walls all along among the servants. Someone had smashed a litre of some incendiary—"molotov" was the ancient word, another of Robret's practical revivals—against one wall, destroying a prized Shandeen tapestry and blackening the ceiling. Smoke filled the hallway even yet, the smell of the *molotov*—and of its victims—overpowering.

Taking advantage of soldiers who should have been upon guard and people dragooned out of offices, still coping with results of the fire, Lia slipped along a wall, heart pounding loud enough to distract her even above the noise, and crossed where lingering smoke was thickest. She entered the abandoned suite. Inside, the thrust-battered body of a rebel slumped over a table, half-buried in tatters of a large map upon which tactical projections and situation estimates had been marked with grease-pencil. The dead man had been in process of stripping it from a wall. In seconds, Lia was across the room to the inner office, the door of which had been left ajar, uncertain what she sought. Access to Morven's sanctum was not a thing to be depended upon twice. The threat represented by alien technology was of the highest priority.

Cursory examination of the room yielded nothing of particular interest. The maps outside were of greater value. She was about to give up, with a sense of peril survived to no good purpose, when, running her fingers beneath an edge of the desk, she heard a faint springing and a portion of the desk's surface slid upward. Inside a small cabinet, open upon the side which faced a person seated at the desk, was an unfamiliar looking object, rather like a lantern lying upon its side, transparent or translucent (Lia was uncertain which) with metal ends, integral base, and what appeared to be a wire handle.

No chair stood behind the desk. Moving one from before it, she sat down. With one eye upon the door—which she had closed and locked—and a comforting (if purposeless) grip upon the yoke of her confiscated thrustible, she extended her left hand and seized the wire handle.

CHAPTER XXX:
THE DUNGEON AND THE TOWER

Robret lay strapped to a mechanical table, clothing removed and minor wounds from his capture dressed. He was conscious, watching Donol with clear, sane eyes which refused any reply save contempt. Upon his chest, a folded serviette had been placed. In its middle, lay a thille.

Feeling deprived of his due, Donol shook his head. Not wasting further words, he glanced about the room, so harshly illuminated as to make his eyes water. It was cleaner than he had ever seen these basement chambers; walls, floor, and ceiling scrubbed until they shone—in all probability sterilized, as well—the junctures of the graniplastic blocks,

bulging under the load they bore, sealed to prevent contami-
nation. Upon one spotless wall a colorful poster had been
affixed, portraying the distorted image of a human figure the
proportions of which were altered to convey the relative
density of nerve-endings in any given portion of the body.
Donol thought it grotesque but of considerable interest.
Upon another table nearby, identical to that where Robret
lay, some thoughtful individual had left a portable thille
reader.

"Excuse me." With a cheerful nod for his brother, Donol
picked up the thille, crossed the room, slid it into the device.
The image was of Morven, seated at his desk. At his side
stood Alysabeth. Donol kept the volume low. Once the
message had finished, he turned, grinning, to confront Robret
again. "Our hosts," he declared, "are generous beyond com-
pare. At least with me. They find ways to provide for my
future, they give me gifts. Presently they will offer me an
advantageous marriage and, in due course, a Drectorhood."

Robret failed to answer.

"As you have no doubt guessed, a betrayer lurks within
Skyan ranks and always has done: none other than your own
brother. You may be interested to learn the visit from the
*Rii*an ambassador was a hoax." He paused to allow reply,
received none, and determined to continue. "Morven and I
believed telling you of the *Rii* would draw you into launching
your raid at a place and time of our choosing. If you judge
that I have allowed myself to be lured from the righteous
Skyan cause, dear brother, you judge correctly. Promise of
unlimited wealth and power have that effect upon me, I
confess."

"Like whatever dark charms that bitch offers!" Robret
raised his head with effort. "Daughter that she is to Father's
murderer, and your stepmother, you incestuous bag of shit!
You will wind up with some embarrassing disease. It is
obvious you already suffer a severe case of blue—"

"Articulate at last," Donol frowned, "and correct.
Alysabeth's influence upon me is considerable, but of a
different character than you might expect. Marriage to the
daughter of the man the Ceo sent puts me doubly in line to
inherit the title of Drector-Hereditary." He moved closer to

his brother, put his hands together, interlaced his fingers, and rested his chin upon them. "I have always coveted your position in the birth order, resenting at the deepest level of my soul the fact that everything, *everything!—*"

Donol paused, drawing a number of deep breaths. "Everything would have devolved upon you, a man constitutionally incapable of enjoying pleasure of any kind. Now all that has changed. The one person remaining in the path of my ambitions is a wheelchair-bound invalid who cannot live much longer and, with all his heart, wants me to possess his lovely daughter and to inherit his position. You see why I could not resist. Who might, given my place?"

Robret let his head fall to the table. Donol smiled. "As if this were not enough, Morven has made me another gift, of your death, which he means to be the most elaborate demise of its sort ever contrived. Technicians, lately arrived from Hanover, will join us when I desire." He indicated the ceiling above the table. "Look upon yourself, Robret, this mirror has been provided to that purpose. Morven is a connoisseur and means this as an example of his subtlest art. He left a message, in your care, as it were, so that even I, the merest amateur, might appreciate what he has ordered done."

At a leisured pace, Donol moved to the head of the table where large cylinders stood upon their ends against a wall, hung with transparent tubes, one ending in a breathing masque. "You will suffer no pain. The means by which some persons will themselves to death will be circumscribed. I believe this a prime feature of Morven's genius. You will experience no distraction from the *concept* of what is being done. This is an unconventional request, the normal course being to enhance pain. Your mind, your senses—eyesight, hearing—will remain functional, perhaps more so than ever."

In the mirror, Donol watched his brother's eyes widen at these words. "Your body will be opened." The eyes showed more fear. Donol smiled. "Each of your vital organs will be removed, replaced by the machinery you see about you. This, for example, insures that blood, suffused with oxygen, continues to circulate after the heart and lungs are gone. Your stomach, liver, intestines, all will follow in inverse order of their importance, so that, at each stage, you will deceive yourself the procedure remains reversible."

Donol's smile vanished as he leaned toward Robret, hissing. "It will not be, for its irreversibility depends upon no petty mechanical detail, but upon my will to see you discomfited. Which is implacable."

The smile reappeared, Donol's tone approaching that of conversation. "You will find you are unable to refrain from imagining I might be dissuaded. Measures will be taken so that you continue capable of pleading, at first for reprieve, at last for swift, clean death." Donol rubbed his hands together and circled the table. "And, dear brother, you will see every moment of it! Oblivion will be denied you! We even possess means to keep you from closing your eyes! From the neck up, you will feel normal. From there down, you will be a hollow shell, sealed up again neat and tidy, dependent upon my will for whatever remaining days, weeks if we are lucky, you enjoy, if that is the word for it." Donol halted, eyes bright, and leaned into his brother's face again. "Never again will you eat, eliminate, draw breath, let alone participate in life's more gratifying functions. I have not been told whether you will sleep. I should not think you would want to. The dreams might be worse than reality. Dependent upon your attitude, you may be allowed, trailing tubes and conductiles, to arise and perambulate. By any practical measure, you will be dead, a biological curiosity. Long after you weary of such an empty—pardon the expression—existence, you may be permitted to finish dying."

For a moment, Robret's eyes were wild, with horror at what he had been told or with murderous anger at his brother. In an instant, they regained a normal, almost sleepy appearance. Donol became alarmed lest his victim faint, depriving him of further pleasure. He reached out and slapped Robret across the face. Ignoring Donol, Robret whispered the name of the girl he had loved and left behind. Donol laughed.

"I looked forward to this, fearing you had formed another attachment." Which would be a pity, Donol thought, considering that Fionaleigh Savage was neither among the prisoners nor the dead. "Pay attention, now. You will find what I have to say of some importance." He watched his brother's eyes.

"You see, while wooing Morven's daughter, I have, by his explicit invitation, had my way with your woman, as well. *Every day!* I force myself upon her, use her in every manner possible, hurt her, demean her, humiliate her, punish her, do you hear, for every advantage you ever enjoyed by virtue of your birth!"

A sick look colored Robret's eyes. Again he struggled to raise his head. "Every perverse appetite Alysabeth stimulates within you—and frustrates?"

Donol hurled himself from the table. "Have it your way," he shouted, "dead man! Hollow man! I shall give you a choice of what to watch when the technicians begin. I shall go to the tower this instant and take your girl again, enthilling it so you can watch, as they eviscerate you, what I shall continue doing to her long after you are wormfood!" Robret's head sank to the table, his mouth working with pain. Donol laughed. "While you wait here, knowing what I do, here is a thought to savor. I planned this a long time. The lots we drew, determining our fates—Arran to certain death, you to ignominy, me to power, wealth, the sweet bodies of your woman and my own—were contrived. You drew the stem I intended, do you hear me, Robret?" This time Donol received no response. His brother's eyes were closed. "Robret!"

Frustrated, Donol slapped his brother's face again. Robret's head rolled. From his open mouth gushed a torrent of scarlet fluid. *"Robret!"*

The eldest brother had bitten his tongue through, and was dead.

Light unbearable. *Heat* impossible. *Sound,* which hammered, not just at Lia's ears but at every square siemme of her body. In the focus of her field of consciousness, a multi-limbed figure moving, swimming, at home amidst the intense and brilliant hammering which was the heartbeat of a living star.

It spoke. *"Acknowledgement, Lia Woodgate, Knowledge-Conveyor and Inheritor of the affiliance Islay upon the planetary body Skye, of mutual existence and psychological visibility. I am a pseudoresponsive communicale, within limits capable of answering questions. My outer envelope is neces-*

sitated by differences between our environments. Without it, I would not survive exposure to your surroundings, nor would you survive exposure to me."

Lia heard herself speak. "Who are you? *What* are you?"

"My enthilleur is Zerushaa, Thinker-Questioner of the nation-state Aahnaash, of the Rii. It is his voice and appearance you experience. He has enthilled me within the central regions of a medium yellow sun, not unlike the primary of your own stellar complex, to convey to you knowledge of his existence, and to propose a transaction of mutual benefit . . ."

A chill seemed to pass through Lia's body. " 'Knowledge-Conveyor' I understand. Why do you call me Inheritor?"

The communicale appeared not to answer her question. *"It is essential that you understand I am more than just a message enthilled earlier in another place. I am also capable of drawing information from those I communicate with and, in a limited fashion, forming conclusions."*

Every moral fiber she possessed was called upon as Lia framed her next question. "You draw a conclusion which leads you to call me Inheritor?"

"Ritual formula of regret, that my capabilities are finite and that additional limitations have been placed upon them by my enthilleur. You, Lia Woodgate, Knowledge-Conveyor and Inheritor, must adjudge for yourself whether I have obtained correct data and make correct inferences. If so, I have come too late to be of use to anyone else of your affiliance."

"Arran is truly dead?"

"Ritual formula of regret, I possess no referent—yes: insufficient data regarding missing Arran, third of the affiliance. You have become the appropriate recipient because you are affiliated, under the customs of your people, with Robret of the affiliance Islay, Drector-Hereditary-in-Exile upon the planetary body of Skye. It is he who is dead."

Lia missed the next comments made by the communicale. Had she not been experiencing what seemed much like a dream, she might well have lost consciousness with the shock of hearing this, even from an uncertain source.

". . . Morven, capable of any act in order to achieve what he desires. The daughter, Alysabeth, is strategically insignifi-

cant. Yet within her, at a tactical level, exists unlimited potential for evil. You are to be warned in her presence. She has already helped subvert the moral well-being of the entity Donol, second of the affiliance."

"You t-tell me nothing new. What of this proposition you offer?"

"I was coming to that . . ."

A shadow fell across her. The first sound Lia heard as her eyes swam into focus was the voice of the Black Usurper. "It would appear Mistress Woodgate has certain skills with locks we were not aware she possessed."

Out of sight, Alysabeth tittered. Aware of her surroundings, Lia sat in the chair she had placed behind the desk—the communicale had vanished—head pillowed upon its surface by her arm, from which the thrustible had been removed. Lifting her head, she saw the weapon lying in Morven's lap.

"Tell me, Lia, have you been enjoying my practical joke?"

"Joke?" She was groggy. The word came in a croak.

"Why, yes. I am learning to program that contraption, and fear you are a victim of one of my small hoaxes. Pardon me, if what I ask is personal, but from your bruises, it appears you have enjoyed an energetic session with young Donol. Is this why you disdain the comfort of your apartment?"

"The message was false?" Lia slipped sideways and fell to the floor, unable to move, sobbing into the carpet despite herself. Morven looked down at the disheveled mess she had become and back across the office, appreciating more than ever the angelic beauty of his daughter.

"Ceo, what a fuss! Call the guard, if you please, call two guardsmen! Get her out. Send her back to the tower and have her better restrained." Alysabeth left to obey. Morven looked down again at Lia, now weeping without noise. "I shall have a word with Donol, once he is through playing with his brother in the basement. He must learn to take better care of his toys."

A bewildering complexity of feelings concerning his brother struggled within Donol as he climbed to the ground floor from the foundations of the Holdings. He dare not examine them now, and likeliest never would.

Passing through the outer office, he noted that although the staff had retired, the place still bore signs of attack. The door to the inner office was ajar. Having suffered the rebels' rude attentions, the hinges had sprung and the catch no longer mated. He paused before entering, distracted by a flashing light upon a receptionist's console which proved no more than a minor failure of the mechanism itself. Lifting a weary, shaking hand to push the door aside, he heard Morven's wheeled chair whine for an instant. He stayed his hand, uncertain what to tell the Usurper of his brother's premature demise, knowing he would be held responsible. Thus, by accident, he overheard—and by chance did not interrupt—what transpired within.

"Alysabeth . . . ." The girl's assenting voice was to Donol's ear false-toned. He stepped to one side. Yellow-tinted light of late afternoon—the sun would set within the hour—flooded the inner office, shadowing the crack through which he peeked. Morven was visible in profile. Alysabeth stood before her father's chair, eyes cast downward, one small hand in each of his. As Donol watched, she lowered herself gracefully to her knees, gazing into his face, her slender forearms resting upon his thighs. *"Relieve me."*

To Donol's horror, aloof and haughty Alysabeth, whom he desired above all women (yet who had, with infuriating consistency, evaded his grasp), loosened her father's clothing with swift, delicate fingers, dropping her head to his lap, demonstrating in the most unmistakable terms her subservience. Morven sighed, closed his eyes, rested his hands upon her pale curls.

"Vindication," Morven murmured a monologue, his daughter being incapable of replying, "I swore to win so long ago at the expense of the presumptuous Islay and his peasant brood, is all but complete. You, my dear, are my angel of revenge. The token I imposed upon myself, of my determination in this affair, is no longer necessary. I, whom it amuses others to call 'Usurper'—they dare not call me 'cripple'—am free to be a man again!" Repositioning himself, he muttered unintelligibilities at the beautiful Alysabeth, who, judging from the noises she elicited, performed to his entire satisfaction. "It will please you to learn that I have begun treatment which will abolish my confinement and extend my life by an indefinite measure."

Donol felt bitterness stir within him. Enough to witness Alysabeth's abject, incestuous compliance with Morven's obscene demands, with what even Donol considered the man's gross appetites (although he shared a full measure of them, himself). Jealousy and disappointment filled him with unbearable pain. That he had been swindled, would not inherit the power and position which were his birthright from an elderly invalid who had rejected life and all it had to offer and would soon be dead—that was infinitely worse.

Morven threw his head back and cried out, hands flattening the curls at the nape of his daughter's neck, crushing her to him as she gathered the fabric of his trousers into shaking, tight-clenched fists. Donol had seen enough. He turned upon his heel and strode from the office, making plans which would give him revenge upon everyone. This, and his angry footsteps, took him to the stairway leading to the tower where vengeance would begin.

Placing a finger in a depression of the new lockplate, Donol fretted as its *ulsic* mechanism assayed traces of perspiration for immunity factors. From one hand a bundle swung heavy at his knee. The lock clicked; the door, built as it was from massive timbers, swung at his touch. As always hoping that Lia would cower into a corner from fear, he entered. The room, however, possessed a decided lack of corners, nor did she retreat. As much as she may have liked to, it had never been within the compass of her character.

Something clinked at her feet. Having had the freedom of Arran's old room, she was, at Morven's order, being punished for her escape (in a sense she was fortunate, the death of the guard having been attributed to rebels), restrained by a collar fastened by a long chain to the wall. The sight of the metal band round her throat stirred him. Battered as she was, with dark circles under her eyes, she stood unbroken in the tattered gown she had once again assumed, at the limit of the chain. He shut the door behind him.

"They think I fail to see," he was abrupt, "that you were given me as a distraction, a consolation prize, taking pressure off Alysabeth who makes countless promises, implicit and explicit, keeping none." Across the room, beyond her reach, stood a cabinet. Here he placed his bundle—it clinked, not unlike her chain—items salvaged from the dungeons which he had earlier retrieved, certain he would discover uses for them. He had intended moving the cabinet to the landing outside. Now, given her collar, being unable to reach them, it pleased him to think she could look upon these items in his absence, anticipating his return. "You, because you despise me and make no pretense, because you fancy that you belong to my brother, believe I shall tire of you." He strode toward her. "Both parties to this deception make a dreadful mistake, Lia, as you are about to learn to your discomfort and humiliation once again. As you will learn as often in future as necessary. As they will learn to their ruin and dismay when the time comes!"

He stood close. She had learned better than to resist; at the first sign he would call guards—he relished Oplytes for the task—to wrestle her into a compliant posture. Taking her by her wrists, he pulled the gown from her shoulders, exposing a breast which he seized, rolling the nipple cruelly between forefinger and thumb where dark ovals, evidence of previous such treatment, were visible. She bit her lip, accepting his abuse in silence, although a single glistening tear, whether of pain or chagrin even she could not have sworn, squeezed from beneath the fronding of her eyelashes and rolled down her cheek.

Donol grinned. Releasing her wrists, he draped an arm over her shoulder, letting his hand trail down her back. He crushed his mouth to her breast, sucking, biting until he discerned a trace of blood. Leaning her back until he almost lifted her, he reached for her skirt hem, crumpling the fabric into rude folds until his free hand burrowed beneath it. The invading hand traveled up smooth flesh, fondling and pinching, levering her thighs apart. Despite herself, Lia whimpered, stiffening as he cupped the mound between her legs, thrusting his fingers into its moist, fragrant warmth.

Holding her thus, he released her shoulder and stretched for a pair of heavy bracelets from the bundle he had left upon the cabinet, beyond her reach but just within his own. Locking her hands behind her, he released his intimate hold upon her, turned and shoved her, face down, onto the unblanketed bed. Pushing her skirt up round her waist, he fumbled at the fastenings of his trousers, threw himself upon her, and seized her by both breasts. His weight bore upon her, bracelets cutting into her flesh, as, without warning, he thrust himself into her as if she were a boy.

This being his favorite way with her, for no reason other than that it caused her greatest suffering, pain, as much from previous such invasions as this, seared her. Lia wept with demolished pride, neither for the first time nor the last. Robret was dead. Worse, she had discovered a compelling reason to endure this, if she could.

Part Five: Loreanna
Yearday 9, 3011 A.D.
Febbe 39, 510 Hanoverian
Octavus 13, 1569 Oldskyan

"Hallo, hallo," cried Henry Martyn,
"What makes you starsail so high?"
"I'm a rich Murchan-starship bound for the frontier,
  The frontier,
  The frontier,
Attack at your peril, star-bandit of Skye."

CHAPTER XXXI:
A FATE WORSE THAN EXILE

Mistress Loreanna Daimler-Wilkinson stood upon a polished floor inlaid with exotic hardwoods, within a shaft of sunlight which fell upon her hair and naked shoulders from a pair of tall windows behind her.

For the moment she was relaxed without altogether realizing it, resigned to what was bound to happen to her—in truth relieved that it would not be worse—possessed of that complete unself-consciousness which can only arise in utter certainty that one is alone and unwatched.

In one small hand she held a fold of her voluminous skirt, as she had done so many times before in this spacious, familiar chamber where she had been taught to dance—and to *listen* to the music—eyes half closed, lips half parted. Her other hand made gentle, preliminary motions to the melody and rhythm beginning to issue from a nearby thille player. This—as with all she had said or done the past fortnight—would be the last time. The thought stirred within her, as it never failed to do, sensations of anguish and futile outrage, which of late (she found this infuriating in itself) had begun to be displaced, or, at least, mixed up, with a certain curious anticipation by which she felt self-betrayed.

Before her, a floor-to-ceiling mirror set between the windows conveyed a view of herself as she turned with an unhurried, flowing motion upon her tiny feet, rising to her toes and down again, coming round to face the image she did not recognize as that of a lovely young girl. She was both fair and freckled, the latter a golden smattering. Her hair, arranged in the elaborate-simple fashion of the Hanoverian elite, was a warm brown-auburn. Although diminutive of stature, she was well proportioned, so that individuals seeing her in surroundings which lent no indication of scale invariably, and incorrectly, thought her taller.

She was delicate of face and form, gifted with a touching natural grace she was unaware existed or was visible to others. Upon the contrary, at this instant in her life, one fraught with change imposed upon her by others, she wondered, and rather doubted, whether she might ever be, to any man she could regard as worthy of respect, the woman whom he might love all his life.

"Will that be all, Miss?" Loreanna started in that manner possible only when one's certainty she is alone proves to have been false. A lifetime's education in restraint kept her from showing any sign of it.

"Thank you, Brougham. I believe so, for the time being."

Brougham inclined his upper extremity. "Very good, Miss."

Loreanna let her eyes see what her mind had emended from the image, of the chamber, not of herself, in the mirror. Two broad double doors, standing opposite the windows (in one of which Brougham stood), led from this place. In addition to serving as a studio for dance practice, it was at other times employed as ballroom, recital hall, and grand dining room. Along an expanse of decorated wall between the doors, dozens of ugly mesh containers had been filled, and with Brougham's always uncomplaining assistance, stacked, unstacked, emptied, rearranged, refilled, and stacked again, during the ten days or so she had been preparing for her hated—and somewhat looked-forward-to—voyage. To one side stood the object Loreanna believed she would miss most, since taking it was out of the question. Her mother's old-fashioned synthechord, covered with protective cloth, was next to the only physical reminder she had left of her dead parents. She had taken lessons, and, in the end, mastered the instrument, only after her guardian had been at considerable expense to find a teacher. She still played almost every day.

Loreanna also found herself seeing Brougham clearly for the first time in years. Looked at as if she had never seen him before—or in this case, as if she might never see him again—he was rather an odd sight. At just over a measure and a half—no taller than Loreanna herself—Brougham and the rest of his species, the *yensid,* had evolved upon a small but massive planet with a gravitic pull twenty times that of

Hanover. This lent them an agility and strength which, upon human-occupied worlds, made them ideal servants.

Just as everything of importance about a human being might be described as dwelling above his shoulders, so everything important about Brougham dwelt below his "hips." Here he made contact with the ground through hundreds of stiff, buff-colored locomotory organs, each a couple of dozen siemmes long, no larger than the wire from which metalloid mesh was fashioned. Here also his nervous system centered. Rising above the twenty-siemme width of his lower body, a wandlike "trunk," shades darker than the rest of him, elevated his sensory organs. It was sensitive to light over a broader spectrum than the human eye (less so to sound—to Brougham, Loreanna's fascination with music remained unfathomable), and to a variety of other energies, some of which humans appreciate only by means of scientific instruments. A third of the way from the rounded tip of Brougham's uppermost extremity, a pair of long, thille-thin arms always looked to her as if they were attached as an afterthought. Despite their silly appearance, they were stronger than human arms, and terminated in deft, powerful three-fingered hands.

Perhaps most significant, in terms of their being ideal servants from a human point of view, was the fact that Brougham's people were, to a remarkable degree, unambitious and noncompetitive. Like intelligent species everywhere, the *yensid* were their world's most aggressive predators. All things being relative, however, and life upon the *yensid* planet being relatively quieter and slower-paced than elsewhere, by a standard more universally applicable, they were disinclined to violent behavior, and adapted well to being told what to do—a quality of mind which no one, especially her guardian uncle, Sedgeley Daimler-Wilkinson, would ever have accused Loreanna of manifesting.

As an alternative offered to what had first been planned for her, she had, without an instant's hesitation, chosen Baffridgestar, a handful of icy, barren lumps circling a dim red clinker in the furthest-flung locale where her family claimed an interest—and thus, it was hoped, beyond reach of political memory or retribution. Of somewhat greater importance, the system was convenient (only in a comparative sense) to the neighboring imperium-conglomerate of Good Yrich, should exile alone not suffice in the Ceo's view and the furies of the 'Droom pursue her even to this ragged end of everything.

The unfortunate inhabitants of Baffridgestar (it crossed her mind that, given troglodytic habits imposed by climate, a more apposite, if denigrating, expression might be "denizens") were dedicated, for lack of better occupation, to the cultivation of ice algae, a commodity useful, but far from critically important, to Hanoverian pharmaceuticals. Their chief recreations appeared to consist of gambling and drug addiction—for which she could scarcely find it in her heart to blame them manio depressive suicide, and occasional mad slaughter which left whole families dismembered in smoking pools of their own blood. Otherwise, with reference to the remainder of the galaxy, nothing of interest or importance had ever happened in the Baffridgestar System, and it was an excellent guess that nothing ever would. Try as she might, Loreanna had been unable to find anything within the wealthy household she and her uncle shared, or offered by any shop or salon she frequented, which had originated there or which had been produced employing any product or process unique to the place. Few Hanoverians were aware it existed. Among those who were—those like her uncle, who derived a portion of his income from it—the first response seemed to be a shudder at its mere description, and the second an attempt to forget it again as soon as they had been reminded.

It was dark there. The system, it was generally agreed, lay steeped in amber twilight so depressing that the starker black of the interstellar Deep was considered a relief. One reference had the cold so terrible that evolution itself had ground to a halt or been slowed so greatly that biological development lagged billions of years behind the rest of the galaxy. Loreanna was uncertain that evolution operated in such a manner. In the first place, it was a random phenomenon for which no universal agenda could be claimed to exist. In the second, it seemed to her that stresses inherent to an environment so extreme ought to hasten the process, rather than retard it. She had noticed that the argument had been made not by a scientist, but rather in an article written by a sociology professor.

Nonetheless, native life forms were held by all informants to lie dormant all but four or five days out of an impossibly long year. Most unspeakable about Baffridgestar was that she would be lying dormant as well. Her income was provided for, modest by Hanoverian standards; lavish by those of where she was going; sufficient so that she would never have to lift a finger to maintain her existence; inadequate, even if she scrimped (which might prove rather easy, since almost nothing existed there to purchase), for passage home across the empty lightyears. Her fate thus arranged fulfilled every concept she entertained of damnation. But Loreanna, as a little girl reading from mythology, had always considered Limbo a worse consignation than Hell.

This thought caused her to shake her auburn curls in violent dismissal. Seeking control of her emotions, as well as reestablished concentration upon more immediate, practical matters, she stepped toward the wall, with its high-stacked crates, attempting again to determine which of her beloved possessions must be left behind, perhaps never to be reclaimed. Nestled in one open-topped crate, among a dozen stuffed animal figures, lay the flofilm microscope her uncle had given her upon her eighth birthday, an example of perhaps the subtlest application made of §-physics. This she would take, since it weighed next to nothing, occupied scant volume, and represented a diverting manner in which to occupy the many empty hours she anticipated lay ahead.

She hesitated over a container of datathilles she had studied not only to satisfy her uncle, but in hope of gaining some greater understanding of herself and of the dark and complicated universe she lived in than might have been claimed by the ordinary run of young Hanoverian women in whom a good general education was regarded as among the least important of qualifications for success in life. Her eye happened to fall upon a particular favorite, Lynn and Zike's epochal *Galactic Political Economy*. She hushed the thille she had left playing and replaced it with the text, accessing a passage at random.

. . . established in the imperia-conglomerate and other polities, known as "charter capitalism," a system of production and distribution consisting of an interwoven partnership between producers and rulers. In previous times and circumstances, this partnership was variously known as "murchantilism," "state capitalism," "corporate socialism," or "fascism," depending upon minor details in the arrangements between partners, or, more importantly, upon which of them predominated.

Loreanna shook her head again. How synchronous, she thought, that she had turned to this lesson at this particular moment. Yet, upon consideration, it was not synchronous at all. She had all but memorized this thille. Here, she realized, were the roots of all her personal difficulties, laid out in remote and dessicated tones, complete with index, scrollnotes, thilliography, and the neat, if tendentious, schoolgirl marginalia she herself enthilled:

Within the Hanoverian Imperium-Conglomerate, it is Ceo and Monopolity, the political partner, predominant, whereas the flagellum *wags the* euglena *in the Jendyne Empery-Cirot.*

Lorcanna smiled at this remembrance of a younger self. It was like this throughout. Here, where the authors had written—

. . . reserving to itself a monopoly upon the production, distribution, and retirement of the principal medium of exchange. The official currency of the Monopolity is the "clavis." Within the Jendyne Empery-Cirot, it is the "gavelle," at present approximately equal to three clavises.

—she had added:

. . . neither supported by anything of value except the willingness of each respective polity, within its territory, to coerce those subject to its authority into employing it.

A notation followed, referring to one of many further comments appended at the end of the text. Grinning to herself, Loreanna found a crate to sit upon and manipulated the knurled bands of which the thille was mostly constructed, turning them against each other and observing the result of her adjustments in the air above the player. She came to the appropriate spot:

> The names of reigning polities, their units of currency, as well as many titles they confer, descend from those of commercial entities founded earlier in history. This is an obscure fact, in general known only to historical and linguistic scholars, and relatively few of the former remain—and even fewer of the latter—since close study of history or linguistics is, for obvious reasons, not much encouraged.

True, she thought, and, as with State and Capital under murchantile socialism, entwined inextricably among the reasons her life was in turmoil. How had it happened that an obscure fact of history and linguistics came to have so direct a bearing upon her personal misfortune? The steps of Loreanna's line of reasoning were many and she retraced them now as she had not been able to avoid doing several times a day over the past weeks.

Step One: truth of any kind—linguistic, historical, or otherwise—is, according to an ancient proverb, the first casualty of war. The imperia-conglomerate had waged war for a millennium over trade routes and colonies, representing markets for goods manufactured in better-settled regions, such as Hanover itself, and sources of supply. Aside: after a millennium, how much was left—linguistic, historical, or otherwise—of the truth?

Step Two: the chiefmost contenders of this era were the mighty domains known as the Monopolity of Hanover and the Jendyne Empery-Cirot. It was inevitable that victory and defeat should shift back and forth between them, decade by decade, century by century, with no genuine resolution in the offing. Before the Thousand Years' War had become quite so formalized, a planet or two, which, for a time, had provided centers for embryonic imperia-conglomerate of their own, had been blasted into cinders, wiped clean of every life form, rendered, for millions of years to come, uninhabitable. Later, §-fields, and their capacity for neutralizing atomic weaponry, had come into common usage. More to the point, the survivors of previous disasters had learned to appreciate that war—with all its myriad convenient justifications for secrecy, taxation, conscription, and suppression of the troublesome individual—is, indeed "the health of the State." Thus it was arranged that victory and defeat should become eternally transitory.

Step Three: temporary victors of any moment were free to grant franchised access to whatever they had won to favored entities with requisite family or financial connection. In that portion of the galaxy under Jendyne control, the process was more complicated. Families and financial empires granted the State its operating franchise, in effect, in a manner roundabout, making commercial concessions to themselves. Under either system, unauthorized individual enterprise was suppressed with vicious enthusiasm.

Step Four: none of this, of course, had ever found direct expression in Loreanna's texts, nor had her tutors ever told her of it in so many words. None had ever conceded, straightforwardly and without euphemism, that, because of the way affairs had been arranged for centuries, all intellectual, technical, and economic progress within the human-occupied galaxy had remained at a standstill for generations, save in those frontier reaches the imperia-conglomerate could not control. Teachers, even of the children of the wealthy and powerful, who made a point of airing seditious opinion, found themselves—provided they were lucky—banished to those frontier reaches, even as Loreanna now was bound for exile for a rather different assortment of reasons. Such areas, as Loreanna knew—and knew she would soon appreciate at closer hand—were many, the present age being, despite the self-induced stagnation of the central worlds, one of broad-ranging exploration. They acted as a safety valve for individuals whose personal furies were left unsatisfied by the opportunity to participate in the Thousand Years' War.

Aside: perhaps, as some contended, always with discretion, a change was coming, widespread revolt which would cure every evil and set every injustice to right. Observers agreed it was too far in the future, even for those who could sense its putative inevitability, for anyone, upon any side of any issue of the day, to be much concerned. Meanwhile, as Loreanna had found recent occasion to discover—and was this Step Five or Step Six? As always, she lost track and gave up counting at this point. One imperium-conglomerate, her own Monopolity of Hanover, had become desirous of a respite. Doubtless the Ceo's purpose was to gain some tactical advantage, perhaps only to gather resources for a subsequent outbreak of civilized savagery. In any event, and whatever his purpose, he had determined to offer, to his best-esteemed and longest-standing enemy, a truce.

One cannot wage continuous war for a thousand years. Such hiatuses were not unprecedented, nor the treachery they often presaged. She entertained not a moment's doubt that, receiving the offer, doddering Ribauldequin XXIII, Ceo of the Jendyne Empery-Cirot (or whoever wagged his flagellum these days) suspected trickery and would be well prepared to trick back. For the time being, through diplomatic channels, he had expressed a certain willingness to listen to the proposition. And thus, following customs older than the Thousand Years' War itself, and in token of all this counterfeit cordiality and nonexistent good faith, an exchange of gifts seemed called for . . .

"Miss?" Brougham reentered the sunny chamber and glanced from the doorway to the pile of crates. A subtle ripple passed through his hundreds of locomotory filaments, his species' equivalent of a sigh, followed by a shrug, a human gesture he had somehow absorbed over the many years he had been a faithful retainer to the Daimler-Wilkinson family.

His young mistress was fatigued by the many preparations for her coming voyage, as well as by stresses engendered at the prospect itself. Not to mention those emotion-charged events between her uncle and herself which had precipitated it. Yet (and she was like her uncle in this) she was unwilling to acknowledge her exhaustion and remedy it, instead, once again, seeking refuge from her troubles in her texthilles. She lay now, her weight supported by one crate, leaning back against another, eyes closed, breathing shallow and even. The player, balanced atop a third crate, had shut itself off.

Loreanna stirred at his mellow-accented voice, not quite emerging from the warm, half-dreaming state into which she had slipped without noticing. Another ripple passed through his supporting filaments as he whisked across the room and lifted Loreanna in his arms as he had so many times before when she was just a little girl and had fallen asleep in exactly this manner.

"Brougham?" her sleepy voice was younger in pitch and timbre than had earlier been the case.

"Yes, Miss?" The alien servant was incapable of anything like a facial expression, yet his tone reflected abiding affection for the human girl.

"It is still daylight, not time for bed. Where are you taking me?"

Brougham made a murmuring sound which served him as a chuckle. They entered the dynalift at the core of the house and ascended. "To your suite, Miss, for a rest. A much-needed one, if I may make so bold as to say so. You may rely upon me to awaken you in good time to dine with your uncle."

The dynalift whined, bathing them in its eerie blue §-glow, before Loreanna was able to sort out something resembling a coherent reply. "Very well, my stalwart Brougham, I shall. I was only thinking, anyway. It was quite warm and pleasant. Now, what was I thinking about?"

"I am afraid," he lied, for he knew what subject had been uppermost in her mind for two almost sleepless weeks, "I could not say, Miss." Exiting the lift, Brougham carried her along a broad carpeted hallway toward the suite of rooms which had been hers since earliest childhood. She was again oblivious to her surroundings as he exercised typical Broughamlike decorum in summoning a *yensid* maid to prepare her for her nap. Yes, he thought, she had been thinking that an exchange of gifts seemed called for. And had his young mistress not spoken out when she did, earning, thereby, the exile she was about to enter, she—Loreanna—would have been that gift.

CHAPTER XXXII:
THE 'DROOM OF THE MONOPOLITY

"Ambathador Frantithek Demondion-Echeverria, of the Jendyne Empery-Thirot!"

At the great doors of the 'Droom, each half a klomme high, the latest Stentor-Honorary gave the nickel-steel floor beneath his feet a ponderous drubbing with his two-measure mace. So vast was the chamber, so noisy and crowded, that the sound, along with that of his voice, might have been lost had not an amplifier been built into the head of the mace itself. A small, neat man—dark, handsome, and well dressed —the official representative of the principal enemy of the Ceo and Monopolity of Hanover stepped past the threshold and melted into the glittering throng.

Another crash, another shout: *"Drector-Extraordinary John Cameron Cronkite-Goebbelth and the Lady Cronkite-Goebbelth!"* A man in a black masque watched the entrance. Nearby, a quieter voice arose at his shoulder, its cultured tones rippling with cynical amusement.

"Thith new thtentor of the Ceo'th." Saint-Lennon deFender-Gibson, Drector-Hereditary of the Hanoverian Isle of Farfaraway, adjusted his glitter-gilded oscarwilde, assumed a stance with one hip thrust outward, and flopped a perfumed handkerchief at his neighbor of the moment. "Quite capable of babbling anything, I tell you, in any of a thouthand different languageth, and underthtands nothing at all in any of them."

It was an opening gambit, an invitation to partake in the perilous two-edged game of 'Droom repartee. DeFender-Gibson lowered his masque, raised a plucked eyebrow, and awaited reply. Behind the masque of black his temporary companion frowned. A player of far more dangerous games, he had never cared for repartee, had never liked this DeFender-Gibson, his gaggle of androgynous friends, nor any of their degenerate affectations, no matter how popular they happened be. According to the tacit rules, a measured rudeness was in order. "Perhaps because he was chosen from the hereditary Drectorhood."

DeFender-Gibson dropped his masque to reveal a painted mouth open in mock outrage, covered the orifice with a soft, nail-enameled hand, winked, and turned to pass the remark along. The man in the black masque turned his back.

"Wanque." He uttered the expression of perhaps childish derision under his breath, dismissed DeFender-Gibson, and resumed watching the colorful spectacle which a mass audience with Ceo Leupould IX never failed to present. The space they all occupied, shoulder to shoulder and, as always, raising an unbearable racket, was simple in conception and design, no more than a cube proportioned with an accuracy of one ten-thousandth of a siemme, and being a full klomme upon each side. This vast space was the 'Droom of the Monopolity of Hanover, the center from which the Ceo's will was imposed upon a million suns. As with all such architecture, it was intended to impress, to belittle and intimidate at an animal level inaccessible to rational analysis those whose fates were decided within. At this it was well suited.

The floor was a single mass of carbon-bearing nickel-iron, the naked heart of a planetoid, cut, rough-planed, and delifted from orbit eleven centuries earlier, siemme by siemme, over the endless period of an entire year, a titanic feat of courage, planning, expertise, and Deepsmanship which in all probability could not be duplicated today. In place, it had been laser-polished to a half wavelength mirror-smoothness. Over the centuries, with continued careful attention, under the subtle friction and persistent pressure of a billion locomotory appendages, it had by gradual degrees, acquired the patina it now wore, a flawless blue of infinite depth. Those standing within the mighty chamber—upon those rare occasions when sufficient room existed to appreciate the phenomenon—appeared to be walking upon water. Knowing more of history than most visitors to the Ceo's 'Droom, the man in the black masque never failed to be amused by this illusion.

Occupying the center of the 'Droom, taking up only a

tenth of the surface of the meteoric steel floor, a dais lifted a single, modest measure. Rather, the floor had been relieved, representing, to those with understanding to appreciate it, the most arrogant feat of machining ever accomplished. This rectangle, five hundred measures in length, two hundred in width, was the Ceo's Table. Anyone, lacking the credentials of a Drector or the Ceo's permission, who dared step onto its gleaming surface would be cut down in an instant by hundreds of Oplytes standing at its perimeter or patrolling overhead upon personal §-field suspensors—representing in themselves a fabulous expense—possession of which was savagely restricted.

At the end of the Table furthest from the great doors at which the black masqued man had earlier been announced by the Stentor-Honorary, an elevation of another measure—two hundred measures wide, fifty measures deep, also integral with the floor—was set aside for the Ceo and his personal retinue. At present, save for guards, it was unoccupied. The vast and noisy gathering in the 'Droom was in anticipation of the Ceo's arrival.

The walls enclosing the 'Droom were no less impressive than its Deep-spawned floor, composed, as they were, of purest silica a klomme square and fifty measures thick. Gigantic spreighformers, requiring the combined output of a planetary system's thermonuclear reactors and early §-field annihilators, had been assembled upon the site and afterward (in some haste) disassembled; the parts destroyed or dispersed out of fear that a fabricator so massive might be employed to create whole warships or other weapons threatening to the interests which had caused it to be constructed. By daylight, the walls admitted an eerie tinted view of vast gardens about the 'Droom which somehow rendered those manicured expanses more remote than the stars and made the building's occupants feel they were standing at the bottom of an ocean. By night, despite their seamless perfection, they seemed to swallow illumination like frozen slices of the infinite Deep.

A klomme overhead, the ceiling of this vast monument to power was the latest addition to the structure, one made, by comparison to the original effort, in modern times. Once a unitary span of glass, albeit less massive than the walls supporting it, five hundred years ago, during a period of economic and political "readjustment," it had been demolished by a single small trajectile weighing less than a gramme, traveling at nine klommes per second, inserted from orbit, with thousands of identical others, by insurgents never identified or apprehended. Now the ceiling of the 'Droom was metalloid mesh, supported by §-beams and suffused with energies more than capable of withstanding such assault. Devices installed upon its under-surface controlled "weather"—for the most part indoor rain—which otherwise would have occurred spontaneously within the enormous enclosed volume. The glow from overhead bathed everything beneath it in a pale blue light, reflected from the mirrorlike floor and absorbed by the surrounding walls.

Additional embellishment, the elaborate ornamentation which otherwise characterized this age, had been avoided, so that the architect's assertion of unanswerable power remained unblunted. To the man in the black masque, it was the most beautiful place in the known universe, and, at the same time, the most horrifying. And the most astonishing fact about the 'Droom, at least to him, was that it had never been intended as a seat of government, but had been built by private parties for individual murchantile purposes a century before the founding of the Monopolitan Imperium-Conglomerate. He shook his graying head and took a deep breath, never lowering his masque.

The cast of characters strutting this mighty stage was mostly human, although centuries upon unwelcoming worlds or floating in the night-black Deep itself, and consequent genetic drift imposed by mutation and natural selection, had modified the meaning of the word. With conquest of the stars, an enormous physical variation had begun imposing itself upon humanity. Some present stood no fewer than three measures tall, having arrived from small, light worlds with little or no appreciable gravity. Many wore metalloid braces to augment their muscles or protect fragile bones, or shuffled about the mirrored floor in walking frames. A wheeled chair or two and one powered stretcher indicated those whose missions at the 'Droom must be urgent to necessitate heroic measures. Others of the far-flung Monopolity, possessed of thick bones and massive limbs, moved with exaggerated circumspection in gravity constituting but a fraction of what they had been born to, attempting to avoid an accidental head-high leap which might embarrass them or earn them a kinergic reprimand from ever-suspicious Oplytes.

The man in the black masque nodded to a colleague he suspected of trying to have him assassinated the previous year, but continued concentrating upon his own thoughts. The rich variety of visible accessory and dress served purposes other than ostentation. For some visitors, attenuate and emaciate or broader and compact, the ambient temperature (in which he felt quite at home) was one of freezing discomfort. They were swathed in thick furs, featherpelts, or quilted kefflar, a poignant reminder of someone he loved and had recently condemned to spend the rest of her life in such repellent swathing. For others the 'Droom was intolerably hot or humid. These unlucky individuals were attired in minimal clothing more suitable for swimming, sunbathing, or erotic play. Some few unfortunates required bacterial or allergenic filters, canisters of supplementary oxygen, exotic trace gases, or other contrivances from which they breathed, at intervals or upon a continuous basis.

Meanwhile, servants—*yensid* in the main, along with a stylish smattering of less-familiar others (some of dubious sapience, no more, he suspected, than bright domesticated animals)—bustled about the cavernous chamber fetching food and drink. The aromas—along with those of bodies, pheromones, and breathing gases—created a sometimes overwhelming olfactory experience even in this well-ventilated space. Those carrying messages or running other errands for their owners and employers were not the only aliens within view.

This day a delegation of "stiquemen" was at the 'Droom. Repulsive in appearance, they remained the most humanlike non-humans yet discovered. In point of fact, they had discovered humanity two generations ago, arriving without prior detection about Hanover itself, not bothering with intermediate stops that any Hanoverian starship would have

deemed necessary in Monopolitan systems closer to their
domain. This was believed to lie beyond the neutral
imperium-conglomerate of Good Yrich, a fact of some importance to the man in the black masque. Another stab of
love and conscience assailed him. For a moment he regretted
the adamancy of his resolve.

Perusing this morning's event summary, an enthillement
for the Ceo's Drectors hand-delivered before dawn by liveried
couriers, he had noted the arrival of one of the stiquemen's
interstellar ships, driven by starsails like human vessels, yet
proportioned weirdly and possessing improvements not well
understood by the few Hanoverians motivated to sufficient
curiosity to investigate them. It was not that the stiquemen
attempted to keep their technology a secret. Those beings—
three measures tall and, preferring to go naked, thille-thin not
just in their extremities (of which they possessed six, not
counting short manipulators growing in hornlike pairs upon
their fist-sized heads) but in their torsos as well—claimed
they were no more than simple explorers and traders. Trade
they did, driving hard bargains and yielding interesting and
valuable commodities in exchange. It was clear that they
hailed from a vital, expanding civilization, innocently eager
to share what it knew for information about how other
species did things.

Even after all this time, few within the byzantine environs
of the 'Droom were willing to take the stiquemen at their
word. To whatever extent they were believed open and honest
in their protestations, for that very honesty they were held to
be—by the more twisted Monopolitan minds he was compelled to deal with every day—especially enigmatic and
inscrutable! He took a breath. Twisted Monopolitan minds?
Who was he to criticize, even in his thoughts? Unless he
found a third alternative in his personal affairs which respected the rights, wishes, and personal sovereignty of an
individual whom he loved, and for whom he wished nothing
but—

"Why bind me!" He was distracted by the sound of a
too-familiar voice. "If it ith not the Executor-General
himthelf, hanging back here with all of uth mere rabble! Pray
tell me—and pray tell my eagerly awaiting lithenerth,

Drector-Advithory old boy, as Piotr Megrim-Boutade would put it, what ith it to be with the gell, gavage or gavelleth?"

The individual who had spoken, pushing an autothille into his face and diverting the current of his thoughts, was none other than Percival Keynes-Bovril, Esquire, an obnoxious snoop employed by one of the many nongovernmental equivalents of the news service he received each morning. Keynes-Bovril wore sky-blue satin tunic and trousers, lace-trimmed at cuffs and collar. Rather than the gainesborough which might have been expected, the masque he had chosen was of himself, and quite transparent.

Lowering his own masque a moment, that this professional back-biter could appreciate the hostile intensity of his expression, Drector-Advisory Sedgeley Daimler-Wilkinson, Executor-General to Ceo Leupould IX of the Monopolity of Hanover, held before his chest the ebon dumaspere he had adopted when, for reasons of significance to himself and no one else, he had retired his ivory truman years before.

"Keynes-Bovril, the lisp you have begun affecting lately—*you will remain silent when addressed by your betters!*—may be all the rage, but it inspires in me an impulse to rearrange your dentition. This may not improve your elocution, but it would work wonders with my blood pressure!"

Keynes-Bovril stepped backward, stumbling against a tray-laden *yensid.* "I—"

The Drector-Advisory interrupted. "I shall yield to the impulse should I hear you utter her name, or refer to any of my family, in public or in private, ever again. Is my meaning clear enough, even for you?"

Keynes-Bovril lowered the autothille, gulped behind his masque, bobbed his head in intimidated acknowledgement, and glanced about to see whether they had been overheard. Raising his eyebrows as if spying some familiar face, he turned, thrust the autothille before him, and hurried away. The Executor-General resumed his own ebon masque and his even blacker thoughts.

The masque was esoteric, but not altogether obscure. Dumas and other nineteenth-century writers were still admired, although the present age, he thought, bore greater resemblance to the sixteenth or seventeenth. Even now he cherished hope that it might provoke revealing inquiry. For a while, having given up the truman, he had considered odysseus, nevadasmith, dreyfus or zola, the more pointed edmonddantes, even the accusing countenance of his dead brother, Clyve. He was acquainted with a widower who wore the likeness of his deceased wife, even a madwoman who had adopted that of a dead pet. Each of these, whatever their respective merit, offered disadvantages with regard to his position at the 'Droom, or might have proven disquieting to his niece, who, in this matter, was blameless. How dearly he wished he could say the same for her more recent and embarrassing lapse. He shook his head, realizing he would not be able to avoid thinking about it, Keynes-Bovril or no Keynes-Bovril.

The fact was that, where her single, and, he regretted, most conspicuous shortcoming was concerned, Daimler-Wilkinson felt himself to blame. His greatest error was that he had not caused the dance to be more emphasized in her education. Perhaps someday he would attempt to tell her this. Was she capable of understanding? Thirty-first-century Hanover, he often reflected, was a milieu of complex, interweaving dances. While Loreanna had grown to acquit herself admirably at the literal sort of dance—even Brougham and his cosapients, suffering utter tone-deafness, adored watching her—he feared his failure had been total when it came to teaching her the figurative.

He reached into a pocket from absentminded habit and an example came to mind. Each day, within the glittering 'Drooms and council chambers of many imperia-conglomerate (according to elaborate and stringent protocol), the most brilliantly conceived, carefully polished, sarcastically pointed pleasantries were exchanged between limp-wristed, expensively perfumed, richly overdressed diplomats and ministers plenipotentiary, in every respect (he admitted with the wry honesty which the privacy of his thoughts afforded him) like himself.

He withdrew his hand, and the object it sought, from his pocket. Almost to the man, each availed himself of one or more perforate-ended inhalers which had originated aboard early starships where smoking with an open flame might prove disastrous. Handsomely hand-wrought, exquisitely embellished, containing a broad spectrum of aromatics—stimulants and stimulus-barriers—according to the tastes of their diverse and various owners, they were the thirty-first-century equivalent (he was aware from his own historical studies which had provided example for Loreanna's) of eighteenth-century snuffboxes. Daimler-Wilkinson raised his own engraved inhaler to his nostrils, breathing the narco-stimulant he preferred. His mind cleared (or he had the impression it did) and he went ahead with his thoughts.

These tokens of conspicuous sophistication were often tucked into lace-ruffled sleeves beside diminutive, elegant, but quite deadly thrustibles. This, he thought, told the tale for an era entire. He himself had soldiered with distinction (and a murderous reputation which still served him) as a youth in the Ceo's wars. Likewise, the perfumed, effeminate DeFender-Gibson, he knew, had commanded the first devastating assault against the poison-atmosphered d'Kramnampach. Keynes-Bovril was rumored to have sired fifty bastards upon Hanover alone, manifesting a differing but undeniable virility.

Dance is an art, he reflected. The medium common to all art is contrast, discernible in the dance being practiced at the 'Droom as effete affectation versus forthright brutality. Those were the parameters of the age, sweeping outward off the pampered, savage capital worlds of each respective imperium-conglomerate, through the dark and endless Deep in concentric rings of apparent—and deceptive—contradiction, like the alternating peaks and troughs which a cast stone sends across a body of calm water.

Thus, at one end of a long, complicated chain of events, powdered, perfumed, and polished politicians promulgated protocol and policy. At the other, in the unutterable blackness of the Deep, starfleets clashed under the iron-spined command of lace-uniformed and lisping officers, re-formed and clashed again. Controlled by the same sort of men—soft at the most superficial level, brutal at the most fundamental—slave-armies clawed and blasted one another for fee-simple ownership of the known galaxy. Oplytes, dreaded devourers, disminded devastators, marched across the screaming faces of entire worlds, raping men, women, and children alike, feeding upon their violated bodies, looting whole civilizations for their mincing masters, destroying whatever remained, leaving nothing behind but cinders. And—even Daimler-Wilkinson was astonished to think it—regardless of the particular styles in vogue, it had been this way ten centuries, a dozen lifetimes, fifty generations, a hundred decades, a thousand years. Possibly it had been this way from the beginning of human history.

The man in the black masque sighed. He had made the right decision after all. It had been extremely difficult, particularly when his niece happened to be a beautiful, intelligent, talented, sweet miniature girl-child of fourteen for whom his love was most unstylishly sincere, just as he had loved her father, his own brother, and had later come to love her mother, his brother's wife. But Loreanna, who sought to disown the facts of reality, was acting out a part whether she intended so or not. When, upon her account, the Drector-Advisory and Executor-General to the Ceo of the Monopolity could be accosted, here upon the floor of the 'Droom, by an insect like Keynes-Bovril, survival itself demanded that an end be put to such intransigence.

A blare of enthilled trumpets announced entry of the Ceo and his retinue. Movement was visible at the opposite end of the 'Droom, as dozens in gorgeous attire—ministers, coattail-hangers, sycophants—were outshone and dwarfed by the magnificent form of Leupould himself. The Executor-General shouldered his way through the crowd. He, as the Ceo's advisor, perhaps even as his best friend, had a place upon the upper dais. The masses buzzed with anticipation.

And, of course, he could always claim he was doing it for her own benefit. He was, in a cruel way, the way which prefers euthanizing its own injured housepets to leaving that distasteful chore to some poor servant.

Another concentric ring-ripple. Another pair of contrasts. Another set of apparent contradictions. Love—and something other than love. Loreanna would have to be disposed of, sent away for her own benefit, if not for that of the Monopolity, even if to a purgatory system like Baffridgestar.

CHAPTER XXXIII:
LEUPOULD IMPERATOR

"Thank the Powers—" the fat man sighed with satisfaction and weariness, "—principally myself, that all the noise is done with for another day. The menagerie's sent away, and I can be plain Leu Wheeler again."

The Ceo of the Monopolity of Hanover interlaced his long, thick fingers behind his bullish neck, stretched his legs, and leaned back in the upholstered chaise his body almost concealed. He was a man of middle years well carried, hirsute to a remarkable degree from the straight black, rather long hair atop his great head, past the curly pelt upon his massive shoulders and chest, to a fur only lighter by comparison adorning his legs and ankles, even down to his toes. Heavy mutton-chop whiskers bedraped his jowls. He turned his fleshy blue-cheeked face, which he was compelled to have shaven twice daily, to address his Drector-Advisory and Executor-General, smiling as he did so, and giving him a broad wink.

"The truth is that I love it, Sedgeley. Each dawn I awaken filled with more enthusiasm than I could ever claim as a younger man, rememberin' all over again who I am, and, long before my appointment aide appears to nag me, precisely what lies before me upon the mornin's schedule."

Daimler-Wilkinson, for all that he had served the Ceo upon an intimate basis more than twenty standard years— and the man's late father another six before that—never felt altogether comfortable seated in his imposing presence. At the moment they were alone. The Drector-Advisory occupied the front edge of a straight-backed chair a few measures away from Leupould, having arrived with him in these less grandiose chambers, as he did every morning at this time, after the mass audience had ended. In a few minutes, a working luncheon with a dozen other Drectors would be served.

Daimler-Wilkinson had long been aware that "plain Leu Wheeler" enjoyed being Ceo much more than his late father, Winthorpe XVII, ever had. Perhaps as a consequence, Leupould had, in his advisor's opinion, proven the exceptional ruler these times demanded. The Executor-General, however, was not accustomed to hearing him proclaim it, even in so private a setting.

The room they occupied was four measures by six, most of it taken up—so it seemed to the more modestly proportioned Executor-General—by the huge individual who was, whatever the history behind his title, absolute ruler of the mightiest empire in the history of any known species, comprising more than a million planet-bearing suns. It was an unremarkable room with a low ceiling and walls the color and texture of an eggshell. It had no windows, a fact of which Leupould often complained, but which gave those responsible for his safety considerable relief when he retired each day from the 'Droom, a crowded, dangerous setting representing the fulfillment of every bodyguard's nightmares. Two doors opened into one of these walls, that upon the left leading (by a long, circuitous route, for this was part of an annex thrown up bit by bit over several hundred years for the convenience of Ceos and those serving them) from the 'Droom itself. That upon the right led to a chamber with large, well-guarded windows, where they would soon eat while making a start upon the day's real business.

The man whose room it was, however, was far from unremarkable. "Plain Leu Wheeler," ninth of that given name to wield power as Ceo of Hanover, stood taller than many an Oplyte charged with protecting his life. To the inexperienced eye, he appeared obese, an appearance he cultivated, since it had the salubrious effect of putting an opposing politician or would-be assassin off guard. Daimler-Wilkinson was one who knew better. He had often observed Leupould lifting weights (until he grew fatigued from watching it) and afterward swim lap after lap to soften the visibility of what weightlifting had given him. Another reason Leupould appeared fat was that it required an inhuman load to give his muscles definition. At either pursuit, Leupould might have been a champion, although he belittled his skills in the scheme of things. He had once informed his shocked Drector-Advisory that striving for such a championship was like demonstrating in public that he was better than anyone at breathing or going to the toilet. However that may have been, next to none of his impressive bulk was fat. He had killed half a dozen of those would-be assassins himself, three his Executor-General knew of with his bare hands at moments when no better weapon was available.

Daimler-Wilkinson shook his head at the remembrance. This was the same man who, "sitting out" his father's long and less-successful reign (while attempting to give every appearance to the contrary), had taught economics at one of Hanover's principal academies. In those rare moments he could spare today, without aid of microscope or any other sort of magnification, he wrote poems with a single-haired brush upon grains of rice, or played the xitherin with such an exquisite touch (it had been claimed; Daimler-Wilkinson had never been any judge of music, himself) as to make grown men weep.

Opposite the doors stood a dozen floor-to-ceiling shelves spreighformed the same color as the wall so as not to detract from items Leupould kept upon them. Among these were autothilles of his family, friends, acquaintances, bits of minerals, botanical and zoological specimens, small sculptures and alien artifacts, other souvenirs from this world or that, and a handful of ancient page-books, each more valuable, the Executor-General guessed, even than the garments Leupould had just cast aside. Entering these chambers, as he did every morning, he had thrown off his spectacular robes, as usual with some deprecating comment. This morning, what he had worn to the mass audience had been delivered from a fashionable old capital-world tailor who affected never having heard of spreighformery, let alone employing it. The price might have supported an ordinary family for a decade. Leupould's quip had been something about "the Imperator's new clothes."

Daimler-Wilkinson had heard him make the same remark upon previous occasions and had given it the chuckle it had once—perhaps—deserved, in part because Leupould did think of new jokes to tell from time to time. Daimler-Wilkinson had never been able to decide whether he served this enormous and difficult man because he was predictable, as consistent and reliable as his father, or for those other moments when, unlike his father, he was unpredictable and brilliant.

The latest addition to the shelves this morning was an elaborate and novel chronometer, a recent gift from offplanet which Leupould had mentioned to him during the audience. Daimler-Wilkinson was uncertain whether it was a genuine antique or a cunning reproduction. A circular display face the size of a man's hand was decorated about its circumference with ancient tally-numbers which scholars called "Roamin'." Two pointers, one short and broad, one long and slender, both embellished to the point of indecency, somehow indicated the hour. This was not the principal novelty of the timepiece. Below the face swung a pendulum which made a rather annoying tick-tock noise, its lower edge fashioned in the shape of a head-knife such as he had seen in the hands of laborers upon certain primitive worlds.

Beneath lay a miniature figure in clothing a thousand years out of date, ankles and wrists bound by fine rings. As it put up a mechanical struggle against its restraints, each swing of the pendulum brought the sharpened lower edge closer to its chest. *Tick, tock, tick, tock, tick . . .*

So clever was the mechanism that he believed he could see the mannequin's eyes widen with each minuscule drop of the descending blade, its mouth forming a tiny O as it "realized" its struggle was in vain, that the hour, and evisceration, approached rapidly. With effort, Daimler-Wilkinson wrenched his own eyes from the hideous timepiece. *Tick, tock, tick, tock, tick . . .*

Leupould was naked as the fabled imperator, his mountainous midsection covered with a light rug, and about to finish his third mug of caff—stiff with cream, sugar, and chocolate so dark it had gone into the mixture black—which served the purposes of sharpening his alertness for the day's duties and maintaining his deceptive bulk. The mug sat upon a small mesh table beside the chaise which also held a servant summoner to which he had rare recourse, and a ceramic dish heaped with ashes and stubbed ends of nicotinettes representing (in his estimate, for, unlike many things he enjoyed, he could find no reason to justify it) Leupould's only genuine vice. Daimler-Wilkinson drank the same caff as Leupould, this being *his* only vice.

A knock came at the right-hand door. This, too, happened every morning. As ordered, without waiting for permission, a security aide poked his head into the room, raising cultured eyebrows in inquiry. Not bothering to rise, as he and his Executor-General would have done on any ordinary day, Leupould raised a giant hand, palm outward. The timing came as a surprise, but neither the event nor its necessity. Nonetheless, Daimler-Wilkinson felt a chill.

"We'll be delayed this mornin', Wendling, kindly inform the Drectors-Hyphenated. See they're supplied with whatever refreshment they desire." He indicated the device lying beside his caffcup and ashtray. "We'll not be long, nor disrupt your well-planned schedule, we assure you. We shall ring when we're ready to be dressed."

"As you wish, sir." The aide withdrew, closing the door without otherwise responding. Given the enormous difference in their stations, it was the closest, Daimler-Wilkinson recognized, the man could come to a pout, and one reason he preferred employing non-human servants.

Even as he winked at his Drector-Advisory again and pondered the most graceful manner in which to broach a subject no one, including Daimler-Wilkinson, would ever know had deprived him of sleep the previous night, Leupould reached for a packet lying beside the ashtray, removed the final cylinder it contained—it had been full when he had awakened this morning—drew upon it, and exhaled smoke. He crumpled the empty packet in his pawlike hand. In keeping with a ritual Leupould had never been aware existed, Daimler-Wilkinson arose and took it from him for later disposal. Leupould would not have servants enter this personal sanctum until he was prepared to leave it, not even to empty his overflowing ashtray.

"Sedgeley, my good and faithful, much as we both wish otherwise, the moment's arrived which you and I have dreaded all mornin'." *Tick, tock, tick, tock, tick . . .*

Daimler-Wilkinson braced himself as if he, not the mannequin, felt the blade about to fall. No question lingered whether he deserved it. It had been his idea, he regretted bitterly, to suggest that his own niece, beautiful fourteen-year-old Loreanna, be offered as a goodwill gift in betrothal of marriage to the doddering, but still technically eligible, Ribauldequin XXIII, Ceo of the Jendyne Empery-Cirot. *Tick, tock, tick, tock, tick . . .*

"I'm glad you don't deny it, nor ask me what I speak of. We understand each other. I s'pose she had to be informed of my decision. But I don't know why, after all your years of service, you'd ever think, once the suggestion was made and accepted, that her preferences in the matter would be inquired into. Tell me, Sedgeley, d'you know what a quintillion is?"

"Sir?" What did this have to do with the subject at hand?

"A quintillion, Sedgeley, in the old, pre-barquode writin' which I find a deal more expressive than the soulless stripes we use today. A 'one' followed by eighteen 'zerocs.' By some estimates, something more than a quintillion human beings exist within the various polities of the known galaxy, perhaps that many within the Monopolity itself." *Tick, tock, tick, tock, tick . . .*

Except for an uncle who had proven less meritorious a protector than he might have been, Loreanna had no family. While she was still an infant, her parents, Sedgeley's younger brother Clyve and his lovely wife Jennivere, had disappeared in the vastness of the Deep while touring their far-flung plantations and mining properties. It had been years, and before the end was in sight had required an enormous amount of money and exertion, before Loreanna's uncle learned, beyond an evaporating shadow of his last cherished doubt, what had become of them.

"Possibly this estimate is exaggerated, sir," he replied. "May I—"

"No, you mayn't, Sedgeley. Not for the moment, old friend. You're correct, it's quite possible the estimate's exaggerated. After all, the ravages of a thousand years' unceasin' warfare, and what's less widely understood, the everyday predations of the governments who wage it, some ten or fifteen times worse than war itself, must take some toll of that figure."

Clyve and Jennivere had been just two victims somewhere between systems. Sedgeley's brother had fallen prey to the ultimate pressgang. Tranquilized within seconds of his vessel's capture, he had been transported to a hidden "factory" world where the unspeakable was carried out upon a production basis. From that moment he never again knew human consciousness nor the feeling of acting upon his own will. In a sense it might have been asserted that Clyve Daimler-Wilkinson had died. *Tick, tock, tick, tock, tick . . .*

"Sir?" Only now did Leupould's words register upon his much-preoccupied mind. "Everyday predations of governments." Had the Executor-General uttered these words, he would likely have been executed without trial.

"Try not to look so shocked, Sedgeley! You know me better, or should. 'Pon the other hand, the estimate of a quintillion may well be too low. To be sure, no method exists of being certain."

Despite himself, Daimler-Wilkinson's mind had begun to wander backward in time. Upon that hidden factory world, listed in no official interstellar chart, along with millions of other victims, Clyve's mind and memories, all that distinguished him from every other member of his species, were erased by "electrotherapy," psychoactives, operant conditioning, and surgery. In another sense, this might have been the moment of Clyve's death, for at this point, it all became irreversible.

What was it the Ceo had just asserted? No method of being certain—but of what? "No, sir, regrettably. If I may—"

"You bally well may not! I've thought this out with great care and postponed the day's work to get it stated. Pray don't interrupt again."

Clyve's body had continued living, swollen with hormones, machine-exercise, and tailored viruses, for such was the purpose of the process. In secret, at unimaginable expense, the hulking thing which had once been a man was converted into a fighting robot, to be transported to more "civilized" reaches, perhaps Hanover itself, and sold for more than its weight in precious metals. Clyve Daimler-Wilkinson had become an Oplyte.

Tick, tock, tick, tock, tick . . . Leupould paused here, awaiting acknowledgement. Realizing he had forbidden any word at all, he continued before his friend could be caught in another error. "Such numbers convey precious little to the human mind. A quintillion? What is that? Eighteen zeroes? What do they mean? Nonetheless—p'rhaps for this very reason—valuable lessons are to be learned from them, regardin' the human condition."

It was no different with Clyve than for centuries with a hundred million others. Popular belief held Oplytes to be "rehabilitated" criminals, mutants, aliens, the product of some advanced petrosorcery. However, contrary to all the myths and rumors, they were former human beings one and all, suffering perhaps the cruelest fate ever inflicted by one man upon another. Victims of a ubiquitous and voracious form of slavery, each had been selected, subjected to elaborate alteration, for no purpose except killing. An amateur athlete, Clyve's misfortune—the basis for his selection—was that he possessed superlative reflexes and a magnificent physique.

Tick, tock, tick, tock, tick . . . Again the Ceo paused, this time for a longer time. Unable to bear the prolonged silence, and the persistent tock-ticking of Leupould's hideous new toy punctuating it, the Executor-General risked speaking. "I see, sir. Pray continue."

"Thank you, Sedgeley, you're most kind. Now, whether consciously or not, the lessons I mentioned are extracted by everyone, upon an everyday basis. They form the unstated ground upon which every decision and transaction is carried out in our thirty-first-century civilization."

Daimler-Wilkinson's search had taught him more about thirty-first-century civilization, and the character of those he lived among, than he had ever wanted to know. When he had learned the truth about Oplytes, he had wanted it broadcast from the top of the 'Droom to a galaxy which would rise in arms to exterminate every slaver plying the Deep. He had been taken aside quietly by the Ceo's other advisors. The Oplyte "secret" was not much of a secret, after all. The pretense served many interests. Small effort was necessary to preserve it. All that was necessary was for certain people to look away, which they were more than willing to do.

"Sir?"

"To wit: a single unit of any commodity in such abundance as to be expressible only in numbers like quintillions can't possess much value in itself. Whatever mankind's self-delusional philosophies have ever asserted to the contrary, there exists, as there always has and always will, an immutable natural law which every murchan has savvied since the day cuneiform accounts were first baked into clay."

Tick, tock, tick, tock, tick . . .

Sedgeley's time and money, however, had purchased him a uniquely terrible experience. A law of physics, as immutable as any the Ceo chose to lecture him about, states that nothing is without cost. An Oplyte's superhuman powers demanded that his brain and body be overdriven, after no more than three or four years' service to his owners, to the point of self-destruction. It was difficult to obtain any Oplyte in particular. It had never occurred to anyone to try. No true individual could be identified among them, any more than with spreighformed caffcups or ashtrays. This would defeat the entire purpose of having "created" them. Each was considered, by supplier and customer alike, to be an identical, expendable, replaceable unit.

"I believe I—"

"The law states, as it always has and always will, that the more there is of anything, the less valuable any single unit of it becomes. This is the Law of Marginal Utility, to which all things everywhere are inalterably subject."

After a prolonged wait, Daimler-Wilkinson had accepted, in a state of growing horror, delivery of a particular used-up, useless slave. Instead of a replaceable unit, however, he saw before him someone he had loved, fifteen years the younger, now white-haired, toothless, wrinkled, noncoherent. Clyve was unaware of his surroundings. His body trembled with an uncontrollable affliction resembling Parkinsonism, and he suffered premature senile dementia. This, as everybody knew, was the fate of every Oplyte.

Tick, tock, tick, tock, tick . . . "Sir, I—"

A scream penetrated the room. Daimler-Wilkinson's head jerked toward the timepiece, where, as the pointers indicated the end of the hour, the swinging blade reached its victim. Miniature shirt and chest were cut through. Minute organs could be seen inside. A hideous scarlet liquid pooled round, splashing across the blade. Daimler-Wilkinson had no alternative but to listen to the enthilled scream as the pendulum swung back and forth through the tiny violated body thirteen times in all—that was the hour, early afternoon—before the head slumped, the blade returned to its original position, the little man's wound healed by a mechanical miracle, blood drained away to be recycled, and the ordeal began anew. They sat in silence for a long while.

With some effort Leupould turned upon his side, to face his old friend and advisor. "I hope with all sincerity that you appreciate what I'm drivin' at, old fellow, for we're quite late gettin' started today—I'm not altogether certain that new timepiece is in good taste, are you?—and I should regret havin' to waste more time explainin' any further."

He arose, cast the rug off with the same gesture as his expensive finery, and seized the summoner for his dresser. "Given the Law of Marginal Utility, in all the starry universe, across the cold expanse of the Deep, upon millions of planets, nothing, Sedgeley, is found in greater quantity—or upon this account is less valued—than a human life."

Tick, tock, tick, tock, tick . . . The timepiece counted minutes before the next atrocity. "Not yours, nor mine, nor those of your brother and his wife—yes, I know all about them— not even your own dear niece, Loreanna."

Tick, tock, tick, tock, tick . . . "If you get my meanin' . . ."

CHAPTER XXXIV:
OF LIES AND LOVE

Brougham knew.

Across an expanse of table which felt like a vast and empty playing field, Daimler-Wilkinson's eyes lay with fond sadness upon his niece, but his thoughts were upon the loyal *yensid* retainer attempting to serve them dinner.

"Do you prefer aircrab and dressing, sir, or jellied marmot?"

"I suppose the crab, Brougham. The Ceo served curried

rikshii at luncheon, which, to my taste, is rather similar to marmot."

"As you wish, sir." Brougham turned to Loreanna. "And for you, Miss?"

Loreanna, lost in her own thoughts, started at the abruptness of Brougham's inquiry. She had been attempting, with no more luck than at any other moment over the past days, to determine whether the guilt she felt toward her uncle might be less justified than her feelings of abandonment and disappointment.

Daimler-Wilkinson observed her state of abstraction. As was ever the case, both the meal and the manner in which it was served were faultless, although he had experienced better appetite. His niece pushed the food about upon her plate, picking at infrequent intervals as if to forestall a solicitous word from the uncle she no doubt felt had betrayed her, perhaps even from the alien she had grown up thinking of as her best—now perhaps only—friend.

Meanwhile, Loreanna had come to the conclusion she always arrived at. Any self-respecting young woman would reject a marriage such as her uncle had proposed, would resent being offered the alternative of exile in a frozen waste and being expected to regard it as a favor.

"Nothing, thank you, Brougham, I shall continue with the preserves."

Something like parental disapproval, resigned but not to be denied, colored Brougham's reply. "As you will, Miss."

The glittering traditional service, old-fashioned dishes and cutlery which had never been within a klomme of any spreighformer, the snowy cloth which was a living organism from some far-off world and could never show a stain, the subtle lighting evoked from wainscotted upper walls by the antenna chandelabrum, all served as reminders of more auspicious circumstances. Loreanna, Daimler-Wilkinson was certain, was thinking that, in a few more days, she would never see these lovely things again. To him they were, bitter mementos, treasured heirlooms though they were of a happier time, long past and long lost, when other chairs about the table would have been occupied by those he loved, other voices raised in conversation or laughter.

Loreanna watched her uncle, wondering what thoughts

occupied his mind. A greater grievance lay behind her outrage than the bleak alternatives of banishment or marriage to a total (and, by all accounts, obnoxious) stranger. The former might prove no more than unpleasant. The latter had been the destiny of many women throughout human history. Somehow both women and humanity had survived. She was, however, troubled by a conclusion, predicated upon girlhood observation of her uncle's rise within the 'Droom—which he, believing her sheltered from harsh reality, had never realized her capable of drawing—concerning the results of mixing two forms of polite and bloody warfare known as politics and love.

"If that will be all, sir, I shall retire to the pantry."

He looked up, startled as his niece had been. "Thank you, Brougham. We shall let you know should we require anything."

Even imperturbable Brougham seemed to suffer under the tension. As Daimler-Wilkinson had found himself thinking when this familiar, circular pattern (he was unsure he would call it "reasoning") had begun, Brougham knew everything of the family tragedy which he, Loreanna's uncle, had never dared convey to her.

He spoke: "Excuse me, my dear, I—would you pass the cinnamon?"

She spoke: "I should be delighted, Uncle."

Again he had failed to say the words which might have extricated them from this speechless nightmare. She had responded, not with "Uncle Sedgeley," or even "Sedgeley" as she had been more inclined to call him until recently, but with a naked label, cold and remote. He accepted the shaker—she seemed careful to avoid touching his fingers—and discovered he had quite forgotten why he wanted it.

Loreanna brushed the interruption aside. Physical intimacy between the genders—although she had never yet experienced it herself—may or may not have constituted the transcendent, all-consuming pleasure of which everyone seemed to speak with such melodious rapture. (If it required so much advertising, what must be wrong with it?) Possessing a theoretical grounding in its blunt mechanics (and its manifold consequences, none sounding at all pleasurable), she felt an inclination not just to reserve judgment in the matter, but to marvel at the capacity in others for temporary insanity.

Daimler-Wilkinson blinked. Where had his thoughts been? Yes: the guilty secret he and the *yensid* had preserved between them so many years, telling themselves—and, when resolution faltered, one another—that it was necessary for their beloved Loreanna's protection. One of them now knew differently, and Daimler-Wilkinson suspected that, to whatever extent the alien possessed something akin to human feeling, Brougham harbored similar doubts regarding the real motive for the course they had chosen. He discovered that his hands were shaking and took steps to regain control, tucking them into his lap beneath the table.

Loreanna noticed the tremor in her uncle's hands, wondering what troubled him so. It did not occur to her it might be the dispute between them. She had come, in recent weeks, to the honest if unwelcome belief that she was the only individual who cared what would become of her. Instead, since her mind dwelt upon similar subjects already, she gave in to momentary speculation that he might be having an affair with some 'Droom lady, suffering the proverbial attendant woes thereof. She was reminded of an ancient song at which she had learned to accompany herself upon the synthechord, *"Plaisir d'Amour,"* for whose timeless, universal wisdom, couched in extinct language though it be—it had been necessary to find another antiquarian to translate them—she felt increasing appreciation. Whatever the pleasures of grunting, sweating, interpenetration, it was certain they were ephemeral.

Hunched with his hands between his thighs, Daimler-Wilkinson felt the present dimmed by images of the past, his vision blurred by unshed tears which put the thought of eating out of the question. As before, it was Brougham who occupied the forefront of his mind. Brougham had stood by as, never recognizing its brother, the shattered thing which had been Clyve had expired in Sedgeley's arms. Brougham had seen Clyve's worn-out body given decent and anonymous disposal in the garden behind the house, into which Sedgeley had never again set foot. Brougham had acted as administrative aide when, employing resources which had been successful in the search for Clyve, Sedgeley had failed to discover any trace of Jennivere. In truth—he had been compelled, each step of the way, to struggle against an inclination to do nothing—he had never expected to, that sort of slave, a young, desirable woman, being even shorter-lived and more disposable than an Oplyte.

Swearing his alien accomplice to what was meant to be a temporary secrecy, he had never told—had never been able to tell—his niece of her parents' fate. When old enough, Loreanna had been informed that their starship, like others, had failed to return from across the Deep. Year after year he had promised his conscience that he would unburden himself of the terrible truth. Year after year, he had retreated from the resolution, until what had seemed at first a mere unsavory task assumed the proportions of an insurmountable obstacle. He looked across at her now, again attempting to state the all-important truth, instead finding his mouth clumsy and full of inanities.

"Have more caff, my dear. I can ask Brougham to brew another pot."

Hearing the edge in her uncle's voice and what she imagined it signified, Loreanna became aware of something she had inferred from reading history: a little love, mixed with the exigencies of politics, was a dangerous thing. "Thank you, Uncle, but I slept through most of yesterday. I greatly fear another cup might prevent me sleeping tonight, as well."

He set the pot down without a flutter, a fact of which he was shocked to find himself proud. Despite the strain to which he had lately subjected her, Loreanna was more beautiful than ever in her low-bodiced, full-skirted gown, her copper hair draped charmingly about her fair, freckled shoulders. He had believed himself a good and loving uncle, a reasonable substitute for the father she would never know. In the years she had lived with him, he had never been tempted to see her as anything other than a daughter, for all her delicate, unself-conscious, enigmatic desirability. He often wondered at this. These were corrupt and decadent times, and he himself no different from others he knew who enjoyed the opportunities corruption and decadence afford. He was a hearty individual with a taste for the flesh, the wealth and power to exercise it, accustomed to the company of women—although his preference ran to blondes more buxom than this miniature beauty he had brought up. Had he possessed her, most Hanoverians, steeped in their own unspeakabilities, would have looked the other way. That approached the status of a Hanoverian pastime. Any minority moralistic enough to point a finger would have been dissuaded by his position in the 'Droom.

Instead he had been a father to her. He wondered now whether the alternative might not have proven better for her. In seeking to protect her he had come close to destroying her. He had denied her the truth, he realized, not so much because he thought her unable to tolerate it—to his surprise and delight, she had grown up made of better stuff than that—but because he could neither bear being the one to inflict it upon her, nor bring himself to delegate the task to anyone less important in her life.

For her own part, whatever troubled her uncle, Loreanna was confident he would weather it. Men seemed to. Women were not so resilient, nor so lucky. She had decided long ago—this conclusion she had reached by methods she believed scientific—that love and sex were simply aspects of another dirty power-game, with women always the losers.

Daimler-Wilkinson shook his head. Lately, through blindness, ambition, inadvertence, and loyalty misplaced, he had injured Loreanna in a manner worse than if he had touched her himself. Most painfully, he was learning a truth as terrible as that which, in intended kindness, he had withheld from her all these years, yet more fundamental and general of application.

Lies, he thought, knowing he was not the first in history to realize it, even of omission, create an inevitable necessity for more lies, until lying is a first recourse instead of a desperate last. They erect walls between those who love each other, so that, when crisis comes, as it had, one can no longer reach the person he has lied to, no longer even recognize her as the person for love of whom the dubious protection of lies was first sought.

So it was that, just as he had never told her of her parents' fate, it had never occurred to him in recent days to explain that, in this most cruel of all possible ages, the future he had labored to achieve for her—marriage of state to an entity incapable, in any physical sense, of injuring her—was, by comparison with most likelier alternatives, a kindly one. Even the alternative might prove easier than life upon the capital world.

For an instant, their eyes met across the table, conveying no more than mutual recognition that each felt helpless to escape unenviable circumstances which almost seemed to have created themselves. He wondered if Brougham, himself a sufferer of one of those likelier alternatives, appreciated what he was trying to do, and wondered why he felt responsible to the creature.

"Sir?" The kitchen door swung aside. Brougham, exercising that mundane but real telepathy which years of intimate acquaintance engender between beings, appeared as if summoned by his master's thoughts. "If you have finished, sir, I shall have these dishes cleared out of your way."

Daimler-Wilkinson glanced at his niece, who appeared to have accomplished as much with her food as she was likely to. He understood exactly how she was feeling this evening. He could not help worrying about her; at his present weight he could afford to skip a meal, whereas she, at hers, could not. Because he felt the same, himself. "Satisfactory, Brougham, and if you would afterward fetch my pipe, I would appreciate it."

"Yes, sir." Brougham supervised a pair of female *yensid* as they cleared the table. The omnivorous tablecloth had made short, discreet work of any spots or crumbs the moment they had been dropped.

At this moment, when she might have offered some word which might (or might not) have changed everything, Loreanna recalled a recent confrontation in which he had enumerated ways, had he not been more considerate of her wishes, she might have been induced to cooperate, through drugs or less-pleasant forms of mind-alteration. An unbearable sense of injustice boiled up within her, expunging any thought she might have entertained of making peace. In thirty-first-century matters of the "heart", she thought with bitter satisfaction, the sanction of the victim—an outward appearance of consent without regard to whatever inward reality it may have concealed—had become all-important. Those perceiving themselves as the more refined elements of society preferred "unpersuaded" women as earlier ones had preferred virgins.

In due course Brougham brought his master's smoking materials. Daimler-Wilkinson had never acquired the Ceo's taste for nicotine. Since Loreanna had been a child, he had come to enjoy a single pipe of cannagrass after the evening meal. It settled his stomach and was helpful in overcoming a chronic difficulty getting to sleep. Accepting the miniature pipe, he watched the *yensid* cut a corner from the small cube of resinous brown essence and sprinkle the resultant crumblings upon the fine mesh in the bowl. He leaned forward to receive the flame, drew the sweet smoke in and inhaled, already beginning to relax from nothing more than years of habit.

Loreanna reminded herself that she was both: virgin and unpersuaded.

In these precarious times, precious little personal security existed, Daimler-Wilkinson observed, returning to the track upon which his thoughts had run all evening. Loreanna should consider herself fortunate. The trouble, he realized, was that, again from a desire to preserve the gentler sensibilities he had sought to ingrain in her, he had taken pains to see she led a sheltered life. She knew nothing of the savagery churning just outside her door. She would never believe that good intentions for her were all that motivated him.

"Uncle?"

Daimler-Wilkinson blinked. Brougham had vanished without his having noticed. The cannagrass must be quite fresh. His chair made scraping sounds upon the carpet as he arose with feelings of disappointment and depression. "Yes, my dear?"

"If you will excuse me, I still have packing to accomplish . . ."

Daimler-Wilkinson allowed himself an inward sigh. Over the years he had been accustomed to having her company these last few minutes every evening. Now she had been finding excuses to leave him at table, and he was beginning to have those bleak, never-again feelings which accompany an irrevocable break. Even had they been a string of paradise worlds, Baffridgestar was, in terms of time and space, a long way away. "Of course, my dear. Perhaps I shall see you in the morning before I leave for the 'Droom."

Virgin and unpersuaded, the thought returned. She who remained the latter might yet remain the former. While it was true, throughout history, that uncounted women had survived political marriages, many more had managed to make admirable lives for themselves without handling from any man. Virgin and unpersuaded equaled "Old Maid." Loreanna intended to do her grim and level best to remain both—and if need be the lattermost—for a long time to come. "Good night, Uncle Sedge—" she answered with an odd expression. "Good night, Uncle."

As she left him, he sat down again, feeling ill. He drew upon his pipe, hoping against experience that it would make him feel better. Save for its bubbling, silence descended upon the dining room.

It was also possible to lie to oneself, he thought, and easiest to do so by omission. The consequences were more difficult to see, not just in advance, but even as they were happening, even after they had ended in one's destruction. However, for a different variety of reasons . . . reasons that had created this aching . . . gulf between himself and Loreanna, Loreanna, Loreanna . . . he had never so much as attempted to discover . . . What had he never attempted to discover? That was it: in what manner had it come to pass that his family, of all families . . . of all families had been disrupted . . . by the travesty . . . travesty of interstellar slavery and death.

Daimler-Wilkinson found his thoughts separated by disconcerting gaps in his sense of time-flow which were the signature of cannagrass, the reason he had sought surcease with the drug in the first place. Now that he had achieved it, he was not certain it was what he wanted. He put the pipe down and took several deep breaths, attempting to reorder his thoughts.

When his mind was alert, working in the interests of Ceo and Monopolity—and not beclouded with the effort of hiding from itself—Daimler-Wilkinson was contemptuous of coincidence. What had happened to Clyve and his young wife might have been random happenstance, the unpredictable conclusion to an inauspicious business-and-pleasure voyage. Operating at uninhibited capacity, the Ceo's Drector-Advisory and Executor-General believed it likelier to represent some connivance against his own interests which, perhaps at the last moment, had gone wrong. No punchline had ever arrived. No agent of an enemy had ever appeared to promise, threaten, or gloat. The whole thing had remained an ugly mystery, and the elder brother's secret, for most of Loreanna's lifetime.

Which was what had brought him to this place and time, forged a bond of conspiracy between him and a servant, and, despite his best intentions, lost him the love and respect of the only living human being he cared for. He was surprised to discover himself taking another draught upon his pipe. Shaking his head, he accepted it, leaned back, driving his emotions back inside where they could not affect him, forgetting as hard as he could.

Alone.

CHAPTER XXXV:
THE DROWNED MAN

Frantisek Demondion-Echeverria, Ambassador Plenipotentiary from the 'Droom of Ribauldequin XXIII, Ceo of the Jendyne Empery-Cirot, to the 'Droom of Leupould IX, Ceo of the Monopolitan Imperium-Conglomerate, leaned back upon his mesh relaxer, sunk within the comfortable gloom of his personal apartments at the embassy upon Hanover, taking solitary pleasure, as he often did, in his many well-deserved titles and responsibilities.

He grinned at the retreating alabaster bottoms of his latest pair of mistresses. *Gone again, my well-upholstered beauties,* he thought as he did each morning at this time, with a melodramatic sigh intended only partially in jest, *no more fun for Frantisek again until tomorrow.*

The feeling was mingled with a degree of pleasant satiation. How much less mischief, he reflected, how many fewer wars might have raged throughout the long, mournful dirge which was the sum of human history, had men of power simply put things off another hour to have a second (or a third) go-round with their enamorata? As he should know, who, in all appropriate modesty, happened to be, if not the principal power behind the Jendyne Chair, then at least one of an elite handful and upon the rapid rise.

He blinked. A small, golden-colored fish swam by at eye level. One of many he kept here, its movements were uncoordinated, frantic with dull-witted terror. Another flash of movement caught his eye as a small brown kitten the girls had recently acquired streaked by, paddling for all it was worth. In an instant it had snapped up the goldfish, devouring it greedily as it drifted a measure from the floor. Demondion-Echeverria laughed and clapped his hands at the sight. Some he knew were not particularly fond of cats, even actively abhorred them. He had never understood such a narrow attitude. This miniature devil had scarcely been here in his special apartments a week, yet it had gamely overcome its most instinctive fears, learning to swim like the otter it resembled and in the process winning the ambassador's heart.

"Of course, my swift, voracious friend," he murmured, "some unfortunates we know of—our esteemed, deteriorating master, Ribauldequin, for example—are incapable of a *first* go-round. I wonder what excuse they find to continue such a featureless existence." A spare man, small of stature and dark of complexion, he enjoyed the effect this place had upon his voice, which came to his ears deepened in tone and timbre, the opposite to that effect observed when breathing mixtures less dense than ordinary air, like helium. "I should say we know our Ceo as well as any minister, as well, let us say, as our upright, prissy colleague Sedgeley Daimler-Wilkinson knows his, which, we are given to understand, is well indeed."

Halfway between floor and ceiling, the kitten licked its paws. At the sound of the man's booming voice, it stared at him curiously. "The sad truth, furry one, is that, unlike the shrewd, prolific Leupould, our own poor nominal ruler is not only impotent, but senile into the bargain." The kitten meowed silently, blinked huge eyes, turned and, attempting to seize and wash its tail, whirled in frustration, the appendage eluding its grasp. It flailed its legs in an effort to stop the rotary motion. "With each passing year, it grows more difficult, diplomat though I am, to conceal my monumental contempt for the fool as prudence dictates. And why not? All things being relative, Ribauldequin is a mere youth, scarcely a hundred years old!"

He dismissed these oft-repeated thoughts and rang for a manservitor. It was past time, however reluctant he felt, to begin today's appointments. One was of some importance. He recalled, thankful for small blessings, that it was acceptable to let that individual see him as he was. Another movement caught his eye. One end of a decoratively stitched waist-tie of his dressing gown had apparently decided upon its own to float to the ceiling. Smiling, he snatched at it as the kitten had its tail (albeit with more success), and wrung it out. Minute bubbles squeezed from the fabric vanished upward. The strip of cloth relaxed, this time staying where he placed it. Nodding to himself, he reached to the table beside him and took up a datathille which would inform him in detail of items upon the morning's agenda.

In its usual deliberate course, the manservitor he had summoned finally arrived. Seeing it as no more than a shadow behind a curtain, the ambassador knew that it would be slow-moving, blank-eyed, loose-lipped, and slack-jawed, like every Jendyne menial. This specimen, the vendor had informed his deputy (who had seen fit to mention it casually), was from Kalforn. It had been discovered carrying a small-bladed folding knife, he believed, although in general he seldom kept track of such insignifica, and dealt with upon the spot, as Jendyne law required, by a constable wielding a lobotomizer.

"And a good thing," he informed the kitten. "Within our Empery-Cirot, this law and others like it, as all laws at root are intended to do—though they are seldom enforced with sufficient stringency—have eradicated the servitor problem." He did not inform his friend (who might not have appreciated the point) that lobotomees were a trifle less imaginative than those left intact. They were a deal closer-mouthed. Neither as fearsome nor versatile as Oplytes—

useless as bodyguards or soldiers, upon the other hand, massed upon plantations, they were unprone to revolt—they were cheaper than the warriors, and, accordingly, more expendable. "Given proper legislation," he added as an afterthought, "which all men must violate daily because it basically outlaws living, they are available in endless quantity."

Drawn by his cheerful, soothing voice, the kitten approached, windmilling its paws, braking to a drifting halt siemmes above his legs. It added another few judicious strokes, settled to his robed lap, and began to give itself another bath. Unnecessarily in this room, Demondion-Echeverria mused, instinct is overcome only within limits, an important point for a man of power to be reminded of. *To business, then, the curtain is about to go up.*

This perhaps overly dramatic thought was nevertheless literally correct. The servitor appeared in silhouette at a curtained portal two measures square, separating this chamber from the ambassador's office. It announced itself—it was laboriously trained not to startle—and drew the curtain. He could now see into what looked like a stage set and adjusted the lighting so that he could be seen, as well. A goldfish swam before his eyes. He and the kitten ignored it. This was not the only such portal in the suite. The building had been selected neither for price nor the neighborhood in which it sat, but for its architecture. Had something suitable not been available, he would have ordered it constructed, for he reclined, suspended in a room filled—and woe betide the servitor who permitted unsightly bubbles to collect near the ceiling—with well-filtered, oxygen-enriched liquid fluorocarbon.

The ambassador's apartments had been designed so that the liquid-filled rooms were at the center, overlooking every other portion of the embassy. They were protected from sudden breach (either of physical integrity or the Empery-Cirot's extraterritoriality) by double walls, and built upon one level to avoid pressure necessitating elaborate decompression.

He grimaced with distaste. Revealed in the stronger light, something bobbed near the ceiling, too large for the filters which handled innocent indiscretions of the sort committed by kittens or goldfish. A second glance showed it to be a slipper, escaped from a dresser drawer. The girls, lucky creatures, spent more time here than he did, but, like all women in his experience, tended toward a general untidiness. He took a deep breath, inhaling oxygen-rich liquid, exhaling it laden with carbon dioxide.

A peculiar substance, fluorocarbon, with even more peculiar properties. Primitive matches, useless in these rooms (the liquid carried heat away too quickly to support flame), still lit after being soaked. Lights, timepieces, communicators, thille players, all operated without fault. Undistracting music wafted through the room. He must commend the technician. After many experiments, the transducers had been adjusted to allow for differences between his current ambience and the air in which the music was enthilled. (He was grateful the same could not be done to his voice.) As with most pleasures of which he availed himself, this served more purposes than one. Buried within the wave-forms of the music—and this, he gathered, was what had offered technical difficulty—a superheterodyning signal insured that anything uttered within the room would be converted by listening devices into gabble, punctuated by painful shrilling. He was free to say, and do, anything he wished, even enjoy an amusing, if one-sided, conversation with a kitten.

He glanced at the jewel-encrusted thrustible lying with comforting familiarity along his left forearm. It was reliable when immersed, a virtue more attributable to the liquid than to the weapon, but all to the good. Otherwise, security considerations might have limited the hours he could relax here even more than doing business with the unenlightened already did.

He took another breath, letting his arms lift and settle back. The pure liquid was lower in density than water, alcohol, even many oils. Unaugmented, it would not have supported his weight. He would have sunk to the floor like a stone. Vitamins and other nutrients added to its buoyant properties, like salt added to water. This was more than just a complicated lark. As Master-Practitioner of the Immortal School Poriferitae (or, as envious others upon Homeworld and Hanover had it, a crackpot cult of the same name), he spent most of his hours each day permeated by this liquid, sleeping in it, breathing it—save in the line of diplomatic duty, he no longer ate at all in the open air—and sporting with his women.

Begun as a course of emergency therapy in his youth, when he had nearly burned to death in a starport attack, the Practice had kept him fit some 370 years—"thus far," he told himself, for with each passing year he came to love life and detest the idea of death more, although, like many a combat veteran, he no longer feared it. Unlike cryogenous suspension, one was not compelled to sleep through most of his extended lifespan and could take pleasure watching those who called him crackpot wither and die. He had been immersed unconscious the first week. How well he remembered his initiation into the Immortal School, the effort required to overcome fear of taking his first deliberate breath of liquid, when every reflex screamed he was about to drown. Many would-be Practitioners unable to cross that threshold were, not without understanding, rejected by the Immortal Poriferitae. He had heard it claimed that many a death attributed to water drowning turned out to have been by suffocation, sheer unwillingness to take water into the lungs.

Now taking that breath was the easiest thing in the galaxy, accomplished several times a day. Yet it was neither the extension of his life, nor any love of swimming, which had attracted him to the Immortal School, nor a desire to imitate aquatic creatures, but the avians. Without machinery or similar aids, he could *fly* within these rooms, fulfilling an ages-old and, he believed, instinctive desire shared by all humanity since the dawn of time.

Yawning, he made a note to enhance the oxygen level. The little fellow buzzing upon his lap consumed rather a disproportionate amount. He wondered again whether the kitten's life expectancy, like his own, would benefit from application of the Principia Poriferitae. It was a pleasant possibility. He could think of no reason why it should not be so. More oxygen was a good idea for another reason. He had been considering indulging in a third girl. If he could not increase the number of hours he had to spare for pleasure, he would increase their quality. He also made a note to the effect

that—with the kitten here, a long-haired one at that—
circulation filters would have to be inspected with greater
frequency.

"Our first chore," he told the sleeping kitten, "will be
perusal of an information digest, notes from the Hanoverians
and other diplomatic missions, supplemented by Intelligence, regarding this proposed truce in the region *n'Worb
m'Divad.*" Making slow, smooth movements so as not
to disturb the cat, he adjusted the summoner to route a message to his clerk. "Consistent with a practice long since become routine," (if not tedious, he thought), "send a copy
of the memorandum I first dictated three years ago straightaway to Homeworld bureaucracy, demanding that explorers
accredited by the Empery-Cirot bestow sensible names
upon new territories, rather than haphazardly adopting un-
pronounceable grunts collected from the savages they find
there."

He placed the communicator back upon the table, taking
care that it could not float way. Where was he? It was no
accident that thought of Daimler-Wilkinson had arisen earlier. It was plain to him, and his intelligence staff, that
Leupould's henchman was a proponent, if not the source, of
the truce offer, whether in his capacity as Drector-Advisory
or Executor-General was not clear. It would be worth taking
trouble to determine which. He retrieved the communicator
and dictated a memorandum to that effect. If the former, the
offer was likely genuine, reflecting some necessity upon the
part of the Monopolity. If the latter, it was probably a ploy of
war and should be addressed with skepticism and appropriate
counter-preparations.

The ambassador had reason to hope it was the former,
although it would not affect performance of his duties.
Despite Ribauldequin's disabilities, Demondion-Echeverria
had plans to accept, in his sovereign's behalf, the offered
truce gift, for he had learned what form it would take upon a recent visit to the Monopolitan 'Droom. As coincidence would
have it, taking pride in a capacity to discern the fullness
of the blossom in the promise of the bud, he had for three
years, since first coming to Hanover, kept almost a proprie-
tory eye upon this particular flower, seeking means by

which to add her (the thought struck him) to his *hydroponic* garden.

Thanks to the Immortal School, his was the aspect of a man in vigorous middle age. Even this was mostly cosmetic (he might have been a youth with equal credibility) adopted for politics. He suffered no such shortcoming as drooling Ribauldequin and could make splendid use of the young and tender Loreanna. Word was that she was unbroached, untapped, however euphemism ran these days, which might prove amusing. He had not spread a virgin in a long while and the fancy stirred him. When he had tired of her he would have her lobotomized as a living trophy, or sell her at a profit to the highest bidder. Such calculated insult would hang upon the truce being betrayed by one side or another, but experience told him this was inevitable.

As he perused the notethille prepared by his staff the previous evening, Demondion-Echeverria chuckled. By another coincidence, if he was willing to contrive it, the highest bidder might be his first appointment this morning. By appearance a vile proletarian tradesman, he was an acquaintance of long standing, almost a friend. Further, if rumors Intelligence had collected were credited, that the bride-to-be had offered her demurral, none too polite, and would be freighted as punishment to some ceo-forsaken colony, his almost-friend might prove to be of use as upon earlier occasions.

He reviewed what he knew of the man, reputedly Hanoverian although of dubious loyalty to ceo or imperium conglomerate. He had observed the fellow taking childish delight, like all his trade, in fancying himself a romantic adventurer. Upon another hand, each profession practiced its pretensions; a diplomat had small room to criticize. Officially, the ambassador knew him to be an often-useful doublespy. They shared certain preferences, he and this starsailor. A year or two ago, the man had, in his presence, expressed lustful admiration for the Daimler-Wilkinson girl. It had been some formal occasion, a reception for stiquemen at the 'Droom, if memory served. Owing him a favor, Demondion-Echeverria had obtained for him a copy of an autothille he had ordered prepared in stealth, the so-called "intelligent" kind which anticipated change and "grew up" with its subject.

Be this as it may, the man was in a mood to reward himself. He had recently returned from an unbelievable ordeal, a prolonged starvoyage in an auxiliary, imposed by direst emergency, word of which had made him something of a celebrity. New found reputation offered practical usages to those prepared to take proper advantage. Like many another public hero, he had not hesitated to augment his notoriety by employing a discreet fame-enhancing agency and had experienced little difficulty obtaining more fresh investors than he had use for, along with a new ship, and was, by all accounts, prepared to sail even now, which well suited the ambassador's plans.

Demondion-Echeverria considered the inconvenience of abandoning his pool of fluorocarbon and thought better of it. Greater psychological advantage might obtain were he to interview the villain as he appeared now. He reached to summon his staff of lobotomized servitors, under supervision of a few deputies he trusted to remain in possession of their minds, to welcome the privateer, then reconsidered. Certain courtesy must be accorded the man if they were to do business with the same cordiality as so many times before. He felt a groan arising unbidden within him, stifling it before it found a voice. However casual his first breath of fluorocarbon had become over the years, his last—or, put another way, the day's first breath of air—was another matter altogether. The ordeal remained, if not utterly impossible (in which case he would have abandoned the Practice), a bother and discomfort.

With a sigh of resignation which he did voice, he lifted the kitten from his lap and hung it, protesting, in the center of the room. He unlatched the belt which held him to the lounger, precaution against drifting in his sleep, discarded his dressing gown, and kicked ceilingward where a pair of colored tabs protruded between plastic-coated mesh-wires. He pulled upon the first. A trapdoor lowered, exposing the mirrored undersurface of the fluorocarbon, broken with wavelets. The second released a pair of tapered plastic cylinders attached to cabelles. He turned a half somersault and slid his ankles into them, tightening straps until he was certain they would support his weight. Giving the tab another tug, he straightened, head downward, feet pointing at the open trapdoor, arms folded across his chest, counting to himself.

At fifteen heartbeats, he began deep inhalation of the oxygen-charged fluorocarbon. At twenty, cabelles reeled him through the surface of the liquid into the air above. Long practiced at this uncomfortable transition, he exhaled by reflex, hard as he could, clearing his lungs. He inhaled air, coughing once or twice to rid himself of traces of the fluid. The exercise with the cabelles precluded an entire day of coughing. Swinging upon well-trained muscles, he unfastened his ankles, lowered himself to the mesh beside the trapdoor, and accepted a dry robe handed him by a manservitor. Demondion-Echeverria did not like it, but he was again a creature of the land.

He set off for the spare suite he despised to find clothes, and afterward to greet his almost-friend, Master-murchan Ballygrant Bowmore.

CHAPTER XXXVI:
THE BRIGANTINE *PELICAN*

Fresh tachyon breezes and nary a sign of stormy weather.

Bowmore stood upon the quarterdeck of the *Pelican*, knee-boots braced comfortably against her complex vibration, metal-ended braids swaying, bejeweled hands together at the small of his back, his one good eye upon his officers. The Deep-born flux thrummed in the rigging of the brigantine, bellying her starsails, filling her entire structure with the music her master loved best. At full strength, the §-field pulsed in visual rhythm with it, for she was running swiftly under all plainsail. He was tempted to set her stunsails as a lark, to see whether his escort had their wits about them. He took a deep breath through his pierced and decorated nostrils, enjoying mesh underfoot again. It was a good feeling to be sure, and better yet possessing advanced knowledge of a profitable and diverting voyage.

Upon the maindeck, his marvelous crew were busy at a thousand labors operation and maintenance of a starship required. The plebeians among them scrubbed meshing, an eternal task the doing of which was more important than the having done. Others, careful experts and those they instructed, cleaned and coiled cabelles. Aloft, two hundred seasoned hands and topmen drilled, belayed, cast away, adjusted, readjusted, made and unmade, no fresh meat among them, a fact for which both he and they were grateful. For once attention might be paid to the refinement of mature skills and to coaxing a final increment of smooth performance from the ship. He thought them capable of setting an enthillement for this run, had they not lacked the benefit of a destination. Happy in their ignorance of this, they shouted at one another in time-honored manner, a lyric to the melody the vessel played about them.

The *Pelican* was as fine a vessel as he had ever had the pleasure of commanding, although, lacking resources any Navy captain would consider indispensable, experience informed him that her condition would deteriorate with time, with never enough hands nor sufficient hours to see to everything. Preparation for the voyage had been accomplished with unusual, almost military, dispatch, at first owing to his fortuitous notoriety, later to the bargain he had struck with his friend the Jendyne ambassador. Odd fish, that one.

Demondion-Echeverría had proven helpful finding him a crew, always the most difficult arrangement to make before a voyage. Bowmore had found himself required to explain why a shipful of slobbering lobotomites such as infested the embassy would not do as riggers and projecteurs. The man had promised to use whatever power and connection he could boast to assemble a full complement of normals, as near to normal as Deepmen ever got. As good as his word, in due course he delivered 430 with a pink-scrubbed, polished look which told Bowmore they were reassigned from the Jendyne Naval Academy. A pity prudence had compelled him to feed their officers to the §-field as they came onboard, assisted by those he had chosen for himself, crewbeings he could trust because they feared him, recruited from the grimy haunts of Port-of-Hanover. A greater pity he had lacked sufficient time (there was never enough time) to extract whatever secret orders they had been given. The remainder, thirty-odd dozen, lay drugged and stacked below as cargo to the "manufacturers" of Oplytes, which should clear his debt upon the ship.

Underfoot, in a cabin from which he had evicted Mr. Owen, his third officer, his principal cargo was tucked in safe, a sight warmer than she would ever be again, were her voyage to funereal Baffridgestar completed. Thanks to the ambassador and himself, it would never be, although, like the crew, she was as yet unaware of it, nor was she likely to thank them for the detour.

"A drugged girl is a damaged girl," Demondion-Echeverria had insisted. "This, so I am informed, is the attitude of the more refined elements, among which I number, if not my sovereign, Ribauldequin XXIII, then his advisors in the 'Droom of the Jendyne Empery-Cirot."

They sat in the ambassador's spacious, comfortable office. Relieved of his thrustibles at the entrance (he had been minded to cancel the appointment; still, enduring it again was likely to win him a handsome profit), Bowmore had accepted the hot drink offered him. Outside, the sky voided itself of the half-frozen slush-gobbets which seemed unique to the capital world. The drink, as well as the intoxicant of which it largely consisted, was welcome. The ambassador, pleading that he had just broken fast, partook of occasional draughts from an engraved inhaler. Over Demondion-Echeverria's shoulder, behind the enormous desk, Bowmore could see, through curtains slightly parted as if by an over-sight, what appeared to be a large aquarium built into the wall. Idly curious, he wondered what sort of animals the ambassador kept.

The man had already apprised him of Loreanna's steadfast refusal to submit to the marriage her uncle had planned for her. Bowmore, possessing many fewer scruples than "the more refined elements" regarding "damaged girls" or anything else, snorted. "But, Your Excellency, there be such a wealth of 'suasive substances t'choose from, an' all the time in the galaxy to experiment, 'board a vessel in transit." The battered veteran of many a Deep-voyage often lost track of time upon a planet's surface, never seeming to recall the lack he had of it aboard ship. "Once conditioned, who's t'know?"

To be fair, the ambassador gave the suggestion full consideration. "I, for one, my dear Captain. And what I know, for a variety of reasons, political, financial, even artistic, can indeed hurt me."

Wrinkling the disfigurement he called a face, Bowmore looked a question.

"Take the matter of pleasure," came the answer. "It is commonly assumed that the prohibition against compulsion represents a hallmark of civilization, or a simple courtesy which might be reciprocated in some agreeable manner."

Greasy braids bobbing, Bowmore nodded, hoping the man would spit it out.

"Centuries ago, and I assure you I do not digress, another such hallmark was an agreement among nation-states to exclusive use of weapons designed to wound their victims rather than kill. This, too, was hailed as an humane advance." The diplomat paused, arising from his desk, thrust hands into his pockets, and began to pace. Bowmore, sitting silent, drink upon one loose-trousered knee, was unconvinced that this was not a digression. Demondion-Echeverria stopped, turned to face him, and extracted a hand, turning it palm upward. "Nothing could have been further from the truth. A wounded soldier consumes more of an enemy's resources than a dead one. The agreement, which many thought to represent disdain for cruelty, was made without regard to kindness, and may even have increased human suffering."

This Bowmore could understand. The eyelid sewn shut over its empty socket gave the impression of a knowing wink. Otherwise he kept his peace.

"It is often the case," the ambassador continued, "that the facts of a culture point in deceptive directions. The interactions of quintillions of beings are scarcely ever what they appear. We live in an age of power, when a majority (women are not alone in this, nor is the motivation principally sexual) discover themselves unable to refuse whatever is demanded of them. Recognition of their helplessness, the expressions upon their faces as they submit—without recourse to drugs or physical compulsion—furnishes a better part of the pleasure of wielding power. Under the discerning scrutiny of a true connoisseur, it cannot be counterfeited."

At this, Bowmore laughed, rendering his features even more grotesque. "Excellency, y'got me. I'm a simple man. I fear me these cerebral pleasures y'speak of with such ellyquence are outa me depth."

Demondion-Echeverria gave Bowmore a shrewd, disbelieving look. "My dear sir," he replied, "I greatly doubt whether anything I have spoken of is out of your depth. My point with regard to the recalcitrant Mistress Loreanna is simply this: why incur unnecessary risk, when her refusal appears immutable. She is, after all, being sent away in disgrace."

"Oh?" It was the first Bowmore had heard this. He was inclined to take it, to whatever degree it was reliable, as argument in his own favor.

"Indeed. And, just as cold pragmatics may be mistaken for humanity, she does not appear to recognize an impressive generosity upon her uncle's part, and is reported, instead, to resent it."

"Ah, now digress we do. Whether she chooses t'go t'Homeworld or exile, it'll be upon Ballygrant's brigantine she'll be travelin', is it?"

The ambassador smiled. "It will not be difficult to arrange. By coincidence, you will be bound for wherever she ultimately decides to go."

The captain nodded. "Ye'll understand, Excellency, it means I can't plan my cargo. What I'd be takin' t'Homeworld varies from haulage t'some colony."

"Let me reassure you, Captain," annoyance crept into the ambassador's voice—as he strode to his desk, he gave the curtain an impatient tug—"you will be handsomely compensated, whatever the outcome. Lay your schemes accordingly. Take any cargo you desire, or none. It is all the same to me, as long as you succeed with our plan to . . ." Here, the diplomat hesitated, searching for a euphemism which might convey his meaning.

"T'kidnap," he supplied, "the niece of Leupould's right-hand henchman."

Demondion-Echeverria drew himself up. "As a representative of the Jendyne Empery-Cirot, Captain, I am given to more delicate phraseology."

"As a politician, you're given t'circumlocution as recreation. Lemme tell you, a Deep-captain finds direct expression much the safer habit."

The man chuckled. "My dear Captain, your point is well taken. In any case, by another coincidence, a corvette will be following just behind your own vessel, out of instrumental range."

"A Jendyne naval corvette?"

"A *private* corvette, shall we say. You will put up a nominal defense, heave to, and hand our little Hanoverian beauty over."

Bowmore nodded. The bands upon his braids made tinkling music.

"From there," suggested the ambassador, "several options arise. If her uncle and his master accept a *fait accompli*—they intended her for Ribauldequin, after all, not realizing he has no use for her—that is well and good. If not, we shall claim she was killed in the confusion of battle or suicided in the §-field. You run no risk, being able to testify that you had no choice under the projectibles of a privateer."

Thus the voyage had commenced.

Bowmore thought the plan through, realizing that any fairy story fit to tell the Ceo and his Executor-General was fit to tell the ambassador, as well. He had looked his cargo over at close hand, realized the thille he had once carried had failed to do her justice, and no longer planned to return her intact to his sometime employer. Let the rapespawn get his own girl.

Belowdecks, a midday meal being prepared could be smelt even here upon the quarterdeck. In this he betrayed humble beginnings, for it was a good, familiar odor to him, evocative of his youth, and made his mouth water, although a worthier repast awaited him and his guest in the more luxurious circumstances of the commanddeck. Thought of satisfying one appetite led to thoughts of satisfying another. He raised his saw-edged voice. "Mr. Preble!"

"Aye, sir?"

Rings and thrustibles glittering, Bowmore signaled the officer-of-the-watch of his intention to go below, strode to the break of the quarterdeck, and, taking the ladder rails in each hand, swooped down, cloak billowing behind him, without benefit of treads and risers. He had been wrong about not having fresh meat aboard. Nothing like such a prospect to put a spring into one's step! Stooping to enter his cabin—no matter how luxurious the quarters, they never afforded sufficient overhead—he saw the table laid with kefflinen and iridium, heard preparations for his meal in the small galley off the anticlockwise quarter of the room. His feet took him to the right, toward a door to an adjoining compartment which, had they not had a special passenger, would have been occupied by his third officer.

He knocked. "Mistress Daimler-Wilkinson, luncheon wants only minutes of bein' ready." No answer being audible, he knocked again. "Mistress—"

"Thank you," her voice came muffled through the door. "I am not feeling well. If it is all the same, I shall lie down a while and take some later."

Bowmore just missed cracking his head upon a rafter. He placed his hands upon his hips. He would not have his campaign frustrated in this manner. Taking several deep breaths, he came to a decision. "Mistress Daimler-Wilkinson, this'll be Last Call. I shan't take no for an answer."

He had awaited silence this time. In what manner had her gentle upbringing prepared her to reply to so uncivil an utterance? Without pausing to find out, Bowmore raised a booted foot and thrust, the full weight of his stout body behind it. The door crashed against the wall and swung again. Before it could close, Bowmore crossed the threshold, shut it behind him, and took three steps to the center of the cabin. Loreanna sat upon the bed, startled upright, hands raised in gesture of defense. Bowmore's scarred visage cracked with a hideous grin. He strode to the bedside and peered down with one good eye, his jeweled braids swinging above her face.

"We run, sweet cuntling, traceless 'pon the black bosom of the Deep. Well past time you paid your fare."

Terrified and trying not to show it, Loreanna fastened her gaze upon his seamed countenance, his breath rank in her nostrils. "I trust you understand what a fatal error in judgment you have just committed, sir."

Bowmore gave a mighty laugh, seized her by one arm, and, enjoying the gasp which escaped her lips, caught the fabric at her breast and tore it. Another brief effort she was helpless to resist and he had stripped it from her shoulders so that she lay bared to the waist. He tossed her onto the bed and stood back, elbow in one hand, chin in the other.

"Small," he informed her with a judicious tone and appraising expression, "but serviceable. More'n a mouthful's wasted, but there are those'll tell you I've a big mouth. By the Ceo's balls, you upperclass bitches are late bloomers. B'time me mother was fourteen, she'd a pair—"

"Why not go molest her, you animal, as you no doubt already—"

Bowmore raised a broad, ring-heavy hand and swung it, catching her a blow upon the cheek with its hairy back. Wide-eyed with pain and fear, Loreanna opened her mouth to scream, but found the same rough hand there first, shutting off her breathing. He pushed her backward, lowered his bulk onto the bed, half kneeling. Holding her down, he mauled her with exploring fingers. At once he heard a pounding upon the doorframe, along with a harsh, excited voice. Keeping Loreanna's mouth shut, Bowmore whirled. "What in the name of obscenity d'you want? It'd better be good!"

"Sir!" Whoever stood outside neither showed his face nor made to open the door wider. The instant Bowmore had disappeared below, yet had not sat at table, whispered word had gone to every quarter of the *Pelican* that the captain was taking his long-awaited pleasure of the Hanoverian passenger. Perhaps when he was through with her . . .

"Speak up!"

"Compliments of the first officer, sir! Sign in the field of an approaching vessel. Intersection fifteen minutes, and no word of who she be, sir! Old hands say she's of a size to be a privateer, sir!"

Bowmore exhaled, arising with a look in his eye combining aspects of annoyance, frustration, and dire warning for Loreanna. "Compliments t'Mr. Borchert. Tell him General Quarters. Mr. Grafenstein to his projectiles. I'll be 'pon the quarterdeck directly. Pass word t'Blackmon the carpenter t'bring his toolbox here 'pon the double."

"Aye, aye, sir!"

"You, fresh meat, stay put! I'll soon take up where I left off!"

Bowmore passed the tool-laden carpenter, gave instructions for securing Loreanna's door, ordered him to wipe that expression off his face, and went upon deck. Not many minutes later he had determined—by instrument, conferral with his officers, and long experience with the subtle, shifting colors of the §-field—that the vessel reaching upon them was the corvette ordered to travel in the *Pelican*'s wake and overtake her. The corvette's appearance, unexpected by everyone aboard save Bowmore, was days premature. He was certain she was sent to fetch Loreanna early by order of a cynical and, in this case, well-advised Demondion-Echeverria. Bowmore was prepared for the eventuality. Judging by the thrum arising from the gundeck, the brigantine's twenty-one projectiles were being charged and manned as ordered. His crew were taking battle stations, clearing obstructions upon the maindeck as they would be doing below, manning the rigging to make sail according to the standing order of battle and the ship's moment-to-moment necessity.

Bowmore allowed himself a satisfied chuckle. His pursuer was due for a walloping surprise. All of the ominous Deepmanlike bustle below and aloft was the merest window-dressing compared to the disaster he was about to wreak upon her. He reached into his pocket for a small, rounded, oblong box he had carried every moment, waking and sleeping, since they had broken from orbit about Hanover. Having thus assured himself, he removed the hand, lifted it, and called a ship's boy, standing by to act as a runner.

"Me compliments to the officer-of-the-watch." The boy, judging from his look, could be no more than months younger than the girl-child below. For a moment he was reminded . . . but the thought was lost in anticipation, as well as the notion that, once the girl was broken, it might be interesting to combine what pleasures he could have of her with whatever might be had of this boy. "He's to allow that ship to overtake us an' the §-fields t'merge. When they've done, Mr. Glass will send across to her captain that there's a change of plans. That's all, say, 'A last-minute change of plans.' Should he or Mr. Preble desire clarification, I'll be here."

"Aye, aye, sir!"

Bowmore could not resist slipping a hand into his pocket again. Here lay proof, had he required it, that an old dog can be taught anew. He had learned much, losing *Gyrfalcon,* and had found time to think during the dreadful voyage afterward. He had changed his ways regarding discipline among his crew—no longer allowed to fight over food or anything else—and his visibility among them. Presented opportunity to start with a fresh ship, crewbeings who knew him only by his recent—and expensive—reputation, he had studied practices of the Hanoverian Navy. It was obvious, from the order of the vessel and the celerity with which she came to General Quarters, that they worked. Whatever worked was the ticket. To the Ceo with whatever was customary or expected. This new philosophy had led him to the object he fondled. Since the tactic had worked before (that he had ended set adrift was irrelevant), he had caused an atomic to be implanted within the hull of the corvette as she lay in orbit near the *Pelican.* As he had improved the method of delivery, so had he improved the method of ignition. It was a remote detonator which he held in his hand, useless until envelopes of the starships merged.

"Signal officer's compliments, sir—"

Bowmore started. "Er, go ahead, boy."

"A message, Mr. Glass says, from the corvette. Many a

threat, sir, amounting to a demand we heave to for boarding."

Bowmore smiled. "Thank Mr. Glass for me. Ask him to return: 'Sheer off, excretory orifice, or I'll blow you into your constituent quarks.' "

The boy gulped—Bowmore savored his discomfiture—not daring to mention that the vessel closing upon them mounted half again the *Pelican*'s projectibles. A captain was supposed to know these things. "Aye, aye, sir."

"Inform Mr. Anderson he should be prepared t'make his best speed 'pon my command." Anderson was sailing master, in theory under Mr. Borchert, in fact the technical authority regarding finer points of working the vessel. This command suited the boy better. Bowmore made a mental note to keep an eye upon a youngster to whom showing heels seemed better tactics than baring teeth.

"Aye, aye, sir!"

Bowmore extended some age-old captain's clairvoyance for a feel of the vessel. Deckmesh and rigging creaked as *Pelican* gave a show of running for it, at no more than half the speed of which she was capable. He need not see belowdecks to know the tension with which projecteurs sat at their weapons, the nervousness of their helpers. Nor must he look aloft to see the same attitudes displayed by riggers, topmen, even officers distributed about the maindeck. With them, traditional black bag in hand, stood Dr. Luttrell, the ship's chirurgeon, and his assistant, Mr. Graham. More ominously they had with them Blackmon the carpenter. All strained forward to catch the first faint wavefronts of his spoken command.

The captain alone was relaxed. He sauntered to the taffrail, all senses open to a sign the §-fields were about to merge. He climbed the rigging a measure or two and leaned out, feeling the tingle of the field upon his face, informing himself of many things and with greater subtlety of detail than instruments could offer: an unmistakable *edgy* feeling, metallic tartness under his tongue, a slight discoloration, like being inside one soap bubble, surfaced with a swimming rainbow, as it fused with another. He lifted the remote, opened his mouth to command destruction of the corvette while he accomplished it himself, when he was jerked from his feet, almost overside by the rail, but recovered and was only dashed to the deck.

Thrusting! It had not come from the *Pelican* or the corvette. Some third party, some interloping bandit, was attacking his vessel!

PART SIX: HENRY MARTYN
YEARDAY 70, 3011 A.D.
MARRE 44, 510 HANOVERIAN
PRIMUS 8, 1570 OLDSKYAN

"SO LOWER YOUR STARSAIL AND REEF UP YOUR MIZZEN,
AND UNDER MY LEE YOU SHALL KEEP.
OR I SHALL DELIVER A FAST FLOWING THRUST,
  FLOWING THRUST,
  FLOWING THRUST,
AND YOUR DEAR BODIES EXPOSE TO THE DEEP."

WITH BROADSIDE AND BROADSIDE AND BROADSIDE THEY WENT,
FOR FULLY TWO HOURS OR THREE,
TILL HENRY MARTYN GAVE TO THEM THE DEATH THRUST,
  THE DEATH THRUST,
  THE DEATH THRUST,
SHATTERED FROM LIFTDECK TO FORETIER WAS SHE.

CHAPTER XXXVII:
THE PORT-OF-HANOVER COMPLEMENT

Cursing, Bowmore tightened the straps of his thrustibles and looked up. Through interpretation of overlapping §-fields, now merged into a shifting, colorful trifold display, he watched the unknown intruder draw near from the direction both brigantine and corvette were headed. It could not have been her best point of sailing. The speed of her approach, from the hue and saturation of the distortion representing her, was almost leisurely, even added to the considerable velocities of the Hanoverian and Jendyne vessels.

No more, yet, was to be seen. Bowmore's practiced eye was accustomed to extracting maximal information from minimal perception. For a corsair, he determined, she was small, little more than a converted caravel, incapable of bearing greater armament than a dozen, medium-sized, half the strength of his brigantine, less than a quarter that of the Jendyne. Nonetheless, he did not relish, as he might under differing circumstances, what he believed was about to happen. The approaching vessel's initial thrusts demonstrated an eerie accuracy and impossible cycling pace, which spoke to him of endless drill and considerable technical preparation. Moreover, it seemed to concentrate upon his rigging, rather than, as might have been expected, reaching through the starsails to the solid target of the brigantine's hull.

Nothing about this unlooked-for assault was to be expected! Bowmore, as was normal and traditional (rather, Mr. Grafenstein, his second mate and projecteury officer), had assigned his least-skilled projecteurs to his least-important projectiles—and, it was ironic, those most difficult to use well—the three low-powered bow chasers situated in the cabins of the commanddeck. The corsair was still no more than an unresolvable dot against the crawling colors of the

§-field and the infinite blackness of the Deep. Yet the air was filled with smoke and the screaming of riggers as, one by one, they were blasted from their shattered spars. By the Ceo's left testicle, someone out there knew how to put bow chasers to good use!

A section of one such spar, trailing loops of cabelle and shreds of starsail, fell with a crash to the quarterdeck, rupturing the mesh, coming within a measure of burying Bowmore beneath it. His first thought was that it must be cleared away. He turned to shout at the sailing master's mate, only to see the man's head struck off as a cabelle, pulled taut by the falling spar, snapped past him like a razor-edged whip. The headless body, a grotesque fountain of carmine, pitched over onto the deck. Almost the same instant, the mesh leapt under him as the crystal core of an overworked projectible flared and the breech exploded beneath his feet, bulging the deck upward and releasing a cloud of hissing cryogenics. Ceo knew how many crewbeings that had cost! It was one of the bow chasers which, along with inferior hands, had also received least maintenance.

Shorn of all but one of her foretier suite, the battered *Pelican* began to wallow dismally. Bowmore was about to summon Anderson, calculating whether he might get steerageway upon her using the mizzentier stunsails and the single fore-and-aft expanse remaining upon the starboard foreyard, when he glanced aft. The corvette was taking as bad a pounding as the *Pelican*. She, too, was remaking sail, and it was clear from the shape they assumed what she intended. With the tatters the corsair had left her, she was attempting to disengage. Thrust through with white-hot fury, Bowmore forgot Anderson, strode to the rail at the break of the quarterdeck and waved to the runner.

"Fetch me Mr. Glass immediately!"

"Aye, aye, sir!"

The boy, covered with grime and splashes of blood—the latter, to all appearances, someone else's—saluted and ran across the maindeck, avoiding death by the narrowest of margins as a huge coil of cabelle and three entangled bodies crashed to the mesh behind him. He had soiled his trousers, the captain noticed, but still functioned. So much for doubts. In a few seconds he returned with the signal officer, the man's heavy lasercom teetering upon his shoulder like an ancient *bazooka,* peripheral equipment draped everywhere about his person.

"Make signal to the corvette, Mr. Glass."

Some whizzing fragment passed them at eye-blurring velocity, tearing a measure-wide section from the taffrail before volatilizing itself upon the field margin. It could as well have been his legs, thought Bowmore.

"The corsair, sir?"

"Not the corsair! D'ye think I wish t'surrender? I said the corvette. Say, 'I've placed a fission bomb aboard ye under me remote control.'"

Glass was a short, muscular man of swarthy complexion, close-cropped hair and beard, the nose of a man half again his size, and a peculiar accent unheard in civilized regions. He gave the captain a peculiar look.

"Send the message, Mr. Glass. Do it from here."

"Aye, aye, sir." The signal officer raised the lasercom like the weapon it was at short ranges, peered into the sights, and aimed at the corvette, mumbling into the transducer as instructed. Finished, he looked up.

"Well done, Mr. Glass, now tell the craven I'll blow him up if he veers or won't give better account of himself."

"Aye, aye, sir."

Grudging compliance being returned, Bowmore dismissed both the signal officer and the corvette. Looking across the wreckage-littered maindeck, strewn with mangled corpses, yet still crowded with the upright bodies of struggling men and women, he realized, with rare empathy, that it must be even more unbearable belowdecks. Smoke poured from hatch covers and ladderwell as the projectibles upon the gundeck began to heat. Meanwhile, the corsair lumbered ever closer, unstoppable, until it was clear she intended passing between her enemies, thrusting as she came.

Having all but destroyed the *Pelican's* rigging, she concentrated upon the decks and less-protected areas of the hull. Now the accuracy and timing of the corsair's projecteurs could truly be appreciated. Battling vessels revolved about the axes of their masts, their projectiles requiring intervals for recharging and cooling lest they malfunction with disastrous consequences. Rotating in a conventional enough manner (it was the only thing conventional about her), the corsair fenced with the brigantine and her reluctant escort, as if, Bowmore realized, her projectibles were personal thrustibles. Not only did she match thrust for thrust as the brigantine's remaining fourteen came to bear, so that, as with a pair of dueling individuals, opposing beams annihilated one another, she seemed to anticipate the actions of her enemy, their very rhythms, thrusting only after they did, microseconds afterward, employing the resultant explosions as weapons in themselves, Bowmore thought, trying to "walk" them backward toward the brigantine. One such secondhand detonation threw him to the deck again as the *Pelican* yawed beneath his feet, afterward groaning with him as they both recovered.

The brigantine could not keep up. Her projecteurs, even granting Bowmore's new philosophy, lacked the necessary discipline to counter this new technique. In a portion of his mind keeping track of such things, he was aware he had lost another four projectibles. Despite the lesser number of her weapons, the corsair was getting off three thrusts to the brigantine's one, meanwhile battling the corvette, with her Navy crew, which did not seem to fare much better. Explosions mocked him with their salute. The brigantine rocked, pitched, rolled, and yawed about three axes at the same time, shuddering with destructive stresses she was never fashioned to withstand. Smoke concealed the opposing arc of the quarterdeck. Debris lay everywhere, the deckmesh sundered in a thousand places. By now, the greater part of *Pelican*'s spars and rigging were overside, vaporized upon the §-field margin or lying in a hopeless tangle upon the main- and quarterdecks. Half his crewbeings were dead or useless to him.

By gradual increment, the corsair's thrusting diminished. At the moment of the final blow (delivered by stern chasers as well manned and aimed as her other armament) a stunned and battered Bowmore leaned upon a few remaining vertical fragments of the maindeck railing, thankful she had passed from between her reeling victims, and out of range. Even if she renewed the attack, it would take her a long while to reverse course and catch them up. She surprised him again by putting off auxiliaries. Suppressing a whimper of frustration, Bowmore half crawled to what was left him of the taffrail at the *Pelican*'s circumference—even less than the inner rail he had just quit—leaving a faint blood track he did not notice until he glanced backward, seeing for the first time that he had taken a sizable fragment of metalloid and plastic in the heavy meat between his left knee and groin. It glistened where it had fused and he saw a trace of smoke. Had the trajectile struck a femoral artery, perhaps no more than three siemmes away, he would never have seen it at all. He focused his attention aft.

The corsair had hove to, training her stern chasers upon her crippled prey, protecting the flock of lesser predators she released. Large for the auxiliaries of a caravel, and a full dozen in number rather than the usual six (he wondered where her captain stowed the extras), each bore a small projectible which it employed to good effect as, oblivious to the tachyon wind, the miniature fleet steamed toward brigantine and corvette.

A shout arose upon the maindeck. *"All hands! Stand by to repel boarders! Projecteurs to the boat and lift hatches!"* The command was not quite legal, the captain being alive upon deck, and for the most part uninjured. Still, the *Pelican*'s projectibles would be of no further use. Bowmore let it pass. Upon the maindeck, First Officer Borchert, having done with shouting, threaded his way through mountains of entwined wreckage to the break of the quarterdeck. "Captain Bowmore?"

Fingering the control in his pocket, Bowmore was attempting to imagine some way—perhaps some clever lie to draw that accursed corsair closer—in which the bomb secreted aboard the corvette might turn this pitiable situation to his advantage. He looked down at his first officer. Borchert was tall, thin as a stiqueman, possessed of a wiry strength and (it seemed to the more sedentary captain) an unnatural degree of energy. The skin of his cheeks stretched tight over the bones. It was clear he longed to continue fighting to the end. "Yes, Mr. Borchert?"

"They will be here any moment. Permission to distribute small arms, sir?" Bowmore thought it through. One practice he had not seen fit to alter was that the arms locker would open only to his fingerprint. Were something to happen to him, the crew would be defenseless, but that was their lookout. He would not suffer another mutiny. Only his officers had thrustibles, and he was unhappy about that.

"I think not, Mr. Borchert. Me poor, valiant crewbeings've suffered cruelly enough. I believe, instead, I'll see whether we can't buy these rascals off." Bowmore could see the man, displeased with the decision, yet perform the same mental calculation he himself had earlier completed. The idea might work, at that. *Pelican's* holds were filled to the hatches with cargo purchased only for appearance, never meant to reach its purported destination, Baffridgestar. "Ask Mr. Glass to signal the corvette. They are to offer no resistance."

"Aye, aye, sir."

Standing with feet spread, hands behind him, as if nothing were more amiss than earlier this morning, Bowmore looked about him. The sailing master, Anderson, was demonstrating all the efficiency which the captain had come, in so brief a time, to rely upon. Sufficient headway was maintained by use of mast, spars, and rigging, along with the few remnants of starsail left to the *Pelican,* that she still might boast of something resembling gravity upon her riven decks. Bowmore hated to think of the broken, tangled mess floating free. Only minutes before, it had borne his brand-new brigantine through the Deep upon rainbow-colored wings. He received a report from Mr. Preble, officer-of-the-watch. The corsair's auxiliaries had left parties at the lubberlift and taken up station—this much he saw for himself—outboard the mizzentier, projectibles trained upon maindeck and quarterdeck. Not far off, the corvette was being afforded similar treatment. She had drifted close enough that he watched as a pile of debris upon her maindeck erupted, whether in warning or for some real or imagined transgression he could not discern, at a thrust from one of the gunboats standing watch.

"Upon your lives throw down your weapons, each and every one!" cried an amplified voice from one of the nearby lesser vessels. *"Stand where you are!"*

Still at parade-rest, Bowmore could hear an increasing racket below as brigands from the corsair climbed forward within the *Pelican's* hull, driving projecteurs, helpers, and all others belowdecks before them. Soon the entire complement was gathered upon the maindeck under the watchful eye of the auxiliaries, and the boarders made their appearance. Bowmore was shocked, counting scarce more than half a dozen, each attired in a vacuum suit and equipped with a plain, utilitarian pair of thrustibles. Ignoring the captain (except to relieve him, with rough efficiency, of his weapons), three of them climbed to the quarterdeck, spacing themselves about the elevated structure, the better to guard their captives.

One of a remaining three—they had brought a prisoner, as well, not wearing a suit—was a giant who strode forward with a smaller companion and something alien which moved, yet looked like a cemetery headstone swathed in kefflar. Flanked by the others, the giant addressed Bowmore.

"Y'realize, don't y'Captain, if you'd but issued weapons t'your crew, y'might've stood a chance. We're that shorthanded, having captured ten prizes—no, this makes a round dozen, doesn't it?—this past month."

His human companion nodded, and of a sudden raised, not one of the pair of thrustibles he affected, but a blue-black metallic object, made a squeezing motion which did not involve his thumb, and squeezed again. With each squeeze, the object unleashed an ear-damaging blast, while pale fire blossomed from its end. Whatever the weapon was, it sufficed, for a hideous dual scream aloft was followed by an even more terrible crash upon the deck at Bowmore's feet. Two of his riggers had worked their way out upon the dorsal mizzenyard, purposing to leap onto the quarterdeck, only to be seen—and thrust in some way—by the smaller of the man-shaped raiders. The larger reached up with a huge hand, seized the crest of his flexible helmet, pulled it off his face, and left it dangling upon his chest.

"*You!*" Bowmore discovered to his utter amazement that he was looking up into the broad, ironic countenance of his former first officer, Phoebus Krumm. Bowmore did not speak further, for he was staring at another sight beyond the giant. As well as it had been hidden, integrated with the structure of the corvette's mast while she was undergoing minor repairs about Hanover, his bomb had been found. It dangled from the hand of Krumm's helmeted companion.

The prisoner they had with them, a dark, sullen young man in the uniform of a Jendyne naval lieutenant, Bowmore guessed was the captain of the corvette. Several epaulinettes which had held the thrustible along his forearm had been torn away in the act of confiscating his badge of rank and personal weapon. Bowmore was about to offer him commiseration, until—

"You ill-begotten mutant spawn of a gavaged she-cur!" The lieutenant launched himself across the deck in a murderous attack upon Bowmore's person. He raised his hands to fend off the defeated officer, not before he felt the man's fingers closing about his windpipe, nails sinking into the unprotected flesh of his throat. He was only dimly aware of the shouting and pushing which started up round him. Gasping, he felt cartilage begin to give with a noise that was sickening in itself, and sank to his knees, violet sparks beginning to dance before his eye, his field of vision growing blacker by the second. Desperate, he struggled like an animal, prying at the lieutenant's hold, but the younger man had lapsed into berserk oblivion, and Bowmore's strength was ebbing. Of a sudden, he felt the hands relax, the lieutenant torn away from him. He collapsed, retching, aware that Krumm had pulled his attacker off and flung him halfway across the quarterdeck to the taffrail.

"I warned you." It was a new voice, level and quiet. Bowmore looked up as Krumm's companion raised a forearm and let go with his thrustible. The lieutenant's anger-ravaged face puckered. His skull burst, spilling blood and brains across the deck. Designator still lit, the thrustible swung round to Bowmore, lingered over his scarred face, and dropped away.

Krumm chuckled. "'Twon't be that easy, Captain. Others ache t'have it elsewhere, but the fact is y'lead a charmed life. Instead of comin' to the prolonged, painful end y'well deserve, you're merely t'be set adrift again."

Still kneeling, Bowmore trembled, his metal-ended braids standing away from his head as he contemplated the horrors of his first such voyage and the humiliation which would be the certain consequence of a second. "Kill me!"

Krumm grinned. "I shall not." He turned, winked at his companions, and grinned at Bowmore. "This time, you'll be spared t'carry a message from my master to the rulers of the Monopolity, whom he has lately sworn to inconvenience. A formal declaration of defiance, or, if y'prefer, of war."

"But what of me brigantine?"

"His brigantine, now. We shall see to her jury-rigging directly, and send her where she'll be refitted and added to his fleet."

"You would place a prize crew aboard my starship?"

"His starship, Captain. I doubt me whether he'll place a crew aboard her when one is already here." Krumm turned and shouted to the maindeck. "Mr. Borchert, Mr. Grafenstein, Mr. Owen, Mr. Blackmon! The pleasure of your company's awaited 'pon the quarterdeck. Resume your weapons. Mr. Glass, if it'll please you, signal the boats so they're not thrust for it."

A grinning third officer was first to reach the quarterdeck, stopping to give the gravestone-shape a good-natured thump upon its keffler-covered top. It responded by attempting to trip him with its undercurving tail, causing him to roar with laughter. Mr. Owen was a curly-bearded individual of girth and substance, a sort of miniature of the fantastic Mr. Krumm. Every opponent who had ever dismissed him lightly had come to a surprised and unpleasant end. He was followed by the first officer, the signals officer, the short, stocky projecteury officer, and, to Bowmore's confusion, the carpenter's mate.

The giant addressed them. "Mr. Blackmon commanding, ye five'll select those y'trust among the brigantine crew. Rig her as best y'can and take her you-know-where. Arrange a crew for the corvette. I'd suggest Anderson t'command, with Preble, Luttrell, Graham, and Stafford. Crewbeings from this ship alone, as I mistrust those Navies." He turned to Bowmore. "Let those who brought her to us take her to her real destination."

"Hello the quarterdeck, look what I've found!" This from a gray-haired man of great height emerging from one of the cabins about the maindeck. By one arm he held an angry and struggling young woman attired in a grimy outfit of Deepman's coveralls several sizes too large for her tiny frame.

While the officers rearmed themselves, the attentions of

the giant and his companions remained upon Bowmore. Without looking down at the maindeck, Krumm shouted over his shoulder. "Bring your find here for all of us to appreciate, if ye will, Mr. Stafford."

Stafford responded with cheerful compliance. It was only when he and the young female had climbed to the quarter-deck that Krumm and his companions turned. Behind the reflective face masque of his helmet, the smaller of the two human figures gasped. The alien stiffened as well. His gloved hand went to something tucked into the front of his vacuum suit. He appeared, insofar as could be seen, to be staring at the girl. "You!"

Stafford released her. She blinked and looked round at the shocking damage wrought by Krumm and his men. Several of these, armed like Oplytes, guarded the *Pelican*'s survivors. Not a spar or splinter of the brigantine remained untouched. The bleeding, broken bodies of the fallen lay everywhere. Paling, she nevertheless took a breath and stepped forward.

"Good day, sir." Clutching her borrowed clothing to her, she addressed herself to Krumm, sparing an accusing glare for Bowmore. "I believe I have you to thank for my freedom, and perhaps my life." With a cautious eye upon the alien which accompanied the brigands, she thrust out a hand which, she was proud to observe, only trembled a bit. "Your, er, officer has told me you are to be addressed as Mr. Krumm. Kindly permit me to introduce myself. I am Loreanna Daimler-Wilkinson. My uncle, Sedgeley Daimler-Wilkinson, is Drector-Advisory and Executor-General to Ceo Leupould IX of Hanover. Unless I am very much mistaken, he—my uncle—will be most generous when I am returned."

With an odd expression, Krumm lifted his own hand to the level of his waist and pointed a thumb toward the smaller human, who stepped forward.

"I regret," the figure in the vacuum suit told her, "that I must disabuse you of a false impression, Mistress Daimler-Wilkinson. You are by no means free to return to Hanover now, nor in the foreseeable future." As Krumm had, he reached to his helmet crest, pulled it from his head, ran a hand over the heat-reddened, sweaty face of a boy in middle teens with eyes which had looked into some unspeakable depth, and shook his hair out, the while continuing to address Loreanna. "You have simply changed hands. You are now the property of—" He dropped the hand and pointed a finger at his chest. Only Krumm knew that, between suit and skin, hung an engraved autothille upon a jeweled chain, which the duplicitous Bowmore had given him before betraying him to the nonexistent mercy of the Deep. "The infamous star-raider, Henry Martyn."

He turned to Krumm. "Pressed men or women who will not sign my articles will be set free in *Nosaer* to make shift for themselves. Put volunteers or officers you cannot trust through the §-field."

CHAPTER XXXVIII:
TEN MONTHS EARLIER

"Pray tell, my dear Forbeth-Wethinghouth, which ith it to be with the gell, gavage or gavelleth?" A titter arose from the unseen audience.

Lightyears, and an altogether different way of life, further away, Arran Islay, soon to be fifteen (and still, upon occasion, surprised to be anything at all), shook his head, emptied of any emotion he might have named. Soul of wit, spirit of his times, unanswerable social arbiter or not, the fictional and famous Piotr Megrim-Boutade—or at least the celebrated parlor-pieces which had been enthilled about him—certainly got about.

Well, thought Arran—he gazed with unseeing eyes through the open door into the next compartment, where a swath of clean red and ivory-white lay draped over a towel rack just above the steaming surface of a hot bath (the one such luxury aboard)—*for that matter, so have I.*

He now knew all about a practice capital-world denizens called "gavage." It referred to the manner in which fowl were force-fed (their feet having been cyanoed to the floors of their pens) so that their swollen, diseased livers might be compounded into an expensive delicacy. More generally, it signified variation after variation upon the act of rape, sexual and otherwise, which all humanity claimed to deplore, yet which, upon evidence, it could not do without, since it represented the very foundation upon which civilization, or more to the point, those in authority over it, depended.

Arran wished he could feel something about that. In the place he looked for his feelings, he found nothing but cold reason. When he had first discovered this condition, he had believed he was being drugged. Yet he had never heard of a medicine which could strip away emotion, leaving a crystal-clear and unbefuddled mind. He doubted it had anything to do with chemicals.

The garishly furnished drawing chamber caught his eye again, but failed to hold his interest. Behind his silver kennedy, the juvenile lead grimaced at a question Arran had once found incomprehensible, as, synthechord playing in the background, the aristocrat in the machiavelli twisted his inhaler delicately and thrust it up his nostril. Arran's scorn was all it had ever been. If Megrim-Boutade could not have lasted an hour in the forest of Skye, he would not have lasted a minute upon the *Gyrfalcon's* gundeck. Something had changed, however, since he had first watched this thille, above all, his grasp of the realities behind the make-believe. The gold-chased thrustible tucked into a ruffled sleeve was a token that Megrim-Boutade, representative of his nonproductive class, would never be required to pass any such test of forest or gundeck. The system was designed to preclude it. Upon Hanover they were always fussing in cultured lisps and egg-shaped tones over trivia, but they ruled a universe entire. Arran had long since abandoned any notion that they were wanques in any meaning of the word.

"... *nay, nor even clavitheth, for I have it upon good authority your enamorata ploth her own courth, toward thome Jendyne gentle of a germane gender.*" The audience erupted with laughter. Arran, sadder and wiser than when he had first heard these words, extracted the thille from the viewer upon his blanket-covered lap and tossed it at a shelf across the cabin. Despite all that had befallen him, he was no more given to purposeless distemper than ever. His was a fury under such control that even he was not aware, as yet, of its extent. Any anger smoldering within him would henceforward make itself manifest in a more lethal and spectacular manner than self-indulgent display.

At his knee lay a less elegant, yet no less deadly, weapon than Megrim-Boutade's. Arran had just removed it; its mark was upon his flesh. Circuits switched so that only the designator functioned, at Krumm's insistence he had practiced daily since regaining consciousness, aiming at a bulkhead for hours until he could no longer control his trembling, overtaxed muscles. Misguided by fingers shaking with fatigue (or rendered clumsy by new tensions to which his kinaesthetics were not yet accustomed), the thille struck the wallow-proof shelf-edge, rebounded from a locker where his clothing was stowed, and fell to the deck. He made no move to correct his error. As he had discovered, should Krumm or either of his plump wives catch him out of bunk, there would be the Ceo to pay. That latter pair of self-appointed nurses had proven every bit as conscientious at what they considered their duty as Old Henry or Mistress Lia—"adopting" him through his prolonged recovery—and would have moved him into their quarters had their husband not put his massive foot down. It had helped that an alternative was available.

For the first time in a long while, Arran found himself thinking, for no accountable reason, of Waenzi, missing his demented squeak, wondering, to no useful purpose, what had become of the coarse-furred triskel. It occurred to him he should feel angry over all he had lost, but it seemed even this capacity had been stolen from him. At home among the everblues, retainers would be harvesting groundberries in the meadow. Birds would be singing . . . He reached for another, more entrancing, thille, one he kept upon a chain about his neck, having learned, with some relief, that Bowmore had no daughter he would own to. Arran had no idea who the little dancing girl was—

A pair of raps within his quarters awakened him from reminiscent study. Through the many-paned commanddeck windows, a ghostly §-field flickered, backdrop for mizzentier yards devoid of starsail. The *Gyrfalcon* lay hove to, somewhere in the trackless Deep. The door opened inward, followed by Krumm, bearing a tray of doughnuts and a tankard the sight of which—rather the shudder with which Arran reacted to the sight—evoked less pleasant memories of Skye. Beside it lay another object the boy recognized. Noticing Arran's expression, the some-time baker set tray and tankard upon a table with raised edges similar to the shelving, gave the boy a broad grin and a wink.

"Feeling a touch better, are we?"

"Mr. Krumm," Arran sighed, "I have always wondered why, whenever an individual falls ill, without apparent cause he becomes plural in number."

"Often wondered the same," Krumm laughed, nodding at the dreaded flagon. "Gulp it quick as y'can, vile though it be. I share the opinion indicated by your expression, but y'must admit it's makin' ye well. Though less rapidly than I expect ye'd hoped for." Waggling bushy eyebrows, Krumm lifted the container. Arran made a face and gave in. Krumm had that effect upon him. "Take it like a topman! Concussion, decompression, traumatic acrophobia, hypoxia, an' Deepchill all be serious matters, even one by one, as I, who've suffered 'em all, should know. An' serious matters—"

"Must be seriously treated. Somehow I have heard this before."

The man shook his head. "Ye'd be scarce rememberin' all the talkin' we done while y'wallowed unconsciouslike, wracked with fever an' drug-delirium, the goodwives thinking you were gonna jump ship." He set the flagon back upon the table, making no move toward the other object upon the tray. He grinned and stepped backward. "Valorously done. The crew an' all the carg—er, passengers are demandin' t'come pay respects to the lad as saved their hides. Before I allow it, we've some discussin' to accomplish." The giant offered Arran a hand. "So outa that bunk. Take caution not t'cause yourself undue strain. We'll talk, an' afterward see to such exercise as y'require." He indicated the steaming tub with the colors bright above it. Arran understood it was warmed by induction from the mast and, having risen from the gundeck (and set his old life aside as belonging to another universe), was scandalized at the sybaritic waste.

"P'rhaps ye can even enjoy a soak in the captain's accommodation, him havin' no further need of it."

The boy felt faint enthusiasm, not so much at the prospect
of a bath, as the end of enforced inactivity. He threw back the
blanket and swung his legs over the edge of the bunk for the
first time in what he had been told was weeks. By the calendar
upon the bulkhead, it was Yearday 143, 3010 by the ancient
reckoning, a year and a day since he had first come aboard
Gyrfalcon. It was also the forty-third day of Octto, fourth
month of the 510th ponderous 708-day year since the founding of Hanover. After the Oldskyan manner, with its brief but
familiar 230-day year, it was Octavus 11, 1568. Whatever day
it happened to be, in whatever year, he was indeed better
than when he had surprised himself by awakening in this
cabin. When he placed his shoeless feet upon the mesh,
he discovered that dizziness and infirmity still afflicted
him.

Krumm straightened and cleared his great throat, all but a
trace of his lower-class accent gone. "Ignoramus that I am, I
am not altogether certain how this is done," he told the boy,
"although I have seen reference from time to time in thilles
and books from the ancient past . . ."

Arran supposed he was about to apologize for whatever
part he had taken in what Bowmore had done. That, or
something, would be mentioned again about the corsair.
Arran found he took small delight in that vessel's destruction,
and even less in that of the lives of those aboard her. But he
was already aware of an amount of gratitude toward him
upon the part of the crew.

"Ignoramus? Sir, you—"

"I've trouble enough beginning this," Krumm shook his
shaggy head. 'It would please me just as well if you didn't call
me 'sir,' Arran Islay, ever again.' He paused, at a loss for
words. Curious, and a bit hurt, Arran nodded, knees weak
with the unaccustomed effort of standing. He watched as
Krumm tapped a hardened finger upon the object in the
tray, with its ancient embossery. The man picked it up. It lay
in his palm like a toy. With a giant thumb, he pressed the
button which released the ammunition cassette, filled with
just short of a dozen diminutive chemenergic cylinders.

It was, of course, Arran's walther-weapon which Krumm had brought him, gleaming blue-black, freshly cleaned, and—frail reed though it was—still workable. Overcoming his apparent (and to Arran, bewildering) embarrassment, Krumm resumed. "Today marks a start, I think me, of what'll prove the most dangerous time of your young life. The crew, grateful for their lives, and disgusted by your treatment at the hands of Bowmore, have, in absence of the rewards you were promised, chosen to give you the carrack *Gyrfalcon*. You are to be owner-in-command and their new captain."

Arran's reaction was a smile in remote appreciation of a fantastic joke. Krumm allowed him no time to enjoy it, demanding that he take the offer seriously. He had an ally. The red and white object draped over the towel rack, having spent the morning enjoying a temperature and humidity closer to that of its native planet than it and its fellows had previously endured aboard the *Gyrfalcon*, curled against the wall until it was half erect, and emitted a piercing whistle. Arran winced.

Krumm nodded. "It understands me better than I understands it. I think it says you should listen."

Sighing with resignation and fatigue, Arran sat again upon the bunk-edge. Over previous conversations, Krumm had explained that—as disgusted as the crewbeings which he, in truth, had always commanded, and convinced Arran had died in an effort to save their lives—he had led the mutiny. Two passengers, Bowmore, and officers loyal to him had been set adrift in an auxiliary, more humane treatment than he had afforded Arran. This had satisfied the crew. In the boundless Deep, between star systems, it had amounted to a death sentence. Krumm had been relieved he need not kill his former captain outright.

At this point, an even more incredible thing had happened which neither Arran nor Krumm was satisfied he understood even yet. During the mutiny, the latter had noticed that the "carg—er, passengers" were restive, attributing it to the disturbance of battle. Uproar among the flatsies had continued long afterward. He managed to learn that they not only knew who Arran had been, but what had become of him. Insisting, to the limit of their communicative ability, that nothing supernatural lay in their insistence (but unable to explain it in terms which made sense), they had maintained that the boy was alive. Upon their account, while Bowmore and his party were being cast off, a search was made aft of the carrack. Stunned by the explosion, with his oxygen supply all but exhausted, he was plucked from the Deep at the last moment, hauled back aboard *Gyrfalcon* by mutinous—and grateful—crewbeings.

Arran spoke. "I see why you insisted I take these quarters. Thank you, Krumm, and I wish you would thank the crew for me. It is the most patently absurd idea I have ever heard. No one onboard is *not* better qualified than I, which, for the safety of all, is reason enough to reject this sentimental offer. Moreover, I have learned the hard way what a captain is."

Krumm had found a chair. Meanwhile, the flatsy had crawled from its rack to join the humans, halting in the middle of the floor to raise its front half, to all appearances as interested in the boy's answer as the first officer. Krumm had the notion, with nothing for supporting evidence, that this one had been delegated by its brothers to keep the boy company every moment since he had come back aboard. "And what might that be?"

Arran was careful. "One of those power wielders who place higher value upon property and profit than people. Not only is a love of money the root of all evil, as the proverb has it, but of all which has befallen me, this poor being, and all my pitiable fellows among the crew." He took a breath. "Since joining the complement, I have watched myself change in ways I neither admire nor understand. I killed three men—it does no harm to admit it—and later something more than three hundred. It appears a terrible trend has been established which I do not wish to follow further. I would not become one such as Bowmore. Although it sounds ridiculous to be required to say it, I will not be captain, of the *Gyrfalcon* or anything else."

Krumm nodded and frowned. Even the flatsy seemed lost in thought. "Were you aware, lad, that the *Gyrfalcon* was considered a lenient berth?"

Arran shook his head. "No, if I could feel anything, I suppose I should be surprised to hear it. So much the worse for sailors aboard less lenient vessels. So much the better for the argument I have just made."

"What of the argument that you cannot blame the flour for the sifter?"

"What do you mean?"

"Just that *Gyrfalcon* was captained by such as those who want a captain look for. A candidate lacking the failings you mentioned, if they are indeed failings and not virtues seen under a wrong-colored sun, would never pass the Monopolitan commission which licenses masters."

Arran's scowl matched Krumm's, wrinkle for wrinkle, yet it was a scowl of effort, conveying no more feeling than the wrinkles in his blanket. "You are saying none of the criminal inhumanities aboard this ship would be possible, were it not that the captain was licensed to commit them?"

Krumm nodded, watching the boy's face. The guardian flatsy shuffled closer, as if aware of Arran's emotional paralysis and concerned. "Son, if I were sailin' by your bearings, I'd be as lost. How came you by a notion that people and property are separate? Those things you value most about people, their lives and liberties, are property—" The boy opened his mouth; Krumm held up a hand. "The property they consider most precious." He stopped to take a breath. Arran looked more puzzled than before. "This ship," Krumm continued, "her cargo—excepting our friend, here—some hard-working soul spent *himself* to make or gain, risking it in hope of bettering himself upon the treacherous bosom of the Deep. A captain carries life itself within his holds, along with the dreams of a thousand lifetimes. Life *is* property, property is life, both indistinguishable from liberty. The root of all evil—aside from forgetting that fact—lies in taking property (such as the liberty of this here flatsy) against its rightful owner's wishes."

Prolonged silence followed for the three of them. When the boy spoke again, his voice was quiet, as if he were still in thought. "Mr. Krumm, when I came aboard, I was upon my way to Hanover to get help for my family."

The man nodded. "So I had gathered."

"I had time for thought as the ship's lowliest crewbeing. More since. Leupould himself approved the black deeds of Morven. The family Islay have no friends upon the capital planet. It was pointless to make my way there."

"My guess'd be you're correct."

Arran gazed out the window overlooking the maindeck, not seeing anything in particular. All he had suffered had been to no good purpose, although he was wise enough to understand that he had only traded one set of hardships for another he might have suffered as a woodsrunner upon occupied Skye. "For a thousand years, two powerful imperia-conglomerate have been locked in mortal conflict. This is what my tutor and sister-in-law taught me, Mr. Krumm. Comprised of millions of star systems, quintillions of subjects, spanning vast areas of the known galaxy, their resources are enormous—everything they can extort from those they rule—but by no means unlimited."

Krumm gave him an odd look. "Might I ask what you're driving at?" He found he must restrain himself from adding, "sir," whether due to the boy's educated accent or something happening this instant, he could not determine. Arran looked Krumm back in the eye, inhaled, exhaled, and set his mouth.

"Not until I finish reasoning it out, if you please." Now Krumm knew. Arran failed to notice the delighted twinkle in the older man's eyes, and the way the flatsy folded itself upon the carpet, well satisfied.

"In our age, as in some previous, every circumstance exists for brigandry to spring into existence. The frontier is unimaginable in extent, little explored. But the basic fact of the thirty-first century is that §-physics has yet to develop the equivalent of lasercom or radio. Communication between systems is no faster than transportation." Krumm nodded, not wishing to interrupt.

"Given the martial and economic situation in which they find themselves, the imperia-conglomerate extend their prowess at minimal cost by issuing letters of marque, adding to a brigand's already rich opportunity. This suits my purpose, as I assume it suits a man who believes no complement would follow a baker, but might a young hero guided by an older, wiser officer?"

Krumm inhaled, exhaled, and nodded. "That was the idea, lad."

Arran laughed, not a pleasant sound. His body trembled with unreleased tension. "Mr. Krumm, I understand the arrangement and approve. Because I trust you, I who should have had all trust burned out of him, I agree to it. I accept the commission you offer me."

Krumm clapped the boy upon the back. "Good lad—" He held his hand up and examined it as if it were something foreign. "I mean, sir."

Arran was inclined to grin, but sobered as thought reestablished itself. "You have swayed me in more than this, for, although we shall live as brigands, it will be to a purpose. I shall not make war, as I believed I might, in the name of persons against property, but against those who live by stealing property—life and liberty—from its rightful owners."

Krumm nodded. "I shall be proud to serve you, Captain Islay."

"I shall take a new name, Mr. Krumm, under which, although I did not know why at the time, I signed onboard the *Gyrfalcon*. That of my first friend, murdered by Morven as he took my native Skye, one who shared with me his love of ancient lore, and died attempting to preserve my life."

"Sir?"

"In his name shall I wreak vengeance until the whispered words 'Henry Martyn' strike terror into the hearts of thieves and hypocrites who benefit from the imperia-conglomerate! *Gyrfalcon* being no fighting ship, Henry Martyn shall take the corsair. Placing a few he distrusts least aboard *Gyrfalcon*, he shall repair the corsair where she lies, rename her *Osprey*, and appoint you second-in-command." He turned and looked at Krumm. "What others call banditry, he shall call vendetta! Taking suitable ships, he will arm them as he can, expanding his fleet rather than selling them. His crewbeings will be satisfied, for what they lose in prize money, they shall make up in plunder."

"Yes, sir!"

"Henry Martyn will raid planetside, razing every article of Monopolitan property! Every field, mine, and factory owned by the vile murchantilists will be reduced to the sort of rubble left by Oplytes! He will search the ashes and execute every last Hanoverian vassal and retainer!"

The boy leapt to his feet. "We sail in search of fortune—
and revenge!"

CHAPTER XXXIX:
SISAO AND SOMON

"'Vast hauling, bemmy! Wanna snap me a spar?"

Krumm shouted from the quarterdeck, fingers entwined at the base of his spine, legs braced against the erratic surge as, with a minimum of starsail, the corsair backed and filled through the perilous, gas-clotted Deep.

It was the third hour of "graveyards," a period of reduced activity when the least numerous and competent of three watches was upon deck. Yet the hour could not be told, as upon the surface of a planet, from the appearance of the sky through the skeletal pyramid of spars and cabelles overhead. Through the pulsing §-field, the sky itself offered a unique display of color and apparent depth, for, over the past days, he and his captain had insinuated their small fleet lightyears into the heart of a forbidding nebula.

Etumalam. Their destination, only a ship's "day" away now, Sisao and Somon, circled one another in the gas cloud some distance from a giant star of harsh yellow-white in which philosophers of science might have found interest, had pursuit of knowledge been fashionable within the imperia-conglomerate comprising human civilization. Its like was not to be found upon any "main sequence." It would be reasonable to assume it was a young star, destined for a spectacular demise. Yet the planets within its influence were old. To the extent any curiosity was ever manifest among the misfits who inhabited them (starsailing officers, doomed to spend their lives avoyaging, often developed esoteric interests; what few naturalists flourished these days were mostly found aboard starships, even those of freebooters fully as subject to physical law and the tedium of long passages as any legitimate vessel), it could be demonstrated, with support of fossils and the like, that the sun which warmed them was no more given to instability than any other.

Etumalam. No one might have seen it in the first officer's imperturbable appearance, but his mind was a battlefield of conflicting feelings, not alone because this was the system where he had once been sold as a slave.

Etumalam. Like their extraordinary sun, the planets themselves were anomolous. Nothing about the otherwise remarkable star they circled (insofar as could be determined) might have led an erudite observer to expect a pair of near-identical worlds, eleven thousand klommes in diameter, pivoting about an imaginary point upon a mutual orbit round it. Even the natural expectation that they might long ago have compromised gravitic differences, settling into revolutions which, owing to geophysical imperfections, caused them to display the same face to one another (as with better-known examples), proved incorrect. Each spun upon its own tilted axis. The pair, as such, spun upon another. This, in turn, followed Keplerian tracks about the inexplicable primary, rendering determination of time, date, or season—without recourse to complex charts or custom timepieces—quite impossible.

Of the surfaces of these worlds, what might have been rendered succinctly which would be accurate and valuable? The most negligible planet is a complicated phenomenon, in particular if, as these did, it harbors life. Having given birth to its own evolutionary sequence, Sisao and Somon each possessed the usual proportions of land, water, desert, and forest; temperate, arctic, and tropical zones with a trifle more water than the average Hanoverian planet; less desert than forest; a touch more of the tropical than the arctic, offset by mountainous equatorial altitudes attributable to the astrophysics of mutually orbiting planets.

What stood out about Sisao and Somon depended more upon their location outside the explored Deep and the borders of established polities, the nature of their inhabitants (chiefly a certain relaxation concerning finc points of the law), and the manner in which the interests of imperia-conglomerate had led them to an attitude resembling tolerance toward the system. A cometary "halo" of unusual density—filled with billions of spinning, sharp-toothed planetary fragments—and the fact the system as a whole was passing through the gaseous remains of an ancient supernova completed its natural defenses. No fleet admiral would risk speeds necessary to spring warningless upon it against a certainty of dashing his vessels to pieces.

Even in this wild outlaw port, where theorists might predict nothing but chaotic violence (and—in that most abysmal variety of ignorance, that of the educated—call the condition anarchy), spontaneous order and organization were to be discovered. *Etumalam* possessed its own complexity of rules, powers, and immunities. Such was not for the likes of Henry Martyn. Krumm remembered the first time they had visited here after the boy assumed command.

"Privateer Council be thrust!" This he had snapped in angry reaction to an invitation to join a guild of freebooters. Its issuers, captains all, had conceived it an honor, for already Henry Martyn had achieved a species of celebrity.

"This arrangement smells of another imperium-conglomerate in the making! I shall have none of it. And it had better stay out of my way!" Shaking their heads (in most cases gray-thrust or snowy), the captains had departed, mumbling and astonished to have their invitation rejected by this boy-child.

To serve the *Osprey's* master as his headquarters upon Sisao—many people must be seen in selling off her plunder and attending her resupply—he had leased an inn at the heart of the small city, two streets from the block (although he had not known it until he and his first officer had gone sightseeing) upon which Krumm had once been auctioned for less than he now received in shares from the capture of a lifeboat.

"A clavis for your thoughts, Phoebus."

Krumm came close to jumping. "Ceo take you, Mathilde, you're the only one I know can sneak upon me like that!" Tillie's laugh was soft. As he turned to face her, he heard the echoing chuckle of his other wife, Tula. "What mischief are you two after committin' 'pon me peaceful quarterdeck?"

Tula gave him a mock frown. "Are we forbidden it? We thought we'd take the air of the late watch, Mr. First Officer Krumm, sir. Not so many feet to get under with the captain away, most officers off duty, and our own dear husband pacing the mesh with time heavy upon his hands."

"You aloft!" he shouted as if arguing with his wife. "What're ye rollerballers about up there? Belay that skylarkin' an' see t'those reefs, or by the Ceo's shrunken dingus there'll be no liberty in *Etumalam!*"

Etumalam. The alien in the mizzenyards waved cheerful compliance to the unnecessary order, carrying on with its duties as before, leaving Krumm to steep in the humiliation attendant upon his own display of temper.

Etumalam. Krumm's wives were accustomed to his moods, as well as the reasons for them, and would not be put off by any such demonstration. "In any case," Tillie insisted, "we wanted to speak with you before we arrived."

Tula nodded agreement. "We wanted to ask you something, Phoebus."

He frowned. In his eyes, love for his wives, concern for their concerns, belied the expression. It was a rare moment, the watch consisting in the main of non-humans, the captain supervising repairs aboard the Jendyne two-decker, and Krumm, accustomed to keeping within himself, for once inclined to talk of things troubling him. "It couldn't wait," he asked, "'til the watch-end?"

Tillie shook her head. "It's been waiting, Phoebus darling, at the end of every watch, while we accumulated courage enough to broach it. Before many more watches have passed, we'll have reached *Nosaer,* and it will be too late."

Nosaer (pronounced "Noss-air," yet which sailors, typically perverse, insisted upon calling "Nose-hair") was an ice asteroid within the halo of Sisao-Somon. Given its size—it was possible to leap, in a vacuum suit, from the quarterdeck direct onto its frozen surface—it was unnecessary to take orbit or lower the lubberlift, for the direction "down" did not exist.

As the twin planets had provided sanctuary to *Gyrfalcon's* mutineers, so here the brigantine and the corvette were led by Henry Martyn's *Osprey.* The corsair would first heave to

—Pelican and *Peregrine* being sent ahead to join others of his fleet—with the purpose of putting off any from the captured ships who, even after persuasion, would not enlist. Also, she would take on water—at a place it was cheap and, owing to lack of gravity, easiest to get aboard—without which the innovative use of her boats became profligately impossible. By long-standing arrangement, those debarking would be picked up by a vessel whose captain was paid to stray off course and keep his mouth shut. In Henry Martyn's view they were upon their own thereafter. He did not consider that he was operating a charity. From the murchan starship, they would, by various means, return home to spread the fame, whether he would have it or not, of their erstwhile benefactor.

Krumm frowned down at the small, plump woman. "And?"

"Not 'and,' dear Phoebus," she replied, "but 'so.'"

"So what does he intend," Tula blurted, "with that girl-child he captured aboard the brigantine, the poor thing?"

Krumm nodded. "I wondered when you two would get round t'that."

"I keep asking Tula, what *can* he do? He's just a little boy, himself."

"That 'little boy,'" Krumm snorted, "ordered a hundred to their deaths just t'begin this run. I won't say they didn't deserve it, but I was that glad I persuaded 'em t'sign his articles an' mean it."

The women made clucking noises appropriate to their personalities and the circumstances. "Will he be angry you didn't carry out his order?"

"He knows all about it. Those were his orders: feed anyone to the field as won't sign up." Krumm pounded a fist into his palm. "That 'little boy' happens t'be the best Old Man I ever sailed under. He doesn't care *how* things're done as long as they *get* done."

This, Krumm thought, was only one of his virtues. In the span before they had waylaid the *Pelican,* with some help from his first officer, the boy had discovered that he was one of those rare, dangerous natural leaders for love of whom men would leap with a glad shout into the maw of death.

True, Henry Martyn—known to a smaller portion of the galaxy as Arran Islay—was a lad of but fifteen, third and lowliest son of an attainted Drector. Krumm had kept close eye upon him as he had risen from stowaway, victim to sadists, gundeck menial, and projecteur's helper, to commodore of a growing fleet. Still he did not altogether understand the boy.

Upon assuming command of the carrack and the corsair he had taken, he transferred to the latter, renamed *Osprey*. Warfare being laid into her very keels, she suited his purposes better than the ship he had first sailed upon. Taking officers and crewbeings with him whom, by virtue of his own experience and at Krumm's suggestion, he deemed trustworthy, and restoring her to fitness chiefly by restarting her collectors and disposing of the radiation-ravaged corpses of her crew, he had turned his attention back to *Gyrfalcon*.

Those left aboard were less to be trusted, and in this way his practice of overarming vessels had begun. He had ordered her fifteen projectibles placed aboard the corsair wherever they fit, behind improvised portals upon boat- and liftdecks, upon the commanddeck calipretted at right angles to the bow chasers. Likewise, the holds soon served as hangars for *Gyrfalcon's* remaining auxiliaries, some of which, more to conserve space than from belligerent design, soon boasted small projectibles—the carrack's chasers—of their own. Later he leavened the ranks of her complement with liberated slaves, victims of pressgangs, and alien life forms.

This developed into a lucky stroke for which he was to feel grateful. Unable to imitate the noises which served them as speech, he had converted them into something he could write and read. In this, he had explained to Krumm, he found the letters Old Henry had taught him more useful than the sparse jottings of barquode. The young man had discovered that the rollerballers referred to themselves as *"seporth."* A numerous and varied people just inventing their own steam engines and combustible gas lighting, they inhabited a young planet (which, to everyone's regret, not even Krumm knew how to find) of violent crustquakes and volcanoes. Human raiders (or Oplytes, the distinction was lost upon the *seporth*) had dropped onto the surface of their world and made off with an entire town. Nor, if *seporth* folklore was to be credited, was it the first time.

While humans made perfect riggers and topmen (perhaps owing to their monkey lineage), accounting for their species' preeminence upon the Deep, rollerballers were ideal projecteurs, impervious to heat and smoke, possessed of fine sensibility with regard to the fussy, dangerous projectibles. As long as he had rollerballers serving upon the gundeck, calling thrusts from beneath much-modified darthelms, Krumm never again lost use of a weapon to core failure or conductile burn.

From Henry Martyn's viewpoint, the flatsies—who referred to themselves as *"nacyl"*—turned out even better. Allowing for an arboreal specialization which had biased the course of human evolution, their flatworm shape was as generalized as that of mankind, lending itself to a broad variety of application. They were faster getting up the cabelles and out upon the spars, spiraling round them like stripes upon a candy stick. Aloft they exhibited limitations. The appendages they used for hands, stubby tentacularities extruding through apertures all over their surface, were no longer than a man's smallest finger. Upon their own world, every artifact, of course, was constructed by means of such manipulators and with such in mind. They professed to admire the longer, stronger limbs of human crewbeings, as well as the adroit tendrils of the *seporth*.

The *nacyl* did not say much about their home, not, Krumm believed, because they wished to withhold information. Some inadequacy in the common vocabulary, suitable as it was proving to the working of a starship, kept them from it, or humans from understanding them. If they were to be believed, their culture, although it occupied a solitary world (if that was what they meant), had advanced in technologic arts beyond the imperia-conglomerate; although to the young captain and his first officer it sounded more like sorcery. It appeared, by virtue of Henry Martyn's rescue, that they could read thoughts, although their denials were strenuous.

Many unanswered questions remained. How, if they were so powerful and accomplished, had these been captured? The *nacyl* (Krumm continued thinking of them as "flatsies," hoping, in frustrated moments, that they *could* read his mind) were unable to explain, beyond bald facts not significantly different from the story rollerballers told. The captain, who spent half his time learning to whistle like a flatsy, would understand someday. Krumm was compelled to imagine a human party of nude sunbathers caught in a surprise attack by savages.

"Murdering those people," Tula objected, "he must hate someone terribly."

Krumm nodded. Punctuated by kinergic thrumming, Henry Martyn's first months as a starbandit had streamed by in a river of blood, his reputation for implacability well earned. Appreciating less and less the alleged differences between contending imperia-conglomerate, he extended his attentions to ships and installations of Hanover's arch-enemy, the Empery-Cirot, to its supporting polities, as well as to those of Hanover and their many lesser rivals.

Everywhere he went, any time he achieved a victory in the Deep, or later, as his prowess and resources grew, upon the surfaces of outpost planets, he liberated slaves—by whatever euphemism they were called to deny the injustice of their estate. Common people, no better off—Hanoverian, Jendish, others all alike, were victims like himself. Whatever retribution he visited upon their masters, he left them unmolested. Often he spent time recruiting those he liberated, persuading them to become shipcrews for his fleet or his eyes and ears upon planets ruled by their masters. He gave special and mysterious assignments to aliens he set free, and to humans whose peculiarities suited them to whatever task he had in mind. Krumm pitied anyone whom the captain calculated still owed him a moral debt. Those who acted for the ceos were not long in responding. Hunted by two dread imperia-conglomerate, Henry Martyn's infamy as buccaneer, starship-robber, and freebooter continued to swell.

Tillie and Tula, accustomed to husbandly idiosyncrasies other than bad-tempered outbursts, waited in patience for

Krumm to break his thoughtful silence. "No doubt, me dear, an' with sufficient reason. Yet he delivered himself of the order as a housekeepin' matter—ye know prisoners in any number, let alone a hundred, are a knotty problem 'board ship—as calm as he'd order the shortenin' of starsail."

"The way he's followed about by those flattie things," Tula shuddered.

"They saved his life," he answered. "He takes comfort in their company, as they do in his, bein' lost t'their own people as they are." Tillie opened her mouth. Krumm interrupted, "An' before ye remind me, yes, Henry Martyn gives many a humane order. Such as his policy with slaves an' pressed beings. But he offers only cold pragmatics for a reason. There's no more humanity in his many kindnesses than there is malice in his many cruelties."

Mathilde Krumm would not be put off. "And the little girl?"

Krumm shook his head. "Tillie, I've driven pressed crews into the yards an' t'duties belowdecks most of me life. I've been, as ye know well, a slave m'self, first sold in the port *Etumalam* we're bound for. That this was not me choice in the matter is irrelevant. Had I dwelt upon me qualms, and not upon the discipline and workin' of the ship, I'd not be discussin' it with ye now, for I'd still be a slave, or, far more likely, good an' dead."

Tillie stepped closer, Tula rested a commiserating hand upon his arm. Even as he spoke, Krumm sensed within himself the poison of moral compromise which, addicting one and all within the imperia-conglomerate, permitted continuation of institutions that ought to have been smashed centuries ago. Compromise was not the only addiction a man could suffer, he thought bitterly. Perhaps he should never have led a mutiny nor rescued Henry Martyn from the Deep. An accommodation he had earlier reached with what he had conceived to be unchangeable had been breached. Forever afterward, anything he undertook which failed to measure up to those moments would smack to him of cowardice.

He shrugged. "We've no more t'say about that lass than of

how he spends his share of what we garner in shipraid, for that's what she be, his share from our attack upon the *Pelican.*" He stared up into the §-field. "Now be hush, darlin' spouses, an' belowdecks with ye. Yonder comes the captain's gig, and over there the pilot in his boat t'take us down t'*Nosaer.*

CHAPTER XL:
THE CAPTAIN'S CABIN

Through the metalloid fabric of the starship about her, Loreanna heard the thump of an auxiliary arriving and being made fast below.

Without being told so—and perhaps for the sake of preserving her sanity—she had decided she was being held for ransom. Having resigned herself to a long wait until the sum demanded of her uncle (or even of the Ceo) could be paid, she had resolved to make the best of her ordeal and to maintain the appearance of composure, so that, afterward, she might hold her head up. In this manner she would represent both herself and the Hanoverian people to these barbarians as the superior stock she had grown up believing they were. Although, of late, she had begun entertaining some soul-disturbing doubts upon this score. However that may be, perhaps Uncle Sedgeley would be proud enough of her, in the end, to relent in the matter of her exile.

To this purpose, she was at the moment sitting—almost content, washed and gowned afresh as she had striven to appear each day from the outset of her captivity—in a straight-backed chair beside the broad, soft, railed bed, mending with skillful care a traveling dress, among her favorites, which the repulsive Bowmore had torn. She was aware that these accommodations, with their unique plumbing and bathing facilities, were the captain's personal quarters, and even cognizant, in a vague way, of the fact that this hospitality, and his continuous absence since she had come aboard, was what had given her an impression her release was, if not in the immediate offing, at least certain to come soon or late. It did not occur to her, perhaps because she had not let it, that the place she had been quartered might portend another sort of fate.

Now she heard thumping upon the maindeck, saw moving shadows cast from beyond the angle of vision which, from this vantage-point, the cabin windows permitted. She looked up from her mending as the cabin door swung open. The young man she knew as Henry Martyn stepped inside and shut the door behind him. Without a word, he strode to the many-paned windows overlooking the maindeck, polarized them until they were purple-black, and shook out curtains in front of them which had been tied back and not let down for years.

She stood. He turned to face her, cupping his left palm over the aperture of the thrustible he wore upon his right arm in a warrior's gesture of well-intentioned greeting the significance of which she did not realize.

"Good afternoon, Mistress Daimler-Wilkinson. Forgive the fact that I have, until this moment, been too busy to pay you proper attention. Remove your clothing." Loreanna took a step backward and discovered, to her dismay, that she had placed a hand over her mouth as if she were the heroine of some melodrama thille. Henry Martyn grinned and stepped forward, taking two deep strides to her one. "I will not repeat myself, girl, do it *now!*"

Swallowing, she raised her other hand, and, where it met the first, began, with fingers rendered awkward by terror, to unfasten the short row of small buttons at her throat. The startling thought struck her that this moment would not have passed much differently had she agreed to give herself as bribe and bride to the Jendyne Ceo.

With a local pilot at the helm, one Lua P'nor, captain-by-courtesy and foremost among those badgering him to join that stupid Privateer's Thing, and Krumm to do the breathing down his neck, Henry Martyn had left instructions that he was to be undisturbed until their arrival at the ice asteroid *Nosaer*. He was free to take his time with the little captive. Yielding to impatience despite himself, he obliterated the distance between them, swept her hands down, and finished off the row of buttons for her. He did not tear her clothing, but, before she was altogether aware of it, he had the short jacket off her shoulders, her blouse as well, the sheer camisole beneath it over her head, and she was standing before him in stockings and her long, full skirt, naked from the waist up, just as she had been before Bowmore.

Above all, she was aware that the hands upon her—his thrustible glittered in the cabin light, cold where here and there it brushed her bare and goose-fleshed skin—had murdered countless men, perhaps brutalized many women. Had it been within her character, she might have fainted, or prayed to the long-dead gods of her ancestors for another interruption, however disastrous. Instead she stood straight, disdaining to cover her nakedness, even with upraised arms.

"Go ahead, sir, mock me." She tried with all her might to keep a tremor from her voice. For all she had despised him as an animal, Bowmore's sneering criticism of what was, in fact, her slim, youthful figure had stung her pride. "Do not hesitate to enumerate the many bovine virtues of which I fall short. Make whatever brutish remark lies foremost upon your mind. But I will have you know that you do this at your peril, for I am niece to—"

"I know who you are," replied Henry Martyn. "We shall have the skirt off, as well." Out of modest reflex, she turned to unfasten her waistband, as she did so spying the mending basket she had placed upon the bed. Suddenly, her knees collapsed beneath her as if in a faint. When she rose again, with his assistance at her elbow, she whirled, startling herself with a snarl, a long pair of gleaming scissors raised in one tiny fist. Henry Martyn clapped a hand about her wrist, squeezing until her hand grew numb. She heard, rather than felt, the scissors fall from her tingling fingers and clatter to the floor where, still holding her, he kicked them under the bunk. Eyes shut tight, she waited for a backhand blow across her face which never came. "No more nonsense," he told her. "Take the skirt off, or I shall take it off for you."

Defeated, Loreanna complied. As she did so, he reached

out, timidly, it struck her afterward, and brushed his fingers across one of her nipples. A shudder, not altogether of revulsion, swept through her body.

"Please . . ." As he pulled her forward, she stepped out of her skirt where it lay upon the floor, clad only in her garters and sheer stockings. "Have mercy, for I am a virgin."

"And you talk too much," he replied, "but I've an idea how to deal with both failings." He stared at Loreanna, fascinated by her moist, full-lipped mouth, having given it much thought. His plans for her were detailed and precise. This first night, for as many hours as it took, he would make repeated use of her in this manner, handling her with cuffs and sharp words when, in his estimate, she failed to please him. He would stroke her hair and caress her when she managed to perform to his criterion. One curiosity satisfied, the next time he came for her, probably tomorrow when they were hove to at *Nosaer,* he would use her as he had first been used, keeping her at it until she was accustomed to that outrage as well. After they cast off for Sisao and Somon, he would begin with something new.

These thoughts singing in his blood and weakening his limbs, he pushed her backward until something struck her behind the knees and she found herself sitting upon the edge of the bunk. In almost the same motion, he unfastened his own clothing so that, stepping toward her, lacing his fingers into the hair at the nape of her neck—she raised protesting hands to push him back, but he was too strong—he might lever her teeth open with a thumb.

"Please . . ."

Of a sudden, having no reason he could account for, he stopped before completing the act he had intended. Looking down at her, what he saw upon her face was an expression of resignation—her eyes were squeezed shut, her body quaking with fear and tense anticipation of his assault upon her—articulate of all the suffering he had himself endured. In short, this lovely creature had composed herself for a dishonored death.

Thus the dreaded Henry Martyn could not bring himself to do to Loreanna what had been done to him, to inflict upon her the merest fraction of pain and terror which had changed his life. She seemed so small and fragile he wished only to protect her, even from himself. He shook his fingers loose from her hair, and sat down beside her upon the bunk, wrapping his arms about her naked, vulnerable form, holding her to him as tightly as he could. After a time, she began trembling violently, making odd choking noises deep inside her throat as if she would not release, in his unwelcome presence, the wail of despair he was certain, from his own experience of life, she was feeling. He held her closer and stroked her hair until the trembling subsided and she began to weep softly into his shoulder, discovering, as he held her, that his own face had become wet with tears.

A considerable time passed.

It was in his mind to say that he regretted having frightened and humiliated her. Feeling an apology was only words, and in the circumstances grotesquely inadequate, he continued, in its place, to sit beside her, holding her without words, until—noticing how chilled her flesh had become, how exhausted she looked, and finding he felt much the same himself—he lowered her to the pillows, lay down beside her, and, still holding her thin, pale form in his arms, covered her with the quilted comforter upon the bunk.

Loreanna's eyes remained shut, but her expression of terror and defeat relaxed by gradual stages. Perhaps without realizing what she did—for he could not imagine it to be an act of deliberation upon her part—she laid a small, white hand upon his forearm where it rested across her midriff, and began to breathe more evenly and deeply. So it was, in the warmth and semidarkness of his cabin, in the comfort of encircling arms which neither of them had felt for so long, they both fell asleep.

Henry Martyn awakened to the startling sensation of soft fingers stroking his cheek. Not until long afterward did he realize that his first thought had not been for the readiness of his thrustible. Instead, he opened his eyes to the sight of Loreanna, propped upon one elbow, looking down at him with an expression he could not altogether fathom. She did not speak.

He had surprised—and frightened—himself by drifting off in this manner. Yet he had spent several days and nights without sleep, almost without pause, at the backbreaking labor of refitting the captured *Peregrine*. This was the first rest he had enjoyed in all that time. She might have killed him as he lay insensible. He suggested as much, and asked her why she had not.

The corners of her pretty mouth twitched upward. "I might have, at that," she told him, "but my scissors were under the bed where you earlier kicked them. You were sleeping so peacefully, I could not bring myself to disturb you by retrieving them. Perhaps another time."

Still feeling exhausted, he grinned, relaxed again, and closed his eyes—until he felt a small, soft hand, not quite as gentle as before, upon his shoulder. Puzzled, he opened his eyes and looked up.

"Please have mercy," she told him, with the same fathomless expression, "for I am *still* a virgin."

A thrill of wondering disbelief, perhaps something resembling joy, passed through his body like a wave of frozen fire. He opened his mouth. "I've an idea how to deal with that, but . . ." He hesitated over what he was about to say, which, in a sense, he considered a half lie. "I believe it only honest and straightforward to inform you beforehand, Mistress Daimler-Wilkinson . . . that this will be my first time, as well."

"You talk too much," she told him. "We shall learn together."

In answer he seized her—ever so tenderly—by the hair at the nape of her neck, and pulled her mouth to his own. Afterward, they did not sleep. He unsealed the outboard gallery windows, battened down for battle and not since reopened, so that they might gaze upon the faraway mist-shrouded glory of the Sisao-Somon System. They lay beside one another, talking far into those hours which, had they been upon a planet's surface, would have been fading into dawn. Loreanna spoke of her Uncle Sedgeley, of her life upon the dangerous fringes of the 'Droom, of power and politics, of her studies of history and economics, of her friend and servant the redoubtable Brougham, and, in a somewhat halting manner, of how she came to be aboard the *Pelican*.

Henry Martyn spoke, with equal diffidence in the begin-

ning, of moonringed Skye, his long-dead mother Glynnaughfern, his murdered father Robret, his brothers Robret
fils and Donol, his tutor and sister-in-law Lia, and in particular of his wise, valorous friend Old Henry, whom he had
never quite been able to think of as a servant. At last he came
to Morven's usurpation. It surprised him to discover his own
interest in everything she had to tell him of galactic politics.
In large measure she approached in theory what he was able
to confirm by virtue of experience. He found her eager and
incisive intellect as stimulating as her beauty. Watching her
speak fascinated him all over again with her lovely mouth. He
was even more surprised to hear himself telling her, at last, of
his first evil hours aboard the *Gyrfalcon,* of the shroom crate,
and of what had happened upon the foul, dark liftdeck.

"Sometimes, Loreanna, I ache in my bones because no one
is left upon whom to revenge myself, save Morven and his
obscene daughter, as yet beyond my reach." She nodded,
trying to understand. "And Bowmore," he added, "whom
circumstance has twice compelled me to set free."

"And if any were left?"

"Man after guilty man would fall to the skill-at-arms I daily
practice. Toward that end would I frequent ports where other
brigands supply themselves and exchange information. I find
myself in possession of a deal of money for which I have no
better use. I have let it be known I am willing to pay for
information bearing upon Bowmore's whereabouts, should
he again survive the Deep, for I swear he will not escape me a
third time."

"I see . . ."

"Still, events have made it plain that my real enemy is the
current of the times which makes possible obscenities like
imperia-conglomerate and the vermin they nurture. Alas this
insight may satisfy the intellect, but it gives me a foe without
a face, and that rankles."

Loreanna found herself swept up in his urge for revenge.
"What of the pair from the capital, the Drector-Honorary
Witsable and Lady Nasai-Ulness?"

He shrugged. "All I can discover is that they boarded
Gyrfalcon sometime after I did, albeit in more dignified

circumstances, and were put off with Bowmore and his officers. They did not appear at Hanover when he did."

"No!" She shrank back with a cry. "You don't think Bowmore *ate* them?"

"It was," he answered her, "a desperate voyage. Who can say?"

She returned to questions about Skye and he to answers, often difficult and painful, rather than futile, grisly conjectures. They spoke of *seporth* and *nacyl*—he realized this was the first time in months that one of the latter was not his constant companion—and of waiting in vain for rescue from the cold and heartless Deep. Although neither of them might have predicted it, it now became Loreanna's turn to comfort her captor within the circle of her arms.

At intervals, their bodies merged again. In the end, all that he might have taken from her, the answers to every curiosity he burned to satisfy, Loreanna gave him freely and more, besides. He did grow violent, after all, but it proved a different sort of violence, three-quarters play, than he had first intended to inflict upon her. Before the night was over, Loreanna came to understand (as perhaps her lover did not; like most men, according to what she had read, he only knew his need and she felt fortunate that he was beginning to know hers, as well) that, just as the animal process of feeding had, over the long course of evolution, been converted from a mechanical matter of fueling the body into an occasion for fellowship and celebration, so those reflexes which served reproduction had begun, with the fullness of time, to perform a secondary function, absorbing, diffusing, transmuting the killer rage with which life was all too likely to fill an individual into something bearable and consistent with continued sanity.

A knock came upon the cabin door. "Nose-hair in sight, sir, and the captain's presence requested upon the quarter-deck."

Henry Martyn sighed and raised his voice. "Very well. I shall be along presently." Rising, he suggested to Loreanna that she remain abed a few more hours. The night which they had spent together, whatever its other virtues—and they had been many—had afforded her scant sleep. As he dressed himself, his movements were clumsy, for he chafed in unaccustomed places. "Rest easy and for as long as you wish. I swear no harm will come to you."

She smiled in a way to melt his heart and settled deeper among the pillows. Reaching for his thrustibles, he recalled with a start what a threatening place a starship could be for a weak, helpless, and, worst of all, uninformed individual. Nodding to himself, he strode to a locker set against a bulkhead, removed a small plastic chest, and returned to the bunk, resting one knee upon it beside Loreanna. He found it difficult to speak.

"This, my . . . my beloved Loreanna, is one possession which was not taken at thrustible-point, with me from the beginning of my life upon the Deep. I give it to you, not just in token of what I feel, which I could not in any case express, but that you may never fear for your life again, having means of defending your own person." She looked up at him with sleepy eyes, not altogether understanding why the gift was so important to him, but knowing nonetheless, that it was. He grinned. "I shall have to wait to show you its operation, but now you need not crawl under the bunk for your scissors."

Loreanna smiled at him and blushed. Arising again, he left her. He had intended showing her what he carried upon a jeweled chain about his neck (no question lingered in his mind that she was the little dancer in the autothille) and asking her about it. Still, it could wait. They would have time. They had time enough for everything now.

She fell asleep with the ancient walther-weapon tucked beneath her pillow.

Chapter XLI:
The *Cormorant*

Loreanna awakened to an unaccustomed quality of light seeping through the depolarized windows and the curtains floating loosely before them. And to a shocking memory of the night before.

Trying to sit up, she experienced a moment of panic, thinking she was restrained. Someone had tucked the comforter under the mattress, and for good reason. A comb which had escaped from one of her bags floated in the middle of the room. She sat upon the mattress but did not indent it. Not only was the *Osprey* hove to, it (*she,* Loreanna reminded herself, annoyed with her trivial concern for exactitude) was under no power at all.

All these things she observed with a small, rational corner of her mind. The rest of her consciousness recoiled at what had been done to her . . . no, that was not quite right. Without question, she had been brutalized and violated beyond any extent she had ever realized it was possible to endure. Yet—hating herself for it—she discovered within her heart a dawning (and, given present circumstances, very disturbing) awareness. She had managed to accomplish rather more than her share of brutalizing, not to mention repeated violation. Her victim, who had several times expressed a doubt that he could long survive such ecstasy as she inflicted, was none other than the murdering bandit Henry Martyn.

In an unenviable state of moral confusion, she remembered hearing or reading of the capability of the mind, for the sake of sheer survival, to compel its owner to identify with a powerful enemy, if that was what staying alive required. Was this such an instance? In all honesty, she thought not. She had enjoyed most of what had happened to her, missed it already, and desired more. She was tempted to attribute this to some inherent evil which, thanks to her Hanoverian education and her perfidious uncle, she had come to believe lurked within the best of men. And, to all appearances, of women.

Dallrane Barnagus-Willhart was afraid.

Night bristled with a billion needlepoints of cruel brilliance. Within the nebula enveloping Sisao-Somon, one might expect the blazing splendor of the great curve-spoked wheel which was the galaxy to be subdued. Yet adrift in the belly of the Deep, Barnagus-Willhart, captain of the *Cormorant,* a Hanoverian caravel of nine projectibles, had never seen a sky crawl with such multicolored glittering. The knowledge that not a thousandth, not even a millionth, of the scintillating razor-chips about him were suns, but mundane, palpable, *dangerous* objects ranging from swift particles of frozen gas to tumbling asteroids the size of continents, reflecting the dazzling radiance of their primary, failed to diminish the terrible glory of the vision.

The vessel he departed having been secured for freefall like his own, Barnagus-Willhart seized a lubberline belayed parallel to the flexible watering main attached to the thirsty starship and launched himself back toward the glare-bright surface of *Nosaer,* sparing a glance for the belligerent-looking frigate floating nearby. The *Skerry,* he recalled, under command of a Captain Sullers Monen, boasted an impressive fifty-seven projectibles. She was half again as large as the vessel he was leaving or his own, their hulls a mere thirty measures in diameter.

It was not his habit to authorize liberty for crewbeings at a stopover. He feared losing them to the pressgangs of other captains. Nor would he ordinarily visit such a body himself. Yet no alternative had been offered him. Although he was weeks away from those wielding power greater than a captain's minuscule authority—those threatening to convert his body into that of a mewling cripple, leaving his brain intact to appreciate the humor of it—never did he doubt their ability to reach across the lightyears and grasp him as they wished. What made the affair more ominous, in a manner he could not put a finger upon, was that all they demanded was delivery of a message to one whose name lately promised to become better known than that of any Ceo, the infamous Deep-raider, Henry Martyn. Having been a signal officer, Barnagus-Willhart had thought it most discreet to see to it himself, balancing the tube upon his shoulder like the ancient weapon it resembled, centering the notorious vessel in its sights:

Compliments of Dallrane Barnagus-Willhart, Master and Owner-in-Command caravel Cormorant, *to Captain Henry Martyn. Request permission to come onboard, purpose of delivering personal message from Skye. Await reply.*

Curiosity was no more habitual with Barnagus-Willhart than granting liberty or accepting risks. He was one among many who never wondered why starships of a million worlds invariably took names from avians of a planet only historians remembered. He never wondered why those power-wielders had threatened to destroy him, nor questioned any right they had to do so. He was anxious to know one thing: how soon it would be over. Perched like an avian himself upon the taffrail of his quarterdeck, a leg twisted into the rat-lines, the lasercom rendered clumsy upon his shoulder by lack of gravity, he had not been required to wait long. Modulated waves of infrared had flashed back over the intervening klommes as soon as he had finished sending his own:

Henry Martyn, Master of corsair Osprey *to Captain Barnagus-Willhart. Advise means of arrival, as will save embarrassment all round.*

The §-field being powered down and the upper decks exposed to the Deep, he had already attired himself in one of the few vacuum suits his starship carried, this being but the second time in his career he had done so. Now he took up a hand-held device resembling a hybrid of beer-stein and dowsing-fork, an annihilator which converted water into superheated steam, aligned its crosshairs with the wheels and valves at the asteroid end of the waterline stretching from his own ship, and closed his fist upon the grip, thumbing the button trigger. Had he been more experienced, he might have chanced thrusting himself across the gap between caravel and corsair, but he was a cautious man, aware of his limitations, and thought it best to follow the waterline down to *Nosaer*, thence upward to the *Osprey*.

He was disappointed to observe, as he remembered being upon two previous occasions, that the jets thrusting backward at outspreading angles could not be seen. He was beyond them before they cooled into clouds of ice crystals. An ironic corner of his mind reflected that, lured slowly surfaceward by the asteroid's minute pull, the water would be sold back to him a decade hence. Still, the jets performed the task of taking him in the direction he desired.

Before he knew it, *ulsic* squawked a warning predicated upon feelers of invisible light. He flipped a lever so that the jets thrust forward, braking his velocity before he could injure himself upon the surface of the asteroid. As the ice boulder swam before his eyes, he caught himself entering a state of hyperventilation. Panic-stricken reference to *ulsic* patches upon one sleeve of his suit told him his oxygen supply was not to blame for the roaring in his ears or the sweat-trickle crawling along his ribs. He was familiar with this particular malfunction, although he knew it by another name.

What he feared was Henry Martyn's reputation. The man (if man he be and not some monster with a human alias) was something of a legend. Yet Barnagus-Willhart's informants had assured him that, long out of touch with events upon his native planet—ring-wrapped, mountainous, forest-covered Skye—he would be eager to learn of the upheavals taking place there. Barnagus-Willhart's task was simply to describe those changes, tell the truth about them. Why should that be so thrusted difficult? The only possible answer lay in a direction into which the captain's curiosity did not extend. Truth always represented unaccustomed difficulty in a culture built upon a foundation of euphemism, this being but another euphemism for a shorter, better word.

Some were more straightforward. The warning in Henry Martyn's reply was no exaggeration. Barnagus-Willhart was searched where *Osprey's* waterlines connected at the planetoid—he was not deprived of his thrustible—halfway along the line, and again upon reaching the end, which entered the vessel not at the lubberlift, as with his own ship, but at a boatdeck airlock. "If not weaponth," he asked the officer at the lock, once he had removed his helmet and the amenities were observed, "what were your men looking for?"

Osprey presented a disconcerting spectacle. But only a converted one-decker herself (the phrase, less descriptive than it might have been, referred to the number of gundecks a vessel boasted), she was no larger than his nine-weaponed *Cormorant*. Yet features of her hull were indicative of the four-decked dreadnoughts whose potency was the very backbone of the imperia-conglomerate. Taking chasers into account, Barnagus-Willhart's first estimate of her strength was forty-six until he noticed that the nine-per-deck "rule" had been violated. *Osprey* carried twelve per deck (with full-sized projectibles remounted as chasers) and twice the number of expected auxiliaries, also—without precedent—well armed.

The giant first officer grinned down at him. "Surprises." Without further explanation, they ascended the ladderwell and crossed the airless, unpopulated maindeck to what he presumed were the quarters of Henry Martyn.

At first, Barnagus-Willhart wondered where the captain was. His curiosity extended that far. Within jury-airlocked doors, two plump women seated him and the officer at a heavy kitchen-style table, hurrying back with drinks in freefall sacks with sipping tubes and a covered plate of pastries. They were assisted by a youngster whom the caravel captain took to be a son to one of them or perhaps a cabin boy, until, refreshment having been served, he floated into a chair of his own and tugged its strap across his lap.

"Welcome, Captain," the boy nodded. "You have met Mr. Krumm, my first officer. These are his goodwives, Mathilde and Tula—did you see that thrusted frigate heave to out there, Krumm?—my signal officer tells me you have brought a message from Skye. From whom, may I ask?"

Barnagus-Willhart was grateful to the blue-eyed, sandy-haired child of perhaps thirteen years, judging by the standard of his own world. This speech had given him time to regain control of his jaw, which had dropped open. The effort was made more difficult by entrance, from the maindeck, of a species of alien he had never seen before, a limbless slab of scarlet and ivory. It folded itself upon the floor at the young captain's feet, to the obvious discontent of the women, making Barnagus-Willhart unsure whether it be person or pet. "Captain Martyn—"

"*Commodore* Martyn," Krumm interrupted. "The corvette hangin' out there be his an' a sizable fleet insystem. Not bein' one t'stand upon ceremony, he don't insist upon bein' called 'Admiral,' though he might."

"Er . . . Com—"

Henry Martyn threw back his head and laughed. "'Captain' will do, sir. Krumm will not permit me to call him by that honorific, though if commodore I be, he should accept. You have stumbled into a jocular old controversy between us. By whatever title, I am anxious to receive your message."

Barnagus-Willhart cleared his throat. "I greatly fear me, thir, it ith not a pleathant one to be entruthted to deliver. It cometh from one who dethcribeth herthelf ath a friend, a Mithtreth Woodgate."

"Lia?"

The captain closed his eyes a moment for the sake of memory, and opened them again. "Through Fionaleigh Thavage, Mithtreth Woodgate'th aide, from whom I have it firththand. Mithtreth Woodgate bidth me firtht inform you of her deduction ath to who—whom?—the infamouth 'Henry Martyn' really ith."

"An impressive intellectual leap, would you not say, Mr. Krumm?"

Krumm appeared, he observed, more wary than impressed. With a nervous glance at the alien, he took a breath. "It giveth me no pleathure to inform you, ath requethted, that Robret Ithlay *fith*, 'by right Drector-Hereditary of Thkye,' ith dead, having been captured in battle and died afterward under quethtioning." The boy's face was impassive, as if he had not heard these terrible words. At his feet, where, in absence of gravity, it had curled itself about a table leg, the alien stiffened as if it understood. "Lacking other reathonable choiceth, Mithtreth Woodgate wath compelled to entrutht thith methage with the captain of the firtht pathing vethel—mythelf."

What Barnagus-Willhart could not say—must not, upon pain too terrible to conceive—was that, having met the rebel girl at Alysabethport, he had been captured lifting to his ship. Being a fellow of fragile sensibility, unable to abide the idea of torture let alone its actuality, all that was necessary to learn what he knew was to describe the implements to be used upon him (he had never even seen them) did he not cooperate. Thus, Lia Woodgate's message had fallen into two successive sets of wrong hands.

The first were those of Donol Islay, surviving son of the attainted elder Robret and apparent successor, to whom, he observed, this boy bore more than slight resemblance. Donol had questioned the *Cormorant's* captain hard before handing him over to the Ceo's deputy upon Skye. Small wonder, he thought now, if in this manner Donol had learned that his younger brother—was the name Arran?—was not only still alive, but had become Henry Martyn.

"From within the confineth of the . . ."

"The Holdings," offered Henry Martyn, "our name for the Islay estate."

"Thank you, thir . . . in her wordth, the Black Uthurper'th headquarterth, Mithtreth Woodgate hath taken command of the woodthrunnerth in the name of her late—I wath warned to be exthact: 'unwedded huthband'—to renew the rithing againtht the uthurpation. If I may be tho bold, intelligently and capably, judging by the ethteem in which the lady ith held everywhere, not the leatht by her adjutant, Mithtreth Thavage." He wondered whether the boy knew of rumors that she had lost her 'unwedded husband' to the girl before his death, whereupon she herself had become mistress to the younger brother. Barbaric lot, these colonials. His message delivered, the captain of the *Cormorant* lingered no more in the presence of the boy, his first officer, the two women, or their living throw-rug than he must before excusing himself.

Careful not to injure herself, Loreanna arose (no dearth of handholds being provided in the cabin for those occasions when the vessel was without gravity, although they had been inconspicuous before now) to wash and dress. If she did as she planned, she might not soon have the luxury again, although the bag into which the shower curtain folded was less pleasant than the tub.

A locker held Henry Martyn's vacuum suit (this ship had more than she had ever heard of) with a checklist and means of cinching it to smaller forms than it had been intended for. Beside it hung a maneuvering engine. To her surprise, the suit smelled fresh as she crawled into it, as if he made regular practice of having it cleaned. Why should that surprise her? Last night, after he had awakened and they had . . . well, in any case, he had not seemed at all dirty or unpleasant as she had always imagined even ordinary starsailors must. Afterward, before they began again to . . . anyway, he had taken trouble to bathe, apologizing over what he had claimed was the grime of three days' labor, although he must have bathed at intervals, even aboard the corvette.

The last thing she took was the weapon he had given her, feeling guilty as she tucked it into a pocket. Hating herself for irresolution, she opened the trap in the cabin floor which led to the boatdeck and made good her escape, even while Krumm was leading Barnagus-Willhart to meet Henry Martyn. Taking a risk she did not altogether appreciate, she hung outside the unguarded airlock, aimed at the closest vessel, and thumbed a button. A trail of glittering crystals marked her path toward a *Cormorant.*

Barnagus-Willhart did not hear the conversation between Krumm and Henry Martyn as it continued for a while after he had taken his leave.

"My sister-out-of-law is tough, Mr. Krumm. Even I am surprised. She has not only survived, she has kept things going, perhaps as a kind of relief from her personal suffering, when everyone else was ready to give up. I must, also with surprise, give Donol credit. I did not believe he had it in him. With Lia's collusion, as we planned long ago, he pretends cooperation with the Black Usurper. He even helps plan a trap for Henry Martyn."

"Might an old starsailor ask, sir, what y'propose doin'?"

"Belay the humility, Krumm. Obviously such a message could not get offplanet without Morven's cooperation. Barnagus-Willhart must have been caught, yet he is obviously healthy. Thus he has been bribed or threatened—"

"Or both."

"And sent upon his way with word meant to lure Henry Martyn home."

"Might'n old starsailor ask, sir——"

"Grrr! We shall lay over, though I regret the wasted time, for repairs and supplies, as well as desperate thinking. I shall make arrangements, including an unexpected visit to the frigate lying out there, let her master lecture me again about the Privateer's Council, and set sail for home."

Beneath the table the *nacyl* stirred and flowed up to the seat of a chair. Tillie was out of the room. Tula glared until it made a sad, whiffling noise which altered her expression. Tentatively, she offered it a bit of the sweet dough, which it accepted and absorbed contentedly. She shook her head and returned to work, a faint smile upcurving the corners of her mouth.

"To the dismay," Krumm argued, "of a crew who could profit from a rest."

"I shall promise greater profit, Mr. Krumm. A chance for different gains than they have had before. They will accept. Now, if you will excuse me, I shall go see whether Lor— Mistress Daimler-Wilkinson—has awakened."

He arose and left, the flatsy flowing after. Krumm, having deduced what had passed between the two young people, nodded and grinned.

Loreanna's doubts did not desist, even as she was handed onboard the *Cormorant*. Crewbeings at the lifthatch responded more to her manner and accent than any surety she had to offer—she had brought some jewelry with her—for her passage. Shown the purser's cabin, she awaited return of the captain. No doubt remained upon one matter: she harbored other feelings—toward what had been done to her, the way she had responded, and the young man who had done it—than propriety expected. It was her relentless regard for truth—for the presence of which within her only she was responsible—that finally saved her from further indecision. It had occurred to her, during the drifting passage between ships, filled with the sound of her own breathing, that she was desired—if so mild a expression served— by Henry Martyn, for herself alone. For her person, her hands, her mouth, her ability to gratify, increasing through the night as his to gratify her had increased. Perhaps even for her mind and heart which had resisted him while they surrendered. Not for any leverage she might bring to some scheme he was hatching.

The caravel was being prepared for the next leg of its journey, which she had been told was to Hanover, small coincidence, given Monopolitan trade routes and colonial policies. As she waited in her stolen vacuum suit, its helmet resting upon her breasts, in the office serving as an anteroom to the captain's, she discovered she had failed, even now, to escape from her dilemma. Knowing she loved Henry Martyn, she was unable to determine what to do about it. A thumping from the next room brought her out of her reverie.

"Back at latht," came a voice, "a free man. They catht our lineth off. We thail within the hour. Help me with thith boot, will you, Grubb?"

"Oy, sir. We've a passenger, ane wealthy one, though temp'rarily down upon 'er luck."

"The Theo you thay! By all meanth find her quarterth. We thhall thee to her further comfort onthe we are underweigh! By the Theo'th dirty underwear, we could uthe a change of luck, ourthelveth, eh, Grubb?"

"Sir?"

"A trap ith being laid, a nathty, clever trup, for a man— more like a boy—whom I ought, by all I live by, to detetht, by enemieth including hith own family! I tell you, the thooner we are away from thith bally nebula, and able to forget Thkyo in the bargain, the better I thhall like it!"

"Yes, sir."

"I would not burden you, Grubb, but do you gueth what that weathel—you know what a weathel is—Donol Ithlay, retherved for a parting thrutht ath we took leave of hith accurthed world? He athked me, *a thtarthhip captain,* to kill Henry Martyn if I got a chanthe, ath if I were a merthenary!"

Astonishment and outrage for Henry Martyn's sake rang through Loreanna's being as she unstrapped herself, arose from the straight-backed chair she had been sitting upon, and pushed herself across the room toward the adjoining quarters. She did not bother to knock.

"Captain—pardon me, I do not know your name—you must take me to the *Osprey!*" Despite the confusion which earlier had troubled her, she faced no difficulty now, dumfounded as she was by the manner in which her moral universe had been inverted. Proper behavior consisted of remaining silent, leaving her erstwhile captor to whatever fate authority decreed. Yet her one determination was to find some way of warning the man she had begun to love.

Seated, half out of his suit and rubbing bootsore feet, the man looked up at her standing in the doorway. "Dallrane Barnaguth-Willhart, Mithtreth, eager to be of thervithe. Ready to convey you to Hanover, ath you athked. I am afraid many reathonth exthitht why I may not comply with your immediate requetht, not all of them contherned with prethervation of my own thkin."

"You do not make yourself clear, sir."

"Thurely you jetht. You thee, Mithtreth . . . but, I do not know your name, either, do I? How awkward. In any cathe, it ith too late. I am afraid the infamouth and dreaded corthair *Othprey* hath jutht catht off, ath we thhall thhortly be doing, raithed thtarthail and departed."

Chapter XLII:
The Ghosts of Somon

Beneath a sky the color of wet iron, underlit by fitful lightnings, a cold wind swept the moss-covered, somehow defeated-looking contours of the Burial Plain of Somon, carrying with it moisture which was not quite rain.

"Burial" in the place-name referred to that of a civilization. Something had lived here, eons in the past, so long ago that archaeologists, amateur and otherwise, were locked in perpetual conflict over whether some particular item which had just been found was artificial or a product of erosion. Whatever it was, this monumental enigma, it had not been remotely human. It had built, loved perhaps, fought (nothing would grow upon the Plain save moss, so altered was the soil by isotopes of war), and died, leaving artifacts so durable no tool known to the imperia-conglomerate would mar their seamless surfaces, so ancient that weather had softened their shapes into unrecognizability.

Waiting for his captain to return, Krumm ran a hand over the opalescent monolith beside him. It thrust out of the tiny-leaved vegetation ten measures. The Somonese steersman of their lighter had told him that this, and twenty-two identical objects within the radius of a klomme, reached into the crust of Somon so deeply that their bases had never been discovered. It made Krumm shudder. That something so unutterably enormous, so inexpressably old, could be reduced to an amorphous memento of its once-powerful makers filled him with horror. The wind lashed wet, straggling fingers across his face, mocking him. The big man shivered, not only at this unaccustomed exposure to the elemental forces of a planet's surface. He was thinking of his captain.

For the remainder of his life, Krumm sensed, Henry Martyn would divide eternity into halves: After Loreanna and Before. The first time took a man that way. Over the past days, the boy had never offered to share, not with even his friend and loyal lieutenant, his feelings upon discovering that she had seized the opportunity of Barnagus-Willhart's visit to flee the *Osprey*, and (it was presumed that this accounted for his silence) his own presence.

Receiving his message from Mistress Woodgate, it was not for Skye that Henry Martyn had set sail. From the beginning, Krumm was aware, the boy had realized his path would lead him homeward, soon or late. Having accepted his captaincy, and again become master of his destiny, he had given the matter much thought, discussed it at length with the giant baker, even undertaken certain preparations against the day. Thus he had ordered Krumm to lay an inward course, away from the enveloping cometary shell of which *Nosaer* was an outpost, toward the outlaw sanctuary of the twinned planets Sisao and Somon, where, rather than the liberty he (and his crew) had long anticipated, he began at once selling valuables for cash, arranging unusual purchases, persuading crewbeings that the enterprise they were about to undertake would be worth any minor sacrifice he asked them to make, and holding a succession of meetings with an odd assortment of individuals, not all of them human.

"And spending rather too much energy, I think me." Krumm had ventured this solicitous if insubordinate opinion during their first orbits within the complicated influence of two worlds, although it was only to his wives he had spoken (the captain having left his first officer out of his planetside arrangements), not only of Henry Martyn, but of a boy who had been called Arran. He had little time to spare for such concerns. Constant adjustments necessary to maintain their position occupied his full attention. "I know the signs. He works himself to death as an alternative to thinking about life."

"Too much time, he says." Mathilde covered a bowl of dough which had not risen to her satisfaction. "Is he that impatient to be away from here?"

"That he be." Krumm bent over a half-consumed mug of steaming caff he had meant to pour here and carry to the quarterdeck. "But not 'til he's done startin' certain machinations. Afore ye ask, no: I don't know what they be. Nor much do I care. He'll tell old Krumm when the time's ripe, and what he plans'll work. That much I've learned of Henry Martyn. The conversation I believe he'd most profit by, he won't have with me, nor anybody else."

The women had clucked and frowned over this sad but undeniable wisdom. Krumm took his caffcup and his troubles to the quarterdeck. For a while he stood at the taffrail, gazing through the §-field at the planets. As with *Nosaer,* it was impossible to achieve stable orbit about Sisao or Somon. Where the icebound fragment possessed insufficient gravity, these boasted a surplus, deriving from two sources, overlapping to cross purposes. This precluded lubberlifting, and constituted the system's final natural defense against invasion. Arriving ships assumed station at a libration point, to be met by variations upon their own auxiliaries. Annihilator-powered, using water for reaction mass, these transferred cargo and passengers to the surfaces below.

Many operators vied for custom. It had been aboard one such vehicle that Henry Martyn had condescended to take

Krumm upon what he explained would be his last errand before leaving Sisao-Somon behind. A buffeting reentry had tinged the leading edges of its stubby wings dull red, coming near to using up whatever courage Krumm had brought along to the excursion. That, and a terrifying descent through a local thunderstorm, had consumed hours and had been nothing like the calm ride in a lubberlift, with its rigid, §-reinforced cabelle to absorb the vagaries and violence of planetary atmosphere.

"Wait for me, if you will," the boy had asked once they had set down in the empty, ruin-cluttered desert, "I shall not be long."

Krumm was glad of the outing, doubly glad it was to Somon, which did not remind him of the ordeals of his youth. He felt frustrated by his captain's reticence. What could he not be trusted to assist with? What secret of Henry Martyn's would he ever betray? As always, the boy was accompanied by a *nacyl*, over whose trailing end the first officer stumbled climbing from the lighter. "*By the Ceo's shorts*—pardon me askin', sir, what is this thing's name?"

He raised an eyebrow, glancing between his friends. "I fear neither of us could say it, as I should know who have given it my best. Clicks and whistles I gather even his own folk find difficult to pronounce."

"You don't say."

"That's the point. He rather fancies adopting a human name."

"And what might that be, sir?"

Henry Martyn grinned. "Phoebus."

The Burial Plain had been an obvious place for a rendezvous. Before too many minutes had seen them huddled against huge artificial stones which seemed to suck warmth from their bodies even more efficiently than wind and rain, another small craft, of obvious alien design vague with distance and weather, swooped out of the overcast and settled upon the mossy ground without disgorging passengers. It was at this point that Krumm had been asked to wait. Boy and alien made their way toward the other machine, the former stooping beneath its backswept wing, and, limned by its golden inner glow, climbed into its belly. Even a hundred measures away, through the whistle and spatter of the weather, Krumm could hear metal and plastic ticking as both vehicles cooled.

Time passed. After what seemed a long wait until Krumm glanced at his timepiece and learned better, Henry Martyn emerged with his *nacyl* companion, lingering to converse with something which resembled another animated bathing towel. Soon, enveloped, as it seemed to Krumm, in a glowing mist trailing off into evaporating tendrils—from reflex, Krumm raised one of his thrustibles in a gesture protective of his captain, realizing, as he did, how absurd it was—boy and flatsy strode and flowed respectively across the damp moss toward the monolith. Krumm had no idea what the light-filled fog was—had been, for now it had vanished. Henry Martyn waved from several measures away.

"I am quite uninjured. What you saw was no more than the residue of a harmless, beneficial virus. Do not be alarmed, good friend."

Krumm disobeyed this order. "A virus, sir?"

"Indeed, what we achieved centuries ago with rare metals and wafers of silicon—the *ulsic*—the *nacyl* undertook with microorganisms. It is their greatest accomplishment, more compact and portable than our contrivances. The virus replicate themselves, saving the necessity of manufacture."

"To what purpose, if I may ask, sir?"

"To what purposes do we put the *ulsic?* They can work cumulatively, combining their minute capabilities, or parallel, creating great calculatory engines, say for navigation. They can enthille and relay messages or be used directly over limited distance. This is the means by which the *nacyl* saved my life, having infected me whilst I was feeding them, because they liked me!"

Krumm shook his head, the idea of infecting one's friends with a virus being somewhat scandalizing, whatever its purpose. By now the boy walked beside him, *nacyl* following, as they approached the waiting lighter.

"One reason we are here is simply to catch up with the latest virus-borne gossip. I am afraid that must serve you for explanation. All will be made clear in the fullness of time. Meanwhile, wake our steersman, for we are free to depart, not only from this funereal planet, but the system it belongs to."

"To Skye, sir?"

"To Skye, sir. May whatever gods still linger in a universe long ago grown weary of them have mercy upon my enemies, for surely I shall not!"

When *Osprey* crossed the ill-defined margin of Sisao-Somon's cometary halo and stretched her figurative wings upon the empty reaches of the Deep, the weather proved no better than upon the Burial Plain. A neutrino storm was brewing, if Krumm was any judge, rare and ferocious, which would test the mettle of both starship and crew. It seemed to Krumm the captain was grateful for an excuse to take command, to issue orders in a harsh shout beginning to betray traces of his full-grown voice, to steer with his own hands the tiller-ball upon the quarterdeck, even to fling himself aloft with topmen to reef starsail and inspect rigging for worn cabelle which could spell death for them all, did the screaming hurricane of particles to which §-permeated mesh was not selectively transparent seize upon them in its mighty rage.

At present, Krumm rolled the tiller under his own broad palm. Two thirds of a klomme above the storm-slanted maindeck, Henry Martyn trod a footcabelle and clung to the outer tip of the dorsal foreyard, supporting himself by his armpits, edging toward a broken cleat upon which the dorsal forestaysail had snagged, cursing like the crewbeings behind him the necessity to do so, yet, inside himself, exulting in the fact that he possessed such strength and courage, as well as frequent opportunity of testing it.

Already the fringes of the storm lay hard upon them. Forward of the staysails, the margin lashed and billowed under the seething assault, throwing off globes of coruscation wherever its energies doubled over upon themselves. The starship heaved and pitched, her entire fabric shuddering in endless, only partially successful adjustment to the asymmetric stresses. The great mast of the *Osprey* dipped and swayed in a titanic figure eight. The yards swung with a peculiar complex rhythm of their own, thrashing against the standing rigging straining to hold them, carrying the crewbeings clutching at them in swooping, stomach-wrenching ellipses as they struggled for sanity and survival.

As he fought to clear and reef his portion of the twisted starsail, Henry Martyn kept a part of his attention upon the §-field chasing itself about the ship in an orgy of swirling color. More significance, he thought, lay in its pattern than could be accounted for by the storm, and he was right. As he bent the gaskets into place about the folded mesh and began edging inboard toward the comparative stability of the forecrotch, he heard a voice, pitiful and piping against the screaming energy of the storm. He could not quite make out the words, but hearing them was sufficient to confirm his judgment. *Osprey*'s course was being intersected by another starship.

He shouted against the storm, which seemed to gather strength with every second, ordering his topmen to the mast, but reversed himself until he clung again to the outer extremity of the yard. Seizing a shroud running parallel to a great diagonal staysail which spanned the gulf between dorsal foreyard and maintier, he leapt from the yard, mindful of the now unstable §-field margin, and, twining the shroud about one leg, let it pass through his hands. He fell swiftly aft to the outboard end of the starboard mainyard. A similar route took him to the crotch of the mizzentier, where he climbed the more conventional ratlines to Krumm's side upon the quarterdeck. Shielding his eyes against explosions of light, he peered aloft, shouting at the giant struggling with the tiller-ball. "Where away, Mr. Krumm?"

The man shook his shaggy head, never taking his eyes from the binnacle, stooping as he watched to shout into the captain's ear. "No tellin', sir! Nor who or what she be! 'Nough trouble upon our hands as is!"

Staggering against a sudden lurch of the deck, Henry Martyn nodded exaggeratedly so that Krumm could see it in his peripheral vision. "I would be pleased to hear you call General Quarters, Mr. Krumm." Krumm's head turned against his will. He stared at the boy, openmouthed. "If you will."

"Aye, sir. Mr. Willis, call General Quarters!"

Throughout the already embattled starship, alarms struggled against the overwhelming noise of the storm as crewbeings, looking about at one another in stunned disbelief, appeared at their appointed stations. Ordering those in charge upon the several gundecks, mostly his canny *seporth* projecteurs, to thrust when they found something to thrust at, Henry Martyn determined to remain upon the quarterdeck, requesting Mr. Krumm to stay beside him. Both allowed themselves preparatory glances at their personal thrustibles and at once returned their attention to management of the *Osprey*.

Nor were they a moment too soon. The corsair reeled under another sort of onslaught as the impact of projectibles was felt everywhere throughout her. Rigging, mast, and spars held through the pounding. They had been stripped and reinforced before the storm. It was soon apparent from the pattern and direction of the kinergic thrusts that *Osprey* had more than one pursuer.

"Four'd be me guess, sir, 'less it's fewer ships better projectibled. 'Pears they chose t'spring their trap a mite earlier than we reckoned."

Henry Martyn shook his head, weary of the need to shout each word. "We have it yet to arrive at the trap, Mr. Krumm. Someone jumped the queue, likeliest that *Skerry* two-decker. By the Ceo's bright blue balls, we shall make that rapespawn Sullers-Masen pay the price of impatience!"

The corsair's many projectibles began speaking for themselves, following his standing order to anticipate, when possible, the enemy thrusting and meet his energy with theirs, so that the annihilations might do greater damage than kinergic power alone. This time, they were only partly successful, although the unseen enemy's rhythm became disturbed and erratic and his rate seemed to fall off. Being a hundred klommes aft of the *Osprey,* they were only beginning to appreciate the full intensity of the weather. A runner, unable to push his small voice past the double fury of neutrino storm and battle, tugged diffidently at the captain's tunic. Henry Martyn turned. Being scarcely more than a boy himself, and slight of stature into the bargain, he did not have to bend far to place the boy's mouth at his ear.

"C-compliments of the liftdeck chief projecteur, sir. We've damage to the lift and stern chasers. Two functional, one out of it altogether."

"And the crewbeings?"

"Seventeen dead, sir, as I was sent forward, wounded as yet uncounted. Chief's a replacement, himself, sir. Travis, the cook's helper."

Henry Martyn set his mouth in a grim line. The pursuers imitated his use of heavy bow chasers, hanging aft of *Osprey* where he might not bring as many projectibles to bear. As he opened his mouth to reply, she lurched in a manner telling him she had taken another deadly blow.

"Very good, Mr. Nolan. Compliments to Mr. Travis. If he lives, he may consider himself warranted. Inform him and the other chief projecteurs upon your way aft that they will have targets soon enough. Now get you below."

The boy stepped back and saluted. His captain could only see him mouth his next words. "Aye, aye, sir."

Henry Martyn turned to Krumm who had spared half an eye for the previous conversation. "Alert all hands aloft, Mr. Krumm. I want the starboard forestaysail loosed, also the port mizzensail, after which they will have to look to their lives. We shall veer and wallow and, if lucky, end up full aback. But we shall get in some thrusting as our main projectibles bear! I shall summon the watch officer myself to assemble a boarding party."

Krumm grinned. "Aye, you want her figurehead among his mainyards?"

Henry Martyn nodded. "Pick us a good fight, Krumm, to the Ceo with the tariff. Choose the largest of our foe. Let her run full upon us. And mind, as she murders us, that you ruin her for life!"

Chapter XLIII:
Battlestorm

"Steady, now!"

Braced with a motley dozen crewbeings upon the narrow platform at the maintier crotch, Henry Martyn awaited the collision. *Osprey*'s projectiles had already spoken to good effect, delivering themselves of a full, rotating broadside before the corsair swung onto a course opposing that of her pursuers and could, before the coming impact, use only her bow chasers.

The captain had made an everyday habit of carrying a second thrustible. He chose now for his boarding party only crewbeings adept at fighting with two weapons (while entertaining certain doubts about his own skills upon this score). He had decided upon the maintier as their jump-off, having evacuated all riggers and topmen from the mast and yards further forward, calculating that little of the structure above was likely to survive catastrophe. In truth, he would be lucky not to drive the mast through the *Osprey*'s hull, spitting her like a homelier fowl about to be roasted.

For once he was unaccompanied by one of the *nacyl* who ordinarily took turns as his advisor, liaison with the other flatsies through the medium of the virus with which they were infected, and something of an extra shadow in Krumm's stated opinion. The creatures were, by virtue of their odd anatomies, unsuited to the rigors of combat. The young captain felt it a shame that his first officer (and wives) were ill disposed toward the aliens. This was one reason for keeping that stalwart ignorant regarding his overall strategy. Nor were any of his comrades of the moment *seporth,* the rollerballers' mass being too great to survive the initial stages of his plan.

Three of the attacking vessels, whoever they had been, were well out of the fight, the struggle between *Osprey* and what he presumed was the frigate *Skerry* having swept beyond them. By the time they returned, as they surely would, the issue would be settled. Had it not been for the neutrino storm still raging all about them in undiminished strength, he would have put auxiliaries off to seize those vessels as prizes. He would still do so, given a chance, if only to pay the bill for this fight and make up to his crew for opportunities they would lose should this endeavor prove successful and they continued to moonringed Skye.

Henry Martyn peered aloft, shading his eyes against the storm-glare. Even with all starsail taken in it was difficult to see forward. Before he was quite aware of the distortion it created, the §-fields of both vessels coalesced and the yards and rigging of each began to tear themselves apart upon those of the other. The racket was unbearable. Both masts groaned, sending a horrible shudder into the hulls of their respective ships, crumpling like foil tubes into their own lengths as foreyards and mainyards tore loose or were smashed from their crotches like the branches of saplings. Standing and running cabelles, loaded far beyond their capacities, tightened with a dissonant thrum into rigid bars, stretched with heartrending screams and let go, free ends lashing about the mast like deadly whips, trailing sparks where they struck the §-margin.

Somehow the young star-raider and his boarding party survived, clinging to the shivering mast, waiting until both vessels ground themselves to a mutually destructive halt. Fragments of rigging and other objects, including several bodies, plummeted past them, whistling in funereal warning as the frigate—being larger and carrying more starsail upon her mizzenyards than the *Osprey*'s officers had thought well advised in the teeth of the storm—pushed the double tangle of wreckage along, reversing the influence of acceleration onboard the corsair. Following his own advice, Krumm had ordered the maindeck crew to tie themselves to every cleat and bollard they could find.

Taking ragged breath, Henry Martyn arose and, without further preparation, flung himself from the platform, spread weapon-heavy arms, and free-fell three hundred measures toward the frigate's triangular port mizzensail, tucking himself into a ball at the last moment to land upon his back, hoping the expanse of sailmesh would hold him lest he break through and incinerate himself upon the after portion of the §-field.

The mizzensail held. Having finished half a dozen diminishing rebounds, and without waiting for his companions, but desiring to get out of their way as they, too, alighted, he scrambled awkwardly toward the crotch of the maintier and down the shrouds to the maindeck. He and his fellows were confronted there, as expected, by a well-armed repelling party. At their head was Ballygrant Bowmore.

The former captain of the *Gyrfalcon* raised an arm in the salute of death, protecting his torso with the secondary field about the axis of his thrustible. Even without the eyelid stitched over his grotesque empty socket and the accompanying scar along one dark cheek, Bowmore's nasal, rasp-edged voice would have been all too familiar. "We meet again, Master Islay. Rather sooner than you expected, I would imagine!"

The ring upon his one pierced ear glittered in the stormlight. Here was an individual who experienced no difficulty making himself heard above the neutrinos' wail. Disdaining his enemy's salute, Henry Martyn put a hand into his coverall pocket, grinning at the man with long, gray, stiff-braided hair in dozens of polished metal stops.

"Boatswain Ballygrant! More appropriate than I might have dreamed! Days ago, I paid a visit to this vessel's captain during which, never being one to discard anything useful, I took pains to conceal aboard her the explosive you attempted to use against the *Peregrine*."

He removed the hand and held up a small squarish object. "As you recall, this is your remote, now rigged in such a manner that, should I release it, these ships and everyone aboard will be blown into incandescence. Give it up. Take off your weapons and advise Sullers-Masen to surrender."

"I have no need of such advice, lad!" A tall, deep-voiced man with only a pair of metal-studded braids to boast of, hanging past a heavy jeweled choker down his naked chest, had just arrived from the quarterdeck and now stood, with a degree of obvious reluctance, beside Bowmore. "I agreed to help," he told the man, "after we pulled you from the Deep, because this young fellow refused to join our Council, declaring himself outlaw among outlaws. I think better of it now. What is the universe coming to? He can destroy my starship with that little thing?"

The murchan shook his head. "What it controls. But not before I've settled him personally!" He cast off his deck-length cloak with its furred collar and edging. A look of horror and denial crept across the frigate captain's features.

"Madness! Better to lose a battle, even a ship, than all our lives! I shall of course surrender, Captain Martyn, what are your terms, sir?"

Henry Martyn grinned again and turned to climb back up to his own vessel. "The best I can afford to give, sir, I assure you. And that, my former captain," he offered to Bowmore, turning to face him a moment, "settles that!"

Bowmore sprang forward in pursuit. "No you don't!"

"No, Captain—" Sullers-Masen attempted to interpose himself.

"Stand aside," cried the murchan, pushing at him. At Henry Martyn he shouted, "Wait! You will not take leave of this ship while I live!"

The young captain hurled himself back to the frigate's maindeck. "Then I shall take it when you are dead!"

Bowmore ripped at the jeweled studs of his billowing, throat-ruffled blouse until he wore only thrustibles, loose-fitting trousers, and knee-high, exotic-leathered boots. His breathing was already furious, from anger rather than exertion. The two rushed together, ready to kill or be killed, but again Sullers-Masen was between them, pleading. "There is no shame in surrender, Captain! The issue has been honorably settled!"

His companion sneered. "It has not been settled for me!"

"But what is one child more or less? Do not be a fool, Captain!"

Again Bowmore pushed him aside. "It is my affair!"

The Skyan boy had stood by, watching and listening. He was, however, ready when Bowmore charged, thrustible leveled at his chest.

Flash! With a casual sweep, Henry Martyn parried the murchan's enraged and desperate thrust, dodging down and to the left, the deadman's switch in his left hand preventing him from using that thrustible. It was obvious that

Bowmore had forgotten his own second weapon as he slashed downward, attempting to follow his elusive quarry's motion, but—

Flash! Bowmore's second thrust was short, trailing sparks across the smoking deckmesh, missing its intended target by a measure. The two combatants disengaged, guards dropped for a moment, both breathing heavily.

"Twice," the boy asserted, "your life was given back to you. This time you should be hauled to Skye. It is what I intended in the end. But since you prefer it this way, rapespawn, then I shall humor you!"

Again they found themselves *en garde,* engaged in what both knew was a struggle of life or death. Beam flashed upon kinergic beam, rocking the deck with explosions, as each thrust was hurled and answered by opposing thrust, once, twice, five times, ten times. Henry Martyn broke off and leapt forward, colliding with Bowmore, pressing his glowing axis to the man's sweat-trickled throat. Bowmore somehow insinuated an arm beneath it, also slippery with sweat, levered the boy backward, and parried a bolt hurled at him. Before they could disengage, Bowmore slashed out, Henry Martyn countering while edging round and sideways. Neither having intended it, they had exchanged positions. Bowmore's back was to the mast.

His adversary slashed and ducked. The murchan chopped an answer, Henry Martyn thrusting the same instant. Bowmore fell back, losing ground. Henry Martyn lunged, attempting—perhaps foolishly—to grapple with the larger man again. Spine pressed against the mast, Bowmore ducked. He and the boy were, for a moment, locked together, shoulder over shoulder. Both took a breath and the *Gyrfalcon's* former master ducked from under, reversed, and laughed aloud, crewbeings of both vessels muttering excitedly without regard to whose side was whose. A ball of fire exploded aloft, the storm, as if jealous, reasserting itself.

With a shout, Henry Martyn leapt forward. Again the fighters, clumsy with fatigue, chopped at one another, both nearing exhaustion, every thought of martial artistry and warrior's finesse long vanished. With nothing more than sheer ferocity, Henry Martyn drove Bowmore backward down the meshing to the break of the quarterdeck. Bowmore suffered a fall, again reversing the field as he rolled to his feet. Wary, they circled one another, exchanging positions once more.

The older man backed up and paused. Feeling an obstruction behind him, he put a foot upon a hatch cover and in an instant was looking down at his opponent from the height of half a measure. Breathing hard and streaming perspiration, he continued to retreat across the hatch as the shouting all about him increased in pitch and volume.

Sweat running into his own eyes, Henry Martyn leapt onto the hatch and, almost by reflex, exchanged a short salute with the man, flash following flash like an exercise in the formal *salon* of death-dealing which neither had ever attended. They exchanged the salute again, both transformed and somehow beautiful in motion, a long rhythmic series this time, until, having retreated too far, Bowmore fell backward off the hatch, landing upon a coiled cabelle.

Not pressing his advantage, a breathless, panting Henry Martyn gestured. "Up!" Half-blind with fatigue, faces wet as if they had been swimming, they grinned, almost one comrade to another. Bowmore rose, siemme by siemme.

The boy leapt from the hatch, parrying thrust after thrust, flash after brilliant flash, driving the man backward until the axes of their thrustibles jammed upon one another, throwing sparks which singed their clothing and, though neither noticed, burnt their skin. They crashed, face to face, eyes locked, the carrack master's broken, double-baubled nose no more than a siemme from Henry Martyn's. The grin was one of strain now, brute exertion against brute exertion. With greater strength than any larger adversary might expect, Henry Martyn pushed Bowmore backward by gradual degrees forcing the man to retreat to fighting distance, thrust, and thrust again.

Another series of blinding multiple flashes filled the air between them, Bowmore now decidedly upon the defensive. Henry Martyn fell this time, struggling to retain his sweaty grasp upon the slippery remote in his left hand. Unlike his opponent, the master-murchan leaned in hard to make the best advantage of it, but Henry Martyn raised his weapon to meet the murchan's. Their gleaming axes collided once again, showering both with brilliant, painful motes of energy, echoing in miniature the fury of the storm still raging round them, almost forgotten, as they fought. An infinitesimal pause. The look which passed between them was one of recognition and of parting, as if each, being at the end of his capacity and resigned to oblivion, realized that only one would walk away from this and live again. The moment ended. Again they hacked at one another.

Bowmore's arm shot forward as if he could augment his thrustible's energy with muscle power. He was answered with an upraised axis. Their weapons clashed a final time. Still upon his back, Henry Martyn forced Bowmore to retreat and arose by sheer strength and determination, launching an immediate attack of his own, a single, slashing thrust. Its object parried, countering with a blur of weary overhand flailing. Henry Martyn, also long since exhausted, parried and flailed himself, wide of the mark, as Bowmore backed away another step.

This time, as Bowmore attacked, Henry Martyn ducked inside his guard, crouching to the deck. He rose and let Bowmore's momentum take him past, turned, and jabbed him in the back with his thrustible, delivering the weapon's full power into the man's kidney. The breathless victor backed away three steps. Bowmore fell to the deck, his eye already glazing, his wide, cruel mouth silenced forever.

"And that, my friend, ends a policy of repeated mercies which should never have begun!" Aware, of a sudden, that he still held the remote in his left hand, he overrode the setting and tossed it into the §-field. It struck with a flash and crackle and disappeared. Speaking to Sullers-Masen, he pointed a weapon-heavy hand toward the object which had been Bowmore. "Get that trash cleared away!"

CHAPTER XLIV:
RETURN TO SKYE

It was a small room. Owing to its shape and the peculiar manner in which it had been decorated, its dimensions were difficult for her to determine. Approximating a circle with a low, domed ceiling, all of its surfaces had been carpeted (if that was the word; "upholstered" came to mind) in light-swallowing black, floor, ceiling, and walls flowing into one another indistinguishably.

Aside from two reclining chairs, low-backed in defiance of the current mode, and a knee-height glass-topped table, the only other feature was a waist-high shelf, carpeted like the walls, running about the room's circumference, including a door which all but disappeared when it was closed. Upon the shelf, with scarcely a siemme between them, stood thille-readers fashioned by the hands of more than a hundred worlds. Above each, hovering against faultless blackness, hung an image, a scene from the surface of one of the millions of planets which comprised the Monopolity.

"Come, Mistress Daimler-Wilkinson," a deep-voiced man spoke, each syllable flat and final in the anechoic chamber, responding to a look of disapproval lying upon her pretty face. "Havin' endured uncountable difficulties and delays, havin' outwitted stolid guards, influence-peddlin' secretaries, all eunuchs of varyin' degrees of literality, to return without your uncle's knowledge, in contravention of his wishes—as well as against my specific orders—you didn't expect to find me a closet egalitarian. You didn't expect me to retire from what our ancestors more frankly termed the 'Bore 'Droom,' to some humble, cluttered office somewhere, to slip out of my finery with a sigh of relief and assume the attire of someone below my station. Or p'raps loll about *au naturel?* I'm the *Ceo,* girl. I enjoy being what I was brought up to be since birth."

After the effort which had brought her, she found she was unable to speak a coherent word, let alone as she had planned. He chuckled, drawing her to a chair, taking the other himself. "You want something, that's clear enough. To you, the power and wealth at my disposal appear infinite, although no one knows better than I their too real limits. I don't blame you, you could hardly feel otherwise, or for wantin' something from the fellow possessing them. Everybody does. I've grown used to it and make allowances."

"Sir, I—"

"You realize, of course, that nothin' is free. I'll want something from you in return—*oh, dear me, child, no!* Not that."

She let her breath out, relieved, but knowing she would have paid that price or any other to obtain what she sought. Having waited too long to decide for the man she loved, it might now be too late to interfere in the trap being laid for him. Having reached her decision, she was discovering herself as unstoppable in its execution as the implacable Henry Martyn.

The Ceo shook his head. "What d'you think I am—don't answer that! Instead, think a moment: I'm the Leupould IX, Ceo of the grandest imperium-conglomerate in the history of the galaxy, in effect the absolute ruler of something like a million systems, with subjects numberin' in the quintillions." He lifted a hand and let it drop to the arm of his chair. "You're an exquisitely beautiful child, without doubt. And I'm a man with a man's tastes, increasingly rare upon this planet. But if I accepted a billionth of the fleshy offers coming my way, I should be a wrinkled old prune like my esteemed colleague Ribauldequin!"

Not knowing what reply to offer, Loreanna, in her wisdom, offered none. She was curious to know how those who plotted, like her uncle, to sway or distract men of power with the lure of sex would take hearing that they—at least Leupould—regarded it as an occupational hazard, foremost a threat to their physical well-being. Having arrived upon the capital world, she was reminded all over again, by observing contrasts between shipboard life and the audience she had just quitted, how such eloquently spoken, overly dressed, cleverly masqued, and terribly good-mannered creatures had planned to use her with what amounted to far greater brutality than ever Henry Martyn had.

"No, my dear, what I want from you, I already have. My luxury, my satisfaction, lies in something which you, lackin' my disadvantages, have never had to value. What I hunger after is reliable knowledge. I struggle after it every day, as my most impoverished subject struggles after bread."

"Sir?"

"D'you not understand? I know what you want and why you want it!" A single antique reader stood upon the glass table between them. He activated a thille within it. Into life sprang another planetary scene, a flower-dotted meadow and blue forest against a backdrop of mountain peaks. Behind them a misty ribbon of silver arched across the great bowl of the heavens. "Somewhat outdated, I fear. They've built a shanty settlement in yon pasture."

Despite this news, Loreanna brightened. "I understand," she responded. "You have no hidden intentions to worry about upon my part?"

The Ceo bobbed his great head with enthusiasm. "Let me tell you it's a relief, a precious moment in which I feel free to relax a trifle. If I didn't—if it weren't—you and I shouldn't be here, most of my time and effort, you see, bein' spent in an attempt, not entirely successful, to determine those very things of people I've no choice but to deal with."

Loreanna nodded, feeling something like sympathy for this great man who was never certain he was hearing the truth— or words of genuine friendship. Thus she was able to tell him, in as brief and simple a manner as she found possible, all which had befallen her and what she had learned concerning Tarbert Morven, Skye, and Henry Martyn. Finishing, she glanced up from her lap to discover Leupould peering at her.

"Mistress Loreanna, you're about to find, perhaps to your consternation, given the time and effort you yourself have recently expended, that you hadn't much to tell your Ceo of your circumstances, or those of Henry Martyn or his planet —what was its name, Skye, wasn't it?—that he didn't already know." Again Loreanna nodded, meekly. Leupould surprised her by throwing back his head and bursting into laughter. "You truly hope that what I claim is true, don't you?

Thrust me, I'm disposed to help you at that! But you must forgive me. I was compelled to give in, just once more, to a lifelong habit of double-checking to see what guilty look a casual remark may provoke."

"I . . . I am most sorry, sir . . ."

The Ceo laughed again. "See here: one confidence, however involuntary upon your part, deserves another. I fear my hesitancy over the name of Henry Martyn's planet was another deception. I am familiar with its situation for the best of reasons. Unknown to anyone else upon Skye, or Hanover for that matter, an individual there has long served as my personal eyes and ears."

"Mistress Lia Woodgate!" It was the Ceo's turn for surprise. The words burst out against her will and better judgment.

"Great Expulsion, how d'you reckon that?"

She had to clear her throat before explaining. "A cultured Hanoverian girl with more comfortable prospects here, off on the raw frontier ostensibly tutoring the sons of a countrified Drector you yourself created, one hated, albeit unknowingly, by one of the Monopolity's most powerful figures?"

Leupould blew a considerable volume of air through his nostrils.

"Who else," she nodded at the table, "could have enthilled that scene?"

"Well," Leupould answered, "one hopes it isn't that obvious to others. It helps, in that regard, that her sympathies are genuinely and entirely with the Skyans. Mistrustful of the reports of 'disinterested' observers, I make appropriate allowance to balance any bias she may manifest."

"You find that easier," Loreanna ventured her new understanding, "than constantly wondering where her true desires and loyalties might lie?"

The Ceo inclined his head. "I trust that this arrangement meets with your unalloyed approval?" Loreanna blushed. "What you've no way of knowin' (it is to be hoped!) is that Lia's also my daughter, upon the wrong side of the blanket as the sayin' goes, and entirely unaware of her parentage. The confidence I place in you is something you may not appreciate until you're older. She's not the only such child I own to, but the onliest I care for. I tell you so you'll understand my personal concern for what happens upon Skye."

"Sir, I do not know what to say . . ."

"Say nothing, ever, of what I've told you. The point is that Lia, fully as indomitable as the Ceo she serves, kept report-in' secretly to me through all her personal tribulations. Until recently. Despairin' of greater satisfaction than revenge, it was her hope that, despite the part she believed I played in the Usurpation, Morven's excesses would not go unpunished."

"Henry Martyn believed you did approve the Usurpation and told me so."

"Say rather, Loreanna, that Leupould of Hanover is not the incompetent fool his Jendyne opposite, Ribauldequin, appears to be. I often suspect even he merely finds it advantageous to cultivate such an impression. He may, in fact, be among the shrewdest power-managers in the galaxy. Say, rather, that I am one who, never bein' certain whom to trust, allows his underlings opportunity to betray their real sympathies and motivations."

"At the cost of how many innocent lives?"

"Among how many quintillions?"

"I have heard this argument before, sir. It is my conviction that each sapient life is unique—the product of unrepeatable combinations and permutations of heredity, experience, and free will—and therefore not properly subject to the Law of Marginal Utility."

Leupould smiled. "Now you know, my dear, why I regard your uncle with respect and affection. He's not afraid to argue with me, either."

Loreanna was taken aback. "Argue? I was arguing with the—"

Laughter: "It runs in the family. Now, since I've no need for more detail of what's happened upon Skye, and since you are uncommonly reticent regardin' time you spent with the notorious Henry Martyn, what further observations have you to offer, pertinent to the circumstances?"

Loreanna gave it thought. "Only that this arrangement between you and your—Mistress Woodgate, more than any skill or passion upon my part—"

"I assure you, those qualities were far from ineffective in your cause."

"Thank you, sir—I think. I was about to say that it explains my relatively easy access to an otherwise notoriously inaccessible—"

"Not altogether, my dear." A section of the carpeted wall, not that through which they had come, swung aside.

"Uncle!"

"Please forgive me," he told her, "for eavesdropping. My reasons for doing so were two in number. The first is that the Ceo and I have a problem. Our protégé, Morven, is becoming something of an embarrassment, being responsible, among other transgressions, for having sparked the legend of Henry Martyn. You have only confirmed what we had deduced in that regard."

"That may be the noblest of Morven's accomplishments," the Ceo nodded, "I rather fancy pirates." Daimler-Wilkinson gave his sovereign a look complaining that the man could well afford to fancy them, having others to clean up the messes they made. The Ceo laughed.

"And the second?" Loreanna asked her uncle.

"The second—oh!" A look of infinite sadness crossed his features. "Why yes. It would seem, in light of the Law of Marginal Utility, that I have dealt an inexpressible injustice to the 'onliest' individual I care for. I had to see how well she had survived the consequence, whether any possibility exists that she might someday find it in her heart—" Loreanna opened her mouth. "Say nothing," her uncle interrupted, "until I have found a way to make amends. I shall begin by paying an older debt, telling you the truth, however painful it may be, regarding the fates of your mother and father."

The Ceo put up a hand. "Tell her later. And don't be surprised but what she knows already. This is quite touchin', but if we're to avoid accrual of even more debt, we've scant time to put you aboard your ship, Sedgeley."

Loreanna turned to look at Leupould. "Aboard a starship?"

"Why yes, my dear," her uncle answered for his sovereign, "a punitive flotilla the Ceo is about to dispatch to troubled Skye."

* * *

"How were you able to make your way down here unde-tected?"

It was a weary young captain who, when battle and storm were ended, had seen to the repair of the *Osprey* using spars and cabelles salvaged from four other drifting and disabled vessels. Mixing his own crewbeings among theirs, as was his habit, with orders to return the prizes to Sisao and Somon as best they could, in due course he reached Skye. Passing himself as a construction foreman, with the name of Captain Bowmore as reference, he transferred to a murchan-vessel standing in synchronous orbit, and with a gang of common laborers, lubberlifted surfaceward. Travel from the equator northward had been similarly contrived. He peered up from the dirty, drink-ringed surface of the table at which he sat, through a layer of smoke, hanging at eye level, which dimmed the already burdened atmosphere within *The Wasted Corsair*.

"Strange greeting, after more than two years, Donol."

A man with thinning hair, wearing expensive clothing in the latest style of Hanover, stood backlighted against the fuzzy globes hanging from the rafters. "Forgive me, Arran. It was a shock learning otherwise when I had thought you dead all this time." He gave him a crooked half smile. "And other preoccupations prey upon my mind."

He sat without asking, continuing conversation only after a dirty-aproned wench had departed with their order. Amidst mindless noise and a dense forest of human forms, still for the most part farmers and herdsmen, although the place never gave up its pretense of being a spaceman's bar, soldiers and officers of the Holdings guard enjoyed the fleshpots, rendered equal in rank and identity by the bleary, smoke-filtered illumination. Prey to his own preoccupations, the younger brother nodded understanding as the elder spoke.

"It would be good seeing you, Arran, were it not so dangerous. You do not want to hear you have grown a measure and become a man into the bargain."

Arran looked about him at the drifting wreckage of human-ity crowding them shoulder to shoulder, animated, to appear-ances, only by the force of their own raucous laughter, amidst stenches of excreta, decaying garbage, unwashed bod-ies, and enthilled blaring someone had mistaken for music. "Growing up is not the most enjoyable of processes, but one can be proud of having survived it. You appear to have survived. And prospered."

Donol shrugged. "For one supposed to be no more than a prisoner, learning all he might from the enemy? I assure you, Arran, any privilege I have earned I regard as a trophy, a measure of my effectiveness as a spy. And any damage my reputation suffers upon that account is not only a necessary sacrifice in our behalf, but a species of protection."

Arran grinned unpleasantly. "I see. What have you managed to learn?"

Again Donol shrugged. "Everyday matters of tactical import, movements, shipments, which I used to pass to Robret and which I now share with Lia, who has astonished everyone by becoming our unquestioned leader. And Fionaleigh Savage, who represents her in the field." He edged closer to Arran, lowering his voice. "The one strategic fact I have concerns an alien philosopher—and a device he has offered Morven, capable of enslaving an entire planet."

He took pains to explain in detail, to Arran's evident growing alarm, underlining the threat they represented, not only to Skyans but perhaps the entire Monopolity. He described the false rendezvous with the alien which had resulted in Robret's capture, with certain convenient emendations.

"The Black Usurper has lately received the actual instrumentality, Arran. He required considerable practice to become proficient, but is about to make use of it now. It is his most closely cherished secret I have managed to ferret out. Now, are you going to tell me how you got here?"

Arran looked at him across the rim of his caffcup. "Is it important?"

"No one among the Hanoverians, none of their vaunted equipment, detected your arrival, Arran. I did not know of it until you sent word through the gardener. We have great need of the ability to come and go undetected."

The younger man raised his eyebrows. "We?"

Donol nodded. "Us—the resistance."

Arran chuckled. "I see. What if you should be captured and tortured? Would the method not then be useless?"

His brother's face reddened and his voice became a hiss. "It is useless now if we remain ignorant of it! You are being obtuse, Arran!"

"I am being cautious. But what difference does it make if a man cannot trust his own brother? I hove to in polar orbit, which Hanoverian defenses are not well suited to detect. It is somewhat like that natural tendency upon which certain predators depend of their prey to be wary of every direction but *up*. I had the lubberlift modified and lowered halfway into the atmosphere, whereupon it released an unpowered aerostat which I piloted the rest of the way. Are you satisfied?"

Donol nodded, licking his lips. "More than satisfied, Arran." As Morven would be, he thought, once informed of this weakness in his defense. Nor had the possible implication, that Arran was alone upon Skye, escaped him. "Is it a large fleet you have brought with you?"

"You are full of questions."

"And you of suspicion and evasion. I only wished to know how soon we might throw ourselves against the Usurper. Forget that I asked."

Evincing world-weary regret that frankness, even between kinsmen, had become so difficult, Arran shook his head and placed a hand over his brother's. "No, it is only right that you be informed. It will be necessary to wait a while. I have been long out of touch and will need to learn much before I act. I only brought the one starship, my corsair *Osprey,* which I afterward sent away into the Deep to await prearranged rendezvous."

Donol smiled. "How gratifying that my baby brother, thrown upon his own resources, has in so short a time become not a mere captain or fleet commander, but famous throughout the Monopolity." He stood. "I hope Old Henry appreciates the honor, as I hope you appreciate the attention you are about to receive upon account of it. Guard! Arrest this man at once! Look to your weapons, he is the infamous starshiprobber, Henry Martyn!"

"I believe we can do better than that!"

Donol whirled. "Drector-Protempore!"

It was indeed the Black Usurper who stood behind him, free of his wheeled chair, flanked by Oplytes and a pair of

human officers, thrustibles at the ready. Before Henry
Martyn could lift his arm from beneath the table, Morven
raised a peculiar object, consisting of a pair of upright,
translucent cylinders seething with light deep at their centers,
fist-sized, connected at one end by a handle and at their other
by an arc of heavy wire which bore at its center a small
parabolic dish. The air pulsed between Henry Martyn and the
device as the light inside the cylinders boiled with increased
fury. He sat unmoving, body rigid, face contorted with agony.
Morven relaxed his grip and his victim's shoulders dropped.
Henry Martyn sighed, his eyes unlit by expression or intelligence. The room had fallen into silence, a few prudent figures
near its edges using the distraction to slip away unnoticed.

"You will arise and go with my soldiers, Arran Islay, doing
everything bidden." Morven turned to one of his officers.
"Take his weapons."

Henry Martyn's chair made a scraping noise in the disconcerting quiet. Offering no resistance, he allowed himself to be
disarmed.

"Alert my technicians. Tell them to sharpen their wits as
well as their probes. I wish this to last many days." He turned
to Donol, holding up the device. "Not that there is anything
we cannot now learn by more sophisticated means. You have
done well, young man. I apologize for surprising you. I
wanted to try this with the most recalcitrant subject I could
imagine. You have earned a reward. Would you care to be
present beside me in the dungeon?"

A smile split Donol's face. "I have looked forward to it a
long time, sir. I mean to enjoy every minute!"

CHAPTER XLV:
THE EXECUTOR-GENERAL

Outsized boots trod the graniplastic flagging.

"I should like," the Black Usurper declared to the small party accompanying him, "to determine how aware of their surroundings subjects remain under influence of this device."

He held up the object with which he had so easily made Henry Martyn prisoner. The twin cylinders, with their swirling interior glow, could have lit the way along this corridor. The parabolic dish cast leering shadows. Receiving no reaction from his companions—Donol, two human officers, half a dozen Oplytes they commanded, and Henry Martyn himself, blank-eyed and obedient—Morven shrugged. He was in too good a mood to permit this occasion to be spoiled. What he had, at so much trouble and expense, accomplished with his daughter over many years, he was about to inflict upon whole worlds in a figurative instant. He supposed that what he felt was glee.

"For example," he mused, "would the young man hear if I were to tell him that this very room—Lieutenant, stop here—is the same in which his late father was tortured to death?"

Even with the most modern environmental controls Morven had imported, the room was cold. Condensation formed and dripped upon the smooth walls. The only reaction he received was that Donol dropped his gaze and swallowed. His brother appeared unaffected by the news. Without word or sign, he simply lay upon the operating table as instructed.

"Where the Ceo are my technicians? They are never here when I need them! They were ordered to meet me here! By the Ceo, I shall strap one or two of their number down and see whether it improves their—what is it now?" A member of his office staff had appeared in the still-open door.

"Sir, a message has arrived by lasercom from Alysabethport! A military flotilla has taken orbit, under command of the Executor-General! Troops have lubberlifted down and §-flyers are reported upon their way this minute!"

Morven stared. *What?*

"Sir, a military flotilla has—"

He waved a hand. "I heard you! What could the fool want?"

The nervous administrator swallowed, answering the question Morven had asked of himself. "I am afraid I really could not say—"

"Get back upstairs and say whatever you are *not* afraid to say! Find out what they want. Stall them! I shall join you directly."

As the fortunate clerk escaped, Morven turned to one of his officers. "Captain, take your warriors to my apartments. Collect my daughter along the way and see that she is well protected. Lieutenant, guard this prisoner—from outside influences, as I doubt he is inclined to run. Donol, stay with him." He held up the alien device. "I will deal with this interruption and return as quickly as I can, do you understand?"

Donol gulped. "Yes, sir."

"It should not take long. We shall lock this door behind us." With these words, and a mechanical clash, he left them.

Self-conscious silence descended over the pair, broken only by a rumble of activity overhead, their own breathing, and dripping along the walls. The officer paced, hands at his back, bouncing upon his toes, essaying a half-mute whistle and thinking better of it, looking from Donol to the figure lying upon the table. At last, he bent over the unconscious form. "The infamous star-raider Henry Martyn, eh? Why, he's no more than a kid! All the same, hadn't we better truss the little bugger up, just to be on the safe side?"

Donol opened his mouth. "The Drector-Protempore—"

A hard fist spread the lieutenant's nose across his cheek and deprived him of consciousness. Deft fingers upon his forearm deprived him of his weapon. A boot heel upon his larynx deprived him of further concerns.

"*Arran!*" Donol screamed the name.

Animated more by fury than by strength, Henry Martyn sprang across the room, seized his older brother by the throat, and pinned him to the wall, his other hand holding the lens of the thrustible within a millimeasure of the bridge of Donol's nose. "Where is Lia? You have three seconds! *One! Two!*"

Donol choked, "Your old room in the tower! I beg you, Arran—"

Keeping his weapon steady, the brigand made rapid search of his brother's clothing. "No key. It is a print lock. Must I drag you there—" he showed teeth, "—or can I just lop off your treacherous hand and take it with me?"

Donol's answer was another scream. "An override thille in a niche beside the door! I swear! But what good is it? We are locked in!"

Henry Martyn released him. Donol sagged against the wall, held up by friction alone. *"You* are locked in, Donol. If you have lied to me, I shall take pleasure doing to you what I just did to Morven's toy soldier!"

He turned and ran a hand along the seam between two graniplastic blocks beside the door. Having played in these chambers as a child, he knew their every secret, few of which he had ever shared with the adults of his family. This knowledge had been crucial in his decision to return to Skye. A loud click sounded and a section of the wall swung aside. Without another word to his brother, he slipped through, letting it swing shut behind him. A louder click persuaded Donol there was little hope of repeating Arran's escape. In this he was proven correct all too quickly, for, cautiously glancing one way down the secret passageway he entered, Henry Martyn just missed a shadowy figure which took his place with Donol in the dungeon.

Remaining as much as possible within a network of hidden passages he had explored as a boy, in the end he had no choice but to abandon it where it was interrupted by some ancient effort at remodeling. Planning to reenter a few measures away, down a well-traveled corridor, he was appropriately cautious. Approaching a right-hand bend, thrustible ready, he clung to the wall, keeping movements quiet, scraping his back along the blocks, stopping to listen. With the greatest care he could muster, he poked his head round for a glance—

And was seized by the hair! Massive gray-green arms whirled him round and slammed him into a wall. This Oplyte and another, with their superhuman hearing and sense of smell, had been waiting for him. He wrenched free, heedless of pain or potential loss of scalp. Before the second giant could seize him, he thrust a bolt of kinergy into its eye, destroying one side of its brain. Compartmented by its conversion into a fighting machine, it was only slowed by what should have been a mortal blow. It might die of the wound, in time. Now it groaned and pawed the air, attempting to grab him. He was busy with the first Oplyte which had triggered an alarm and also tried to sweep him into its grasp. Repeated thrusts at its chest and solar plexus proved futile. Before he was aware of it, his designator flickered and died, along with all kinergic power. With seeming defeat of the rebels and Morven's attention elsewhere, his troops had grown lax. The idiot officer who had owned this thrustible had not kept it at full charge!

Now the slave-warriors' amplified strength and reflexes were set against a merely human will to live and remain free. At a basic level, this was what they lacked, the very capacity taken away to make them Oplytes. Despite their daunting power and speed—and a fearsome reputation serving as a weapon in itself—Henry Martyn, who, as Arran, had fought a hundred imaginary battles in this corridor, did not give up as many another might have. He ducked the wounded creature's treelike arms, luring his healthier pursuer into its half-blind, entangling grasp. He seized upon the straps of the damaged warrior's thrustible. They came away. Provided he had time, he now had a weapon meant for use against the semi-artificial fighters.

The first Oplyte pushed the useless one away and came for him, never raising its thrustible. It must have orders to take him alive, although how Morven knew of his escape so soon . . . no time for that. Lifting a weapon much heavier than his own, he centered a crimson splash upon the Oplyte's face. The bolt took its victim in the forehead. It staggered, sank to its knees, and collapsed. Before he could take another breath, six more entities exactly like it marched round the corner and stumbled upon him.

"Good evening, Captain! Or ought I address you as young Master Islay, now you have returned home after so long an absence?"

Henry Martyn opened his eyes, not without effort, for they felt as if they were cyanoed shut. He essayed to sit up but did not succeed, his head being only one part of his body throbbing with pain. His right arm was in a sling. He lay upon a divan he did not recognize, within what had been his father's office, a silky coverlet pulled over his legs. Upon a nearby table a carafe sent wisps of steam and the wonderful aroma of caff into the air.

"The former," he croaked, for it was all he could manage at the moment, "which I chose and earned."

Two men stood before him, one tall and gray, uniformed in a paramilitary fashion sometimes affected by Hanoverian aristocrats. Henry Martyn guessed that his black masque portrayed the half-mythical Malcom Ten. The other was slight, attired in stylish and expensive civilian clothing of Jendyne cut. He wore a forthright and unmistakable richelieu. As his eyes began to focus, Henry Martyn saw that it was the Hanoverian who had spoken and who now knelt to assist him with the caff, which was heavy with milk and sweet flavoring.

He drank deep. "Who in the Ceo's name are you?"

"In the Ceo's name, indeed." The gray man stood again, set the carafe upon the table, took a step backward, and swept his masque away. "My boy, I am Sedgeley Daimler-Wilkinson, Drector-Advisory and—what is more important at the moment—Executor-General to Leupould IX."

Henry Martyn blinked. "Daimler . . . Wilkinson?"

"You are familiar with the name? Pray permit me to introduce my esteemed colleague and official enemy, Frantisek Demondion-Echeverria, Ambassador Plenipotentiary of the Jendyne Empery-Cirot to the 'Droom upon Hanover, who accompanies me as an observer. Ambassador, *the* Henry Martyn."

The man doffed his masque, bowed without a word, afterward standing with arms folded across his chest, a scowl

upon his dark face. Henry Martyn extended a hand, noticing
for the first time that he wore other bandages and in places
tingled from disinfectant fields. More, he had been deprived
of his—rather, the Olpyte's—thrustible, and neither of these
two carried one he might take. "Some effort has been spent
reviving me. How long—?"

"How long have we been here," Daimler-Wilkinson asked,
"or how long have you been unconscious? I gather we arrived
almost upon your heels. As to the latter, my people dragged
you here—somewhat zealously, I might add by way of
apology—about an hour and a half ago, after an exhaustive
search of the premises and what I am told was an impressive
battle below. Young man, you have cost the Ceo rather a
pretty clavis this day. Do you actually recall biting through
the carotid artery of one of my Olpytes?"

Henry Martyn shuddered. "No," he lied.

"Be that as it may," Daimler-Wilkinson continued, his
voice acquiring a trace of irritability, "you proved difficult to
come to grasp with. In the same span, three light divisions of
the Ceo's Olpyte legions took a whole world rather more
easily from supporters of the man you call the Black
Usurper."

This time he did manage to sit up. "What has become of
him?"

"We hear he escaped into the forest, looking for a vantage
from which to bring our occupying forces under his sway,
employing some alien weapon he is rumored to possess. In
absence of your brother, who seems to have disappeared as
well—I have people searching for them now—this weapon
was one of the items I wished urgently to discuss with
you."

"And Lia Woodgate?"

Daimler-Wilkinson drew a chair up beside the divan. The
ambassador threw himself upon a settee across the room
where he sat scowling. "I have," the Hanoverian reflected,
"very special instructions regarding her. She was not in
her . . . quarters. I sincerely hope to discover her safe and
sound."

Henry Martyn nodded, sharing his hope. In any case, many
dire reckonings would be paid before this was over, and he
did not intend letting some idiot Ceo interfere. "'One of
the items.' What else do you wish to discuss with me,

Executor-General, my trial and liquidation as a rebel and freebooter?"

"Dear me, no!" The man laughed as if it were the furthest thing from his thoughts, which it was. "Upon the contrary, my boy, it is my earnest desire to enlist, upon the behalf of my Ceo, the sympathies and cooperation of a celebrated . . . shall we say 'adventurer'?"

Henry Martyn raised an eyebrow. "Sympathies?"

"And cooperation. I intended, wherever and whenever we found you, to offer you, straightaway, the Ceo's amnesty and a full pardon—"

"The same as offered my brother by the Black Usurper," he snorted. "It appears each side, in whatever capital-world dispute this represents, wishes its own pet Islay for some obscure reason. Well let me assure you, Executor-General, I have not the faintest interest which faction finishes uppermost in any political struggle. My experience is that the Monopolity—and your Empery-Cirot, sir—are but two varieties of the same disease."

"Sedition!" Demondion-Echeverria gasped the first word he had spoken in Henry Martyn's presence. "This creature is nothing more than a common murderer! Upon Homeworld we have ways of dealing with his ilk!"

"Yes, Frantisek, I know you do." Daimler-Wilkinson turned back to the figure upon the divan. "My friend refers to electronic cerebrectomy. Upon other occasions, he wonders why the Empery-Cirot suffers a chronic death of talent and initiative in these latter days." The Executor-General sighed. "Even you must realize, my boy, that, in the real universe, our imperium-conglomerate represents the least of many greater evils. It is the only proven defense against not only Jendyne predation—you will excuse me, Frantisek—but the threat of anarchy which endangers any civilization."

"It becomes necessary to point out that I am not your boy," an angry Henry Martyn shook his head. "Also, save your apologia for someone upon whom it may prove effective. I am a ship-robber, representative, as it were, of that anarchy you mention. Moreover, knowing something of defenses, proven and otherwise, and being a businessman of sorts, I remain unconvinced of your proposition upon pragmatic grounds of contract, profit, and loss."

Daimler-Wilkinson blinked. "Sir?"

"You argue that you protect civilization from predation. Yet what do I owe a protector," Henry Martyn demanded, "who keeps his part of the bargain—a bargain, I might add, which I had no part in arranging, to which I was never offered a chance to consent or refrain from consenting—with confiscation and conscription, the very predation you claim to protect me from, in short, with nothing but the bargain's betrayal?" From the ambassador a series of half-articulate mutterings was audible. For his own part, the Executor-General opened his mouth to offer one of many conventional answers upon the subject. "Not to mention endless sophistries," Henry Martyn added before he could speak, "designed to redefine that lattermost word away?"

Daimler-Wilkinson closed his mouth. Henry Martyn lifted the coverlet, swung his legs across the divan, and rose to his feet. "What have I left," he asked, "to offer a defender who defends me—from enemies he made for me—by taking more away than they could? What am I free to say of a liberator who defends liberty by placing it in protective custody?"

The brigand folded his good arm about his sling. The man sighed and shook his head. These searching questions were the same as he had often asked himself (in mental privacy) for which he had never found adequate answer.

"You are an even greater idealist," he offered at last, "than I was given to believe. Albeit one who backs his ideals with intelligence and a palpable courage. Allow me to appeal to both, your idealism and your courage, for they are rare. You cannot help having seen how our rather overcivilized young men today lack—let us use olden words—the 'grit' or 'gumption' you manifest every minute. My bo—Captain, it was your sort who made Hanover great for a millennium. Yet even now, at its peak, the rot begins to show. Your imperium-conglomerate needs you if it is to survive another thousand years."

"Your imperium-conglomerate, sir. And I observe, in passing, that it was not to my intelligence you chose to appeal. I repeat, I am an outlaw."

"By your light, I am a contract-defaulter," Daimler-Wilkinson chuckled. "One outlaw to another, what may I offer in exchange?" He held up a finger. "Shall I hand you a traitorous brother for whatever you consider justice?" He held up a second finger. "Shall I play a thille I brought of my Ceo promising to restore all Islay properties to you?" He held up a third finger. "With title and power of a Drectorhood, not for this world alone, but the region of the Deep surrounding it? It would hardly be unprecedented. Someday, visiting the 'Droom, you might appropriately affect the visage of Sir Henry Morgan, an outlaw who forged a similar bargain with his sovereign."

"Were I to wear a masque, it would likelier be of Jean LaFitte, an outlaw who rejected the same bargain." Henry Martyn shook his head. "Make clearer why you need me badly enough to offer these things."

This was too much for Demondion-Echeverria who leapt up, threw his hands wide, and shouted: "Why do you let him speak to you in this manner? Give him to me! What I leave will be happy to cooperate!"

"He merits an answer, Frantisek." Daimler-Wilkinson shrugged, "Strategic reasons, Captain Martyn. Skye itself is of no value. Yet, fearing Jendyne interference, with due respect to the ambassador, and an increasing alien presence in what has become, through a degree of neglect, an unstable region, the Ceo is anxious to find a competent, popularly supported governor—"

Henry Martyn nodded, "One well able to supply his own firepower?"

Daimler-Wilkinson's smile verged upon a grin. "Yes, and perhaps, in the process, rid himself of an increasingly bothersome freebooter by some means other than the lengthy and expensive one of hunting him down."

"Or attempting to gain his confidence through the ancient hardfellow-softfellow game, with the help of your 'official enemy'?"

Demondion-Echeverria threw back his head and laughed. "Pay me, Sedgeley! I wagered it would not last half an hour! Pay me my thousand gavelles!"

Daimler-Wilkinson gifted Henry Martyn with a look of rueful admiration. "Clavises, Frantisek, and I shall pay you once the captain has answered."

Henry Martyn took a long while. "Living the life I have

thus far lived, I shall suffer no one to call me master, nor ever call another by that name."

"Well spoken, sir," Daimler-Wilkinson smiled, "and in future I shall make bold to quote you. Yet it appears that I confront futility. Permit me a final inducement." He strode to the desk, leaned over and pressed an annunciator lever. "Will you please send in my niece?"

CHAPTER XLVI:
THE CEO'S HAND

"Arran!"

Nodding with satisfaction, Daimler-Wilkinson watched an emotional reunion between Loreanna and Henry Martyn. Unable to avoid melodrama, she rushed to his arms and afterward made fussing noises over his bandages. In his own way, the young man was no less moved. Their undisguised joy at finding one another confirmed everything the Executor-General had suspected of the pair. Having established what would doubtless prove useful leverage, he left them to their embraces, pulled a chair round the desk, and gathered his wits as he had been unable to before. At last he steepled his fingers and cleared his throat.

"Where were we?" Employing the distraction to fullest advantage, he pressed his former line with Henry Martyn as if it had not been rejected. He believed all men desire power, the noblest only seeking means by which to justify the craving. With analogy and historic example, he amiably countered each of Henry Martyn's earlier protests, invariably to the effect that someone will always be needed to rule. "You must not judge others by standards you set, Captain. Ordinary folk require governing. It may be stifling to you. To them it is vital, as their need for food, clothing, and shelter. Evil it may be, as you insist. It is the archetypal example of necessary evil."

Now that Loreanna was restored to him, Henry Martyn

was willing to look away from his beloved only briefly. Nevertheless, accustomed to thinking upon his feet, to giving orders and making plans in the heat of battle or the teeth of storms, he was less defenseless than the Executor-General believed. He released Loreanna, took a breath, a step forward, and framed an answer.

"I wonder about this phrase, 'necessary evil.' You do not suggest that a person may coexist with cancer—simply to name another widely acknowledged evil. Whatever the quality of rhetoric supporting it. Nor can he long endure 'a little bit' of cancer, believing it somehow consumes his capacity for illness and protects him from all other diseases." He looked from Daimler-Wilkinson to Demondion-Echeverria, from one wielder of power to another. "Nor would any but the most venal quack regard cancer as a 'necessary' evil."

The ambassador sniffed. "What do you offer as a substitute?"

"What does any conscientious physician offer as a substitute for cancer except its complete obliteration?"

Daimler-Wilkinson frowned. "The aptness of your analogy, Captain—"

He was interrupted by pounding upon the door. "Sir," cried a messenger who followed it into the room, "word from the starport brigadier! An armada—Jendyne, he says, sir—has arrived in stationary orbit off Skye!"

"The Ceo you say! How many, how armed, and how disposed?"

"Thousands, sir, heavily armed. Three, four-deckers, starships-of-the-line, dreadnoughts, arrayed in almost a solid ring and signaling one another by . . . I recollect the word was 'radio.'"

"Radio?"

Despite an implied breach of courtesy, Daimler-Wilkinson glanced at the ambassador who spread his palms, displaying innocence. Himself a student of obsolete technology, Henry Martyn supplied, "Electromagnetic communication, short-ranged and lightspeed. Highly effective within limits."

The messenger nodded. "Almost the brigadier's words,

sir, now I hear 'em again. Electromagnetic impulses, some bein' relayed t'what appears a thousand vessels more, hove to somewheres in the Deep beyond instrumental range of the planet! In orbit, sir, they caught our minimal—"

"—and complacent?"

Not bothering with Henry Martyn's wry suggestion, the Executor-General waved a hand to silence him. "Our minimal what?"

"Deckwatches, sir. Caught off guard, they did. Boarded half our ships. They've issued an ultimatum to the rest: surrender or be destroyed."

Daimler-Wilkinson examined the messenger, Demondion-Echeverria, and, with an odd look, the young ship-robber beside his niece, one good arm about her shoulders. "Jendyne, did you say?"

The messenger gulped. "B'look of 'em, sir, yes."

Daimler-Wilkinson leaned back, placed his steepled fingers to his lips, regarded those about him shrewdly, and leaned forward. "Quite a coincidence. I wonder what Henry Martyn would—never mind, I know what I shall do." He pointed a finger. "Seize me that man and have him thrust upon the spot! Have his body sent to this armada in answer to their ultimatum!" He pointed at Demondion-Echeverria. The two Oplytes who had dragged in Henry Martyn burst through the doorway past the messenger, spilling him onto the floor. One took the ambassador by his arms. The other placed its thrustible at his temple.

"What's that?" For a moment they were all distracted as a roar buffeted the windows and, heavily curtained as they were, the glare of flames became visible. Loreanna swept the drapes aside. Fire had broken out in Newtown and seemed to be consuming the entire shabby settlement.

"Never mind that," her uncle ordered as a chorus of screams added to the roar, "others will deal with it. We have important matters at hand. I am sincerely sorry, Frantisek, but I am also sure you understand—*now what?*" Even as the Jendyne Ceo's man prepared about to breathe his last—of air or any other substance—certain actions, high aloft in stationary orbit, had manifested themselves in a noisy crackling within the Black Usurper's desk.

"Pardon, Executor-General, I believe that is for me." His face lit by the flames outside, Henry Martyn approached the desk, glancing over his shoulder at the Oplytes holding a thrashing, cursing Demondion-Echeverria. "Pray do not let me interrupt your duties, gentlebeings." Leaning over the desk, he pressed a concealed button, waited as the hidden cabinet raised itself through the surface, and removed the weird, glowing object he knew he would find within. Without hesitation, he laid a hand upon the *Rii*an communicale. "I am listening, Mr. Krumm."

"AYE, AYE, SIR!"

The young brigand jerked away with a yelp. Krumm's words, he was aware, were audible only within his mind, received by the same sort of *nacyl* virus which had sent them. He was surprised, given their perceived intensity, that the entire planet, let alone those in the room about him, had not heard them. "Easy! This is not another demonstration for our enemies of *Rii*an prowess and ineffability. Just an ordinary conversation!"

Thirty-five thousand klommes overhead, Krumm stood upon the quarterdeck of the *Osprey,* making noises of embarrassment as he hastily requested that the signal gain be reduced by one of the flatsies—*nacyl*—and the virus in its circulatory system. *"Sorry I am, sir, to have forgot it! You'll be happy t'learn, to a ship and a bein', the Hanovers have meekly allowed themselves t'be boarded. They're greatly surprised, rather than the Jenny cutthroats they expected, that we're squads from Henry Martyn's modest fleet!"*

Henry Martyn chuckled. In his mind's eye he saw hordes of hardened men and women, dangerous children, aliens of many species, swarming aboard vessels of the flotilla, claiming them under Krumm's command. He relayed what he knew to the others in the room. Even with a city burning just beyond the windows, the Executor-General must have seen them, too. With a gesture, he released Demondion-Echeverria who, glaring about him as he straightened his clothing with brisk, furious motions, looked from Daimler-Wilkinson to Henry Martyn.

"My dear Sedgeley, would it be presumptuous to suggest that you seize the genuine culprit? Dismaying odds aloft to the contrary, arrest of their leader would stop what is happening in orbit."

Sliding a hand into a trouser pocket, Henry Martyn wrapped it about the comforting, familiar shape of the walther-weapon which, despite their passionate greeting, Loreanna had thought to pass him. Firelight gleamed along its polished sides. The Oplytes tensed. He discouraged any sanguine ideas upon their part by giving the mysterious (if not very potent) weapon a gentle wave in their direction. Before they made matters worse, Daimler-Wilkinson called them off with an absent shake of his head, all the while thinking as quickly as he could. A glance at Loreanna, who looked defiance back at him, confirmed where the weapon had come from. He looked back as if to say, *well struck, my dear, and I deserved it.*

Meanwhile, Henry Martyn prudently equipped himself with a thrustible from one of the guards. "I fear, Ambassador, my arrest would not affect a thing. My crewbeings serve me by serving their own interest." He handed the walther back to Loreanna, turning to Daimler-Wilkinson. "Each one would have had to be arrested in order to stop this, an advantage they enjoy over those who believe in the supremacy—or indispensability—of authority."

"Why," the Executor-General asked, one eye upon the window and hundreds of refugees beginning to stream out of Newtown, "do I doubt, despite your formidable reputation, that you control thousands of heavily armed three- and four-deckers, starships-of-the-line, dreadnoughts, et cetera?"

"You are correct to doubt it," replied Henry Martyn. "Ours is a small fleet, augmented, to be sure, by the armed craft of various friendly trading captains, and by numbers of unbeinged inflatable drones which I recently had fabricated in the Sisao-Somon system."

Daimler-Wilkinson nodded, resigned. It was annoying the way his niece gazed upon this dangerous puppy with such awe. "A fleet which has been feigning these arcane communications with a greater fleet which does not, in fact, exist?"

"Nonetheless," Henry Martyn told him, "it produced the desired effect. With or without your Ceo's leave, by ancient usage as well as my more recent practice, I now command the world which was always mine by right!"

Hearing dried leaves crackle beneath his feet, Morven was suddenly aware he had not been outdoors and afoot for thirty years.

In one hand he held the device, delivered by the same mundane means as the communicale, which he had privately dubbed his "persuadible," disdaining to bear another weapon in the belief that this was the function of a servant. At the moment his daughter performed that humble service, walking beside him, adding to the racket. "Creeping" might have been a better word, he thought, for their slow, blind progress through the forest edge about the Holdings.

Uppermost in mind was a dire need for transport to the base Alysabeth's dead husband had named for her, then a starship of any size, the intent being to employ alien technology not just to seize command of the intruding force or recapture the estate, but an entire planet. The device had only just arrived, its first test interrupted by invasion. Yet in their desperate estimate, it might allow them to reverse the deteriorating situation.

Meanwhile, an Oplyte contingent and increasing numbers of brigands were turning over every leaf in their pursuit and had to be avoided. At long last—when their clothing had been dew-soaked to the hips, and they were cold, hungry, and exhausted—they found what they had been looking for.

One of Daimler-Wilkinson's flyers lay in a clearing within sight of the Holdings, backlit in orange-red by what could not yet be the dawn, even had the direction been correct. Newtown must be set afire. Morven shook off the distraction. It was a transport, not remarkably different from the draywherry which had brought them here, save for *nacelles* holding projectibles or thrustibles (whatever they were called when this size, he thought) giving it the appearance of a huge creature sleeping with its legs beneath it. It still hovered siemmes above the ground, even in this somnolent state. More to the point, the crewbeings and soldiers it had carried were nowhere to be seen. It was guarded by two Oplytes, for whom he held effective treatment in his hand.

He arose from the soggy grass where they had been hiding.

Alysabeth's teeth were chattering, her hairdo had collapsed, and, in the light thrown by a fire at the stern of the transport, her lips appeared blue. "Remain here," he told her, "until I have made certain of those soldiers."

Striding across three dozen measures separating him from the campfire, he stood some distance from the Oplytes, raised the artifact, and squeezed its lever, bathing them in eerie light. To his immense satisfaction, they stayed where they were, hunkered behind the flames, their eyes expressionless as always. "Do not move or make a sound!" he ordered. "Alysabeth!"

"Here, Father!" Her harsh whisper had come from close behind him. She had hurried to catch up. He turned and saw that her color was improving.

"Follow me aboard, but have a care. We may find more of the creatures inboard. If not, we have a clear run ahead, and the rigorous military training of my youth should serve me well in—"

Looking over his shoulder, Alysabeth's eyes had widened. Before he could turn, he felt a rough hand upon his face, another upon his arm, stretching his body as if it were bread dough. The palm over his mouth kept him from echoing his daughter as she screamed. The other Oplyte had seized her. It had never occurred to her to use the thrustible she wore. Morven twisted to face his captor, raised the alien device and brought it down upon the warrior's head, shattering both cylinders, releasing their contents in glowing wisps, but doing his adversary no discernible damage. He struck again and again until the soldier tired of the annoyance and broke his arm.

"Father!" The other Oplyte threw Alysabeth to the ground, spread her legs, and, one hand upon her chest to keep her, knelt between her knees. Morven knew real horror when his own assailant spread him the same way.

Having no better occupation, and deprived of a world to ravish and burn freely, the Oplytes had set fire to Newtown, which fulfilled their fondest wishes by sending forth a screaming flood of refugees and flames a hundred measures into the sky. By dawn the broad plain before the Holdings would be empty again of everything but ashes and the crumbling skeleton which was all burnt metalloid leaves behind. Before a year passed, two at most, the meadow would be green and filled with flowers.

In the wood, Lia searched with infinite patience for a group of Oplytes forming ranks for departure and reassignment elsewhere upon Skye, just as she had searched for Donol when he had failed to make a promised visit to the tower. She looked down at his limp, bloodstained body and was surprised to feel nothing. Perhaps she would in days—or years —to come.

The moment arrived. Using the best command voice she could muster, taught her in a hard and thorough school to which a very important man—who did not know that she knew who her father was—had ordered his daughter sent, she strode from the wood into the garish firelight, for the moment leaving Donol where he lay.

"Field Agent Woodgate." She spoke the syllables, harsh but low, to a non-human warrior which attempted to seize her, as it and its fellow monsters had seized hundreds, perhaps thousands, this night, only to withdraw a broken wrist. *"Priority Code Ceo's Hand."*

Ignoring its injury, it snapped to attention, reflections of the city flames flickering along its battle harness. Of a rare new breed of Oplyte officer, recently being tried in the elite corps, it was a hybrid, lacking the speed and strength of an ordinary Oplyte, the initiative or compunction which might have made it human, unable to boast of any third quality compensating for either deficiency. "Your orders, Ceo's Hand?"

"You will find a body in that patch of woods yonder, still alive."

"Yes, Ceo's Hand!" It sent two of its creatures to retrieve Donol, groaning his way back to consciousness as they dragged him to one of the transports. He should begin screaming soon and should be suffering pain, as well. Considerable pain. That ought to help keep him awake.

Ceo's Hand, indeed, she thought. She looked down at her hand, which had often done the Ceo's work and would again in future. Tonight it had done its own work, with another of its little homemade knives, another esoteric skill she had been taught, castrating Donol Islay.

"I shall require transport to the landing pentagrams immediately—no, not in that vehicle, some other—and afterward offplanet as quickly as possible. And Captain?"

"Yes, Ceo's Hand?"

"I want you to see personally that this thing stays alive while you use it, as my gift to you, for as long a time as possible, until you have eaten every bit of it."

"Thank you, Ceo's Hand!"

CHAPTER XLVII:
SKYE OF GOLD

"Truly, things have not turned out that badly, have they, Uncle?"

Breathless with anticipation, beautiful Loreanna, no longer Mistress Daimler-Wilkinson, but with joy and without question Henry Martyn's woman (and Arran Islay's, she realized, as well, whatever that might prove to mean), saw her uncle aboard the golden draywherry, battered but still glittering, ghostly by ringlight, which another Henry Martyn had so long ago adorned. Demondion-Echeverria, already aboard, made no polite pretense of not listening to the private conversation between his colleague and his colleague's niece.

"I would say the estimate," her uncle spared a wry look for the Jendyne ambassador, "rather depends upon one's viewpoint. Being freighted hastily offplanet in the middle of the night, without the dignity of leave to remain until morning—and in a farm waggon, of all conveyances—smacks of ignominy, would you not agree?"

The ambassador could identify with Daimler-Wilkinson's feelings and was himself grateful that he had come to Skye at the behest of the Hanoverian Ceo rather than his own, and only as an observer. Fighting thoughts that wished to stray elsewhere, Loreanna shook her head. "You are not an honored guest, Uncle, but an unsuccessful invader. Moreover, as I have recent occasion to appreciate, day and night are all the same within the bosom of the Deep." Nonetheless, her smile was kind. "The only viewpoint I own is that of one who must bid you farewell. I suspect the Ceo will understand, if that troubles you. Affairs here would inevitably have concluded the same way had he come himself. I shall enthille a message and tell him so."

The Ceo was indeed what worried Daimler-Wilkinson. Fancying pirates as he professed, possibly Leupould would be amused by what had transpired upon Skye, however displeased he must officially appear. Which reaction, personal or political, to humiliating failure upon the part of his Executor-General would most likely determine that worthy's fate? Sharing his niece's opinion with regard to the eventual outcome, nonetheless he wondered, with an anticipatory shudder, what Baffridgestar was like this time of year.

Events now moved relentlessly, as if by their own weight, toward some momentous conclusion he would apparently not be here to witness. The fire in Newtown had already burnt itself out. Among themselves, the rebels seemed to hold a sense of unnamed excitement. Hours had passed since Henry Martyn's complicated ruse had been revealed. His forces continued to make planetfall in great numbers at the starport—a new name would be found for it, now—to hunt for Morven's stragglers, aided by woodsrunners, villagers, and (it rankled the Executor-General) some elements of Hanoverian soldiery lately persuaded to join the famous star-raider.

"Many of his crewbeings will be staying planetside, I should imagine." Joining the two men within the draywherry —their pilot had as yet failed to make his appearance— Loreanna poured tea from a portable service she had carried with her. She seemed nervous and preoccupied, anxious to have done with this and be elsewhere. "At present they are sorting out genuine deserters from the spies you had planned leaving behind."

"He will have no one left to work his ships," her uncle replied, taking the cup she offered, "and this pleasant woodland world will be overwhelmed with people—and other things."

"I rather doubt it, Uncle. It is what he promised," she observed as she sipped her tea, "as a substitute for the usual prize brigands seek. Yes, even some *nacyl* and *seporth* will remain. Skye will be the first home many of them, human or otherwise, have known. It is a large world, and their places will be taken by a greater number of Skyans wishing to travel to the stars."

"While I, the Ceo's personal representative, am rudely, unceremoniously booted off a world under Hanoverian sovereignty by a mere . . ."

"Freebooter?" Despite herself, Loreanna giggled. "Does this look rude to you?" She threw a glance about the comfortably appointed draywherry. They had just quit the paneled library office where a sumptuous breakfast had been served while music played and a fire burned in the grate. His niece had eaten little, having been called to the communicator several times during the meal. "I understand that, as soon as he returns from looking at something in the woods which Mr. Krumm wished him to see, he will come to wish you bon voyage, whereupon you will be free to return to Hanover—if, as he says, you believe that the most prudent course. This is what he wishes, Uncle, what he planned, and assured at great personal risk by entering a rather obvious trap."

Daimler-Wilkinson snorted. "He did not look for our presence here, it was a complete surprise!"

"It is the policy he purposed following all along, whoever claimed to represent the Monopolity upon Skye." She raised an admonitory finger. "He still desires to send a message to Hanover, which Captain Bowmore somehow failed to deliver. I daresay he is rather pleased that it happens to be you to whom pragmatics compel him to show mercy, rather than certain others."

Daimler-Wilkinson nodded his satisfaction. "Yes, even the ruthless Henry Martyn seems to have acquired some restraint of late, I suspect as a result of his violent and emotional experiences with you."

Scarcely concealing her impatience, she shook her head. "I would not stake my life upon that theory, Uncle. Not in the way you mean. He will continue to be what he must be, merciful or ruthless by turns as practicality requires of him.

Rather say that your niece has learned profoundly from the sometimes splendidly, deliciously ruthless Henry Martyn, and hopes to continue her lessons in future. Violent emotional experiences are not a bad thing, altogether. True, perhaps, he feels he has regained some measure of humanity he feels he lost—"

"In no small part, thanks to you, my dear, I have no doubt of it." He nodded toward the ambassador. "For which two great spheres of influence shall be grateful for a long time to come."

She frowned. "Be that as it may, Uncle, I warn you, he will never grow soft like the fops you complain of. I know him. It was only by heroic effort, against what has long since become reflex with him, that he refrained from thrusting the Ceo's personal representative when he first laid eyes upon you in his father's house. For him it constituted one usurpation too many."

Daimler-Wilkinson sat up. "The presumption of the whelp!"

"A whelp who has you by both spheres of influence, Uncle Sedgeley!"

She almost jumped from her seat. The words were not Loreanna's, but arose from the ladderhatch. Henry Martyn was muddy from head to toe, the sling upon his arm filthy. Blood spatters lay across his other sleeve. Krumm climbed the ladder behind him, filling the hatchway as, at their feet, flowed one of the bandit's *nacyl* companions. Henry Martyn strode up the aisle, bent to kiss Loreanna—who gave him a look fraught with expectation—and straightened to face her uncle.

"My message is a simple one, sir," he continued, his voice level, "I bid you and your unclean minions and mass-murderers begone, not only from the planet Skye, but from this entire region of the Deep. If not, then by all that is unholy in a universe brimming with obscenity, I swear I shall bring long-overdue revolution to Hanover itself. And, whatever else may come of it, not one stone of that planet shall I leave standing upon another!"

The cabin lay silent a long while. Ignoring this annoying, overhanging air of unfulfilled awaiting as he usually ignored air altogether, Demondion-Echeverria found he could be quite philosophical about not having acquired Loreanna. Given a measure of ruthlessness upon her part fully comparable to that of Henry Martyn—not to mention her apparent taste for weaponry—he was vastly better off.

A voyage of some weeks lay ahead. It would be well to introduce his Hanoverian friend to the mysteries of the Immortal School. Sedgeley's was an intelligent and stabilizing influence in the galaxy. The Practice would extend a useful life—did Leupould not see fit to end it after hearing of events upon this planet—and give them something personal in common.

They would need it. If this threat to bring anarchy down upon Hanover were taken with a fraction of the seriousness it merited, life was going to become interesting and difficult for the established powers in the not-too-distant future. Perhaps it was time to begin thinking about ending a Thousand Years' War which diverted their attention from matters more important.

At last, the troublesome individual who had created the silence broke it. "I would have said all of this earlier, had we not been interrupted and my attentions urgently required elsewhere. Now matters are out of my hands for the time being. May I have some tea, my darling Loreanna, and a cup for Mr. Krumm, I think, as well?"

Krumm nodded enthusiastic agreement. He threw a grin and a wink at the girl, as if sharing some mysterious private joke with her, found a seat which protested under his weight, and affectionately scratched the alien upon what served it as a head.

"Even with this small armada of yours—" Daimler-Wilkinson gave a polite cough, attempting to regain some measure of his dignity, "—this may prove a difficult edict to enforce, young man, against the massed naval power of the Hanoverian Imperium-Conglomerate."

"You would be well advised to believe him, Uncle," Loreanna suggested as she poured, "when he speaks in this manner without raising his voice." Unable to contain herself further, she turned to Henry Martyn. "And what, if I may ask, have your various searches produced?"

Suddenly appearing weary and much older than his years, Henry Martyn stared into his teacup. "Broken, gnawed, marrow-split bones, left behind in an abandoned Oplyte camp. I have reason to be certain they are the remains of Morven and his evil daughter Alysabeth."

Suppressing a shudder, Loreanna looked a different sort of question at him than had earlier been the case. He passed it to his first officer. Krumm fumbled in a grimy camouflage-patterned kefflar bag slung over a massive shoulder. Daimler-Wilkinson cringed within himself (nor was he alone in this), dreading to see what grisly trophy of the Usurper had been retrieved. Still grinning, Krumm produced the battered "persuadible" which, for man and daughter, had proven the deadliest possible failure. The *nacyl* took the object in its stubby tentacles, turning it as if examining something once familiar, now much altered by circumstances.

"It is my hope," Henry Martyn offered in the same uninflected tone he had earlier employed, "that in the last, terrifying moment of their lives, they realized it was all a deliberate hoax, conceived by myself and executed by my comrades, to forestall many less-sophisticated but more brutal measures upon the Usurper's part by rendering him complacently dependent upon miracles."

Another silence ensued. "And of Mistress Woodgate," Daimler-Wilkinson asked, drawing odd looks from Henry Martyn and his niece, "is there no word?"

"Nor," Loreanna added, some measure of her excitement having evaporated, "of your brother, Donol?"

He shook his head. "Nor, I have come to suspect, will there ever be."

Loreanna reached out to place a comforting hand upon her lover's forearm. Daimler-Wilkinson had quite another reason for the look of concern and loss in his eyes. "And what is to become of you, my dear?"

"I had almost forgot!" Of a sudden, she was bright and lively once again. From a pocket of her gown, she handed him an engraved autothille upon a jeweled chain. Henry Martyn smiled. Her expression had become one of rejoicing. "For you, Uncle Sedgeley, from both of us." She raised adoring eyes to Henry Martyn, who now grinned from ear to ear, momentarily a boy again, and took her hand. "Since he has asked me, I shall sail the dark, endless currents of the Deep with him, or else live the rest of my days in happiness, upon this, our liberated Skye, its halo for my wedding ring."

Henry Martyn pointed upward. "And here, unless I am mistaken, in answer to all your unasked questions, are the first of our wedding guests, four hundred *nacyl* fighting captains, their stout crews, and their new apprentices, late of the Jendyne naval academy!"

An unfamiliar roaring hum filled the air. Through the open meshwork of the draywherry, Daimler-Wilkinson at first thought dawn lit the sky in golden contrast to the dusty silver of the moonring. Yet it was still many hours until sunrise. Then he realized that the Ceo would have little to blame him for, after all. Somehow it seemed like small comfort.

Overhead, from horizon to horizon, the sky filled with hundreds of alien vessels descending—without benefit of cabelle, starsail, or rocket blast—directly toward the planet's surface. Each pulsed with inner light in quality resembling the eerie blue flicker of §-glow, yet brighter, stronger, daytime brilliant, challenging the night-black Deep, bearing the first real progress for mankind in a thousand years.

"In either case," declared Loreanna, suffused with a certain glow of her own, "upon Skye or in the Deep, I shall be with the man I love, forever."

THE DRAGON REBORN

Sequel to *The Great Hunt*

Book Three
of
The Wheel of Time

by

Robert Jordan

Praise for *Eye of the World*

"A powerful vision of good and evil...fascinating people moving through a rich and interesting world." —Orson Scott Card

"Richly detailed...fully realized, complex adventure."
—*Library Journal*

"A combination of Robin Hood and Stephen King that is hard to resist....Jordan makes the reader care about these characters as though they were old friends." —*Milwaukee Sentinel*

Praise for *The Great Hunt*

"Jordan can spin as rich a world and as event-filled a tale as [Tolkien]...will not be easy to put down." —*ALA Booklist*

"Worth re-reading a time or two." —*Locus*

"This is good stuff...Splendidly characterized and cleverly plotted...The Great Hunt is a good book which will always be a good book. I shall certainly [line up] for the third volume."
—*Interzone*

The Dragon Reborn
coming in hardcover in August, 1991